T0129210

SPENDING THE NIGHT TOGETHER

Flynn picked his duffel off the ground and started in the direction of one of the bunkhouses.

"Flynn," Gia called. "You can stay in the house."

A look passed between them, Flynn silently saying, *Are you out of your mind?* But instead of protesting in front of Annie, Flynn nodded.

"Show me where you want me," he said.

She was tempted to lead him to the master bedroom.

Gia took Flynn into the house.

"Are you trying to kill me, woman?"

"Annie didn't have anywhere to go. It's bad enough that tonight she's planning to couch surf. What's the deal with this Zeke guy?"

"He's a loser and a user . . . always taking Annie's money. And it's not like she has much. It's good of you to take her in." He brushed a lock of hair that had come loose from her ponytail behind her ear.

"I'm happy to have her oversee the farming venture, but I'm sorry you're losing the apartment."

"I'm not here full-time and can sleep in the bunkhouse . . . don't need a lot of creature comforts."

"Flynn, I've got an entire second floor of en-suite bedrooms. Take one."

He pressed her against the wall and boxed her in with both hands. "What if I want yours?"

She shrugged. "You're the one who made the rules, not me."

His mouth quirked. "Where's that Winchester? You setting me up?"

Then he dipped his head and kissed her until her toes curled. . . .

Books by Stacy Finz

GOING HOME

FINDING HOPE

SECOND CHANCES

STARTING OVER

GETTING LUCKY

BORROWING TROUBLE

HEATING UP

RIDING HIGH

Published by Kensington Publishing Corporation

Riding High

Stacy Finz

LYRICAL SHINE
Kensington Publishing Corp.
www.kensingtonbooks.com

LYRICAL SHINE BOOKS are published by

Kensington Publishing Corp.
119 West 40th Street
New York, NY 10018

All Kensington titles, imprints, and distributed lines are available at special quantity discounts for bulk purchases for sales promotion, premiums, fund-raising, educational, or institutional use.

Special book excerpts or customized printings can also be created to fit specific needs. For details, write or phone the office of the Kensington Sales Manager: Kensington Publishing Corp., 119 West 40th Street, New York, NY 10018. Attn. Sales Department. Phone: 1-800-221-2647.

Lyrical Shine and Lyrical Shine logo Reg. U.S. Pat. & TM Off.

First Electronic Edition: December 2016
eISBN-13: 978-1-60183-709-7
eISBN-10: 1-60183-709-7

First Print Edition: December 2016
ISBN-13: 978-1-60183-710-3
ISBN-10: 1-60183-710-0

Printed in the United States of America

*To my pals: Wendy, Leah, Miriam, and Amanda,
you're the best.*

ACKNOWLEDGMENTS

Thanks to the law enforcement officials who helped me wade through the intricacies of white-collar crime. Any mistakes, technical or otherwise, are mine.

And a special thanks to everyone who made this book happen: My agent, Melissa Jeglinski of the Knight Agency, editor John Scognamiglio, production editor Rebecca Cremonese, and all the other folks at Kensington Publishing who worked tirelessly on the entire series.

Chapter 1

There was a man in Gia Treadwell's shower. A strange, naked man. She'd come into her master suite to unpack her suitcase and heard the water running. Figuring the cleaning people had inadvertently left it on—not good in a drought—she went into the bathroom to turn the faucet off. That's when she saw him through the clear-glass shower enclosure, scrubbing his back while singing at the top of his lungs in a wobbly, deranged baritone. Something about Tennessee whiskey.

On the vanity, next to a shaving kit, sat a pistol.

She froze, let out a bloodcurdling scream that anywhere else would've brought in the National Guard, and ran for her life.

But it was a huge, unfamiliar house, situated in the middle of nowhere, and by the time Gia found her way to the front room, feet from the door, the shower intruder was hot on her trail.

"Calm down, lady." He fumbled with the buttons on his jeans while simultaneously dripping water from his bare chest onto the hardwood floor.

She quickly sized him up and came to the petrifying conclusion that he could crush her like a bug. At least six two, he had about seventy or eighty pounds on her, every ounce of it solid. Judging by his muscled arms, he could snap her neck with one fluid motion. Or just shoot her.

What if he was one of the men who'd sent the death threats? There'd been more than a dozen, some so graphic she'd had to double security before selling her penthouse.

But Gia was a New Yorker. Resourceful. Able to survive the mean streets of the city—and the wolves of Wall Street—on her wits

2 • *Stacy Finz*

alone. Too bad she'd left her can of pepper spray in her purse on the bed in the master bedroom along with her car keys.

She remembered a self-defense class from years back. The teacher had told a room full of attentive women that when under attack they should grab anything that could be used as a weapon. One of the students had bragged that she'd beaten a subway mugger into submission with an umbrella. Scanning the room, Gia's eyes fell on a rifle hanging on the wall like a trophy. It was displayed under a moose head, clearly the weapon that had been used to kill the poor animal. She pried it loose from its bronze hanger and pointed it at shower man.

Unconcerned that she had a firearm aimed at his center mass, he gave her a brazen once-over. Then he motioned his head at the gun. "I don't think it's loaded, but you should never point a weapon at someone unless you mean to shoot him."

"I'll shoot you." It was a bluff. If push came to shove, Gia didn't think she could pull the trigger.

Again, he eyed the rifle with indifference. "Yeah, I don't think so. Otherwise you would've removed the safety."

"Give me your pistol," she said. He looked confused. "The one in the bathroom."

"I don't have it." He held out both his hands. "Feel free to pat me down."

She wasn't getting anywhere near him. "Back up real slow."

He glanced behind his shoulder. "Where we going?"

"Into the bedroom."

"Yeah? Sounds good." He flicked his gaze over her, eyeing her from head to toe. The guy thought he was a real comedian. "Why don't you let me—"

"Not now." She needed to concentrate and was reevaluating the bedroom idea. But that was where her cell phone was. Gia hadn't seen a landline since she'd gotten here. She lifted the rifle so that the muzzle was pointed directly at his chest.

He rolled his eyes but mercifully kept quiet. They made it to the master suite without incident and with one hand Gia held the rifle against her shoulder, using the other one to search her purse for the phone.

Eureka! She punched 9-1-1 with her index finger, put the phone on speaker, and dropped it on the bed so she could resume holding the rifle with both hands.

"9-1-1, what's your emergency?"

Gia would've sworn she saw her captive snicker. She promptly ignored him and told the operator her situation. The cavalry was on its way, thank goodness.

"You think I could put my shirt on before the cops get here?"

"No funny stuff." She followed him into the bathroom, ordered him to stand against the wall, and warily removed his pistol from the vanity.

"What are you doing with that?" Now he wasn't so funny.

"Taking it for safekeeping."

"Okay, that one's loaded." He lowered his voice like he was afraid of spooking her. "Let's sit down and talk it out like two adults. But first, put the gun down."

She shook her head. "Not until the police come. Go ahead and put on your shirt. I won't shoot you unless you come at me. I promise." Gia placed the pistol in her jacket pocket.

She watched him pull a T-shirt out of a monogrammed leather satchel. Pretty nice luggage for a feckless squatter or a deranged stalker—whichever he was—but she wasn't taking any chances. Not after what she'd been through.

He saw her take note of his case, dragged the tee over his head, and said, "If you'd given me a chance to explain—"

"I'll let you explain, but not in here." She didn't like her chances in the bathroom. Too many sharp objects and too many opportunities for him to overpower her.

"You must be having a seriously bad day."

She couldn't tell whether he was being sarcastic or trying to placate her but responded, "You don't know the half of it. What are you doing?" She poked the rifle at him just so he understood she meant business. And to think she'd counted on being safe here.

"Take it easy. I just want to put this on." He shrugged into a western shirt and snapped it closed. She supposed he wanted to look respectable for the police.

"Let's move back into the living room."

"Yes, ma'am," he replied.

Once in the living room, she motioned for him to sit on the couch. She preferred not having him tower over her. He sat, stretching his long, denim-encased legs wide, resting his head against the brown leather as if he didn't have a care in the world. She sat across from him on the chair.

"Why is it you look so familiar?"

"How would I know?" She knew of course. "I've never seen you before in my life."

"Well, you've seen all of me now," he said, flashing a straight row of pearly white teeth.

"I wouldn't be so proud of that." She let her gaze lower to his crotch, pretending to be unimpressed. "You walk here?" She hadn't seen a vehicle in the driveway. If she had, she wouldn't have been caught off guard.

"I drove. My truck is on the side."

She got up, inched her way around the sofas without taking her eyes—or the rifle—off him, approached a large picture window, and pulled the heavy drapery aside. Sure enough, a shiny Ford F-150 hitched to an equally shiny stock trailer sat parked on the road that led to the barn. Her stomach dropped. Maybe he was a worker, not a stalker. Someone Dana, her real estate agent, had sent to make sure everything on the property was in order. Still, what the hell was he doing in her house? In her shower? Workers didn't have carte blanche to her private quarters. Dana never would've given him permission for that. She knew how protective Gia was of her privacy and personal safety. Especially her safety.

Yet he didn't seem too concerned that she'd called the police. Nor had he tried to subdue or evade her. Gia wasn't so deluded as to think she actually had the upper hand here. As he'd pointed out, she didn't even know where the safety was on the rifle.

Okay, perhaps she'd overreacted. Then again, who takes a handgun to the bathroom with him?

"I'm a little jumpy these days." She returned to her chair.

"I hadn't noticed," he drawled.

Hey, buddy, if you'd been through what I have . . .

"Start explaining," she said. "Who are you and why are you in my house, using my shower?"

He'd started to answer when sirens rent the air. It was about time, though the ranch was a good fifteen minutes from town. Perhaps living so far away hadn't been such a smart idea, given the state of her life these days. She could hear her pulse pounding, surely the aftermath of the adrenaline rush.

Her prisoner actually had the audacity to yawn.

She started to lecture him on his insolence when the police, including the chief, burst into the house.

The chief surveyed the scene and stopped short. "Hey, Flynn." He dropped his pistol into its holster, carefully removed the hunting rifle from Gia's hands, and passed it to one of his officers.

"Hey, Rhys." The man . . . Flynn . . . got to his feet and nodded at his rapt audience. "Nut job here went off half-cocked."

"That's not true. He was in my shower . . . with a pistol." She carefully took Flynn's gun from her pocket and handed it to Rhys.

Rhys let out a breath and looked at Flynn. "You had a semiautomatic in the shower?"

Flynn snorted "My Glock was on the sink. I'd just come back from riding in the hills. You never know what you'll run into up there."

Rhys let out a breath. She'd only met the police chief once but got the distinct impression this was one of the trials of being a country cop that he didn't particularly enjoy. According to Dana, he'd once been a big-time narcotics detective in Houston.

"Gia, meet Flynn Barlow." The chief said it as if the name would clear up everything. Well, it didn't. She didn't know Flynn Barlow from Adam. More than likely, though, Flynn Barlow was starting to put together who she was.

When Rhys saw that the name Barlow wasn't ringing any bells, he said, "He's the guy who's leasing your property . . . for his cattle."

Shit!

He was *that* Flynn Barlow. The previous owner, who was now serving time in prison, had made a deal with Barlow's family that their cattle could graze on the thousand-acre ranch. As a term of the sale, she was forced to stick to their agreement.

"I don't remember the lease including rights to my shower," she huffed, but she was starting to feel foolish for her over-the-top behavior. But he'd had a gun, she reminded herself.

Rhys looked pointedly at Barlow.

"Old man Rosser said I should make myself at home until the new owner took over. The T Corporation"—Flynn glared at Gia— "wasn't supposed to arrive for another week."

"Well, the T Corporation is here, so don't use her shower anymore. Problem solved." Rhys turned on his heels and was about to leave when Gia stopped him.

"Escrow's been closed since fall. This is my place." She'd even purchased the furniture and the artwork, such as it was. She glanced at Bullwinkle hanging on the wall. "Mr. Barlow had no right coming into my house."

Rhys pinched the bridge of his nose. "We've established that. Are you saying you want to press charges? Is that how you want to play this?"

After the past six months she didn't know how she wanted to play anything. That was why she'd blown off her meeting with her agent in New York and traveled to Nugget a week early. She'd needed peace to feel safe again. With the death threats, the surprise visits from the feds, the grand jury hearings, she was constantly on edge. That was why finding Barlow in her shower had been so frightening.

"No, of course not. But this house is off limits, Mr. Barlow." It was supposed to be her sanctuary.

"Got it," he said. "I'll just get my bag and boots from your bathroom and move on."

Rhys waited for Flynn to gather his things while Gia sat in the living room. The police chief probably thought she was a lunatic.

"You up for good now?" he asked her.

She nodded. For the second time in less than eight months she'd been told she was in the clear. But as long as her ex-boyfriend, Evan Laughlin, was missing, people would always suspect that she'd been part of his scheme. At least here in this Sierra Nevada railroad town, on this large parcel of land, she could hide from her former life. A life that had been abruptly ripped from her thanks to Evan and her stupidity about men.

"Is there really a T Corporation?" Rhys leaned against the mantel of her enormous fireplace, curiosity written in his body language. His backup had already taken off on another call.

She'd incorporated and bought the ranch under the phony name to hide her true identity, afraid that the media would catch wind of her multimillion-dollar acquisition. Buying a fancy estate while mired in the largest financial scandal in history wasn't exactly prudent. But from the start, Rosser Ranch had called to her, representing everything she'd ever wanted in life. Security, roots, and the opportunity to fulfill a longtime dream.

"Of course there is," she told him, knowing she wasn't really answering the question. Last summer the town had discovered her true identity. But she'd never made it clear whether the T Corporation was a bona fide business or that she was its sole stakeholder.

"What is the corporation going to do with the place . . . or is it just you?"

Saving her from having to answer, Flynn came into the room carrying his leather satchel.

"I'm sorry I scared you," he said, appearing somewhat contrite, though she suspected it was an act. With his perfect white teeth, chocolaty brown eyes, and cleft chin, the man obviously thought he was George Clooney and could talk his way out of anything. "See you around."

God, she certainly hoped not.

Rhys followed Flynn out the door, leaving Gia alone in blessed solitude. She heard gravel sputter and watched out the front window as both men rode up her long driveway in their separate trucks. The place was all hers and Gia began aimlessly wandering the rooms of the eight-thousand-square-foot log home, taking in the soaring ceilings, the gorgeous hewn beams, and the views of endless fields, mountains, and the Feather River.

She'd planned to move in last fall, right after escrow closed. But the feds, who'd originally cleared Gia of collusion in Evan's Ponzi scheme, had stunned her by reversing themselves and bringing her case before a federal grand jury. Jurors had ultimately failed to find enough probable cause to indict her. Nevertheless, her lawyers had advised her to stay in New York for the duration of the hearings.

Now she was here. Finally home, even if the place still felt foreign. She'd only been to Nugget a few times, once as a kid and then as an adult to scout out property.

Far from the ocean and with its freezing winters, this part of the state wasn't the most coveted. But she'd liked what she'd seen. It was the way she remembered it from all those years ago. The last vacation before her dad had died from a massive heart attack. The town, which consisted primarily of a commercial district built around a verdant square, and the obligatory Main Street, wasn't all that charming.

Yet, only four hours northeast of San Francisco and less than three hours from Sacramento, it still managed to attract tourists. The whole setup fit in perfectly with her long-term plan. All of it except Flynn Barlow and his cattle. But what could she do? His lease had been a condition of the sale and she'd wanted Rosser Ranch more than anything she could remember.

Gia continued to walk from room to room. The house dwarfed her New York penthouse, which she'd sold for a hefty sum. The first thing she'd do here was get rid of the animal-head trophies. Ray Rosser had been a big-game hunter and liked showing off his prizes. His last kill had been of the human variety, landing Rosser in prison for life.

Despite its ginormous size, the house was warm, like a ski lodge. In the kitchen, a caterer's dream, there was a big basket on the center island. Gia read the card from Dana and unwrapped the cellophane to find a treasure trove of local delicacies, including chocolates, jams, beer, and two tickets for a train ride through Gold Country. She would thank her real estate agent later that evening, during dinner. The two had plans to meet at the Ponderosa—the only sit-down restaurant in town.

Small-town life would certainly take some getting used to. In New York she could eat at a different restaurant every day for years. But there was no turning back from this new leaf and even if Gia could, she didn't want to. Not after what she'd been through. There was something that felt inordinately innocent about this mountain town.

Yeah, she laughed to herself, a place where a person felt perfectly entitled to sneak into her house and take full advantage of her shower.

Still pent up from the ordeal, she decided to take a stroll down to the barn. The sun was out and the air warm—a beautiful April day. She supposed spring came earlier in California than it did on the East Coast. The walk did her good after being crammed on an airplane all morning and then in a car for the forty-five-minute drive to Nugget.

She took her time hiking down to the paddocks and stable, stopping to admire a patch of yellow poppies and the clear blue sky. Nothing like the layer of smog that hung over Manhattan like a smoke cloud. The property went on forever. And despite the drought, there were plenty of lush, green fields, which Gia attributed to recent rain showers. Across the pasture, she saw cows—dozens of them—and let out a huff of frustration. The animals would put a crimp in her plans. But as she always said, where there's a will there's a way. Gia had plenty of determination left in spite of everything that had happened in the last several months, including losing a multimillion-dollar franchise. Her television show, her syndicated column, her financial self-help books, and her high-paying public appearances were all gone. Dust in the wind.

But Gia had this, she thought as she gazed out over miles upon miles of breathtaking land. The smell of bark and wildflowers and fresh grass . . . and something else. She would've sworn it was the musky scent of horses. But Rory wasn't due to arrive until later in the week.

That was when she heard a soft neighing and followed the sound into the stable. There, in the end stall, was a black gelding. The quarter horse had to be at least sixteen hands high with a coat as shiny as a newborn foal's. The big fellow was throwing his head as if happy to have company. The question was, where had he come from?

She flashed on Flynn Barlow's stock trailer and the answer became all too clear. Apparently the SOB wasn't satisfied to just steal the use of her shower; he'd helped himself to her barn as well.

The last man Gia knew with that kind of chutzpah had not only stolen her money and ruined her career, he'd stomped on her heart.

Chapter 2

By the time Flynn got to Highway 70, Gia's identity hit him like a lightning bolt. Funny how he'd watched her on television for years but out of context couldn't place her.

Her financial show had always impressed him. Beauty and brains, a lethal combo where he was concerned. Who would've guessed she was crazier than a loon?

Then again, who would've guessed Miz Money Wizard would sleep with a crook?

Flynn had been watching the Evan Laughlin case play out in the media with a keen eye. It was just the sort of case he handled, first as an FBI agent, then as a federal prosecutor, and now as a defense attorney. Smart lady like that should've seen right through an investment fraud of that scale. Promises of 50 percent returns in ninety days. *Yeah*, Flynn laughed to himself, *and I'm Santa Claus*.

He could see why the feds were looking at her hard. In their position, he would've suspected she was either an accessory or an early stakeholder who'd made plenty of cash off the new investors and kept her mouth shut when she realized there were no legitimate earnings. That the whole thing was a house of cards.

Though he'd read somewhere that her lover had bilked her out of half her fortune before absconding with twenty billion dollars from thousands of investors, it could've been a cover the two had cooked up to make Gia look innocent. In a case of this magnitude who knew what to believe?

Too bad, because he'd really admired her. On her show, geared toward the average Joe, she broke down everything from the complexities of retirement funds to the pros and cons of reverse mortgages in simple, layperson terms. His own mother, who was financially illiterate, had learned how to follow the Dow by reading one of Gia's *Investing for Dodos* books. With all the self-help crap out there, someone like Gia Treadwell made a difference.

And bank.

She'd turned herself into a small media empire. The show alone had probably catapulted her into the seven-figure income bracket. The books, public appearances, and syndicated column were just gravy.

But Flynn had learned long ago that some people were never satisfied. Greed could be a powerful motivator. Whether she was involved or not, it would be best to keep a wide berth. And after this morning he didn't think that would be too difficult. Gia had made it abundantly clear she didn't like him.

He shook his head; the crazy broad should keep away from guns.

Flynn headed to his family's spread in Quincy, about a forty-minute ride away. Most of the time, he lived in Sacramento, where he ran his law practice. But his parents were getting up in years and he and his brother were slowly taking over the family's cattle operation. With the spring calving, he was living up here almost full-time, racing back and forth between Quincy and Rosser Ranch. Because of the drought they'd leased the Nugget property for more grazing land so they wouldn't have to cull their herd. Between the two ranches, the Barlows, unlike a lot of California cattlemen, were doing okay. As long as the price of beef held, they'd even make a profit this year. He had enough good people running the law firm that he could get away with telecommuting most days. Sacramento was close enough for him to make his court dates.

About ten miles out of Nugget, Flynn got a flat. He pulled over at the first turnout, hopped out, and found what he thought was a barbed-wire puncture in the front right tire. One of the casualties of ranch life. In the bed of the truck he found the jack but took one look at the spare and let out a frustrated breath. The tire was low on air, not safe for towing a twenty-four-hundred-pound stock trailer.

"Ah, crap," he muttered, then grabbed his cell from the cab's console. A few seconds later he had the local tow service on the phone, told the owner his location, and flipped down the tailgate to wait, wondering how the day had turned out so shitty.

Hey, he reminded himself, *no one died*. A vision of Gia holding Rosser's Winchester on him roused a chuckle. Nutjob lady didn't even know where the safety was. He was sitting there soaking up the sun when a Ford, traveling east, turned off the road and parked next to him.

"You need a ride?" It was Clay McCreedy. They'd known each other since they were knee-high boys, competing at the Plumas County Fair for the best 4-H steer.

Even though Flynn had grown up in Quincy, he knew a lot of people in Nugget. The beauty of a rural county was that everyone roamed the same mountains and knew everybody else.

"I'm waiting for a tow. Tire's flat and my spare isn't much better."

"You call Griffin Parks at the Gas and Go?" Clay got out of his truck.

"Yep."

Clay grabbed a seat next to Flynn on the tailgate and said, "I could hitch your trailer to my truck and park it at my place until you get your tire repaired. I don't know if the tow truck can handle them both."

"I'd appreciate it."

"Not a problem. How's things?"

"Good. Met your new neighbor." Flynn grinned at the thought of the little blonde walking in on him in the shower.

"Gia Treadwell?"

"Yup. You meet her yet?"

"Not formally. But ever since last summer the whole town's been talking about her. You think she was in on her boyfriend's scam?"

"I couldn't tell you, Clay. But innocent until proven guilty." Flynn wouldn't publicly hypothesize about her; it wasn't right.

"You know what she's planning to do with that ranch? There's a lot of concern that she'll turn it into a shopping center. That land is zoned agricultural."

Flynn laughed. "A shopping center . . . in Nugget?" The population, even when the weekenders descended, wasn't more than six thousand.

"You know what I mean."

Flynn did. Farm and ranchland was shrinking all over the Golden State. Strip malls and track homes now dotted what used to be fruit and nut orchards, ground crops, and grazing land. "Our meeting was short and not very friendly. I doubt she'll be telling me her plans anytime soon."

Clay raised his brows. "What happened?"

Flynn told him about the shower incident and how Gia had called the cops on him. Clay got a good chuckle over the story. It had been a long time since they'd gotten a chance to talk, so they spent the time catching up on each other's families, friends, and the cattle business.

When Griffin arrived, Clay helped Flynn unhitch his trailer. They hooked it up to Clay's truck. Then Griffin attached the hook and chain from his tow truck to Flynn's Ford.

"All set?" Griffin asked. The tow-truck driver was not only the proprietor of Nugget's sole gas station but owned a planned community on the edge of town where he was slowly selling off second homes to vacationers.

Flynn had heard through the grapevine that Griffin was part Native American and came from a small tribe that owned one of the largest gambling casinos in California. Apparently the guy would rather rescue stranded motorists than count his money. Hell, nothing wrong with that.

"Yep. Thanks for coming to get me." Flynn waved goodbye to Clay, climbed into Griffin's rig, and rode back to town with him.

It turned out the tire was destroyed. Griffin couldn't get a new one until the next day, so Flynn was stranded there for the night. He would've bunked at Rosser Ranch but under the circumstances didn't think he'd be welcome. Instead, he walked over to the Lumber Baron Inn. The hulking Victorian took up a quarter of the town square and had been completely refurbished a few years back. The interior was as elegant as any hotel in the city.

"Hey, Maddy, got a room?"

Maddy, the inn's owner, looked up from the check-in desk and smiled. "For you, of course. But why are you staying in town and not at Rosser Ranch?"

"The new owner is there now." He left it at that. Because Maddy was married to the police chief, she'd find out soon enough that Flynn and Gia had gotten off to a bad start.

"How are things?" she asked while searching for an available room on her computer monitor. In spring the inn did a brisk business.

"Good but busy with the cattle."

"Yeah, Clay too," she said. "I guess it's calving season."

"Yup. How 'bout you?"

"Busy too. This year we're getting extra summer help. It's too much now that we have Gold Mountain."

Flynn had heard that she and her brother, a San Francisco hotelier, had purchased and restored the old cabin resort fifteen minutes away. "How's that taking off?"

"Like gangbusters. This is our second summer and it's booked solid, many of the same guests who came under the old ownership. We thought we'd lose a lot of them because we jacked the price up after an extensive remodel. But the guests are happy with the new amenities."

"That's great. Good for you and Nate."

She grabbed a key off a hook. "Looks like 206 is available. Let me take you up."

"You have a laundry service?" He only had the clothes he'd worn that morning while riding fences. They were pretty rank.

"Absolutely. There's a bag in your closet. Just send it down when you get settled in." She walked him up the flight of stairs and opened the door to a spacious room with a king-sized bed.

"This is perfect, Maddy. Thanks."

"It's our pleasure to have you as a guest." She left him to unpack.

Because all he had was a duffel of dirty clothes, Flynn quickly transferred them to the laundry bag. He took in the room, sticking his head in the bathroom. Pretty luxurious digs. He ran the laundry down to the front desk, came back up, and called Clay to let him know that he wouldn't be collecting his stock trailer until the next day. Then he spent a couple of hours checking in with his law office, reading emails, and returning calls.

Sometime after six he decided to hit the Ponderosa. He was hungry and could use a drink. For a week night the place was swinging. Flynn snagged a stool at the bar and ordered a Jack Daniel's neat. Not five minutes later the police chief walked in and took the seat next to Flynn.

"Heard you're staying at the inn," Rhys said.

"News travels fast in Nugget."

"It helps that I know the innkeeper."

Flynn chuckled. "Maddy working late?"

"Nah, I'm about to pick her up. Just thought I'd drop by to say hi because we didn't get a chance to really chat this afternoon." Rhys tossed his head back and laughed.

"The woman's crazy, you do realize that?"

"I don't know, Flynn, if I found some random dude in my shower..."

"Hey, that's a damn fine shower. She wasn't supposed to show up for another week."

Amused, Rhys said, "Do me a favor and make peace with the lady. I like a quiet town and I have a feeling with her around it's gonna get noisy."

"What do you mean by that?"

"You know who she is, right?"

"Gia Treadwell."

As if on cue, Gia and another woman walked into the restaurant. Both men watched as they were escorted to a table in the middle of the dining room.

Flynn turned back to Rhys. "The feds still looking at her?"

Rhys lifted his shoulders in a halfhearted shrug. "It's not like they would share that information with me."

Flynn suspected Rhys knew more than he was saying. Before coming home to Nugget, Rhys was a rising figure in Houston PD's command structure. Savvy guy. And, unlike the rest of Plumas County, he was tightlipped. Back when Flynn was still law enforcement, Rhys might've confided in him. But not now that Flynn had gone to the other side. And he respected the hell out of Rhys for it.

"I've gotta roll," Rhys said. "Take it easy."

"You too."

After Rhys left, Flynn ordered a steak. "And bring over a couple of drinks on me to the two ladies over there," he told the bartender, and hitched his head at Gia's table.

"You mean Dana and the Rosser Ranch woman?" When Flynn nodded, the bartender said, "They like margaritas."

"Whatever they want." It was a peace gesture.

He watched the drinks get delivered and the server point him out. The two women stuck their heads together. Flynn assumed Gia was telling her friend about their run-in. By tomorrow it would be all over town. Gia glanced his way and nodded. It appeared that was all the thanks he was going to get from her. Fair enough, he supposed, and cut into his steak when it arrived.

He was just sopping up the last of his meal with a piece of bread when Gia approached.

"Thanks for the drinks."

"You're welcome."

She was actually better-looking in real life than on television. Before, when she'd been holding the Winchester—and his Glock—he'd been too preoccupied to notice. But her eyes were bluer, her lashes longer, her lips fuller, and her face more heart-shaped. "We good now?"

"I wouldn't say that. You left your horse in my barn."

"You met Dude, huh?" He'd forgotten about that. "Look, I didn't think you'd be here for another week. Trailering him back and forth . . . that's a lot to ask of the poor guy. Besides, what do you need a barn for?"

"I need the barn for my own horse."

He jerked his head, a little surprised. "You have a horse?"

She didn't answer, just glared at him. Gia Treadwell was dead set on disliking him.

"There're like fourteen stalls in that stable. You need them all?" Jeez, why was he arguing with her? It was her barn.

She stood there for a while, contemplating. "I suppose it's fine."

It was not the answer he was expecting. "I'll pay for Dude's board."

"Don't worry about it."

Before Flynn could insist, she abruptly turned and returned to her table, giving him an excellent view of her backside. He'd never seen her ass on TV. From this angle it looked pretty good.

Chapter 3

Gia thought Flynn Barlow was a real piece of work. Obviously, all he thought he had to do was buy a woman a drink and turn on the charm and she'd melt for him. That wasn't going to work with her. She'd only agreed to let him keep his horse in her barn for the sake of the animal. Plus, Rory could use the company. Gia had been boarding the mare at a stable near Central Park with lots of other horses, so it might be lonely in the big barn, alone.

"What did he say?" Dana asked.

"That he didn't think I'd need the barn. He's about the most presumptuous person I've ever met."

"Okay, but you've gotta admit he's really nice-looking."

Oh, Flynn was better than nice-looking, and she'd seen the full monty. "He's all right. As long as we don't have to interact, we'll be fine."

How often did a rancher have to look after his cows anyway? It wasn't like he was milking them. Gia returned to their earlier conversation.

"I still think you and Aidan should get married at the ranch."

Aidan was an arson investigator for Cal Fire. He and Dana had fallen in love last summer while Gia had been in Nugget shopping for property. In the midst of all Gia's upheaval, she and Dana had forged a wonderful friendship.

Dana squeezed her arm. "You're so sweet. But my parents are excited about having it at their home. I don't want to disappoint them."

"I can't believe it's only a couple of months away," Gia said. "You ready?"

"You know me, the queen of organization. Still, I've never felt more disorganized in my life. Thankfully, Samantha Breyer is lending me a hand." Samantha was Maddy's brother's wife and did the event planning for his hotels.

Gia was still learning who everyone was. In New York she recognized a few residents in her co-op by face, but that was it. Not like here, where you even knew the names of everyone's dogs.

She watched Flynn across the dining room, flirting with a busty brunette at the bar. He was way too sure of himself as far as she was concerned. Evan had been cocky but much more reserved. Flynn acted like he owned the world. Case in point: her shower, her barn, and definitely that barstool. If aloof Evan could manage to bilk clients out of billions, she could only imagine what charming and overly confident Flynn was capable of.

No need to worry because she didn't plan to get close enough to find out.

"Hey," Dana said. "You seem distracted."

Gia reined in her thoughts. "I'm just taking everything in."

"Culture shock, I'm sure." Dana laughed.

For a long time Gia had been running in the fast lane, hanging out with television executives, doing lunches at New York's top restaurants, and rubbing elbows with elite financiers. Nugget . . . well, it was different. Ranchers and railroad workers made up the bulk of the town and the only sit-down restaurant was the Ponderosa, with its gold-rush saloon motif and an attached bowling alley. It was nothing like Bedford, the tony New York bedroom community she'd grown up in until her father had died.

"Yeah," she told Dana. "But a good one. People here at least leave me alone."

"I hate to burst your bubble, but that won't last. Everyone is curious about what you plan to do with Rosser Ranch, and of course there's your . . ."

"My involvement with the biggest con artist in modern history?"

Dana shrugged sheepishly. "People are curious."

"You haven't told anyone about my program?"

Gia had confided in Dana about her plan to turn Rosser Ranch into a residential program for down-on-their-luck women. It was something she'd been mapping out in her head for years, just waiting for the right opportunity. She wanted to name the program after her mother, who knew intimately the travails of being financially dependent on a man and then left with nothing.

"Of course not. I can keep a secret. Everyone's so worried you'll turn the place into a subdivision, they're likely to be relieved."

"That's what I'm hoping." Gia nudged her head at Flynn, who'd moved on to chatting up the bartender. The brunette looked put out. "I also need to get rid of him."

"A deal's a deal, Gia. His cattle get to graze until the first frost. Then he'll move them somewhere warmer."

"What if he doesn't?" If Gia wanted her plan to work, she needed to start exercising it now.

"Ray Rosser gave him a year's lease. Nothing you can do except coexist." Dana glanced over at Flynn and smiled. "There are worse things in life than having to coexist with Flynn Barlow."

"Really? I can't think of any."

"Oh, come on. You two just got off on the wrong foot. People in town adore the guy. His family has lived in Quincy since dinosaurs roamed the land. I've never met them. but from what I hear they're good people."

Everyone had thought Evan was a Wall Street pillar. As it turned out, the only thing he was supporting was a hidden bank account with other peoples' hard-earned money.

"We'll see," Gia said, wanting to change the subject.

A server came to the table and asked if they wanted dessert. Gia got the carrot cake. What the hell; it wasn't like she had to watch her weight for the camera anymore.

Dana declined. "As it is, I'll be lucky to fit into my wedding gown."

"You'll get into it." Gia eyed her slim friend, who beamed. Dana was so giddy in love it was sickening. Except Aidan was one of the good ones.

Dessert came and Gia pushed an extra fork Dana's way. "It wouldn't kill you to take a taste."

Within ten minutes they'd inhaled the entire slab of cake.

"I should probably get home," Dana said.

"Yeah, me too." Gia had gotten a tip on some value stocks and wanted to check them out before the market opened in the morning.

She and Dana paid the bill. On their way out, Flynn swiveled around on his stool.

"Catch you later," he said.

Not if she could help it.

* * *

Rory came at the end of the week in a horse trailer fit for a Triple Crown winner. Gia spared no expense for her baby. She celebrated the reunion the next morning by taking the mare on their first Rosser Ranch trail ride. Both she and Rory were used to the designated equestrian trails in Central Park, not so much the open range. Fearful of getting lost, Gia stuck to the fence line. Though officially spring, it was chilly this morning, and in some spots layers of frost covered the trees and ground like white crystals.

Across the fence, Gia caught glimpses of life on McCreedy Ranch. She assumed the owner, Clay McCreedy, would be her biggest adversary regarding the residential program she wanted to start. According to Dana, he wasn't someone to go up against. His family had been ranching here since the Gold Rush and they had a lot of influence in Nugget.

Besides, the land was zoned agricultural. A halfway house geared toward helping women become financially self-sufficient didn't exactly scream farming. To make it work, she needed their blessing. But she had a strategy for getting around the zoning and just needed to work out the details.

"You're up early."

She swung around on Rory, startled. So lost in her thoughts, Gia hadn't heard Flynn come up behind her. He was in full cowboy regalia: a Stetson swooped over one eye, a field coat, chaps, and boots. The only thing missing was a six-shooter, but he probably had that pistol of his tucked away somewhere. Dude gave Rory a once-over, then blew out a long-suffering snort. Apparently the gelding was as arrogant as his owner.

With the toe of his boot, Flynn nudged Dude closer and scratched Rory behind her ears. Rory let out a happy nicker. *Traitor.*

"Nice sorrel," he said and eyed Gia's English tack. "But you might want to trade that pancake saddle in for something a little more practical. They've got some real fine Western saddles over at Farm Supply." And then he grinned as if he knew he was antagonizing her.

In response, she yawned in his face. "Herding the doggies?"

One brow went up. "The doggies? Do yourself a favor and don't use that term. Seriously, people will laugh at you."

"Good to know," she said and started to rein her horse away.

"Leaving so soon?"

"Do you purposely do that?"

"What?" he asked.

"Try to provoke me."

The jerk grinned again. He actually had the nerve to look her in the eye and flash those obnoxious white teeth of his. "It's just so damn easy."

She was on the verge of telling him what an ass he was when his phone blasted "Home on the Range."

"Gotta take this," he said and tugged the cell out of the pocket of his field coat.

Gia loitered for a few minutes, hoping to catch his end of the conversation. For the life of her, she didn't know why. It wasn't like she was interested in anything about him. When she couldn't glean the gist of his discussion, she moved on, urging Rory into a canter.

A good distance away from Flynn, she tightened the reins, wanting to take the ride at a slower pace. There was nothing like seeing her property from the back of a horse. The sun peeked through the clouds, promising another stellar Sierra Nevada day. Bright orange poppies covered the fields like blankets. From up on the ridge she could see the Feather River running high with melted snow from the mountains. Everything smelled crisp and clean and woodsy. She still had to pinch herself to prove it was hers. That she was here, away from the prying eyes of the feds and the ceaseless harassment of the press. And that she owned a slice of paradise.

After buying the Fifth Avenue penthouse, Gia had thought she'd arrived. "Movin' On Up," just like the theme song to that old sitcom, *The Jeffersons*. The apartment was a symbol of her unimaginable success. But it had never really been her. The yards of travertine tile, the crystal chandeliers, and the Bauhaus art, so cold and sterile. Conspicuous consumption to the point of being vulgar.

Not that Rosser Ranch was modest by any stretch of the imagination. It boasted a thousand acres of prime riverfront land, a custom log house the size of Rhode Island, and amenities too numerous to count. But it didn't feel ostentatious. It felt real and warm and welcoming. It felt like the perfect safe haven for downtrodden women trying to get back on their feet again.

By the time she made it to the stable, Flynn was there, brushing Dude. *Great!* The cowboy was like a bad penny. He'd taken off his jacket and had hung it from a hook while he groomed the horse. Gia couldn't help but watch his sinewy arms move back and forth over Dude's coat, his biceps straining inside the sleeves of his chambray shirt.

As she began to dismount, he magically appeared to help her down.

"I don't need assistance." She clenched her teeth.

"I didn't say you did. But I'm a gentleman."

She highly doubted that, but it seemed petty to protest. He gripped her around the waist and lowered her down as if she weighed nothing. And when he let go she felt a tiny jolt of disappointment.

Flustered, she immediately set to work removing Rory's saddle and going through the routine of grooming her own horse. Flynn silently led Dude into a stall and walked to the back of the barn to a towering stack of alfalfa hay that hadn't been there before. With a hay hook, he twisted the wire on one of the bales until it snapped, removed a flake, and put it in Dude's feeder. He went back for a second flake and dropped that one into Rory's rack.

"I have my own hay," she said.

"Consider it my contribution for keeping my horse here."

Since alfalfa ran close to three hundred dollars a ton, she didn't argue. "Thank you."

He nodded, leaned against the wall, and watched her finish with Rory. "Where'd you keep her when you lived in New York?"

So he'd figured out who she was. Gia knew it had only been a matter of time. "A stable near Central Park."

His eyes lapped the barn. "I can't imagine anything better than this."

"It's pretty great," she admitted.

"A lot of folks had their eye on this ranch when Ray put it on the market. No one could afford the price tag." His words weren't quite accusatory, but there was innuendo there. She should've been offended, but she was used to it. The FBI and the Securities and Exchange Commission had interrogated her ceaselessly about the ranch.

"Yes, well, I used to make a lot of money," she blurted out and then could've strangled herself for sounding defensive. For responding at all. Gia didn't have to justify herself; she'd purchased the place with her hard-earned investments, the proceeds from her penthouse, and savings. Every last dime of it.

"Not anymore, I guess." He paused to study her reaction. "The property taxes alone will cost you a fortune."

She squinted at him. "I've got it covered, not that it's any of your business."

"Nope, it sure isn't. But if you ever want to sell . . ."

"To you?" She laughed. "A wrangler's salary must be good."

He pushed himself off the wall. "It's *honest* work." This time there was no innuendo, just flat-out condemnation.

"You don't know anything about me, so keep your judgment to yourself." Gia led Rory into her stall and put down fresh straw. She wasn't going to let him provoke her. The day had started out too nice and she had bigger fish to fry, like making a living.

"You're right, I don't," he said. "Innocent until proven guilty. Look, in the next couple of months I'll be around here a lot. The cows are calving, I'll be branding, castrating, and auditing. I'm hoping we can forge some kind of truce here."

"Really? Because accusing me of being a thief seems like a funny kind of ceasefire, don't you think?"

"I didn't accuse you of anything. And you're the one who held a rifle on me. But, hey, I'm willing to forgive and forget." He started to say more but heard a motor and the crunch of gravel.

They moved to the door and saw a dark sedan coming up the road. Flynn studied the car for a few seconds and Gia saw his gaze move to the logo on the license plate. She couldn't make it out from this distance.

"You expecting company?" he asked.

"No." She craned her neck to get a better look inside the car. The windows were tinted and most locals drove trucks.

"Wait here out of sight," he said as the car came to a halt and two men in suits got out.

Ordinarily she would've told him to pound sand, but something about the authoritative way he'd told her to wait made her heed his directions. She slid behind the barn door, watching and listening from a small concealed window that was open. Flynn met the men as they approached the stable.

"Flynn!" one of them said, sounding surprised.

"Hey, Jeff." Flynn bobbed his head in greeting to the guy who hadn't said anything. "What brings you fellows all the way up here?"

"I'm gonna ask you the same thing," Jeff said.

"I lease this land to run my cattle. Now your turn."

"We understand a Gia Treadwell owns the property and lives here."

"That would be correct. What can she do for you?"

"You her lawyer, Flynn?"

Gia thought Jeff was being facetious. By now she'd figured out that her visitors were feds, either FBI or SEC. New York . . . California . . . they all looked the same. American cars, cheap suits, crappy wing tips, and a buttload of attitude.

"Nope."

"Then where is she? We were up at the house, but no one answered. . . . Her car's still there."

"Y'all have a warrant?"

"Ah, cut the shit, Barlow. We're just here to introduce ourselves."

"Yeah," Flynn said and moved closer to the agents, his broad shoulders blocking Gia's view. "I'm gonna have to ask you fellows to leave. This is private property."

"Give me a break, Flynn. We just want to ask her a few questions. What the hell crawled up your ass?"

"Just a little thing called the Constitution. I believe all questions should be directed to her attorney."

"For Christ's sake," Jeff said, and the next thing Gia knew, both agents were heading to the car with their tails between their legs. "Screw you, Barlow. Forget about coming to the house for poker."

When they left, Gia walked out of the barn. "You know those agents?"

"Jeff Croce, but not the other one. He must be new."

"How do you know him?"

Flynn just stared at her for a few seconds but didn't answer. "You better let your lawyer know they were here today. They won't let up."

"I don't have a lawyer anymore," she said.

Flynn reeled back. "Why the hell not?"

"Because I thought this crap was over . . . and they cost too much."

"I'd suggest you get one." He went back inside the barn, came out a few seconds later with his jacket, and headed for his truck. "See you around."

Gia stood there, watching the puffs of dust trail behind his Ford as he drove away. The man certainly was an enigma. A swaggering jackass one minute, her champion the next. He'd been the first person who wasn't on her payroll to stick up for her in a long time. And that meant a lot, even if she didn't want it to.

Chapter 4

Even though Flynn couldn't help poking at Gia like a schoolboy with a crush, the last thing he needed was to get sucked into her problems. But when the Sacramento FBI agents had shown up at her place, he couldn't let her twist in the wind. Guilty or not, she deserved due process. And, for God's sake, a lawyer.

What kind of irresponsible person fires her attorney because of lack of funds and buys a multimillion-dollar ranch? Only someone who thought her innocence would prevail. Not that Flynn was saying Gia was innocent. But he'd come to learn that that was the thought process of innocent people.

I've got nothing to hide, so what do I need a lawyer for? If he only had a dollar for every time he'd heard that naïve statement, he'd be a rich man.

In Gia's case, he'd acted out of habit and a sense of duty. But from here on in he was out of it. Private practice meant he could pick and choose his clients and Gia wouldn't be one of them. Better to stay away from pretty women he was attracted to, who were up to their eyeballs in trouble. It was bad enough he'd see her on the ranch from time to time.

He looked at his truck dash clock. If there wasn't a traffic jam in Roseville, he'd make his apartment by noon, just in time to shower and change before his one o'clock appointment with the CEO of a social media start-up. The client was being investigated by the IRS for tax fraud. The only thing the kid was guilty of was smoking too much pot and letting incompetents mind his books. Flynn would straighten it out.

For a Friday, traffic on Interstate 80 was surprisingly light. Usually folks were headed to the Bay Area for a weekend of fun. He got to his loft apartment in record time and parked in the underground lot. The building was conveniently located near both his office and the courthouse. And having grown up in an ancient farmhouse divvied up into a warren of small rooms, he thought he'd like the urban feel of open space and tall ceilings. Turns out he didn't. He rarely stayed here these days, preferring the rural Sierra to the crowded city.

Instead of bothering with the elevator, he took four flights of stairs to his apartment, stripped off his clothes, and jumped in the shower. He finished putting on a suit and tie and hit the answering machine on the way out.

"Hi, Flynn. It's Laurel. I haven't heard from you in a while and thought we could catch dinner this weekend."

"Yeah, maybe," he muttered to himself, thinking Laurel, who he'd been seeing on and off, might be a good distraction.

Call him an idiot, but ever since Gia had held that Winchester on him, his head had been full of her. She had a smart mouth and a sweet ass. And he was a sucker for both. Not so much for someone who aided and abetted a swindler, though. And while he was willing to give Gia the benefit of the doubt, it was best to stay clear of the whole mess.

He took the stairs back down to his truck and the city streets to his office, an entire floor of an old high-rise near the courthouse.

"Well, fancy seeing you here." Doris came around from her desk and gave Flynn a big hug. He'd stolen her from the U.S. Attorney's Office when he'd left. No one could juggle the phones and type as fast as Doris. Better yet, she could cull out the crazies faster than a shrink. "You come from the ranch?"

"A different ranch, but yeah. Went home first and showered."

"You clean up nice." She pinched his ass. Because she was somewhere north of sixty, no one batted an eye.

He sifted through the pile of mail on her desk. "Anything good?"

"A couple of checks, which have been deposited."

"Remind me to give you a raise, Doris."

"And a bonus," she said and tossed him a cheeky grin. "Boy wonder is running late."

That's what Flynn got for rushing. These start-up kids were self-entitled shits who couldn't care less about other people's schedules. But they kept him on hefty retainers, so unless they really took advantage, Flynn didn't complain.

"Toad here?" he asked Doris.

"He went out to grab lunch."

Lunch for Toad could mean a drive through Taco Bell or a lei-surely afternoon at the Lusty Lady. Flynn had lured the detective away from Sacramento PD, and although Toad didn't know a damn thing about white-collar crime, he had a way with witnesses. People, espe-cially women, told him stuff they wouldn't say in a confessional box. And it wasn't because of his looks. He was bald and squat and he had a neck like a bullfrog, hence the name Toad.

For all other investigative work, Flynn relied on Bellamy Brown, a forensic accountant he'd rustled from the IRS who could sniff out missing money like a bloodhound. There were two other attorneys in the firm and between the three of them, they pulled in corporate clients from all over the West.

"I'll be in my office, Doris. Tell me when the little shit gets here."

"I surely will."

Flynn sat at his desk, booted up his computer, and scrolled through his email. There was a cattlemen's meeting later in the month he'd like to miss but wouldn't. An invitation to a legal luncheon he'd def-initely miss and a note from his brother, reporting on the calf count on their Quincy ranch.

The intercom buzzed and Doris's voice came through. "Tim Casserly is on line two."

"All right, thanks." Flynn picked up the phone. "Timmy, what can I do for you?"

"What's up with you and Gia Treadwell?" Well, that hadn't taken long.

"Not a thing. I lease her land for my cattle. My family made the deal with the former owner; she just inherited it."

"The former owner who's serving time for shooting a cattle rustler?"

"The very one." Ray Rosser had pleaded guilty to second-degree murder. At his age, Ray was never getting out of prison.

"Pretty fancy place, from what I hear. Jeff said you kicked him off the property."

"Nah, I just asked him to leave. It was all very civil until he told me I couldn't play poker with you guys anymore."

Tim laughed. "You representing her?"

"Nope. What do you want with her, Tim?"

"Are you freaking kidding me? The woman's boyfriend ran off with billions. A lot of people in high places got ripped off."

"You couldn't even get an indictment." A grand jury would indict a ham sandwich, as the saying goes. The fact that they didn't get one and were still haranguing Gia told him there was more at play here than the Ponzi scheme. "You think she knows where Evan Laughlin is? Because from what I read in the papers, Ms. Treadwell was ripped off too."

"Hell yeah, we think she knows where he is. Could be she's harboring the money in some offshore bank account. How else did she afford that fancy ranch?"

"Tim, the woman's a millionaire in her own right. Doesn't seem like much of a stretch for her to buy a place like that."

"Maybe so," Tim said. Flynn could hear him drumming his fingers on the desk. "We know she liquidated a lot of her assets before closing escrow. Then again, a smart lady like her knows how to give herself cover. How do we get in there to talk to her?"

"You're asking me?" Flynn chuckled. "You're a freaking assistant U.S. Attorney. You know what you have to do. Go through her lawyer."

"She doesn't have one, which makes her fair game to talk to. If we can't get onto her property, we'll corner her in that little town . . . what's it called?"

"Nugget," Flynn said. The FBI could try, though he didn't know what good it would do. Gia had already made it through countless interrogations and a federal grand jury—the last step in a criminal investigation. That's why he didn't get why they were still going after her. In any event, she wasn't likely to spill her guts now. "What are you telling me for?"

"It would help to know her schedule, where she goes and when."

"Did you forget that I work for the other side now?"

"You said you're not her lawyer."

Flynn let out a sigh. "I don't know her schedule, and even if I did, I'm not getting involved." Lazy is what they were. Special Agent Jeff Croce and his partner didn't want to make the three-hour drive in the hopes that Gia would leave the ranch that day. They wanted everything set up nice and easy. Even though playing along could help butter up Tim for favorable plea deals when it came to Flynn's own clients, he didn't want any part of it.

"You're going to have to find your own snitch, Tim. For all intents and purposes, Miss Treadwell is my landlady."

"You suck, Barlow. See you at poker." Tim hung up.

Doris came over the intercom again. "Your brat is waiting in the conference room."

Gia sipped her coffee, nibbled at a piece of toast, and scanned the *Wall Street Journal* online, toggling back and forth between the newspaper, Bloomberg, and CNBC. It was eight o'clock East Coast time (five in California) on a Monday and ninety minutes until showtime. She studied the futures markets and the market indexes, looking for trends. Read what the analysts had to say about various stocks and reviewed economic calendars for new reports. The bottom line was she was looking for good trading opportunities. She had to refill her coffers. That's why she planned to get back to her roots. Day trading.

For most people it was a crapshoot, like going to Vegas and putting all your money on red. For Gia it had been a windfall. While other people got waitressing jobs to put themselves through college, she'd spent her time between classes day trading. By her senior year she'd amassed enough money to pay back her student loans and put herself through business school. When she'd left Harvard with an MBA she'd had enough cash to set herself up in Manhattan, buy a new wardrobe, and send a nice chunk of change to her mother.

She got hired at Locktrade as a junior broker, but the money was shit. No way could she continue to pay her pricey New York rent. So in her down time, she traded in the round-the-clock markets, making more in the first few months than she made at Locktrade in a year. Eventually she made the jump to Lehman Brothers as an investment banker and learned very quickly that her clients were lemmings—investing in whatever the "it" thing was at the moment. The returns were crap and most of them managed their money like infants. Acquiring a lot of debt at high interest. *Hey*, they'd say, *that's what it takes to live the American dream.*

No, it didn't. Gia knew better than anyone the kind of trouble bad financial decisions could get you into. It had probably killed her father. Forty and a heart attack. It had put Gia's mother and her in the poorhouse.

One night, during a dinner with a group of girlfriends, she'd started in on how people didn't have the first clue about managing money or saving for a rainy day. She'd launched into a diatribe about every-thing everyone was doing wrong and soon found herself making budgets and doing financial planning for her inner circle. They were a group of young, ambitious, and well-educated women living hand to mouth. One of those women just happened to be a booker for the *Today* show and got Gia a guest slot on a financial segment Matt Lauer hosted. After that she became a regular guest, as well as mak-ing appearances on *CNN Money* and Fox Business.

That's when CNBC approached her about doing her own show, *The Treadwell Hour: Financial Advice that Will Set You Free.* She gave notice at Lehman Brothers and moved into the CNBC offices, where her television ratings shot through the roof. The books and syndicated column came later, and before Gia knew it, she had her own financial self-help franchise. But it all came tumbling down when Evan's crimes were exposed.

No one wanted financial advice from an "expert" who'd been bilked by her own lover. Then there was the fact that in many circles, Gia was still suspected of conspiring with Evan in his Ponzi scheme. Some of his victims had lost their entire life savings, even their homes and retirement funds.

So now it was back to day trading. Gia stared at her monitor. The markets had just opened and, as usual, the first thirty minutes were highly volatile. She sat back, waiting to pounce. By late morning she was looking for reversal opportunities, also known as shifts in price trends. She looked at the clock, set to Eastern Standard Time, hoping to make her profit target before noon. Pretty soon the big money would go to lunch and the market would slow down. As three thirty approached, she was considerably up. By four, when the markets closed, she called it quits with a nice pot of profits.

And it was only one o'clock in California, giving her the rest of the day to play. She was halfway to the stable to visit Rory and take a ride when she saw a pickup cresting her driveway. It wasn't one she recognized, leaving her to wonder whether the feds were back for a second stab at her. The truck was covered in dust, the tires caked in mud, and the man behind the wheel wore a cowboy hat. There was a dog in the passenger seat with its head stuck out the window. On sec-ond thought, probably not a fed. She turned back to the house, where the man had stopped and was getting out of the driver's seat, holding, of all things, a basket covered in lacy fabric. The picture was somewhat incongruous. He was a rugged, strapping guy and the basket looked downright dainty hanging from his arm.

"Hey there." He shielded his eyes from the sun. "I'm your neighbor, Clay McCreedy."

Ah, the famous Clay McCreedy. "Pleased to meet you."

"I was just waiting for you to get settled in before dropping by. My wife, Emily, had a meeting in town. She wanted me to extend her apologies and said she'd come over to introduce herself just as soon as she could. In the meantime, she baked you this." He handed her the basket.

Gia peeked inside. It looked like a tart. No one ever brought her tarts in New York. "Thank you. Would you like to come in . . . have a cool drink?"

"Sure," he said, somewhat taken aback by her hospitality. People always thought New Yorkers were unfriendly.

She opened the door and led him toward the kitchen.

He stopped in the great room and gazed at the walls. "It's been a while since I've been inside. Ray did like his big-game trophies."

"You know anyone who wants them?"

He chuckled. "Why? You don't like 'em?"

"God no."

This time he let out a full-blown laugh. "I think my wife would be right with you on that one. They're worth something, though. You might want to put an ad in the *Nugget Tribune*. It's the local online newspaper." Gia knew the *Trib*'s owner, Harlee.

"Good idea." They continued into the kitchen, where Gia put the basket down on the center island. "Does this need to be refrigerated?"

"You know, I have no idea. Let me text Emily." He whipped out his phone and with one finger tapped out a message. "She'll get back to me. You're gonna love it. My wife is a world-class baker and all-around fantastic cook. She writes cookbooks, she's so good."

"Really?" It was nice to hear a man speak so highly of his wife. "What kind of cookbooks?"

"You name it. Her last one was about the cuisine of the Sierra Nevada, but she often works with big-name chefs who aren't so great at putting their recipes in writing for the home cook."

"No kidding? What an interesting job."

"Yep. We turned a converted barn into a test kitchen. Occasionally a TV crew will come in and film her and one of the chefs. Of course it's nothing like what you're used to . . ." He trailed off, obviously realizing his faux pas. People as far away as China knew about her fall from grace. It had been splashed all over the tabloids and reported daily on TMZ.

His phone chirped, distracting them from the awkwardness. He read from the screen. "She says you can leave it out overnight. Then it's gotta go into the icebox."

"Great. What would you like to drink? I've got soda, juice, Perrier . . . tequila."

"Tap water would be just fine." He gazed around the kitchen the same way he had in the living room.

"I haven't had a chance to put my mark on the place yet," she said while getting him a glass of water. "A lot of my stuff is still in boxes."

"I notice you got a horse delivered on Friday. Your driver took a wrong turn and wound up at my place."

"I'm sorry—"

"No worries. It happens all the time around here. Some of these roads don't even show up on GPS. Was this horse of yours an impulse buy?"

She laughed. "Yeah, about ten years ago."

He looked surprised—and delighted. "Dana never said anything about you being a horsewoman. Then again, Dana led us to believe you were the T Corporation."

"That was at my instruction, and I think under the circumstances you can understand why." She gave him a pointed look. No need beating around the bush. The sooner everyone was comfortable with her infamy the better.

He grinned. "Fair enough. So you ride, huh?"

"Dressage and some jumping."

"Dressage is pretty fancy for what we've got around here. Most of the horsewomen in these parts barrel race. But you'll do." He winked, the charmer.

"Flynn already made fun of my saddle."

"I bet he did." He grabbed a seat on one of the barstools. "He's just an old cowboy, not real sophisticated like the rest of us."

She laughed. "So you raise cattle, huh?"

"Just like Flynn. My family's been doing it since the Gold Rush. They sold beef to the prospectors."

"That's amazing." She let out a little sigh of awe.

"Unfortunately, we're a dying breed."

She cocked her head to the side. "Why's that?"

"It's cost prohibitive. The land's worth more for development, feed costs are through the roof, and our kids don't want to work their asses off for small gains."

"That's too bad." All those iconic images of cowboys riding the range on the Western plains flashed through her head.

"Yup. It's a special way of life and as long as I'm alive I plan to keep it going. Hopefully my sons will too. And you?"

Now for the real reason he was here. Clay McCreedy wanted to know what Gia planned to do with the ranch. "I don't think I'll be running cattle after Flynn's lease is up." *Keep it vague*, she told herself. "But I'd like to grow some things."

His brows inched up. "Oh yeah, like what kind of things?"

"I'm not entirely sure yet. You have any ideas?"

He was now looking at her like a city slicker who wanted to play at farming, which she was. But at least she'd mollified him that she wasn't turning the place into a resort.

"Biggest crop up here besides timber is alfalfa," he said.

"Really? I was thinking about produce, nuts, and maybe grapes for wine." It was hard to get excited about growing hay. Wine on the other hand . . .

"Not a lot of that around here because of the freezing conditions. But alfalfa and meadow hay were more than a seven-million-dollar crop last year. That was partly because the drought drove up demand. Still, it does pretty well for the county."

Okay, it was getting a little more exciting.

"People do grow some vegetables and plenty of folks raise honey . . . if you want to diversify. But I'm a rancher, not a farmer, so you're talking to the wrong guy. Flynn knows a lot of farmers in these parts. Tell him what you're thinking."

She actually had a consultant coming to the ranch to talk about options. But the real purpose of the farm was to create a loophole around the zoning rules so she could turn the ranch into her residential program. If the women were producing an agricultural product, neighbors might be less likely to complain. In the meantime, she didn't intend to fully disclose her plans until she got to know the residents.

"I'll do that," she said.

"He's a good guy, even if he is from Quincy."

"Is there some kind of rivalry between the two towns?"

"Only in good fun," he said. "What else you planning to do so far away from the big city?"

He was still fishing, but Gia couldn't blame him for being curious. She wasn't exactly your average girl next door.

"Honestly," she said, "recuperate from the past months of upheaval, ride Rory, and live a normal life."

His expression softened. "I hear ya and I wish you well in that endeavor. Ride over to McCreedy Ranch. The boys will show you some nice trails up in the state park."

"I'd definitely like that. And I would really love to meet your wife."

"Absolutely. We're a tight-knit community around here, always looking out for one another." He pulled a wallet from his pocket, fumbled through it, and handed her a business card. "The house number is on there, and my cell phone. You call anytime if you need something."

She found a pad of paper and a pen in one of the drawers, jotted down her numbers, and gave it to him. "I'd appreciate it if you didn't share this with anyone outside your family."

"Of course not," he said, and something about his character made her believe him. But Gia's judgment was shaky at best. Case in point: Evan Laughlin. "You meet Lucky and Tawny Rodriguez yet? They're your other neighbors."

"Not yet." But she'd heard about the champion bull rider and his boot-designer wife.

"You will. They're good people, you'll like 'em." He got up and put the hat he'd rested on the countertop back on his head.

She walked him out, watched him drive away, and went inside to have a piece of that tart.

Chapter 5

Midweek, Flynn made it back to Rosser Ranch. He wondered if Gia would continue calling it that, though the locals probably would never stop. The place, in his mind, would always hold the name of Gia's predecessor.

He threw flakes of hay to Dude and Rory. Since the previous Friday, Gia had been feeding them. Nice of her, although he suspected it wasn't so much a favor to him as a kindness to his horse. As he watched both equines munch away, his stomach growled. He'd left at dawn's early light and hadn't had time for breakfast or even a cup of coffee.

Perhaps he'd go into town and grab something at either the Ponderosa or the Bun Boy. While the Bun Boy didn't have any indoor seating—it was just a drive-through with picnic tables—the mornings were warmer now for eating alfresco. It would give Dude time to finish his hay before Flynn rode him to the back forty to check on the cattle. He was about to get in his truck when Gia came down the trail from her house carrying two mugs.

"One of those for me?" he asked, joking. When she nodded, he was surprised.

It must've shown because she said, "It's in return for running the men in suits off my property. Again, how is it you knew them?"

"Small world." He blew out a breath, took one of the mugs from her, and sipped. "Mmm, good stuff."

She eyed him for a few seconds and kept whatever she was thinking to herself.

"What've you been up to?" he asked just to fill space.

"Day trading."

He creased his brow. Brilliant financial lady like her should know better. "Isn't that kind of risky? Isn't investing all about the long-term?"

"In most cases, yes. But I'm pretty good at it."

He figured what she wasn't saying is that she needed money. Not at all the actions of a person sitting on a pile of stolen cash. Then again, the loot had likely been stashed away and couldn't be touched without raising flags.

"I never saw you mention day trading as a viable financial plan in any of your books," he said.

"You've read my books?" She looked stunned.

"My mother does. But I've been known to leaf through one or two. Good stuff."

She smiled. It was the first genuine one he'd seen from her and it about knocked him over like a mad steer. It was that powerful.

"What does your mom do?"

"She's a housewife and helps my dad run the ranch. It started with her wanting to set up college funds for her grandkids. She'd seen you on TV, bought one of your books, and the rest is history."

"You have kids?"

"My brother's kids," he said and took another sip of coffee.

"That's nice ... that she likes my books ... thanks for telling me."

"She liked your show too," he added. "Was angry when they canceled it."

"It appears she's in the minority. Most people wanted to see my head on a pike."

He nodded. "A lot people lost money in that scam. How did someone like you fall for it?" Flynn knew he was pushing it.

At first he didn't think she would answer. She just stared past him to the empty horse stalls.

"To fall on the old cliché: Love is blind. I trusted him ... not in my wildest dreams could I imagine him stealing from me or anyone else. At least I was conservative when it came to investing with him. Others invested all they had."

"Yet you're day trading," he said a mite too sanctimoniously.

"You wanna know the truth? It's like you said, I couldn't really afford this property. But I had to have it. The whole world was falling in on me and this ranch was the first place I felt safe. Really safe. Like everything here would make everything else all right." She gazed up at him and shrugged. "It's hard to explain."

"I get it. How much you in the hole for?" He was getting mighty personal.

She let out a puff of air. "I paid cash for the ranch . . . but I have things I want to do . . . and those taxes you were talking about. And . . . well . . ."

"Money's tight?" When she nodded, he said, "Sounds like you need to get a job."

"I've got one." She grinned. "Day trading. If things keep going the way they've been, I should be flush by summer."

Foolhardy if you asked him, but she wasn't.

"I guess Ray's buying cigarettes in prison with my grazing-rights money," Flynn said. Rosser got to keep the proceeds from the lease as terms of the agreement, even though Gia now owned the property.

"Dana thinks he's giving the money to his wife and daughter. If that's the case, I don't have a problem with it." She said it like she had empathy for them.

If the rumors were true, the sale of the ranch had been a windfall for the Rossers. Enough to pay Ray's legal fees and then some. "I think they're doing okay."

"I hope so. It sounds like Ray was a pretty difficult man."

"That's an understatement."

"I thought your families were good friends."

He knew she was referring to the sweetheart deal the Barlows had gotten on the lease. "I helped him out once. He was returning the favor."

Flynn had written up a living trust for Rosser. Turned out Raylene wasn't his only kid. Ray didn't exactly want that news getting out, and in these mountains word had a tendency to travel. Of course as Ray's attorney, Flynn was required to keep his mouth shut. But he'd worked it out so that the specifics of the trust could never be leaked. Only when Ray died would his beneficiaries find out.

"As far as my family," he continued, "there was no particular love for the Rossers. We both ran cow-calf operations, that's all."

"Cow calf? Is that what Clay McCreedy runs too?"

"Yep. All that means is we keep a permanent herd and sell the calves for beef. Clay's is one of the finest."

"I met him on Monday. He seems like a nice man."

"Yup, great guy. Now there's a family that mine has been friends with forever."

"It's amazing how everyone here knows one another, how you're entwined since birth."

He laughed. "Sometimes it has its drawbacks, but for the most part it's good to be part of a small town where everyone looks out for one another." He nudged his head at her riding outfit, a pair of skin-tight pants—Flynn thought they called them jodhpurs—knee-high equestrian boots, and a short-sleeved, fitted T-shirt. It was sexy as hell but completely impractical for the dusty trails of the Sierra. "You going riding?"

"Yep." She looked at her watch. "I made my profit target more than an hour ago."

He knew she was talking about trading stocks. "Well, don't let me keep you." It was high time he got to work too, though he was still considering that breakfast.

Gia led Rory out of her stall, took her over to the tack area, and groomed her with a curry comb before saddling up. He had a hard time—hard being the operative word—watching her move around in those tight pants. Every time she bent over they outlined every curve of her ass while the snug top rode up, exposing a nice expanse of creamy, smooth back skin. Weren't the English supposed to be prudes? Those jodhpurs, or whatever the hell they called them, were better than porn.

Quickly turning away when he thought she'd caught him ogling her, Flynn pretended to be busy with Dude. Ah hell, he needed to get out of the barn . . . away from her. He put a lead on Dude and, just like Gia, began the ritual of saddling him.

But he was faster, which stood to reason because he'd been doing it daily since he was four. He put one foot in the stirrup, hoisted himself up into the saddle, and guided Dude out the door. "Catch you later."

"Yep, see you around."

He spent an hour riding fences. The ranch was huge and no longer employed a staff of hands to check for breaks and holes. All it took was an opening for a few steers or cows to wander out, wind up on the road, maybe get hit by a car, or roam into another rancher's herd. Although his had the Barlow brand, it was a hassle recovering lost cattle. He found a few places where the wood had rotted or the barbed wire had become loose. As soon as he got the necessary supplies, he'd come back and make the repairs.

He spent another hour checking the herd in the south pasture. It was a beautiful morning, mild enough to get away with a lightweight denim jacket. In the distance, a red-tailed hawk glided across the sky, its broad rounded wings spread wide. It was hunting, and Flynn stopped Dude for a few minutes to observe the bird swoop into the field, catch breakfast, and quickly take flight. He loved everything about spring mornings in the Sierra. The serenity, the fresh, dewy smell, and the way the light played on the mountains. Breathtaking.

But he wanted to get those fences fixed by noon so he didn't have time to dawdle. Reining his gelding around, he headed back to the stable. There was no sign of Gia, which he hated to admit disappointed him. This morning they'd made decent strides toward being civilized with each other. Hell, she'd been damned friendly, considering their past encounters. Frankly, Flynn had been surprised how open Gia had been about her finances, the day trading, Evan Laughlin.

Love is blind. Nice line, even if it was a cliché.

And pretty personal stuff to tell a near stranger. Perhaps it was part of her cover. None of it made any sense to Flynn, and he'd always been good at reading these things. In the Bureau his uncanny ability to see through the bullshit had made him a crack agent and after that, his aptitude for putting the pieces together had made him an even better prosecutor.

Disappointed or not, the less he saw of Gia the better. She was a little too tempting.

He unsaddled Dude, got him situated, and headed to town. There was a line at the drive-through for the Bun Boy, so he parked, went to the window, and ordered two egg sandwiches, hash browns, and coffee. When they called his name, he took his food to one of the empty picnic tables. Everyone seemed to be on the go this morning.

He was halfway through one of the egg sandwiches when Donna Thurston, proprietor of the fast-food joint, wandered over. He'd known her for years.

"Flynn Barlow, you ought to be ashamed of yourself, sneaking in and out without saying hello."

He grinned. "I wasn't sneaking. I just didn't see you."

"How're your parents? I haven't seen them in ages, not since the Plumas County Fair."

"They're good," he said. "Busy."

"Your ma still jarring that delicious honey?"

"You bet." They kept two dozen beehives on the ranch in Quincy. His mother swore that due to the lavender and cloves she grew her honey was the best in three counties.

Donna looked up at the clear blue sky. "Farmers' market starts next week. She planning to have a booth?" They held two a week—Wednesdays and Fridays—in the square while the weather held.

"I believe so." She'd been making the forty-minute trek every spring and summer for the last six years. Barely breaking even, she mostly did it to socialize with the Nugget friends she rarely got to see.

"Well, good," Donna said and sat herself next to him on the picnic bench. "What've you been up to?"

"Calving season. I've been spending a lot of time at Rosser Ranch."

"With that Gia Treadwell?" She raised her brows. "You think she buried the money somewhere on the property?"

"What money?" He played stupid.

She shot him a look. "All that money Evan Laughlin stole. I've got two conflicting theories on it. The first one: She's in it up to her eyeballs; she and that Laughlin fellow, a modern-day Bonnie and Clyde."

"Yeah," Flynn said, trying not to sound too amused. "What's your second theory?"

"Laughlin seduced her right out of her bank account. You ever see the man? He looks just like Hugh Jackman. Now what kind of red-blooded woman could resist a man like that?"

"Hmm," Flynn replied, not that interested in how good-looking Laughlin was. He was a crook, which made him ugly in Flynn's eyes.

"Well? What's your theory, former G-man?"

"I don't have one."

"You're no fun."

He laughed and started in on his second sandwich. "What's going on around here?"

"Not a lot. And I'm praying for a noneventful summer, not like last year."

Last summer there'd been a series of arson fires in town. No one had been seriously hurt, but the blazes had caused some of the buildings considerable damage. The region's new arson investigator had solved the case and last Flynn had heard, the firebug was doing time.

"Everyone's excited about Dana and Aidan's wedding, even though it'll be in Reno," she continued.

Flynn didn't know Dana or Aidan, but he nodded as if he did. Otherwise he'd be here all day while Donna gave him their entire life stories. "You going?"

"Of course I am. How about you?"

"Didn't get invited."

"I could certainly fix that, Flynn Barlow. How else will you meet a nice woman? Everyone knows weddings are the perfect place. I bet Dana has lots of single girlfriends from college who'll be there."

"I'm actually seeing a stenographer in Sacramento." He wasn't really, but it would keep Donna off his back.

"Hey, Flynn." Sloane McBride, one of Nugget PD's finest, sat down across from him and Donna at the table. "How goes it?"

"It goes." He eyed her heaping tray of food. "Doesn't your chef husband cook for you?"

"He's in San Francisco at the mother ship." Brady worked as the executive chef for Breyer Hotels. Nate Breyer, the owner, lived part-time in Nugget and owned the Lumber Baron with his sister, Maddy.

"You going to my brother's wedding?" Sloane asked.

"He wasn't invited," Donna said.

"I could make that happen." Sloane popped half a hash-brown patty into her mouth and said, "Wanna go?"

"I don't know him or the bride."

"So, free food. Brady's catering it. And Dana's parents have a mansion. There's plenty of room."

"I'll think about it." Flynn scrunched up his garbage and tossed it in a nearby trash can. "In the meantime, I've got to get to Farm Supply, buy material, and mend some fences. It was nice seeing both of you."

"You too," Sloane said on a full mouth. It looked to Flynn like her uniform was getting a bit on the snug side. The extra weight looked good on her, like she was in love and happy.

He kissed Donna on the top of her head.

"Don't you go being a stranger," she said.

"I won't."

He crossed the picnic area, strolled across the parking lot, got in his truck, and drove to the other side of town to Farm Supply. The giant Quonset hut carried everything but the kitchen sink. Western wear, home goods, chicken coops, sheds, feed, tack, seeds, plants, fencing, you name it.

"Hi, Flynn." Grace Miller, who owned the feedstore with her husband, Earl, waved from the front counter.

"Hey, Grace. How you doing?" The problem with small towns was you lost a lot of time exchanging pleasantries. Not a whole lot he could do about it. Unlike Sacramento, where capital workers were brusque and always in a rush, incivility in the country was a hanging offense. Everyone stopped to make small talk. "How's Earl?"

"He's out back if you'd like to say hello."

Flynn suspected the barbed wire was also outside. "I'll do that," he said and made a beeline for the nursery. In back, there were a series of smaller Quonset huts where they kept hay, bags of grain, and building supplies. Nothing like a lumber store, but enough for small jobs.

Earl was directing workers unloading feed sacks off a semitruck with a forklift. He waved to Flynn, who walked over.

"Delivery day?"

"Yep. How are things over at Rosser Ranch?"

"Good. Just have a couple of fences to mend and came over to get some barbed wire, fence posts, and a bag of concrete mix."

"You should find everything you need over there." Earl pointed to one of the buildings, too preoccupied with the delivery to chitchat, which was fine by Flynn. "Let me know if you can't find what you need."

"Will do." But Flynn found it all, loaded it on a flat cart, and paid at the register.

"How's your ma, Flynn?" Grace asked as she ran his credit card.

"Good. I think she'll be here next week for farmers' market."

"We'd love her to join our cooking group, the Baker's Dozen. Now that we've got a commercial kitchen . . ."

"She might be interested." His mother was a good cook and as far as he knew didn't belong to any cooking clubs in Quincy. It was just that in the winter getting to Nugget in the snow could be hairy. He didn't like his mother driving in bad conditions. "I'll tell her to call you."

"You do that."

He loaded his supplies in the bed of his truck and drove back to

Rosser Ranch. First spot was along the highway. Flynn pulled into a turnout and restrung new barbed wire where the old had come loose, then moved on to the next weak spot. That one required a new post and he mixed the cement in a spare bucket, using water from a tank he kept in the back of the truck for the cattle. It was mindless work and for this one he turned on his truck radio to the local country station, humming along to a Dixie Chicks song.

The work took longer than he'd thought it would. But by four he'd got it done. Next, he decided to drive over to the stable, return some emails from his laptop, and make sure things were running smoothly at the office. Then he'd feed Dude and head back to Quincy, maybe pick up dinner at the little Mexican joint in Cromberg. At the ranch he stayed in a small efficiency apartment. It didn't have much of a kitchen. Although welcome to eat dinner with his parents in the main house, he usually saved that for Sunday nights and family gatherings, when his brother, Wes, his wife, and the kids came over.

He found a shady spot by the barn and pulled his laptop from the backseat. The computer automatically signed onto the ranch's Wi-Fi; evidently Flynn had used it before. He scrolled through his emails, deleting the junk ones and opening those that seemed important. Wes wanted to discuss buying a new bull. A good breeding bull with the right lineage cost a pretty penny. They could weigh the pros and cons over a couple of beers. The two brothers were close, but between work, running cattle, and life, there was little time for hanging out. He returned the message, suggesting a couple nights that week for a get-together, and was about to go on to the next email when someone tapped on his window. He looked up to see Gia and opened his door.

"What are you doing?" she asked.

"Catching up on work. Thought I'd hang out long enough to feed Dude his dinner, then go back to Quincy."

"I'll feed him for you. Just hay, right?"

It was tempting. He could do his work from home. "I'm already here and don't want to take advantage. You've been feeding him for me quite a bit as it is."

On the days he didn't come, she handled Dude. Although he provided hay, it wasn't a fair trade because he got board too. He could always pay Clay's kids to do the feeding before and after school.

"It's no big deal to throw him a flake when I'm feeding Rory," she said. "Around five, right?"

A few days ago she'd wanted to shoot him with the Winchester. Now she seemed to want to be his friend. He assumed it had to do with him booting Jeff and the other agent off her property. That had just been a defense-attorney reflex. Next time he wasn't getting involved.

"That's all right." He held up the computer in his lap. "I need to get this done." Hell, maybe she wanted him off her property so she could dig up her money. Donna was a kook, but she might be on to something.

"Suit yourself," she said. "I didn't realize cattle required computer work."

"It does." Tons of it. Everything from breeding and birth records to profit-and-loss statements. It was like any other business. "This is for my other job."

"What's that?" she wanted to know.

"I'm a lawyer."

She jerked her head in surprise. "You are?"

Yeah, lady, I graduated first in my class from Stanford. He rolled his eyes.

"Uh, I just meant . . . I thought you . . . you know . . ."

"That I herded *doggies*," he mocked.

"What kind of lawyer?"

"Estate and corporate." He left out the criminal defense part. Now that she knew, she'd look him up on the Internet anyway.

"Where do you practice . . . uh, besides your truck?" That little bite was back, like she was embarrassed that he'd put one over on her.

"Sacramento."

"Is that how you knew those FBI agents?"

"Yes. How'd you know they were FBI?"

"They left their cards on my door. They've been calling ever since."

"My advice to you is that you don't talk to them without representation." And here he was, sticking his nose in it again.

"I thought that once the grand jury didn't indict me it would be over." There was a weariness in her voice that tugged at him.

"You want it straight?" He studied her face. "Until the authorities find Evan Laughlin it'll never be over, Gia. Get yourself an attorney."

"You think I was involved, don't you?"

"It doesn't matter what I think. I'm going to say it again . . . a lawyer, Gia. Get yourself a good lawyer."

"I wasn't involved and they'll never find Evan because—"

"Stop! There is no privilege here." He wagged his hand between them. "We are not attorney-client. Anything you tell me could eventually be used against you."

She shot him a menacing glare. "I'm innocent! Try using that against me." Gia turned back to the house in a huff.

Guess they weren't going to be friends after all.

Chapter 6

That was the last time Gia would try to be nice to Flynn. She thought they'd reached a turning point when he'd run the FBI agents off her ranch. Clearly his lawyer genes had just kicked in. He probably thought he'd get sued for malpractice if he didn't do it. In the future she planned to steer clear of him. Gia had had about as much judgment as she could take.

Obviously there was no controlling what people thought of her, but for sanity's sake she wanted to avoid the haters. Nugget was all about peace and safety and finding friends who were trustworthy. Men, it just so happened, were very low on that list.

In the house she showered and changed into a pair of designer jeans, a white blouse, and a fitted blazer. Residents in Nugget didn't dress up the way they did in Manhattan to go out. Still, Gia saw no reason not to clean up and at least look somewhat fashionable. She was meeting Harlee and Darla, the local hairstylist, at the Ponderosa for happy hour. Dana had introduced them last summer, when Gia had been looking for land. Dana would've come too, but she was busy with wedding stuff.

She did one last check in the mirror before leaving and made the fifteen-minute ride to town. There was a parking space right in front of the restaurant, something so foreign to a New Yorker that it made her want to auction the spot off to the highest bidder. Inside the Ponderosa, country-western music played on the jukebox and Harlee and Darla waved excitedly from a table across the dining room. The place was full and a few diners stared and whispered as she made her way back.

"That felt like walking the gauntlet," she said as she plopped down in one of the chairs.

Darla immediately poured her a margarita from an icy pitcher. "They're just curious . . . you being new and all, right, Harlee?"

"Of course."

They all knew that was a lie, but it was generous of Darla and Harlee to try to spare her the humiliation of being a suspected criminal in her new home. "It's okay. I'm used to it."

"When do I get the story?" Harlee prodded.

Like everyone else last summer, Harlee had found out that Gia was the mysterious T Corporation. Being an intrepid reporter, she'd planned to rush the scoop to print. Instead, Gia had offered her a deal. An exclusive interview—the first one since the shit hit the fan—as soon as the criminal investigation cooled down. In return, Harlee had promised to hold off writing anything. Because of the death threats, Gia hadn't wanted the public to know where she was moving. Still didn't.

"I'd give it to you now," Gia said, "but the FBI has started snooping around in my life again. They came to Rosser Ranch the other day."

Harlee and Darla moved in closer so their heads were nearly touching.

"What do you think they want?" Harlee asked.

"I don't know for sure, but I'm guessing they're looking for Evan and they think I know where he is."

"Do you?" Harlee asked.

"Of course not." Gia's voice rose above the music. "If I knew, I'd bring him in myself."

Harlee held up her palms. "Sorry, but I had to ask."

"Flynn says I need a lawyer."

"Flynn's a lawyer; hire him," Darla said.

"Wrong kind." Not that she would hire him anyway. Gia took a fortifying slug of her margarita. It was so icy it gave her brain freeze. "He prepares wills and living trusts."

"He used to be an FBI agent." Darla refilled Gia's glass.

Gia's stomach knotted. FBI? Oh boy. It all made sense now. That was how he'd known the agents who'd come to the ranch. It had nothing to do with him being an estate lawyer. Ah Jesus. The FBI had made her life a living hell and he was probably an informant for them. A snitch.

Anything you tell me could eventually be used against you.

"How do you know that?" Harlee asked Darla.

"He came in last month for a trim and mentioned it."

Gia knew Darla and her father's barbershop was gossip central.

"Maybe he could help you," Harlee said.

He'd made it pretty clear he wanted to do just the opposite. "I don't think so."

"Then you'd better get someone. Someone good."

Fat chance finding a top criminal defense attorney in Nugget. The town had a population of roughly six thousand people, mostly ranchers, railroad workers, and small-business owners. Not a lot of white-collar crime here, at least not that Gia knew of.

"You know anyone?" she asked Harlee, who'd been a big-time reporter in San Francisco before buying the *Tribune*.

"I could make a few calls."

"I'd appreciate it." In the meantime, Gia would call her old attorney for a reference. Even though he could continue to represent her, his services cost an arm and a leg, and it would be better to have someone in California now that she lived here.

A server came and the girls ordered nachos with the works, potato skins, an order of chicken wings, and another pitcher of margaritas. Gia could barely eat. She was too sick over the latest revelation about Flynn. It was like having a spy on her property. Even though she had nothing to hide, it was an invasion of her privacy. Her life had already been examined under a microscope. By the feds, the press, the grand jury, and the public. She'd moved here to find solitude because she couldn't take anymore. Flynn might be in private practice now, but he'd been part of the agency that had helped tear her life apart.

The thought weighed so heavily on her that she could barely sleep that night, and the next morning she knew exactly what she had to do. After a quick shower she searched through her contact list to find Flynn's cell number, called him, and got his voice mail.

"This is Gia. I'm not sure if you're coming to the ranch today, but I need to talk to you as soon as possible. Please call me." She left both her cell and home numbers.

After pouring a cup of coffee she headed to the stables, hoping to run into Flynn there. Trading today was out of the question; not when she felt so blindsided. Realistically, Flynn didn't owe her any information about himself. But it seemed that he'd gone out of his way to withhold his background from her. After Evan she only wanted to surround herself with people who were absolutely trustworthy.

There was no sign of Flynn at the barn so she threw both horses flakes of hay and returned to the house. At noon, tired of waiting, she jumped on her computer and found the number for his law office in Sacramento, called it, and asked for Flynn.

"He's in court today. Would you like to leave a message?"

"Will he come back to the office after court?"

"Yes, he has a four o'clock appointment."

"No, thanks. I'll try back later."

Better yet, she'd surprise him with a visit . . . confront him about the whole thing. Lay down some ground rules. She jotted down his office address, changed into something more suitable for the city, and made the three-hour trip to Sacramento. She'd never been to the state's capital, but it was a cakewalk to maneuver compared to Manhattan. There was even a parking lot.

Flynn's building was old but well maintained. She took the elevator in the lobby to the fourth floor. His office, which had two other attorneys listed on the door, occupied the entire space.

A woman with a gray bob and soft blue eyes greeted her at the front desk. "May I help you?"

"I'm here to see Flynn Barlow."

"Uh, do you have an appointment?" She started scrolling through her computer monitor and Gia considered telling her she was Flynn's four o'clock.

"No. He runs his cattle on my ranch . . . an emergency has popped up."

"Oh my." The woman, who according to her desk plate was Doris, glanced at the clock. "He should be back from court any second but has a meeting." She pointed at a glass conference room where a distinguished middle-aged man sat. Gia hadn't noticed him when she first came in.

"That's okay. I'll wait."

"But if it's an emergency—"

Doris didn't finish her sentence because Flynn came through the door.

He was in a suit and tie and carried an expensive briefcase. Gia tried to distinguish him from the faded-Levi's, Stetson-wearing cowboy. As much as she hated to admit it, both looks suited him well. He was without a doubt an extraordinarily handsome man, even if he was a duplicitous one.

"Gia?" He did a double take.

"There's been an emergency with the cattle," Doris said. "You want me to cancel your four o'clock?"

A flush crept up Gia's neck. She could feel the heat like a sunburn. It wasn't an emergency with the cattle, though she'd sort of intimated that it was. Out of guilt she said, "It's not that big of an emergency. Go ahead with your meeting. I'll wait."

He put down his briefcase and folded his arms over his chest. "Exactly what kind of an emergency?"

"It's more of an emergency between you and me," she said and gave him a moment for it to sink in. *I know who you are . . . or used to be.*

He scrubbed his hand through his hair. He knew she knew. "You drove all the way here for that?"

"You should've told me, Flynn." She tried to rise to his height, but even in her three-inch heels he dwarfed her.

"It's on my website, Gia. All you had to do was look. Why don't you go home while you still have sunlight and we can talk about this later?" He glanced at the conference room and gave the man inside the one-minute sign.

"I'll wait." She needed to get this off her chest.

"Suit yourself." Flynn picked up the briefcase and went inside the conference room. She watched him take off his jacket and hang it on the back of a chair.

Doris, whose interest had been piqued, asked if Gia wanted a drink.

Yeah, a good stiff one. "A glass of water would be nice."

Doris got her the water and Gia wandered the office, examining the artwork—Western scenes of cowboys and cattle. She read Flynn's bio: the one she should've memorized on his website. It really was a nice office. Tasteful and masculine without being stuffy or overly muscular.

A man came out from behind a closed door. Unlike Flynn, he was wearing jeans and a golf shirt. Truth be told, he looked sloppy. The shirt was loose and Gia suspected he was trying to cover his prodigious gut. It wasn't working. The jeans were saggy and his tennis shoes looked well worn. He turned and gave her a once-over. Not in a disrespectful way, but like he recognized her.

"Hey, you're Gia Treadwell. I love . . . used to love . . . your show. How you doing?"

"Fine."

He smiled at her with tobacco-stained teeth, the grin so warm and genuine she couldn't help but be drawn in. "You waiting for the big guy?"

She presumed he meant Flynn and nodded.

"I'm Toad." He stuck his hand out for a shake.

"Excuse me, what did you say your name was?"

He laughed and that too . . . well, he just seemed so nice. "You heard right. Toad. It's an old nickname that just stuck. I'm an investigator here. Hey, I was thinking of buying my nephew a couple of shares of Gamer Guy stock for his birthday. Thought he'd get a kick out of it. Safe bet, right?"

She shook her head. "The company's way overinflated. How old is he?"

"Twelve."

"Get him Disney stock. It's a much better bet."

"Disney, huh?" He scratched his chin.

"Good revenue growth and solid stock price performance." She was just thrilled that someone was asking her opinion as opposed to clutching their purse like she'd steal it.

"Really? I hadn't thought of Disney. I'll buy a few shares today."

"Wait until tomorrow and buy in the middle of the day; less volatile."

"Hey, thanks." Toad eyed the conference room. "He shouldn't be much longer."

"I'm in no rush."

"You staying around here?"

"Not here, three hours away."

He glanced at his watch and grimaced. "You're gonna hit rush hour, which around here isn't pretty."

She shrugged. There was nothing she could do about it. Perhaps she'd kill time getting dinner.

"I've got to take off, but it was nice meeting you. And thanks for the advice."

"Nice meeting you too, Toad." She felt awkward saying his name. *Toad.*

"Hopefully I'll be seeing you around."

Hopefully not. After today she wanted to have as little to do with Flynn Barlow as possible. Instead of being rude, Gia simply nodded. Toad said goodbye to Doris and left. Gia busied herself staring at her phone, reading her personal emails. These days it was mostly her mother who wrote.

A short time later, Flynn and his client came out of the conference room. Flynn walked him to the door and shook his hand. Gia had to say he seemed very professional, not the cocky, loose-limbed, smart-mouthed cowboy who'd helped himself to her shower.

He walked over to Doris's desk, said something Gia couldn't hear, and directed her to follow him into his office. It was even nicer than the reception area. There was a large mahogany desk and two upholstered wing chairs on one side of the room and a tufted leather sofa and a cowhide rug on the other. Bookshelves filled with law tomes lined the walls and there were photographs of Flynn and people she didn't know.

"What's up, Gia?" He actually had the nerve to sound annoyed.

"What's up is that you lied to me." She squinted across the big desk at him. "Why didn't you tell me that you used to be an FBI agent?"

"First off, I didn't lie to you. I'm under zero obligation to provide you with my résumé."

"So you can just come on my property whenever you want and spy on me for the feds?"

"Spy on you? For an educated woman you say some truly stupid things. I'm a criminal defense attorney, Gia. You think I'd have a practice like this"—he spread his arms wide—"if I was still working for the government, acting as its informant? You think that would instill a lot of faith in my clients, especially the ones accused of tax evasion, embezzlement, and money laundering?"

"You said you were an estate lawyer. Another lie."

"It's not a lie. I help ranchers, farmers, and vineyard owners with their succession plans; it's a large part of my practice. You think you might be overreacting again, like you did when you found me in your shower? It seems to be a habit with you. You're irrational."

Well, he'd be irrational too if his ex had turned his life upside down. "Forgive me if I have trust issues these days."

"You're forgiven." He leaned back in his chair and gave her a sardonic grin, accentuating the cleft in his chin.

"No matter what I do it seems to make very little difference. Despite the fact that a federal grand jury couldn't find one iota of wrong-doing on my part, I'm still being investigated. I've lost my livelihood and I get threats, even though I was a victim of Evan's scam too. I moved to seclusion to avoid all that. Now I find out that you were once part of the agency that has made my life a living hell. An agency I have come to detest and distrust with every fiber of my body."

"I no longer work for the Bureau and wasn't an agent when they first started investigating you. So your blame is misguided. Do you know where Laughlin is?" He quickly held up his hands. "Don't tell me. But if you do, you could probably make it all go away . . . with the right lawyer."

Why do people keep asking me that? "I don't," she said, despite his warning. "If I did, I'd find him and ring his thick neck."

"Look, you have nothing to fear from me." He eyed her handbag. "You have a dollar in there?"

"Probably. Why?"

"Give it to me."

"I will not."

"Gia, just give me the goddamned dollar. You'll be happy you did."

She was starting to get where he was going with this and rifled through her wallet until she found a buck.

He took it and stashed it in his top drawer, then smirked. "Now repeat after me, 'Thanks for the consultation. Although you're the most brilliant attorney I've ever had the pleasure of meeting, and by far the best-looking, I can't afford your services.' "

"I absolutely will not."

Flynn chuckled. The pompous man liked messing with her. "No need. I'm now officially bound by attorney-client privilege. If I violate it, I get disbarred. You happy?"

"Definitely about you getting disbarred."

He shook his head. "It's weird because you seem so smart and mature on television."

"It's all an illusion." Her lips curved up into a tight grin. She felt somewhat mollified by their little exercise. But Evan had made her distrustful . . . okay, and a little paranoid.

Flynn certainly thought she was unhinged. First by holding a rifle on him and now driving three hours to bitch him out over being a former FBI agent. Even Gia could see where he would think she was unstable. She didn't used to be like this.

"You have an attractive office," she said, trying to sound nice . . . reasonable.

"Thanks." He looked at his watch. "You going home tonight?"

"Yes. Don't worry about Dude. Dana and Aidan are feeding him." She'd called Dana on her ride to Sacramento, assuming that by the time she got home it would be past the horses' dinnertime.

"The couple getting married?" Flynn asked.

"Mm-hmm. Dana was my real estate agent. Aidan works for Cal Fire. They're very reliable."

"Two minutes ago you wanted my ass in a sling, now you're worried about my horse."

"I would never take out my frustrations on an innocent animal."

"Good to know. But I hired Justin and Cody, Clay's kids, to start doing it for me next week so I don't put you out anymore," he said, his face buried in a file. "Uh, it's getting late."

Gia got to her feet. She certainly knew when she was being dismissed. "Is there a good place to eat around here? Toad said the traffic's bad. I thought I'd kill some time."

"So you met Toad, huh?"

"Nice guy."

"There's a good Italian place down the block, Mexican two blocks over, and a few good places on J Street. Want me to draw you a map?"

"I'll find it."

He got up from his desk. "I'll let you out. Doris probably locked up when she left."

At the door Flynn pulled a key from his pocket and turned it in the deadlock. She was halfway down the hall to the elevator when he called to her. "In the evening the neighborhood gets a little sketchy. Give me a second and I'll walk with you."

"I'm from New York, Barlow. I can handle it."

"Yeah, yeah. Just wait for me."

She went back inside while he put on his jacket and grabbed his briefcase.

"You parked in the lot?"

"Yes, but I thought I'd walk to the restaurant."

"I'll walk with you. Which one do you want to go to?"

"How's the Mexican?"

"The Italian's better."

"Italian, then."

They walked to the end of the block, her heels clicking on the sidewalk. The neighborhood seemed perfectly safe to her. He stopped in front of a place called Don Giovani and opened the door for her. The restaurant was loud and busy. Servers rushing around, bartenders clinking glasses, and patrons standing elbow to elbow in the waiting area.

"Thanks," she said. "See you around."

He waved to the maître d'. "Tony, you got a table for two?"

"For you I do." Tony grinned, grabbed two menus, and showed them to a small booth in the back.

"What are you doing?" she asked when Tony bustled away to help the next customer.

"I just realized I'm hungry. All I have at home is two-week-old Chinese food and canned chili. Besides, who'll walk you back to your car?"

"Oh please."

"Hey, you're free to get your own table." Right, in a place packed like a sardine can.

She let out a sigh of resignation and perused the menu, starved. "What's good?"

"Everything. I usually get the chicken parm."

She got a salad, the veal piccata, and a glass of Chianti. A whole bottle was more what Gia had in mind, but she had to drive. Flynn got a beer and went with his regular.

"You live near here?"

"Not too far." Way to be vague. Maybe he thought she'd break in and steal the passwords to his bank accounts.

"Sacramento isn't as big as I thought it was," she said.

"It's spread out, like the rest of California."

"Do you like it . . . Sacramento?"

"I like the mountains better," he said and took a drink of his beer. "What made you choose Nugget?"

"My family visited on our last ski vacation before my father died. It was our first time visiting California."

Flynn frowned. "How old were you when he died?"

"Thirteen." She took a sip of wine.

"That must've been tough."

More ways than he could imagine, Gia thought. "Yep."

"You must've really loved it to come back all these years later."

"Honestly, I could barely remember what it looked like." But she remembered how secure life had been in that moment in time and how safe and perfect the world had felt on that vacation. Perhaps she was trying to re-create those feelings. "But when I was looking for land, Nugget came up in some of my searches. Unlike most of California, it was affordable."

"Why'd you want so much land?" Flynn asked, moving his beer when the food came to make room.

"I didn't." She waited for the server to leave before continuing. "But when I saw Rosser Ranch . . . there's really no earthly way to explain it . . . it was in my soul. The first thing I'd ever wanted that made me feel desperate to have it, like I knew it was part of my destiny. That probably sounds crazy to you."

"You kidding? My family has been ranching for generations . . . we're all about the land. But you couldn't have chosen a worse time to buy something so showy."

She stopped eating and let out a breath. "I know; boy do I know. Initially I just wanted some acreage and a decent house where I could get away from New York and hide." Use it as a base to start her residential program and find her center of gravity again. "I set up the T Corporation, hoping to keep the purchase secret."

As far as she could tell, the general public still didn't know about Rosser Ranch, but the feds obviously did.

"It's not like I didn't have assets before Evan and his Ponzi scheme. I owned a four-million-dollar penthouse, a piece of property in upstate New York, and had stock investments."

"I don't think anyone is shocked that you could afford Rosser Ranch. But in the court of public opinion . . . not so good buying a fancy ranch while your boyfriend's victims are struggling to survive. It's a little like *let them eat cake*, you know what I mean?"

She nodded. "Yeah, I know. And believe you me, if I could make the victims whole again, I would."

They finished dinner and Flynn walked her to her car. If it wasn't for the fact that they didn't trust each other, it would've felt like a date. Self-conscious, she found herself staring down at Flynn's black cowboy boots rather than having to make eye contact. The toes were pointy and the black leather was polished to a high shine. Different from the scuffed ones he wore on the ranch.

"You sure you want to drive all the way back to Nugget?" The sun had dropped. Gia estimated she had less than an hour left of daylight.

"I have to be up early. You staying overnight?" On Fridays he usually showed up at the ranch.

"Yep." He locked gazes with her while they stood in the gravel lot, next to her car.

A wave of sexual tension passed through them. After her combative behavior, Gia doubted he'd invite her over to his place. Oddly enough, though, she sensed he was considering it. But just as quickly his body language changed and a chain-link fence went up between them.

"I'll wait while you start your car," he said.

She should've been relieved—the wounds left by Evan hadn't even scabbed over yet—instead she felt an acute disappointment.

Chapter 7

"Flynn, can I ride Dude?" Cody McCreedy asked.

"Nope. You've got your own horse." Flynn had forgotten to text the kid that he'd be at Rosser Ranch Saturday morning and would feed Dude himself. "Where's your brother?"

"We split it. Because I'm a morning guy and Justin's not, he takes the evening feedings."

"Sounds smart." He paid them $120 a week for the chore. They could do it and divide the money any way they wanted as long as Dude got fed.

"Emily told me to invite you for supper. We're having fried chicken and mashed potatoes."

"Can't pass that up." Cody's stepmom was a cookbook author, well known in gourmet food circles.

"She invited Miss Treadwell too. Dinner's at six. I've gotta go now." He wound up the hose, hopped on his bike, and Flynn watched the boy—he must be a teen by now—fly down the road, bouncing on the ruts.

He put a saddle on Dude and spent much of the morning following up on the herd. There were a couple new calves in the lower pasture. Everyone, mamas included, looked healthy and happy. He checked the water supply, content that there was plenty. Still, it'd be nice if they got a few spring showers. With the drought, the Sierra remained mighty parched. Not only was it expensive for ranchers, who had to supplement pasture with hay and grain, but it was a fire hazard. It didn't take much for these wooded mountains to go up in flames when they were as thirsty as kiln-dried timber.

Riding up and down the hills, looking for strays, he thought about dinner. He'd hoped to steer clear of Gia and might've declined the invitation if he'd originally known she was going. It would be rude now. The thing was, he was attracted to her. He couldn't imagine a man who wouldn't be. Under normal circumstances he'd go for it . . . for her. But her life came with too many complications.

When he got back to the barn it was around four. He would've liked to have cleaned up before going to the McCreedys and knew the bunkhouses on the property had showers. But because of his and Gia's first meeting, he was reluctant to use one without her permission. So he sent her a text, even though it would've been quicker to just walk to the house, knock on the door, and ask her. She was there; he'd seen her car.

Cowboy up, he told himself. Yet he leaned against an empty stall and waited for a reply. And waited. *Ah, screw it.* He hiked down the road, took a turn at the driveway, went up the porch, and rang the bell. A few minutes later he spotted an eye in the peephole, then the door swung open and Gia faced him in a robe and a towel twisted around her head. She smelled like soap and talcum powder and Flynn wondered if she was naked under all those yards of terry cloth.

"What do I wear to the McCreedys'?" She didn't bother with *hello* or *how you doing, Flynn?* "In Manhattan, on a Saturday night, I'd go with an LBD, always appropriate, always in style. But here . . . I don't want to look overdressed."

"What the hell's an LBD?"

She snorted. "Little black dress."

He'd like to see her in one of those but shook his head. "Jeans and a blouse."

"Really?" She looked disappointed. "How about a shift dress?"

He didn't know a shift dress from an LBD. "Sure, just nothing too fussy. They're ranchers." Though Emily had moved here from San Francisco after Clay's first wife had died.

"You're going, right?"

"What, you need me for moral support?"

"Sort of, yeah."

He supposed it wasn't easy getting to know her new neighbors under the circumstances. "Yeah, I'm going. It's fried chicken. You mind if I use one of the bunkhouse showers?"

"No, I guess not."

"Then I'll see you over there," he said and started to leave.

"What time are you getting there?"

He lifted his shoulders. "Cody said dinner was at six."

"Okay, then I'll see you at six."

He went to the barn, got his go-bag from the back of his truck, and trekked over to the bunkhouse to find a shower. The bunkhouse bathrooms were basic, but the water flowed hard and hot. Just what he needed. In a small mirror over the sink, he shaved off the day's scruff and changed into a fresh pair of jeans and a western shirt. Unfortunately, he only had the one pair of boots, but he rubbed them clean and drove over to McCreedy Ranch. A couple of dogs circled his Ford, barking up a storm. Flynn opened the driver's door and let the dogs sniff him, scratching one behind his ear.

"You're a good boy, aren't you?" The pup returned a high-pitched whine of pleasure and followed Flynn to the porch. The other one got distracted by a squirrel.

Cody opened the door before Flynn could knock. "You're here."

"I'm here. Smells good." Before he got as far as the living room Clay pushed a drink into his hand. "Jack, right?"

"Yep. How you doing?"

"Good." Clay looked down the hallway. "Gia didn't come with you?"

"Nah, she's coming on her own." She was probably hiding behind a bush, making sure Flynn was here first.

"Come into the kitchen, say hello to Emily." Clay led the way.

"Where's Justin?"

"He's got a date."

"Shit."

"Shit doesn't even begin to cover it."

Flynn laughed. The boys were growing up. He opened his arms wide for Emily. She untied her apron, took it off, and gave him a great big hug.

"I've hardly seen you, Flynn."

"I've been driving back and forth between here, Quincy, and Sacramento so much my tires are bald. Seriously, I spend more time in my truck than I do on the range or on my practice. Thanks for having me, Em."

"You're always welcome here. Where's Gia?"

"I'm sure she'll be along any minute."

"I thought you'd come together."

He could've offered. Gia probably would've appreciated it, but then he'd be defeating the whole distance thing he was trying to maintain. "You meet her yet?"

"No, but Clay has. Should we be nervous?"

Not about Gia stealing the silver, he wanted to say. *But don't do any investments with her.* "Nah."

"Clay says she wants to farm." Emily glanced over at her husband, who was dredging a chip in a bowl of dip.

News to him. "Then she's told Clay more than she's told me."

They heard a car pull up and the dogs sounded the alarm again. Clay told Cody to call them off and show Miss Treadwell in.

"Flynn, help yourself to some crudité."

He stood over the bowl with Clay and munched on vegetables. Gia came into the kitchen in a yellow sleeveless dress that skimmed her curves and landed right above her knees. Lord praise the shift dress. She handed Emily a bottle of champagne and Clay introduced them.

"That's from me too," Flynn called, realizing he should've brought something.

Emily chilled it while he and Clay drained the rest of their drinks. Clay made Flynn another one and asked Gia what she'd like.

"Wine would be great if you have any."

Emily took over from there, pouring Gia a glass of white and peppering her with questions about Rosser Ranch and living in Nugget. Flynn caught Gia's eye. *You okay?* She gave him an imperceptible nod and Flynn returned to his conversation with Clay. For the next thirty minutes they talked about the price of beef.

Emily moved everyone into the dining room and started bringing out truckloads of food. Salad, chicken, mashed potatoes, grilled asparagus, and homemade biscuits. Flynn's mouth watered.

"This looks wonderful," Gia said. "And thank you for the tart. I never knew anything could taste that good."

"I'm glad you liked it. Do you cook?"

"The closest I come is dialing for delivery."

Clay chuckled. "Good luck with that here."

"You should join the Baker's Dozen," Emily said. "We're a local cooking club that meets once a month at the Lumber Baron's kitchen . . . Maddy, Sam, and Nate let us use it and it's state of the art. We'll teach you how to cook."

"I might just do that."

Flynn pulled a chair out for Gia. *Just good manners*, he told himself. Clay helped get the rest of the meal on the table and Emily called for Cody, who'd disappeared. And they sat down.

"Dig in, everyone." Emily passed the platter of chicken.

For a while they ate, with just the sound of chewing and the clattering of flatware filling the air. Eventually, as they stuffed their stomachs with some of the best food Flynn had ever tasted, conversation resumed.

"Clay says you're interested in farming," Emily said to Gia.

"I'm thinking about it. There'll be a learning curve of course. And right now I have cows running across my land." She looked at him meaningfully.

"It's cattle, not cows." He raised beef, not milk.

If she planned to make her living in agriculture, she should at least get the verbiage right, though he suspected this farming thing was bullshit. The time it would take for a relatively small start-up farm to be profitable—if it ever was—didn't seem to jibe with her get-rich-quick day-trading plan. And if farming had been her goal, she should've bought land in the Central or Salinas Valleys, not in a place that was frozen most of the winter. He supposed it could be a vanity project. These days small farms were like trendy restaurants. But he doubted Gia did anything without knowing what she was getting herself in to. And as hip as farming had become, it was excruciating work where the whim of the weather could make or break you. People did it because it had been in their blood for multiple generations, not because they thought it would be a financial windfall.

"What crops are you thinking of planting?" Emily asked.

"I'm not sure yet, but I have a consultant coming next week."

Flynn looked straight at Gia and cocked his brow. *Not buying it.* She stared back with an expression that screamed, *screw you, Flynn Barlow.*

Any time, sweetheart.

"So you're not considering using the property for something nonagricultural?" Emily asked, and Flynn had to hand it to her for getting right to the point.

"I can't, right?"

It was classic obfuscation—answer a question with another question. The property was zoned agricultural, but local government could lift the zoning if someone persuaded them that their nonagricultural project would bring a lot of revenue to the city. It happened all the time.

"Not technically," Clay said. "And we're hoping you won't."

Gia looked down at her plate. Flynn could tell she was definitely keeping something from them. Even more reason to stay away from her; she was conniving.

Emily changed the subject and the conversation turned to the weather, the upcoming farmers' market, and Dana and Aidan's wedding. Later Emily brought out dessert: homemade ice cream and fresh berries from the ranch. Flynn was stuffed but managed to shovel in a hearty helping.

Afterward he and Gia got up to go at the same time.

"I'll walk you to your car," he said.

"I came over on foot . . . needed the exercise."

"Then I'll drive you home."

"I'll be fine to walk back."

Flynn glanced out the window. "Not much of a moon out; you won't be able to see."

She relented, giving Flynn the impression she didn't want to make a scene.

"Let's go." Flynn thanked his hosts and said his goodbyes.

Gia made a plan to attend the next Baker's Dozen meeting, which surprised him. She didn't strike him as the domestic type. When they got outside the air smelled of pine and rain. Flynn looked up to the sky, hoping they'd get some.

"Hop in." He held the passenger door open for her and tossed his laptop case in the back.

She climbed up, showing a great deal of leg. Long and shapely. Gia caught him looking and quickly tugged her dress down. He got behind the wheel and took it slow down the McCreedys' long driveway, careful not to hit one of the dogs.

"You going back to Sacramento tonight?" she asked.

"Quincy. I've got to come back in the morning . . . check the new calves."

Silence filled the cab until they got to Rosser Ranch Road. "Why don't you stay in one of bunkhouses? It'll save you a trip."

He was surprised by the offer, though it made a hell of a lot more sense than him driving back and forth. "You don't mind?"

"The bunkhouses are just sitting there. I think one of them even has a washer and dryer, if you need to wash some clothes."

"Why are you suddenly so accommodating?" He got the feeling she was working him.

She paused, let out an audible sigh, and said, "I've made enough enemies in the last eight months to last me a lifetime."

"You trying to get me in your corner . . . for that farm you're planning?" It took everything he had not to snicker.

"You can cut the sarcasm. I definitely plan on growing something on this land. If it weren't for your cattle," she enunciated *cattle*, "I would've started by now."

"Yeah, what are you planning to grow? Marijuana?"

"That was a cheap shot," she snapped. "What, Ponzi schemes weren't good enough for me, now I'm a drug lord?"

She was right; it had been a cheap shot. Besides, the way the laws were changing in the rest of the country, weed would soon be a legal crop in California. "You know anything about farming, Gia? It makes gambling look like a safe bet." Despite it sounding gratuitous, he added, "You'd be better off continuing to lease the land for grazing."

"I have a plan," she said defensively.

"Okay. Let's hear it."

"I'm not ready to talk about it yet, not that it's any of your business."

Right again. It wasn't and he'd vowed not to get involved. So why was he sticking his nose in her future plans? Because he wanted to get in her pants, even though there were plenty of willing, less complicated women who'd be happy to afford him that pleasure, like Laurel. He just didn't want any of them.

Gia heard a noise around midnight. She was lying in bed, trying to focus on the words in her novel instead of picturing Flynn in the apartment above her garage. There'd been no bedding in the bunkhouses so she'd given him use of the private guest quarters. Bad idea because she couldn't get any sleep, wondering what he was doing, what he was wearing, and whether he was thinking of her.

She'd caught him several times during dinner checking her out, like he might be interested. The truly mysterious part was that she was interested too. As adversarial as it was between them, she was attracted to him. And now that he was bound by confidentiality she contemplated doing something unthinkable, even mortifying: making a bootie call.

The noise came again. Gia thought it sounded like a car door closing, though she hadn't heard an engine. Maybe Flynn had forgotten something from his truck. She got out of bed, padded across the Navajo rug to peek outside the window. In the pitch darkness she couldn't see anything. She'd have to go to the mudroom to turn on the motion lights, which for some unfathomable reason she'd shut off.

Pushing the drapery aside, she continued to press her face against the screen, hoping her eyes would adjust enough to see what was going on. A few seconds later lights illuminated the driveway. Either Flynn had flipped them on after he'd gone to his truck or he'd heard the noise too.

"Hey, what the hell do you think you're doing?" she heard him shout.

That's when she saw the flash of a camera. And another flash. And two more. Flynn came down and yelled at someone pointing a telephoto zoom lens at Gia's bedroom to get off the property.

The cameraman ignored him and kept on shooting. It took a beat for it to register that the man was photographing her. And in a thin tank and shortie pajama bottoms no less. Flynn ripped the camera out of his hand.

"That's my property." Spit flew from the man. Gia thought he was going to hit Flynn and grabbed the phone to call 9-1-1.

"You'll get it back when you get off mine." Flynn moved into the guy's personal space, and Gia could see the moment in which the photographer went from being disgruntled over his camera to being intimidated.

"I thought this was Gia Treadwell's place." The man backed away until he bumped up against the door of his car. A Ford Escort.

Gia recited the license plate number to the 9-1-1 operator, who was in the midst of dispatching an officer.

"Sorry, mate," the photographer said. "I've got the wrong place. If you'll just return my camera, I'll be on my way."

"You can pick it up tomorrow at the Nugget Police Department," Flynn told him.

"Ah, come on, mate."

Flynn grabbed a fistful of the man's shirt. "Next time you decide to drive up a private road and point your zoom lens in a woman's bedroom, you're gonna lose a lot more than a camera. Got it, mate?"

Gia saw Flynn press his knee into the man's groin, punctuating his point. The guy swallowed hard, got inside his car, locked the door, and drove away.

Flynn cursed under his breath and turned to the window. "You okay?"

"Yes. Come around." The house was shaped like a U and the master suite was located on the ground floor in the left wing, adjacent to the garage, with giant French doors that opened to the pool.

A few seconds later Flynn tapped on the glass. She let him in, staring up at his bare chest. All he had on was a pair of jeans. In his haste to get outside, he hadn't put on a shirt or shoes or even buttoned the top of his fly.

"Was he FBI or a reporter?" she asked, not entirely sure where to point her eyes.

"Definitely not FBI."

He'd know, she thought. He pulled the SD Card out of the camera and shoved it in his pocket. Damn, the man could rock a pair of jeans.

"More than likely some shitty tabloid," he continued. "Mainstream photographers don't typically trespass in the wee hours of the morning and stick their camera lenses into people's bedrooms." He took in her sleepwear, letting his eyes linger on her tank top. "But you'd know more about that than I would."

She wasn't sure if he was talking about the fact that she used to work for the NBCUniversal News Group or that she'd been the target of the paparazzi in the past.

"I thought this was behind me." She sighed out of sheer frustration. "Even in New York the hardcore ones who tried to break into my secure building moved on after the grand jury hearings. And when I got here . . . it was quiet."

She went back to her bed and sat on the edge, feeling unsteady. "Why is this starting up again?"

"There's a lot of pressure on this case. Jesus, Gia, your boyfriend bilked a former secretary of state out of nine million dollars. There were aristocrats, movie stars; the list of victims is a veritable who's who, not to mention middle-class folks, people whose entire pensions were invested and lost. Like I told you before, it's not going away until officials find Evan . . . the money."

He took the place next to her at the foot of the bed and they sat there for a few minutes not saying anything. She could feel his denim-encased thigh against her bare leg and didn't try to move away. It felt too good.

"He's my *ex*-boyfriend and despite what you think, I don't know where he is. One day he was here and the next he was gone. Just disappeared in a puff of smoke . . . just like my money and everyone else's."

"How much you lose?"

"About five hundred thousand." She shrugged. "It grew to a million in just six months." *That's when I should've known. If it seems too good to be true, it usually is.*

"With those kinds of returns why didn't you invest more?"

"Because I believe in diversifying. My father put all his eggs in one basket. When he died he was broke. Seriously cleaned out. The house was mortgaged to the hilt and all his credit maxed out. My mother and I had no idea that in those last days we were living off the life insurance he'd borrowed against."

He nodded and Gia breathed him in. He smelled like clean sheets and virility.

"You need to lock the gates at the entrance to your drive," he said. "We both have clickers."

Feeling secure here, she hadn't thought it was necessary. Not until today. "Okay."

In the faint distance she heard a siren, then saw strobing blue and red lights through her window. "The police are here."

Gia got up and started to move out of the bedroom toward the front door. Flynn grabbed her arm and eyed her tank top again. Gia looked down to see her nipples standing at full attention and felt her face heat.

"You should put on a robe or something," he said.

Without a word she disappeared into her walk-in closet and got fully dressed. When she came out he was gone. The doorbell rang. Gia made her way through the house, turning on lights as she went, and greeted Rhys at the front door.

"I got a call that you had a trespasser," he said.

"Yes. Come in." She hadn't expected the police chief to work these hours.

She led him to the kitchen and put on a pot of coffee. "I gave his license plate number to the 9-1-1 dispatcher."

"Yep. Wyatt's out looking for the car. You get a look at him?"

"Flynn got a better look. The man was taking pictures when I saw him so I couldn't see his face. He had an Australian accent, though."

"Paparazzi?" Rhys asked. From her brief observations, Chief Shepard was no country-bumpkin cop.

"That would be my best guess."

"Mine too." Flynn came into the kitchen. He'd put on a shirt and boots. "I took this from him." He handed Rhys the camera. "It looks expensive. I told him he could pick it up at the police station."

"You take that little doohickey out of it?"

"The SD Card? Yeah."

Rhys turned to Gia, who was getting mugs from the cupboard. "He physically accost you?"

"He took pictures of me in my bedroom. I don't know if that counts as physically accosting me. But it certainly felt like I was being accosted."

Rhys nodded and she couldn't tell if he thought she'd brought it on herself. *That's what you get for being involved in a global Ponzi scheme.*

"For now on close the security gates," he said, his voice holding a hint of an accent. Southern with a twist. It must've been left over from his time in Houston. "When I got here they were wide open. This place have security cameras? Ray was certainly paranoid enough to have them installed."

"Yes, they're mounted to the house. But they've been turned off and I don't know how to make them work."

Rhys looked at Flynn, who replied, "I'll take care of it."

"Are you going to arrest him if you find him?" Gia asked, because no amount of gates and security cameras would keep the tabloid reporters out. As soon as he got his camera he'd be back—with friends.

"Damned right I'm gonna arrest him. Ordinarily criminal trespassing is a misdemeanor, but I know California has some kind of antipaparazzi statute that jams it up these guys' asses if they're caught trespassing to take pictures. I'll have to look into it. We had a similar problem when Emily first moved here, but that got taken care of pretty quickly."

A wave of relief washed over Gia. At least the chief sounded like he was taking her problem with the press seriously. "I appreciate you coming. I'm sorry if I got you out of bed."

"Nope. I'm working the graveyard shift this weekend, plus it's my job. You gonna be okay?"

"I'm fine."

"You got Flynn," Rhys said and grinned, leaving with the camera.

When she heard his police SUV drive away she said, "He thinks we're sleeping together, doesn't he?"

"Yup."

"You're not bothered by that?"

"Why would I be? I can't imagine any guy who would be."

"Because A: we're not. And B: the whole me-being-a-thief thing . . . I might kill you in your sleep to steal your wallet."

"I always sleep with one eye open. Old habit. And Gia, I would've thought by now you'd figured out that you can't control what people think. Good night." He strolled out, leaving her to wonder whether he was interested . . . in sleeping with her.

Chapter 8

When Flynn arrived at Rosser Ranch the following week, a man with a ponytail and a Toyota Tundra was there. He stood with Gia in the middle of a field, not far from the barn.

Flynn loitered by the split-rail fence, watching and eavesdropping as the ponytailed guy filled a box full of dirt. The samples would be tested to determine the soil's nutrient content, though Flynn thought the ground was too wet from last night's showers for an accurate reading. But he was a rancher, not a farmer.

Gia hung on the man's every word, which annoyed the crap out of Flynn.

"You the farming consultant?" Flynn asked and stuck out his hand. The guy shook it with the grasp of a limp noodle.

"Flynn owns the cattle," Gia said.

"Ah, I prefer to call them methane machines," ponytail responded.

"Yeah, I prefer to call them food." Flynn was well aware that raising livestock contributed to greenhouse gases. It also provided protein to the world. He was willing to let the scientists hash out the dilemma and set the priorities. But not some skinny turd in Birkenstock boots with a hipster beard.

The consultant ignored Flynn, walked a few feet away with the sampling probe, and, for Gia's sake, said, "We'll take one more and that should be good."

Flynn checked his gear. He only had five full sample boxes. He should have twenty per every ten acres. Even Flynn knew that.

"How long you been farming?" Flynn asked, trying to sound friendly, not judgmental. "Sorry, I didn't catch your name."

Ponytail puffed up like the Pillsbury Doughboy. "Reynolds Cooper.

About five years. I'm with Urban Farms Unlimited. I'm sure you've heard of us."

Nope. But the name spoke for itself. And while Flynn was all for planting gardens in vacant lots in inner cities, Rosser Ranch was a thousand-acre parcel in the rural Sierra Nevada. "Five years, huh?"

Reynolds finished getting his slices of soil, closed the box, and stowed it with the rest of his stuff. "I'll send it to the lab and you'll have results soon."

"Thanks for coming all the way out here," Gia said and walked Reynolds to his Toyota.

Flynn hung back, climbed up on the fence, and waited for her to see Reynolds off. Apparently she was serious about planting crops. He watched her stick her hands in the back pockets of her jeans as Reynolds pulled away. Since the photographer incident it had been a real battle staying away from her. The fact was, Flynn had it bad and that wasn't good.

"Hey." Gia walked toward him as he enjoyed the sway of her hips. "You hated him, didn't you?"

"Pretty much."

"It was the methane comment, wasn't it?"

"Nope. He doesn't know what he's doing, Gia."

"What are you talking about? He comes with amazing recommendations."

"Maybe as a master gardener. If you're serious about this, you need an expert in agriculture. The guy should've taken three times as many soil samples and not right after it rained. How much you paying him?"

Gia refused to answer.

"Ah jeez." Flynn brushed his hand under his cowboy hat. "Cut your losses, honey. You want someone good, I'll get you Annie Sparks. She's got a bachelor's in plant science and a master's in ag managerial economics from UC Davis, is a third-generation rice farmer, and drives a Ford. She's the real deal, Gia. Reynolds is a poseur."

"How do you know this Annie?"

"I'm her family's estate lawyer." He got down from the fence. "Talk to her. If you still prefer Reynolds, he's all yours."

"All right," she said begrudgingly and Flynn wondered why he was even trying to help. "When do you think she can come?"

"I'll try to fast track it for you. But Annie is in high demand."

"Thank you."

He nodded. "You been having any more trouble?"

"Not since I've been keeping the gate closed. Hey, let me ask you something: What did Rhys mean about having a similar problem with reporters and Emily? Is she that famous a cookbook author?"

Flynn kicked the dirt with the toe of his boot. "Nothing like that. It's a sad story. Before coming to Nugget, Emily had a little girl who was abducted from her backyard. That was seven years ago and they still don't know where she is."

"My God, that's horrible. Do they know who took her?"

Flynn shook his head. "Nope. It's a cold case. But a couple of years ago a death-row inmate at San Quentin bragged about killing her and throwing her body down a well. It turned out he was trying to get leniency. The press swarmed Nugget. From what I understand, most of the reporters were pretty respectful, but there were a few bad apples."

"I had no idea," Gia said. "I think I might've read something about it because it sounds sort of familiar. I probably didn't pay as much attention because it was on the West Coast. What a nightmare. What about Clay?"

"Hope's father was Emily's first husband. I get the feeling the marriage couldn't survive the tragedy. I used to see a lot of that when I was in law enforcement."

"Why did you leave?" she asked.

"I needed a change and more time to help with my family's cattle operation. I'm thirty-nine years old and I figured if I was ever going to start my own practice it was now or never."

"Do you like it?"

"Yep. It's good work." Damn, she looked so pretty standing in the late-morning sun. "Have people started gossiping about us yet?"

A blush went up the side of her neck. "I haven't been out much. Dana came over for dinner and she didn't say anything. You having second thoughts about sleeping with a criminal?" She smiled.

He was having second thoughts about *not* sleeping with her. But where would that lead?

"Rhys ever catch that photographer?" Flynn asked.

"No. The car was a rental and the guy never went in to get his camera. I'm heading to the farmers' market so I'll check in at the police department . . . just in case."

Flynn looked at his watch. "It's a little late; all the good stuff's gone."

"I just wanted to check it out. I went to one last summer, when I first came to Nugget to shop for property, and loved it. All the food and crafts, plus I want to buy some rocking chairs from Harlee's husband."

"Colin Burke?"

"I think that's his name. You know him?"

"Only by reputation. His furniture is a big deal from what I hear."

"You want to come?"

He was sorely tempted. "I've got too much work around here."

"All right. I'll see you around, then."

He watched her walk back to the house in her designer jeans, expensive leather boots, and ridiculous floppy hat. Gia Treadwell was a financial wizard, a television celebrity, and maybe a criminal, though he was starting to doubt it. But she definitely wasn't a farmer.

Gia strolled the rows of booths, hoping to find Colin. With it getting warm, she wanted to put his rocking chairs on her porch to sit outside in the evenings with a glass of wine. It was still too cool to swim. Even though the pool was heated, she was trying to save money on gas and electricity, which was exorbitant given the square footage of the house.

The day trading was going well, but she'd need plenty of capital to carry out her plan for the farm and residential program . . . and something else she had in mind.

As she wandered through the aisles of the farmers' market, checking out the produce, canned goods, and an assortment of colorful wares, including baskets and birdhouses, she got the distinct impression someone was tailing her. After looking over her shoulder a few times she convinced herself she was being paranoid. The square swarmed with locals, nothing sinister.

A middle-aged woman with gorgeous silver hair and big brown eyes handed out samples of honey. Gia stopped to take a taste.

"Wow, this is good. How much is a jar?" She propped her sunglasses on her head to see if there was a price tag.

"It's twelve ninety-five," the woman said and proceeded to stare until recognition shone on her face. "You're Gia Treadwell, aren't you?"

Oh boy; Gia braced herself for a scene. Evan's victims were far and wide. Even if this woman hadn't lost money in his scam, she was bound to know someone who did. Someone who'd had to file bankruptcy or was forced into foreclosure. She thought about slinking away, but it seemed rather cowardly. This was her town now; she may as well face the music.

"Yes," she said softly, feeling the gaze of Owen the barber and his cronies on her. They sat a few feet away on benches in front of the barbershop, watching. Dana had told her that the clique of elderly men was known as the Nugget Mafia and thought of themselves as the town's powerbrokers. One of the men was Nugget's mayor.

The woman jumped to her feet. "Can I have your autograph? I asked Flynn to get it for me . . . oh, you know how men are? Shoot, had I known you'd be here I would've brought one of your books." She searched her booth for something for Gia to sign.

"Will this work?" She held up an adhesive label. "I use it to tag the honey jars. But I could stick it in one of your books when I get home."

"Uh . . . sure." Gia was surprised that someone still wanted her autograph. It used to happen all the time but never anymore. "What's your name?"

"Patty . . . Patty Barlow."

As in Flynn Barlow? Gia had caught the woman's earlier reference to him, but how had she missed the family resemblance?

"How are you related to Flynn?" She fumbled through her purse, looking for a pen.

"I'm his mother."

Gia gulped. That's right; Flynn had mentioned his mother was a fan. Yet he'd never said anything about her selling honey at the farmers' market.

She wrote on the tag: "You've got yourself a real sweet investment" and signed it "Gia Treadwell."

"Here you go," Gia said. "And I'll take a jar of honey."

"I'd give it to you," Mrs. Barlow said and smiled. "But like you always say, 'Don't sell yourself short.'"

"That's absolutely right."

"I used to love your show." Flynn's mom lowered her voice. "I was so angry when they canceled it. You want me to write a letter to the network?"

"I'm afraid I don't think it would have much impact. But thank you."

"Those stupid, stupid people. How could they lump you in with that evil man?"

Gia felt her throat clog. She didn't know Patty Barlow, but she already adored her. Words escaped Gia so she responded by squeezing Mrs. Barlow's arm.

"Don't look now, but you've got the fuzz at your six," a man whispered in Gia's ear, making her jump. "My guess, they're fan-belt inspectors."

Gia whipped around. "You scared me."

"Owen, why are sneaking up on people?" Mrs. Barlow asked.

"I wanted to give her time to escape."

Mrs. Barlow leaned over the table and scanned the market. "I don't see anything." She swatted Owen. "Don't call the FBI fan-belt inspectors. Flynn used to be an agent. Now get on with you; go cut some hair and leave Gia alone."

"No, wait." Gia stopped Owen. "Where are they now?" Owen wasn't crazy; she'd felt eyes on her before and should've gone with her gut. She was being followed.

Owen surreptitiously perused their aisle. "Over at the rhubarb and strawberry stand."

Gia snuck a peek and sure enough, it was the agent Flynn had called Jeff, and Jeff's sidekick. This time they were dressed in jeans and polo shirts. Great. Most of Nugget was at the market and would have a front-row seat to them harassing her. Well, not if she could help it.

"Mrs. Barlow, it was lovely meeting you and thanks for the honey." She stuffed the jar in her oversize bag. "Owen, we haven't really had a chance to meet, but I appreciate the heads-up." She looked over at his crew, still loitering in front of the barbershop. A leathery guy in a polyester western suit gave her a thumbs-up. Whatever that was supposed to mean.

"You need us to get you out of here?" Owen asked. "Dink's Lincoln Navigator is over at the curb."

"Uh . . . I'll handle it," she said, getting the feeling they didn't care whether she was innocent or guilty; they were just hoping for some excitement in the slow-paced town.

She slipped around the corner of Mrs. Barlow's booth, doubled back, and found the agents at a flower stand on the other side of the market. They were either bad at surveillance or they weren't too concerned about losing her. "You guys looking for me?"

The two agents exchanged glances and Jeff said, "We'd like to talk to you for a few minutes. Could we go someplace quiet?"

If she was going to do this without a lawyer present, she at least wanted witnesses. Reliable witnesses.

"Sure. Follow me." She led them across the grassy square, through the clusters of people, to the sidewalk, and straight into the police station.

The agents grew tense and Jeff said, "I think the Ponderosa might be more relaxed. We can get a drink."

"Nope. I'd rather do it here."

A woman wearing a cordless headset, who looked like Velma from the old *Scooby Doo* cartoons, greeted them. "Can I help you?"

"Is the chief here?"

"You have an appointment?"

Ah, give me a break. Gia stared at her imploringly.

"I'll get him."

A few minutes later she returned with Rhys.

"Connie said you were looking for me." He took note of the agents and bobbed his head in greeting.

"These are special agents . . ."

"Croce and Donovan," Jeff said, pulling his wallet from his pocket to show Rhys his badge and identification. Donovan did the same.

For a second Gia could've sworn she'd seen anger flash across Rhys's face, but it was gone so fast she thought she might've imagined it.

"They'd like to talk to me," Gia said. "And I'd like you to sit in." She didn't know why she trusted Rhys Shepard any more than she did the federal agents, but she did. Maybe because she was just beginning to trust Flynn and he and the police chief were friends.

"Yep." He took measure of the two agents, who didn't seem at all happy about this turn of events, and smiled. "This way."

Jeff stalled. "You have a card, Chief?"

"I do. I gave it to your supervisor when he gave me his word that y'all wouldn't be making any surprise visits." He smiled again, but this time there was no mistaking that it wasn't a nice smile. And right then Gia got the sense that the chief wasn't as laid-back as he appeared to be.

He led them into a small conference room and took the seat next to Gia. The two agents sat across from them and Rhys slid two business cards across the table.

"My number's on there," he said. "Next time call it."

Gia had no illusions that Rhys Shepard was championing her cause. This was a turf war, plain and simple. She did like the fact, however, that she had turned them against each other. It made her feel less like the fox and more like the hunter.

"Before we start, I would like to say that I've been completely cooperative with you people, yet you still continue to stalk me like I'm a common criminal." Gia squinted across the table at the two agents. "I would like Chief Shepard to take note that once again I'm being completely cooperative."

"So noted," he said in that laconic way of his and leaned his chair back against the wall.

Surprisingly, Agent Donovan took the lead. Gia had just assumed he was Jeff's junior. "Do you recognize this photograph, Ms. Treadwell?"

She looked at a computer printout of what appeared to be security footage. The image was fuzzy and Gia stared at it for a while. Rhys leaned forward and also studied the picture.

"It's of Evan and me taken at the Four Seasons at Seven Mile Beach on Grand Cayman two winters ago." Gia sucked in a breath. She knew how this looked and wondered why investigators had only discovered the trip now.

"What were you doing there?" Donovan asked.

"We were on vacation."

"So you chose to vacation in one of the world's major offshore financial havens?"

"No, I chose to vacation in a place that wasn't twenty degrees."

"Did you have any meetings while you were there?"

"Define meetings," she said, not trying to be obtuse, but she didn't want to get something wrong and have them say she'd lied. The truth was, half of Wall Street vacationed in the Cayman Islands during the winter. It was less than a four-hour flight from New York and there were plenty of package travel deals. She and Evan had drinks and dinners with plenty of associates.

"Did you come together with anyone involved in banking, hedge funds, or any other financial institutions?"

"Yes."

"In what way?"

"For goodness' sake, I can't remember everything we did while we were there. But we met some of our friends, friends of friends, and associates at restaurants and bars. I think we snorkeled with someone from Goldman Sachs."

"How about with anyone who was local?"

"You mean from the Caymans? I don't think so, but my recollection of something that happened more than a year ago is hazy at best."

"Think hard," Donovan said.

She didn't like his tone. "Agent Donovan, I would tell you if I remembered, but I don't. It wasn't like Evan and I were together every hour of the day."

"Explain that."

"What do you mean, explain that?" What the hell was there to explain? "When you and your wife go on vacation, do you spend every waking hour together?"

"I don't have a wife," he said. *Big shocker there*, Gia thought. The man was a troll.

"You know, I think I'm done here." It was like before. They grilled her and grilled her on things that were totally irrelevant. She started to gather up her purse.

"Ms. Treadwell, we appreciate you talking to us, we really do," Agent Croce said. "I think we're making some headway here and if you'll just indulge us a little bit longer, we'll be out of your hair. What do you say we take a breather for a second?" He turned his gaze to Rhys. "You have any cold drinks?"

Rhys rolled his eyes, picked up the phone, and asked someone to bring in a couple of sodas. Gia didn't want a beverage; she wanted to go home. But she stayed anyway because she wanted to know what the agents were up to and why her trip to the Caymans with Evan was suddenly of interest.

The *Scooby Doo* woman came in with a bunch of soft drinks. Donovan gestured for her to take her pick. She intentionally chose the only nondiet.

"Thanks, Connie," Rhys said. Connie left and closed the door.

The agents tried to make small talk with Rhys, who was cordial but not friendly. She got the distinct impression that he wasn't too impressed with their interviewing skills.

Croce cleared his throat, signaling that the break was over. "I'm gonna be real straight with you, Ms. Treadwell; we think Evan Laughlin was laundering money out of the Caymans. We believe that during your vacation he made contact with someone who was helping him move the money. We were hoping you might be able to shed some light on that."

"I don't know anything about it." And if she did, wouldn't that make her complicit?

"You said you weren't always together. Could you help us with that—days, times, where you both went? We're trying to establish a timeline."

"I can't be specific . . . it was a vacation so it wasn't like I kept a calendar. I do know that I spent a good part of one of the days at the hotel spa. Another day he went fishing on one of those charter boats and I get seasick. . . ."

"Do you know the name of the charter company?" Croce broke in. He was taking notes.

"I don't."

"Can you remember any other point when you were apart for a length of time, like say at least an hour?"

"He ran in the morning and I went to the gym and one day I went shopping and he stayed at the hotel. As far as dates and times . . . I couldn't tell you. Like I said, we were on vacation and trying to be spontaneous. So if that's all, I need to get going."

"Thank you, Ms. Treadwell. This was very helpful," Croce said. He was apparently the good cop.

She started to get to her feet when he said, "Just one other thing." He slid another grainy photo across the table. "You recognize this man?"

Her heart hammered in her chest and she sat back down, trying to look calm while she pretended to study the photo. What the hell did

Rufus Cleo have to do with any of this? "Although he looks vaguely familiar, I don't. Why?"

"You sure you don't know who he is?" Croce asked and flashed a smile that didn't quite reach his eyes.

"Yes, I'm sure."

"Okay, then," he said. "We'll be in touch."

Gia had no doubt of that because Croce had just caught her in a big fat lie.

Chapter 9

"You did what?" Flynn paced back and forth across Gia's front room as she painstakingly explained her impromptu meeting with the Bureau boys.

"I lied to them. I got nervous and without stopping to think about the consequences—how it would look—I said I didn't recognize Rufus Cleo in the picture. Clearly the agents think Cleo had something to do with this. And they were asking all kinds of questions about our associates, about money laundering, about who we had dinner with in the Caymans. I don't know what came over me . . . I just got scared. I thought if I admitted to knowing Cleo it would somehow implicate me."

"This is why you never talk to the feds without a lawyer." He combed his hand through his hair. "Ah Jesus Christ, Gia."

"I'm in big trouble, aren't I?"

"That depends. Can they link you to Cleo?"

Gia closed her eyes and slowly nodded her head. "I was on the board of his charitable trust."

"Then yes, you're in trouble." Big trouble, and so was he because he didn't want to get involved and here he was, getting involved.

"What do I do?" she asked.

"You get a lawyer, like I told you to do in the first place."

"How will a lawyer get me out of this? I lied, Flynn."

He sat next to her on the couch and forced himself to keep a fair distance. She was scared and he wanted to soothe her, which would be a mistake. They both needed to keep their heads on this one and, unfortunately, his little head had a mind of its own.

"If it were me, I'd go back to the feds and say my client had a memory lapse when the agents showed her the photograph." He turned to face her. "You said the photo was grainy, right?" Gia nodded. "I'd say: 'The quality of the picture was so terrible that at first she couldn't identify the subject. But after thinking about it, she now recalls that it was the late Rufus Cleo. She remembered because she used to serve on his charity board.'"

She snorted. "They'll see right through that."

"Yep. But better to clear it up now than when you've been charged with fraud, money laundering, theft, and perjury."

"Oh God, am I going to be charged?"

"I don't know, Gia. How did Evan know Cleo?" He shouldn't be asking these questions. They were for her attorney to ask.

"From the financial world. Cleo went through Evan to get me on his board. But I wasn't aware that Cleo was in the Caymans, staying in the same hotel as us. That's why I was so surprised when the agents showed me the picture . . . and why I panicked."

Flynn wished he had the photos to see the time stamps. Although he suspected the feds had the times and dates down pat. And probably a lot more. The fact that Gia, Laughlin, and Cleo were at the same place at the same time was hardly a smoking gun. Everyone knew Seven Mile Beach was a playground for financial types. All three of them could've had drinks at the bar and no one would've lifted an eyebrow. But the part that raised a million red flags was that Cleo was found in his Manhattan office shot in the head a few weeks before the FBI went to arrest Evan Laughlin and found that he'd absconded. The murder had been splashed all over the news. And just when Flynn had tired of the endless coverage of Cleo's death, the press had latched on to the Laughlin story, and how he'd committed the largest investment fraud in U.S. history.

As far as Flynn knew, no one had ever linked Cleo's murder to Laughlin's Ponzi scheme, but he was betting the feds had something to link the two, something more than just the fact that the two men had vacationed at the same hotel.

Cleo was a well-known philanthropist and a certified public accountant. At the time of his death he'd been going through a nasty divorce. There'd been speculation—at least in the press—that the ex had had him bumped off to circumvent a prenup.

Flynn watched Gia worry her bottom lip until he couldn't stand it any longer. "Best advice I can give you is to rehire your old lawyer. He's familiar with the case and that'll save you money in the long run." Her face had lost its rosy complexion from the morning. She was now white as a sheet of printer paper.

"I don't want him."

He cocked his head to the side. "Why not?"

"Because he kept telling me to make a deal with the U.S. Attorney. A deal for what? I didn't do anything wrong, Flynn. I truly believed Evan was aboveboard. For God's sake, he worked for one of the most respected investment houses in the country. His clients were educated and wealthy people, even powerful unions." She stopped and stared up at him with eyes so guileless that he wanted to believe that no one could be that good an actress. "What you said about going to the agents and admitting that I knew Cleo . . . it seems like sound advice. And more credible if I do it quickly. Because you know these guys, would you represent me? Just for now. Just until I figure out a game plan. I'm desperate here."

Flynn leaned his head against the back of the couch and pinched the bridge of his nose.

"Only until you find someone else. And until then, Gia, these are my ground rules: From now on, you talk to no one about the case unless I'm present, you understand?" When she nodded in the affirmative, he continued. "No lies between us—I don't like surprises. And no sleeping together."

She jerked into a rigid position. "Who said anything about sleeping together?"

"Ah, give me a break. We've been dancing around it since you found me in your shower. The other night, when that pinhead with the camera showed up, you wanted me so bad I could feel it from over the garage."

"You're either seriously delusional or you're transferring your own feelings onto me."

His lips curved up. "Cowgirl up, Gia; you're attracted to me, just admit it. And I definitely want you, have since you held that Winchester on me. But as long as I'm representing you, nothing's gonna happen. Those are the rules. Take it or leave it."

Color returned to her face. "Believe you me, it won't be a hardship."

Maybe not for you.

"And by the way," Gia said, "I met your mother. She's sweet and lovely and it's hard to believe you're her son."

He chuckled. "Yeah, I get that a lot. You meet her at the farmers' market?"

Gia got up, rummaged through her hand bag, which she'd left on a side table, and held up the jar of honey. "I bought this."

He smiled. "Good stuff, huh?"

"Amazing. I may just raise bees and hire your mom to make honey."

"She'd be better than Reynolds, that's for damn sure. You never did tell me where you dug him up."

"I told you, he came highly recommended. Did you talk to your friend?"

"Yeah; I tacked her number up in the barn." That was before a panicked Gia had waylaid him on his way out. "I've gotta go. I'd like to settle this Cleo thing tomorrow, which means a drive to Sacramento. In the meantime, I'll have Doris send you a representation agreement."

"Okay," Gia said. "Do you want me to write you a check?"

Yes, if I were smart. "We'll settle up at some point. And, Gia: no secrets, you hear me? I catch you in one lie and we're done." The last thing he needed was for her to make a fool of him in front of his former colleagues.

"Starting when?" she asked, following him to the front door.

Ah, for Christ's sake, what was he getting himself into? "Starting now!"

She grimaced. "Okay, then you'd better sit back down. I need to tell you everything."

Just when he'd started to believe her innocence bullshit... He wanted to kick himself for being swayed by a pretty face and a great ass. This time he took a chair instead of the couch. "Start talking."

"This is the thing," she said, nibbling on her fingernail. "You're wrong about the shower. While I lied about you not being impressive"—she let her eyes fall to his crotch, as she had that first time—"I also thought you were rude, arrogant, and extremely presumptuous. However, in the interest of full disclosure, in a moment of deep weakness—and too much wine at the McCreedys'—I did want you the night you stayed over the garage... for cheap sex and nothing more. So there's my confession. Are we all good now?"

Good—and hard.

"Yep. See how telling the truth will set you free?" He got up and walked out before doing something stupid like bending her over the sofa.

After Flynn left, Gia went down to the barn to spend some quality time with Rory and to retrieve Annie's number. She found both horses in the corral with their noses in the grass. Since the rain, the meadow seemed greener and everything smelled fresher. She remembered once reading that scientists called the scent "petrichor," created when rain hit the ground, releasing plant oils and actinomycetes into the air.

Rory came up to the fence and nuzzled her hand. The beggar was looking for a treat. Gia usually brought apple or carrot slices. Not this evening, though. She'd been too distracted, thinking about Flynn's edict that they not sleep together. *We've been dancing around it since you found me in your shower.*

Guilty as charged.

She thought Evan had drained her sex drive, actually obliterated it. Guess she was wrong because every time she saw Flynn she wanted to pull him into the bushes and rip off his clothes. But he was absolutely right. As long as he was her lawyer he couldn't be her lover.

The specter of being convicted and sent to prison for a crime she hadn't committed was too real. And if anyone could undo the blunder she'd made that afternoon it was Flynn. He had a relationship with the agents. As a former agent himself, they trusted him. Hell, they even played poker together.

So, yeah, sex was out of the question.

She went inside the barn, found the note with Annie's number, went back to the house, and gave her a call. Annie came bright and early the next morning.

She wasn't what Gia expected. Younger than someone with a master's in ag managerial economics. Her hair was stuffed under a beaten-up straw cowboy hat, there was a tattoo of Cesar Chavez on her left arm, and she wore combat boots and a cropped pair of cargo pants. She had a turquoise Ford pickup that looked right out of the movie *American Graffiti* and a broad smile that made Gia like her instantly.

"You've got a great place here," Annie said. "Flynn wasn't kidding about the house."

Gia knew it was impressive, despite its rustic attempt to be otherwise. It made her wonder whether Annie knew her story . . . if she was already passing judgment.

Annie gazed out over the land, shielding her eyes from the sun with her hand. "Flynn said you've got a thousand acres. How much of that do you want to plant?"

"Not all of it." Gia didn't have to know a lot about agriculture to know that the start-up cost to farm the entire property would cost a fortune. Plus, she had the cattle to contend with. "Just enough to look serious."

Annie gazed at her strangely. "*Look* serious?"

Gia pretended to be joking; she still wasn't ready to tell anyone except Dana the real plan. "Clay said people grow alfalfa here. What do you think of that idea?"

"I think it's a good idea. The weather is good for it and Plumas County has a proven track record." Annie stuck both hands in her back pockets. "But I think you should diversify."

Gia smiled because Annie was definitely talking her language. "What else do you think I should grow?"

"Let's walk while we talk." They headed to the same pasture Reynolds had tested and Annie bent down and stuck her thumb in one of the holes he'd made with his soil probe. "Nice." She wiped the dirt on her pants.

"You could do a large block of alfalfa," Annie continued, "and a second block of meadow hay, which, according to my research, does well here. But I also think you should do Christmas trees. There's good business in it. Besides the trees, you can sell cuttings and wreaths. A fancy wreath can go for as much as fifty bucks. The trees are low maintenance and this is the perfect climate. I'm thinking balsam fir, Douglas fir, and Scots pine."

Christmas trees? Gia had never thought of that. "How long does it take to grow a tree?"

"About eight years for a tree ranging five to seven feet. You can plant fifteen hundred trees per acre. Most growers replant two hundred new trees each year to replace the ones they sell."

"I don't have eight years."

Annie laughed. "Gia, as you well know, any good investment takes time to germinate. Besides, you'll have the hay. That's a much shorter turn around, but you'd have to plant in the fall and you'll have to irrigate, which is costly. My suggestion, because you're starting from scratch, is to go organic. There's a high demand for organic hay and low supply."

Jeez, she was impressive. Reynolds hadn't discussed any of this with Gia. He'd been more programmatic, wanting to test the soil and examine weather patterns. She supposed Annie didn't have to because she actually knew what she was doing.

"How soon would we have to plant the trees?"

"Right now. But we'd have to find seedlings that are dormant."

"Well, that'll be a problem because Flynn has grazing rights for the year. I suspect he'll move the cattle when it starts snowing, but . . ."

"Flynn." Annie shook her head and grinned. "He's always a problem."

She said it in such a teasing, lighthearted way that Gia wondered if the two had been romantic . . . were still romantic. It was pathetic, but Gia felt a little sick about it. Annie was one of those mother-earth types—with her healthy skin, lithe frame, and musical voice—that men like Flynn really went for.

"There's plenty of land here, Gia. I'm sure we can persuade Flynn to let us use a portion of it for Christmas trees."

"Are you two close?" Gia asked, trying to sound casual.

"Pretty close, yeah."

Okay, what did that mean? "He said he did legal work for your family."

"Mm-hmm. We . . . my parents . . . own a rice farm near Yuba City. He helped with their estate."

"Is that how you met?"

"Our families have known each other for years. Flynn was brought in to be a peacemaker."

"Uh . . . contentious, huh?" Gia didn't want to pry, but she was curious about Flynn's role.

"It usually is with farmers and their succession plans. Rarely is everyone on the same page and things can get vicious fast." Annie left it at that and Gia didn't want to press.

"Say I work things out with Flynn and the cattle, how much would the start-up costs be for the trees?" The idea of a Christmas tree farm appealed to her. Gia saw a lot of ways in which women in her residential program could get involved. The wreaths were a stroke of genius.

"That would depend on how many acres you wanted to plant."

Gia had no idea. "Want to go inside the house and have a drink? I've got a steep learning curve ahead of me and I'd rather approach it with something cold."

"Let's do it."

They talked for hours. Annie was an amazing listener and Gia found herself opening up about the FBI investigation and how she'd hired Flynn to represent her in the short-term.

"I'm sorry this is happening to you," Annie said. "I don't know much about your situation, but it does appear to me that you're being turned into a scapegoat for your ex-boyfriend. Unfortunately, women make easy targets, especially strong women."

Gia got the sense that Annie had some personal experience in that area.

"What I don't understand is why you want to farm," she continued. "You could do better financially using your stock trading skills. Farming on the scale we're talking about isn't hugely profitable. I mean, I get wanting to use your land. Heck, I commend you for it. But compared to a television celebrity's income, the Christmas trees and hay would simply be a sideline."

"First off, I'm no longer a television celebrity. But to answer your question, I'm not looking to get rich off the farming." What the hell, Gia thought, she may as well confide in Annie. At some point soon, she'd have to unveil the idea of her residential program to her neighbors and Annie would be a good sounding board. "I have a bigger plan; the farming is a small part of it."

"What's that?"

"I want to set up a residential program for women in dire economic straits and teach them how to be financially sufficient. I'd like to use the farm as a business model to teach everything from budgeting to prioritizing bills. Hopefully, the farm will be successful enough to subsidize the program."

Gia talked fast, detailing her plan, afraid that if she came up for air Annie would voice disapproval and accuse her of using the farm to circumvent the zoning rules. When she finally finished, Annie surprised her by beaming gamma rays of sunshine.

"Wow, what an amazing idea. It'll be like your show, but on a much more personal level. How will you choose the women?"

Gia hadn't figured that out yet, but that was the easy part. It was getting the plan past Nugget, starting with her immediate neighbors, that worried her. "I still have to work that out. How do you think it'll play with the locals?"

"I'm not from here, but my experience growing up in a rural area is that people can be skittish about anything new. They may be nervous about the women you'd be bringing in."

Given that Gia herself was the target of a criminal probe she figured "nervous" was an understatement.

"I would have Flynn help you win them over," Annie said. "Everyone loves Flynn."

Gia wondered if that included Annie. Every time Annie mentioned Flynn, Gia had trouble keeping the green-eyed monster at bay. Annie was too young for him, Gia chided herself.

Yeah, like when had age ever stopped a man?

Case in point: Evan had been ten years her senior. Flynn had said he was thirty-nine, only four years older than Gia. Totally age appropriate.

Enough with Flynn, Gia told herself. She had to keep her eye on the goal, not on her lawyer.

"What's the next step?" Gia asked Annie.

"It depends on how you want to proceed. Perhaps you should first feel out your neighbors before spending money on tilling the land, buying seed and trees, and putting in irrigation, which is no small investment."

Gia sighed, knowing she had an uphill battle. "You're probably right. But I want to show them this is every bit an agricultural venture. If I can set up a meeting, could I hire you to speak about the farming end of it?" Gia knew Annie would add tons of credibility. No question the woman knew her stuff.

"Absolutely. I love this idea and will help any way I can." She gathered up her purse and the crop reports she'd brought to show Gia. "I've got to get going."

Gia walked her out, thanked her for coming, and watched her drive away in the turquoise Ford. Back in the house, she was clearing away the dirty glasses when the phone rang. Initially, she thought to ignore it. Reporters had somehow gotten hold of her new number and started calling again. But it could be Dana. They were planning a trip to Reno for Dana's wedding gown fitting.

She glanced at caller ID, saw it was Flynn, and immediately picked up.

"Your ears must be burning," she said.

"Why's that?"

"Annie and I were talking about you."

"She came already?" He seemed surprised.

"She was here all morning and has really great ideas, which I need to talk to you about." Gia put the glasses in the dishwasher.

"Okay. I met with Croce, Donovan, and Casserly on your situation."

"Who's Casserly?"

"Assistant U.S. Attorney. We need to talk about that too."

That didn't sound good to Gia. "Is it bad news?"

"It's not great news, but I suppose it could be worse. Let's not do it over the phone, though. I've got to come out tomorrow to vaccinate some of the calves and for a cattlemen's meeting." Flynn's deep baritone voice reminded Gia of his mother's honey. Smooth and silky.

"Where are you now?"

"Twenty miles from Quincy. Traffic was a bitch getting out of Sac."

"Why don't you come here and stay the night?" His end of the line went silent and Gia was sorry she'd asked. "I'd rather not wait until tomorrow for my bad news."

"Yeah, okay. I'll stay over the garage." He made sure to emphasize "over the garage." "I'm starved, though. You want to meet at the Ponderosa?"

She'd had enough iced tea with Annie to fill an SUV's gas tank and wasn't the least bit hungry. "Sure. What's your ETA?"

"About ninety minutes. I'm gonna stop home first to shower and get some clothes."

For a second she flashed on Flynn naked in her own shower, then made herself block the vision of his hard, wet body. "I'll meet you there around six, then."

Gia took a bath in her spa tub while gazing out at the gorgeous Feather River and Sierra mountains. The place was so private she didn't have to draw the drapes. It was like being one with nature. Wrapping herself in a bath sheet, she got out of the tub and searched her walk-in closet for something to wear. Most of her clothes—pastel suits and monochromatic dresses—were left over from her TV days and were totally impractical for Nugget, where dressing up meant putting on your best pair of cowboy boots.

But she wanted to wear something other than jeans and a T-shirt so she chose a color-block sleeveless crepe dress she used to wear with a matching jacket on the set. Without the jacket it looked springy and flattered her figure. She dressed it down with a pair of flats, although high heels would've drawn more attention to her legs, which as far as Gia was concerned were her best feature. But she didn't want to look like she was trying too hard.

She drove to the square and bumped into Owen on her way into the Ponderosa.

"We saw you go into the police department yesterday with those agents." He bobbed his chin at her. "Rhys is as closemouthed as a mute. So, did they get you under the bright lights? Make you spill your guts?"

Clearly the barber watched a lot of television. "They asked me about a vacation I took two winters ago with Evan. I told them what I knew." And lied.

"Are they gonna find the guy?"

Gia shrugged her shoulders. "I don't know. He seems pretty well hidden."

"Do you have him stashed in Ray's big house? Plenty of room to hide someone in there."

"No, of course not." She didn't know why she was even dignifying his question with an answer.

"I've got my eyes on you, missy."

"Good to know." The old guy was dotty.

She went inside the Ponderosa and Flynn waved to her from the back. The restaurant was crowded. One of the owners came over with a menu to seat her.

"Thanks, but I'm with him." Gia pointed to Flynn.

"I used to devour your show." The woman put the menu away.

"Thank you," Gia said, a little taken aback. She'd been in the restaurant and the adjoining bowling alley a number of times since she started looking for property in Nugget and neither owner had ever said a word to her. They'd always been friendly to whoever she was with: Dana, Harlee, or Darla. But that was it.

"I used to be in marketing and public relations and it used to drive some of my celebrity clients crazy when strangers would make a fuss over them in public, so I hope I'm not violating your privacy. But I figure now that you're a local . . ."

"Hey, these days I need all the love I can get." She smiled and stuck out her hand. "We haven't officially met. I'm Gia."

"Sophie. And my partner is Mariah. She's home with our daughter tonight."

"The dark-haired woman, right?"

"That's her. How's it going on Rosser Ranch?"

"It's going. I'm thinking of starting a Christmas tree farm." May as well start spreading part of the word.

"Really?"

"It's just a lot of talk right now, but I like the idea."

"There's someone else in Nugget who grows them whose name escapes me at the moment. I'll find out and let you know. It might be worth talking to him."

"Absolutely. So you used to be in marketing, huh?" Gia thought someone with that kind of background could come in handy.

"Before Mariah and I moved here, yeah. Now we run this place."

Judging by the packed tables, the Ponderosa was successful. The food was good, but in Gia's opinion it was the atmosphere that pulled in the crowds. Warm and casual, the Western equivalent of *Cheers*.

"I'd better get back there." She pointed to Flynn again.

"I'll get you that tree grower's contact info."

"Thanks, Sophie." Gia strolled toward Flynn, who, despite his attempt to cover it up, was giving her the once-over.

"Nice dress," he said when she reached the table and pulled out her chair.

He was in his usual: jeans, flannel shirt, and cowboy boots. His hat hung from a hook on the wall next to a half dozen other Stetsons. Having spent much of her career around Wall Street guys, she liked Flynn better in Western attire than a suit. But the truth was she liked him in everything.

"How was your day?" she asked.

"Busy. Yours?"

"Annie is amazing. Thank you for recommending her."

"She's pretty great," he said, and Gia tried to gauge his expression to determine what exactly their relationship was—or had been. Nothing. Complete poker face.

"She thinks highly of you, that's for sure."

"That's nice to hear." He looked down at his menu.

"How exactly did you say you know each other?"

"Through our families," he said. "What're you getting?"

"Uh . . . a salad. How about you?"

"Steak." He flagged over a server. "Could we get a couple of drinks? Jack neat for me and whatever Gia wants."

"A glass of chardonnay," she told the waitress.

When she left, Flynn said, "What did you want to talk to me about?"

"Uh-uh, you go first. Did they buy that I suddenly regained my memory when it came to Cleo?"

He leaned back in his chair, inadvertently showing off the breadth of his chest and his mile-wide shoulders. His hair was damp from his shower, but he hadn't shaved, sporting a five-o'clock shadow. And before he delivered whatever bad news there was, she had the intense urge to kiss him. She didn't of course, but she was probably going to spend most of the evening thinking about it.

"I doubt it," he said. "But they pretended to. They're not planning to give up, Gia. They think you hold the key to finding Evan." He paused and studied her face.

"Don't tell me to make a deal, Flynn. Like I've already told you, I don't know where Evan is. It turns out that I knew very little about the man, least of all where he would run and hide billions of dollars' worth of stolen money."

Flynn held up his hands in surrender. "I'm not telling you to make a deal. I'm telling you to stay on your toes because the feds aren't going away. My guess is that they're trying to get a court order to track your phones and your bank accounts."

"That's fine. I hope they enjoy the weekly calls to my mother in Boca Raton. They can have at my bank accounts, though I don't know what that'll tell them other than that I'm close to broke."

"How's the day trading going?"

"Good." She smiled. In the last few days she'd made a lot of money. But she'd need every dime of it to pay her property taxes and get her project off the ground.

"Be careful with that."

"There's nothing illegal about what I'm doing." She folded her arms over her chest.

"Other than it's felony stupid. You of all people should know what a gamble it is."

She certainly didn't need him telling her how to make a living. "So the bad news is that the feds are tapping my phones and tracking my money?"

"Probably. That's what I would do if I were them. The worse news is, they're getting a lot of heat to solve this case, to find the money, and pay back investors. And you're convenient, Gia."

"What does Cleo have to do with it?"

"I don't know. That's something they wouldn't talk about. But again, if I had to guess, they've somehow linked Rufus Cleo's murder to the Ponzi scheme. Maybe he'd figured it out and threatened to blow the whistle. But that's just conjecture on my part. Do you know if he was an investor?"

"I have no idea. There should be a list; can't you get it?"

"I can try," Flynn said. "In the meantime, Gia, I can't emphasize enough how important it is that you not talk to anyone about this. Not without me. And even then I don't see any benefit of being cooperative anymore. Croce and Donovan will go through me from now on and I'm planning to tell them that you're moving on with your life. No more interviews."

"Don't you think it'll make me look guilty if I don't cooperate?"

He rubbed his chin. "Nope. At some point it just becomes harassment. Now promise me that from now on you say nothing."

"I promise."

The server returned with the drinks, took their orders, and went back to the kitchen.

"Let me ask you something, Gia. Is there a chance Laughlin will try to contact you?"

"No way. I may not have known him the way I thought. But he certainly knows that I'm the kind of person who would immediately turn him over to the authorities."

"If he does contact you, that's exactly what'll we'll do. Turn him over. But Gia, never meet him or any of his associates in person, you hear me?"

"You think he's even in this country?"

"I don't know where the hell he is. But if Cleo's death is somehow wrapped up in this, it's not safe. There's also the fact that the feds will be watching your every move."

"I won't. Anything else?"

"That about covers it." His eyes swooped over her. Gia could tell he liked her dress.

"One of Clay's boys came over to feed Dude as I was leaving. I don't mind doing it, you know. Not as long as you're providing the hay." She smiled.

"It's not your job to feed my horse."

"We do, however, have to talk about your retainer."

"No worries, darlin', we'll get to that. Now tell me what you needed to talk to me about."

"Okay, but I don't want anyone to hear."

The waitress reappeared with their food. Even though Gia wasn't hungry, Flynn's looked delicious and her salad looked boring. He saw her eyeing his plate, cut off a piece of steak, and put it on her plate.

"It's McCreedy beef," he said. "Not as good as Barlow's, but it'll do."

She took a bite. The meat was fabulous. "Annie thinks I should grow alfalfa and meadow hay—and Christmas trees."

"Christmas trees, hmm."

"You don't think I should grow Christmas trees? What do you have against Christmas?"

"Nothing. Don't get defensive. I just hadn't thought of it. But, yeah, it absolutely makes sense."

"She says I need to start planting seedlings now, because it takes eight years for them to grow to five feet."

"Okay." He was globbing sour cream on his potatoes, which made Gia's mouth water. He cut one of the halves and put it on her plate.

"How do we deal with your cows? I don't want 'em eating my trees."

"What kind of acreage are we talking about? And where on the property do you want to put this tree farm?" Flynn asked.

"I don't know the answer to either question. We're still in the planning phase."

"As long as there's enough grazing pasture for my cattle, I'm not concerned about it. We'll fence off what you want to farm."

"What do you consider enough grazing pasture?"

Flynn glowered with impatience. "You've got a thousand acres, Gia; we'll make it work." He leaned across the table, close to her ear, and said, "This is what you didn't want people to hear?"

She was surprised he'd given in so easily about the land and didn't want to push her luck. Not here. "No. There's more, but we should talk about it at home. Later."

"Then eat up." Clearly he wanted to hear what she had to say.

More than halfway through his steak, he said, "This doesn't have anything to do with us not sleeping together, does it? Because that rule hasn't changed."

She put her finger to her lips. "Hush. People can hear you. And no, it doesn't have anything to do with that. Is that all you can think about?"

"Pretty much." His lips quirked into a half grin as he took in her dress again. "But it's not gonna happen."

"Of course it's not," she said, then whispered, "After Evan, I'm never having sex again." Although with Flynn it was all she could think about.

He scowled. "I don't want to talk about that dirtbag."

"Works for me."

They finished eating, passed on dessert, and Flynn covered the bill.

"Shouldn't I pay, because this was a legal meeting?"

"It was off the books." Flynn waved her off. "I'll follow you home."

They walked out together and Flynn made sure she started her car before getting in his truck. All the way back to Rosser Ranch, Gia thought about what a different breed Flynn was from the men she knew in New York. He was an old-style gentleman. It should've bugged her because she'd worked hard to assert herself as an independent woman—none of this the-man-pays-for-dinner crap and *I'll follow you home*—but she liked it. She didn't get the sense that he thought he was smarter or higher on the evolutionary ladder than she; he was just mannerly. Perhaps it was a cowboy thing, because in New York the men were all too happy to let her foot the bill.

She pulled into the garage and Flynn parked in the driveway. By the time she walked through the house and opened the front door, he'd grabbed his duffel and was headed up the stairs to the guest quarters over the garage.

"Hey, aren't you coming in?" she called to him.

"I just want to put my stuff away and say hello to Dude. Put on a pot of coffee and I'll be over in a bit."

In the kitchen the answering machine blinked. Lately, when the machine flashed, it gave her heart palpitations. She pressed the button anyway.

"Gia, it's Mom. Call me as soon as you can. The FBI came by the condo today—"

She quickly shut off the machine and laid her face in her hands. Flynn was right; this was never going away.

Chapter 10

Flynn walked to the barn. He needed a little distance from Gia and to get his head twisted on straight. There was too much flirting going on between them and nothing good could come of that, not while he was her attorney. There were ethics and rules.

He was also losing his objectivity. It was one thing to give her the benefit of the doubt but another not to keep an open mind to the possibility that she was dirty as sin. Instead, he kept telling himself that criminals sitting on billions of dollars of cash didn't talk about planting Christmas tree farms. Not unless she planned to launder the money through the farm, which was as ridiculous as it was brilliant. But with the feds keeping eyes on her the way they were, every dime she spent would have to be accounted for. No cash transactions.

He'd need records of her day trading, because that seemed to be the way she planned to pay for her agricultural endeavors.

Dude neighed at the scent of Flynn. He found a bag of baby carrots near the grain feed and helped himself to a few, offering the treats to his gelding with the flat of his palm.

"How you doing, boy?" Flynn scratched the horse behind his ears. "We'll go out tomorrow, get you a little exercise."

Dude shoved his muzzle into Flynn's hand, looking for more carrots or scratches.

"Greedy fellow."

Clay's boys had been doing a good job. Dude's stall was clean and his water fresh. Flynn checked on Rory, who had thrown her head over the stall to see what was going on. Both horses liked to come in at night instead of grazing in the paddocks.

"You're a nosy girl, just like your owner," he told the mare. Gia's veiled attempts at digging into his and Annie's relationship had both amused and turned him on. At least in some areas she was very much transparent.

After Evan, I'm never having sex again.

She would with Flynn as soon as he stopped being her lawyer. And then she'd forget all about Evan Laughlin.

He gave Rory one last pat and hiked back to the house. The sun was starting to set, painting brilliant pinks, oranges, and blues across the sky. The earth still held the pungent scent of the recent rain. Flynn wished for more, especially if Gia used some of the pasture land for farming. Christmas trees; he smiled and scratched his head. Somehow he couldn't picture America's premier financial guru driving a tractor. Then again, she'd look damned good on top of a John Deere. Damned good.

He knocked on the door and let himself in, finding Gia sitting at the breakfast bar in the kitchen.

"The FBI has started harassing my mother," she said without preamble.

He cocked his hip against the counter. "Where does your mother live?"

"In Florida. Boca Raton."

"Did she talk to them?" He zeroed in on the coffeemaker, found the mugs, and poured them each a cup.

"No. She hid in her house, afraid to answer the door. I don't want them bothering her. She has nothing to do with this. She didn't like Evan; hated him, in fact."

"Smart lady."

"Can you make them leave her alone?" she asked, her voice cracking.

"Probably not. They'll likely be sniffing around all your family, friends, and associates. They can try to talk to anyone they want. No law against it." No sense sugarcoating it. If they wanted to, the feds could make Gia's life miserable.

"They've already interviewed everyone I've ever had a conversation with. When does it border on harassment?"

Flynn sat next to her, put his hand on the back of her neck, and rubbed the muscles there. "They want to flush Evan out, which means making you cooperate."

"For the last freaking time, I don't know anything."

"I believe you, Gia." Or at least he was starting to.

"You got enough money to send your mom on a cruise for a couple of weeks?"

She made a sound in her throat as if she thought he was nuts. "So now she has to go into hiding?"

"It was just a thought. You could always have her come here. They won't harass her on your property because they've been told they have to go through me."

"That feels good," she said as his hands continued to knead the knots. "How about my shoulders?"

He moved his hands down and worked on her deltoids. She let out a moan of gratitude and he went instantly hard. Okay, bad idea. But he didn't want to stop. His fingers itched to unzip her dress and touch her bare skin. Fondle her breasts and squeeze that perfect ass, which he'd been admiring since that first night in the Ponderosa.

She pulled her hair away to give him better access and he nearly groaned out loud. Gia sure wasn't making it easy on him. Or, depending on how he looked at it, she was making it too easy. He stepped behind her barstool, hoping to hide the growing bulge in his jeans.

"Better?" he asked.

"Mm-hmm."

"Good, because we've gotta stop now."

"Why?" Gia leaned her head back and smiled into his face.

"You know why." He reached for her hand and pressed it against his crotch.

"Uh-oh." She giggled and squeezed his package.

"How much wine did you have at dinner?" He moved her hand and stepped away.

"Not nearly enough. You know, they have a name for men like you."

"No more!" He returned to the stool next to her and took a slug of his coffee. "What do you want to do about your mom?"

She sobered quickly. "I don't know yet. I'd send for her, but she has an active social life in Boca. What would she do here?" Gia stared out the big picture window. As beautiful as Rosser Ranch was, it wasn't a thriving senior community.

"Why did she hate Laughlin?"

"She didn't think he treated me well. But you know how mothers are. They want men to put their daughters on pedestals."

"How did he not treat you well?" *And how did a smart woman like you fall for a con artist?*

"She thought he only wanted me as a trophy because of my celebrity. And in the end she was right. I opened a lot of doors for him."

"You were never suspicious of him?" he asked, trying hard to understand why she hadn't seen through his duplicity.

"Not as an investment banker." She shook her head. "I actually thought he was mediocre in that area, solid but not taking the world by storm. Evan was the opposite of slick. Looking back on it, that's probably what made him seem so trustworthy."

"Then what were you suspicious of?"

"His feelings toward me. He told me he loved me often enough, but it always seemed like hollow words, like something he knew I wanted to hear. I never really felt it where it counted." She pressed her hand against her heart.

"Why did you stay with him, then?"

She shrugged. "It was familiar and comfortable and I wanted to believe it was real."

It bothered Flynn that she'd been in love with Laughlin. And there was more to it than the fact that the man had been a no-good grifter. There was a jealousy factor that Flynn wasn't quite ready to explore, especially because he'd known Gia less than a month. It seemed a little soon to be territorial about a woman.

"What was the last thing he said to you?" It was a question he used to ask witnesses when he was an FBI agent. Sometimes those last words could help crack a case.

Gia thought about it for a while. "Evan had just gotten out of the shower and I was rushing off to work. He called to me, 'Remember, we have dinner with Porter and Joan tonight. I'll meet you at the restaurant.'"

"And then he never showed?"

"Right. The next morning someone from the SEC was pounding on my door. You know the rest."

Gia got up and refilled their coffees. He drank, not worried that the caffeine would keep him up. It wasn't like he'd be able to sleep with Gia lying in bed only yards away from the guest apartment.

"I told you mine," Gia said. "It's your turn to tell me yours. What's the deal with you and Annie?"

He laughed. "There's no deal. Our families are friends. Annie's my friend."

"You never slept with her?"

"Not that I would tell you if I had, but no, we never slept to-gether."

She squinted at him as if she thought he was lying. "Why not?"

"Because it's not like that with us."

"So what's up with her family? It sounds like there are problems there."

"That I can't talk about," he said and drained the rest of his coffee.

"Attorney-client privilege?"

"Yup. And it's none of your business. So what did you want to tell me that needed to be said in private, besides the fact that you're desperate to sleep with me?"

"For a guy who says sex is off the table, you sure bring it up a lot."

She was right about that. He was playing with fire, but he couldn't seem to stop flirting with her. "Someday I won't be your attorney." He winked at her and watched her face flush.

"At the rate the FBI is harassing me I'll need a lawyer for the rest of my life. And you seem to know what you're doing."

He knew what he was doing, but sometimes that wasn't enough. "What did you want to tell me?"

"That I need your help with something that has nothing to do with the law."

"If you need me to build a fence, rope a calf, or bulldog a steer, I'm your man." He grinned.

"None of the above." She got up again and turned off the coffee-maker; the carafe was nearly empty. "I need you to help me persuade my neighbors to rubber stamp a project I'm planning."

"What's the project?"

"You promise you'll keep it confidential?"

He brought his mug to the sink, rinsed it out, and put it in the dishwasher. "Yeah, as long it won't get me disbarred."

"It's nothing like that," she said. "I want to start a residential pro-gram for down-and-out women and teach them how to be financially independent. They'll run the farm and I'll provide them with classes on how to enhance their earning potential, how to budget their money, how to invest, stuff like that." She spent the next hour giving him the details.

"Where will you get these women?" He liked the idea but didn't think her neighbors would if the participants were right out of Frontera State Prison.

"I'll put the word out on social media, go through social services and the Welfare Department. My name may be mud, but I don't think desperate people will pass up a chance for room, board, a job, and a way to better their life."

"You thinking this will be something that'll resurrect your public image?" *It certainly wouldn't hurt it*, Flynn thought.

"I've been planning this long before Evan and his Ponzi scheme. . . . I've been planning this since I was twenty. But yeah, it wouldn't hurt my public image. It would be nice to stop getting death threats."

"Why since you were twenty?" Flynn wondered what the impetus was.

"It's when I made my first million dollars from investing my student loans in the stock market." She laughed. "I know you're appalled. But it worked out, didn't it?"

"I hope that's not what you'll be teaching these women because you may as well take them to the nearest racetrack. Okay, you made your first million. That still doesn't explain why you wanted to go into social work." Especially because she'd spent her next years in the financial world and on television, making more money than most people could imagine.

"My life wasn't always this." She spread her arms wide at the yards of granite countertops and the pricey appliances. The house was a showplace. "When my father died he was up to his neck in debt. . . . He'd made some very bad investments. My mother had no idea we were living off his life insurance. She'd always let him oversee the finances, convinced he was better and smarter than her. Ha. I think I would've done a better a job and I was just thirteen. After the funeral the world started caving in us. We lost everything. The house, my mother's jewelry, the country club, even the furniture."

"What did you do?" The story hadn't been in Gia's Wikipedia entry. As far as Flynn knew, this wasn't public information.

"The only skill my mother had was keeping house. Eventually, a family hired her to keep theirs. But until then, we lived hand to mouth, sometimes sleeping in the car, often relying on soup kitchens. It was a long way to fall . . . from Bedford to homeless." She stopped and studied his reaction. "Does it shock you? Does it make you think I would steal investors' life savings . . . their retirement?"

"No. But it helps me understand what drives you." It was impressive how much she'd accomplished. "I'm sorry, Gia. No one should have to go through that."

"I didn't tell you so you'd feel sorry for me. It's ancient history. I told you so you'd understand how important this program is to me. If my mother had been better equipped . . . well, things would've been different."

"Look," he said, "I like the idea and I'm happy to help any way I can. But I'm not a local—"

"But you sort of are," Gia interrupted. "People here like you."

"You'd be much better off getting Clay on your side. His family was among the first settlers of Nugget. He'll have sway."

"Will you help me talk to him?"

He didn't see how that would hurt. But he wouldn't force it down Clay's throat. "Yeah, because I can't seem to resist you. Where will you put these women? And what if they have kids?"

"I've thought about that," she said. "I'm going to spruce up the bunkhouses and the cottages on the property. The bunkhouses for the single ladies and the cottages for families. It won't be fancy, but it'll be a roof over their heads. They'll have their dignity."

That last part made Flynn's heart twist. Everyone should have dignity.

He looked at his watch. "You know it's one in the morning? I've got to be up and out by six."

"To give the cows shots?"

His mouth quirked. "They're cattle, Gia, not cows. Come over to the squeeze chutes in the morning and watch. You want to fit in around here, learn how it's done."

She walked him to the door. "You have everything you need up there?"

"Yep." Although he'd like her in his bed. "See you tomorrow."

"Good night."

He got halfway out the door when he turned back. "Gia?"

"Hmm?"

"Besides the fact that I want to sleep with you, I'm starting to like you. From what I see, you're a good person. But if you're conning me . . . don't! You won't like the consequences."

* * *

Gia forced herself out of bed at the crack of dawn, showered, and pulled on a pair of jeans and a hoodie. The idea of watching calves get vaccinated wasn't all that thrilling, but she wanted to see Flynn in action. He was an amazing rider; she'd noticed that from the first time she'd seen him astride Dude. Nice seat, she giggled to herself. Flynn had a way of making her revert to her teenage years, back when a boy could make her giddy.

Last night's declaration had made it clear he didn't fully trust her, which was fine because she didn't fully trust him either. How could any woman ever fully trust again after Evan? But she'd like to get back on the horse, so to speak. She'd always liked sex as long as it was with someone safe and respectful. Flynn felt safe. And he was one of the most respectful men she'd ever met.

Perhaps today she should start looking for a permanent attorney, she joked to herself. Unfortunately or fortunately, depending on her priorities, he seemed to be a good lawyer. How could you beat having a defense attorney who was a former FBI agent and a federal prosecutor? Talk about cred.

She pulled on a pair of boots she'd recovered from her urban cowboy phase and headed for the "squeeze chutes," if only she knew where they were. A while back she'd noticed a metal structure—a pen with gates and ramps—near the hay barn in the south pasture and suspected that was the place.

Sure enough, a group of men on horseback had gathered, including Flynn. He waved his hat at her and she climbed up on the fence to watch. They'd already rounded up a small herd of mamas and their babies and had corralled them in a fenced in area near the chute.

"Am I safe here?" she called to them.

Clay rode up. "You ever seen this before?"

"Can't say that I have. But Flynn suggested I watch. It doesn't hurt, does it?"

"Nah. It's like getting a shot at the doctor's office. In a couple of weeks Flynn will dehorn 'em and castrate the males. That might hurt a little."

She would be sure to miss that part of the program. Clay's boys were helping, but Gia didn't recognize the other rider. "Who's the guy in the black cowboy hat?"

"That's Lucky Rodriguez. Around here he may be just as famous as you."

Was he wanted for investment fraud? Gia wanted to ask. "Ah, the rodeo star."

"Champion bull rider." Clay grinned and called out to Flynn. "Hey, Barlow, introduce Gia to Lucky."

The two men trotted over and Lucky swiped off his hat and bent over the side of his horse to give her a bow. "Welcome, neighbor."

"Nice to meet you, Lucky. I'm Gia."

"My wife, Tawny, and I have been planning to come over to introduce ourselves, but the cowboy camp is booked solid this month." His lips curved up into an amazing smile. "Who the hell would've thunk it?"

Dana had told her about the camp. Apparently it was a dude ranch, but Lucky didn't like calling it that. "Congrats on your success."

"We're certainly not complaining. But I'll be bringing the welcome wagon over real soon . . . my daughter, Katie, too."

Lucky and Clay rode off to shoo a stray into the pen.

Flynn caught her yawning. "You only half-awake?"

"Yeah. I don't know how you keep these hours. Is there even coffee in the guest apartment?"

"Yep, it's fully equipped. You're not working the markets this morning?"

"Nope. I came to watch you instead. I might get a couple of trades in before lunch." So far she'd had a good week. "When does the fun start?"

"In a few minutes. You didn't bring a hat?"

"No. What for?"

"The sun's gonna get you with that fair skin of yours." He took off his and dropped it on her head. The hat was huge and fell over her eyes. Flynn made a few adjustments. "There you go," he said and rode away.

A smile rose to her lips and she pushed the Stetson back so she could see better. Clay opened the corral and Flynn herded one of the calves toward the chute. He and Lucky flanked each side of the little guy. Once the calf went in the chute, Clay's oldest boy, Justin, pulled a lever that held the animal's head in place. With another lever, he squeezed the bars of the chute closer to the calf's body, keeping it still for the vaccination. The whole thing took less than five minutes and when they were done, Justin opened the chute and the calf ran out.

Flynn reunited the critter with its mama, moved her out of the corral, and the two wandered off to freedom. Pretty soon the guys were like a well-oiled machine, moving calves in and out faster than Gia could keep track of. She thought it was nice that the neighbors helped out and wondered if Flynn did the same for them.

Occasionally he'd look her way and wave. Gia waved back, and a few times she caught Clay grinning. Clearly, he thought they were an item, which was kind of embarrassing because she and Flynn barely knew each other. She wouldn't want the good folks of Nugget to think New Yorkers were slutty. It was bad enough they thought she'd helped steal billions of dollars.

By eight o'clock they were done. Lucky and the McCreedys rode off to their respective properties and Flynn cleaned up the unused syringes and the rest of the medical supplies.

"You gonna make me breakfast?" he called as she scrambled down from the fence.

"If you trust my cooking, sure." She could probably manage toast, bacon, and a couple of fried eggs.

He pointed to his truck, which he'd parked in the pasture and was loading. "You want a ride?"

"Nah, I'll walk back." It beat the treadmill in the basement.

"Okay. I'll let Dude loose and meet you at the house."

At home she put on a pot of coffee, grabbed the eggs and bacon from the fridge, and a carton of orange juice. Flynn had beaten her back, but he'd gone up to the garage apartment to wash up. She got the bacon going and put down two settings at the center island. The house had a breakfast nook and a formal dining room, but the island worked better because everything was so spread out. The kitchen alone outsized most New York apartments.

Flynn came in through the mudroom.

"I hung your hat in there," Gia said. "Thanks for letting me borrow it. How do you like your eggs?" She popped a few slices of bread into the toaster.

"Sunny-side up." He grabbed a piece of bacon off the plate she'd set out and poured them each a cup of coffee. "What did you think of Lucky?"

"He seems nice." She finished the eggs and plated them.

Flynn covered them in pepper, took a bite, and sopped up the runny yolk with his toast. She liked the efficient way he ate. There was something very manly about it.

"When do you think I should call a meeting about my proposal?" she asked. "Annie said she'd come to talk about the agricultural points."

"No one will have a problem with your tree farm or growing hay. That's the easy part," he said. "You talk to your mom today?"

"Not yet. I'll call her later." She looked at the time. "She's probably playing golf. What time's your cattlemen's meeting?"

"This evening. I was thinking about going into town and getting a haircut."

"From Owen? The man's nuts. One day he's offering to be my getaway driver, the next he's telling me he's watching me, as if I might steal his wallet when he's not looking."

Flynn let out a laugh. "Yeah, he's different. But folks in the Sierra are. I wouldn't be offended. Chances are he likes you or he wouldn't bother with you at all."

"I'm friends with his daughter, Darla. If I were you, I'd have her cut your hair. She's very good."

Flynn got up and stuck two more slices of bread in the toaster.

"You're still hungry?" The man ate like a horse and didn't have an ounce of fat on him.

"Yeah. That was hard work this morning." He grinned. "Want another slice?"

"I'm stuffed," she said.

"You sure you want to set up this residential program? It may help redeem you in the public eye, but there are easier ways to do that."

"After everything I told you last night . . . I bought this place to do it. It's important to me."

Gia didn't like talking about how the bank had foreclosed on their house in Bedford and how they'd slept in shelters. But she would do anything to save someone else from poverty . . . from the misery she'd suffered.

Flynn came back with his toast and put his hand on her back. Even through her sweatshirt she could feel the warmth and strength of his touch. "I get it. But you've got your hands full right now."

"This has nothing to do with the case."

"All right, I'll drop it." His hand left her back and she felt bereft without it. His touch helped to shore her up. "What are your plans for the day?"

"Dana and I are going to Reno for her wedding dress fitting."

"Ah, the big wedding I've been hearing so much about."

Gia started to clear away the dishes. "Yep. It's big news in Nugget. I'm happy for Dana. Aidan is a great guy and she was my first real friend when my life blew up. We were in the Lumber Baron together last summer when an arsonist set it on fire. Did you hear about it?" When he nodded, she said, "Dana got smoke inhalation and had to go to the hospital."

"So Aidan's the arson investigator who caught the culprit, huh?"

"Uh-huh. He and Chief Shepard."

"I'm glad you weren't hurt." He came up behind her as she was rinsing dishes and just stood there. "What do you do at a wedding gown fitting?"

"Drink wine, ooh and ah over the bride, and try on stuff. I gather you've never been married."

"Nope." He was so close she could feel his body heat.

"How come? You're almost forty."

"I don't have anything against marriage. . . . It's hard to date and get serious when you're running around chasing bad guys. On my days off I was helping with the ranch and before I knew it I was old."

"You're not old; far from it," she said and squeezed around him to turn off the coffeemaker. "Wasn't there anyone special?"

"There were lots of special women. Just not special enough. How about you? Before Evan, was there someone you were serious with?" He propped his hip against the counter, waiting expectantly.

"Not really. I dated, had boyfriends, but like you, my career came first. And because I don't want to get married there was no pressure to get serious."

"Why don't you want to get married?" he asked, looking at her as if she were alien. "All women want to get married."

"A: That's a generalization. And B: It's sexist. I don't want to share a bank account with another person. I don't want to make financial decisions by committee. And I don't want to be dependent on someone else." Like her mother was on her father.

"You make marriage sound like a business merger. What about wanting to make a home with someone you love?"

"Wow, aren't you the romantic."

"Maybe." He gave her a crooked smile that she felt to the tips of her toes. "I had good role models. My parents have been married forty-five years. We still catch 'em making out in front of the TV. So your mom never remarried?"

"Nope." Iris had been too busy surviving.

"Did she and your dad have a good marriage before he died?"

How good could it be when he took their life's savings and squandered it in bad investments without telling his wife? She shrugged. "I was a kid."

Flynn studied her but didn't press; then his phone rang. It sat on the island where he'd been eating, next to his wallet and keys. He reached over, grabbed it, and checked the display.

"I've got to take this."

He wandered into the dining room, where Gia could hear him talking in a muffled voice. She caught words and snippets of conversation. It sounded to her like it was work, but it was hard to tell. She finished tidying up and continued to eavesdrop.

"That was Toad," Flynn said, coming back into the kitchen. "Your ex-boyfriend managed Cleo's money. His assets are listed at more than a billion dollars."

Gia took in a sharp breath. Cleo was one of the biggest philanthropists in the world. His charitable trust gave away millions of dollars in grants to human rights organizations, research centers, even public libraries. "Oh God, Evan stole it all, didn't he?"

"Dunno. But if Cleo had discovered the fraud and threatened to go to the SEC, that would be a good motive for killing him, wouldn't it?"

Gia's eyes widened at what Flynn was suggesting. Evan...a murderer?

Chapter 11

On the way to the barbershop, Flynn popped into the police department. He had plenty of time to kill before his meeting and Gia had left to go to Reno with Dana. Despite the complications of it, he liked hanging out with her. Not just because she was beautiful. He knew a lot of beautiful women. But because she challenged him. Their back-and-forth was better than being in a courtroom.

Connie, the receptionist and dispatcher, stood up behind her desk to greet him.

"Is Rhys around?" he asked.

"Why is it that no one ever comes to visit me?"

He'd only known Connie since he'd started grazing his cattle at Rosser Ranch, but he liked the way she bossed Rhys around. She sort of reminded him of Doris, though she was young enough to be her daughter. According to town gossip, she was seeing the cook over at the Ponderosa.

"I'll take you to lunch after I'm done talking with Rhys and getting my hair cut." He would too.

She leaned into him ever so slightly. "I'm on to you, Barlow."

"Oh yeah? How's that?"

"Everyone wants to get in good with the gatekeeper."

He laughed. She was sassy and he liked that too.

"Let me get the chief for you."

A few minutes later Rhys came down the corridor and motioned for Flynn to follow him back to his office. "What's up?"

Flynn made himself at home in one of Rhys's lumpy chairs. The room was small and cluttered, the way a police chief's office should be. "Not much; just curious what you thought of that meeting the other day with Gia and the FBI."

Rhys sat pensive for a moment. "I'm not at liberty to talk about that; in fact, I'm not even confirming it happened."

Flynn stretched out his legs. "Gia's retained me as her attorney."

"That so? Then why did your client lie about not knowing Rufus Cleo?"

"She didn't lie. Her memory escaped her. On her way home she remembered who he was."

"Ah, so that's the story you're going with. Because even I recognized the dude and I'm just a humble country cop."

"Fact is, she served on the board of his charitable trust."

Rhys laughed. "Look, it's not my jurisdiction and it's not my case. I was surprised when she asked me to sit in."

"She trusts you and she doesn't trust them."

"Wise woman. No offense, Flynn, but the Bureau is really pissing me off. I don't like them mucking around my town . . . my residents . . . without giving me a heads-up. It's common courtesy."

"Hey, you're preaching to the choir. When I was an agent I wouldn't have big-footed you like that. We're on the same side; tell me what you thought."

"We used to be on the same side. Not anymore."

"We're both on the side of justice."

"Yeah, yeah," Rhys said. "I thought she was good until she lied. I saw Croce's eyes light up like Christmas. They want her; they want her bad. Does she know where Laughlin is?"

"Of course she doesn't. She's been cooperating since the get-go."

"Do yourself a favor, Flynn: Don't get sucked in by a pretty face."

"I represent lots of pretty faces," Flynn said.

"But you like this one, I can tell. If she's clean, I'm all for it. Love is a fine thing. But if she's not . . ."

"I'm her lawyer." Flynn got up. "And who said anything about love?"

Rhys walked him out. "You want to come over one night for dinner?"

The folks here certainly made him feel welcome, even if he *was* from Quincy. "Sure. How's that kid of yours?"

Rhys beamed like a proud papa. "Emma's perfect. You're around all the time; come join one of our pickup games."

The chief had turned the blacktop behind the police department

into a basketball court. Every afternoon they played ball with whoever showed up.

"I may do that."

Flynn walked over to Owen's. There was already someone in the
barber's chair getting a haircut. Flynn took a seat and thumbed through
his phone, reading emails. Toad was running background checks on
Cleo.

"You sleeping with that financial wiz?"

Flynn popped his head up, wondering if Owen was talking to him.
The barber brushed the hairs off the neck of his customer and looked
at Flynn expectantly.

"Gia?"

"Yeah," Owen said. "Everyone says you're sleeping together."

"Well everyone's wrong, though it's none of their business."

"No need to get your back up, boy."

Flynn just shook his head, knowing any effort to deny it was fruit-
less. He spent a lot of time at Rosser Ranch and people liked to talk.
Owen finished with the customer at the cash register and indicated
that Flynn was next.

"Where's Darla?" he asked as he hopped up into Owen's chair.

"She has the day off. We like to coordinate it so we're not working at the same time." Owen snapped a cape on him. "You want to go
short?"

"It is short. I just want a trim."

"Back in my day men wore buzz cuts. Nowadays you're all trying
to look like Fabio."

Flynn wondered how Owen even knew who Fabio was. He'd
probably seen him in one of those I-can't-believe-it's-not-butter com-
mercials. "All I need are the edges cleaned up."

Owen started snipping. "I tried to help your girl escape from
those fan belt . . . uh, FBI agents the other day."

"She's not my girl. But yeah, she told me."

"Big mistake her talking to those agents like that."

"Why's that?" Flynn just went along with Owen's stories for the
hell of it.

"Those guys will twist your words." Owen got out his clippers
and began crisping his sides. "You think she's hiding Laughlin on
Ray's property?"

"It's her property now and no, I don't." Why mention that he was at the ranch nearly every day and that he would know? It only added fuel to the gossip fires about him and Gia.

"Is it true the scoundrel also stole her money?" Owen asked.

Didn't the old guy read newspapers? "You'd have to ask her."

Owen spent the next twenty minutes focusing on Flynn's hair, occasionally throwing in a piece of town gossip. Flynn didn't know most of the people involved but pretended to anyway, figuring it would get him out of the barbershop quicker.

The door jingled open and Donna came in. "Here you are. I've been looking all over for you. Trevor saw your truck parked on the square."

"Let me finish with him before you jaw his head off." Owen waved his clippers at her.

She made a face at him, helped herself to coffee, and spit a mouthful back into her Styrofoam cup. "This is disgusting. Griffin has better coffee at the Gas and Go and that stuff is one notch above swill."

"Then why don't you drink your own?"

"We stop serving coffee at the Bun Boy after one." She walked back to the bathroom and came back empty-handed.

"No one asked you to come over here." Owen brushed Flynn's neck, removed the cape, handed him a hand mirror, and spun the chair around for a view of the back of his head.

"Looks good," Flynn said and got up to pay at the cash register.

"My turn now." Donna said and shot Owen a dirty look. "I need a lawyer."

Owen suddenly perked up, interested.

Flynn took Donna by the arm. "What do you say we do this somewhere in private?"

"You need an office here is what you need," Donna replied but let Flynn lead her across the square to one of the empty picnic tables at the Bun Boy.

"Are you in trouble with the law again, Donna?" Flynn winked.

"Trevor and I want you to do our wills. We don't plan on dying anytime soon, but last week Sally May Jordan over in Graeagle found two lumps in her breast. When the good Lord says it's time to go, you want to be packed and ready."

"Okay." As far as Flynn knew, the Thurstons didn't have any children. Regardless, good estate planning was important. "Depending on how you want to divide your assets, you may want to consider a living trust. But you and Trevor and I can sit down and talk about the options. In the meantime, I'll send you some literature explaining the process and a worksheet to fill out."

"Do we have to come to your office . . . to Sacramento?"

"Nah, I could come to your house one of the days I'm up to deal with the cattle. Just make sure you fill out that worksheet; it'll save us time." Flynn took down her email address so he could have Doris send her the paperwork.

"What's going on with you and that Treadwell girl? From what I hear you're up there every night."

"It's calving season, Donna."

"Spring ain't just for calving." She jabbed him in the chest with her finger. "And if you want to hear my ten cents"—he didn't—"the poor woman got taken for a ride by that oily, albeit fine-looking Evan Laughlin. My guess is one look at him and Gia dropped her panties and handed over the goods."

The comment rubbed Flynn the wrong way. He knew that was the way Donna talked—no filter on that one—and meant no harm. If anything, she was standing up for Gia. But the idea of Gia "dropping her panties" for Laughlin made him want to rip the guy's throat out. The idea of her with Laughlin at all . . . well, it put him in a foul mood.

"Donna, Gia's been through enough," he said. "Don't make the situation worse by spreading rumors about the two of us. There's nothing going on."

"Maybe there should be. You two would make beautiful children and your mother wants more grandbabies."

He inwardly groaned. Nugget was worse than Quincy. "Let's focus on your will."

The last vision he wanted in his head was him and Gia making babies. He had enough trouble keeping his hands off her.

Chapter 12

Flynn had been missing in action for a week and all Gia could think about was seeing him again. The ranch was too big to rattle around alone. Although no snoopy FBI agents or pushy reporters had shown up, she felt safer with him there. And despite his overall bossiness—*"Don't talk to anyone without me present"*—and his flagrant disapproval of her day trading, he was great company.

And she'd be lying if she said she didn't like looking at him. Flynn could be the poster child for the perfect male specimen. Not too pretty but beautifully masculine. Rough, chiseled face, lean, muscled body, and a cool confidence that she'd first mistaken for arrogance. She suspected a lot of his self-assurance came from his law enforcement background.

But what she liked most about him was that he was a good communicator. No game playing. Flynn spoke his mind. Some of the back and forth between them was as good as sex, which made her wonder what the actual sex would be like. Flynn had made it perfectly clear that he wanted her, but unlike most of the men she'd known he could show restraint when the occasion called for it. He was a grown-up.

Evan, six years older than Flynn, had been an overgrown child. Impetuous, self-centered, and prone to fits. When they'd first started dating Gia had been nominated for an Emmy. CNBC bought a table for the event, but there were only enough seats for members of her staff and network executives. Quite frankly, she hadn't known Evan long enough to have him sit through the disappointment of her losing. That year the award for economic and financial reporting had gone to *Frontline*. And it wasn't as if the ceremony was that exciting.

Not like the Academy Awards or the Golden Globes. No glitz, no glamor, just a lot of TV industry people talking shop.

Still, Evan had practically thrown a temper tantrum at not being asked. She suspected that if Flynn had been in the same position, he would've understood and supported her from home. But more than likely she would've invited Flynn.

Stop thinking about the man, she chided herself.

Instead, Gia occupied herself by staring out the window. The day couldn't be any more gorgeous. It had started out overcast, but the sun had come out and the temperature had risen to somewhere in the seventies. Too nice to stay inside. Gia considered saddling up Rory, but Annie was on her way. She'd found dormant Christmas tree seedlings from a good nursery and Gia had decided they should plant regardless of whether Nugget agreed to her residential program or not. Today they planned to pick the best spot for the tree farm and to take soil samples because Reynolds's had come back inconclusive. As much as Gia hated to admit it, Flynn had been right about him. The so-called farmer was a poseur.

She grabbed her hat from the mudroom and started to head for the door when the phone rang. Checking caller ID, she picked up.

"Mom, everything okay?"

"I'm fine, dear. I'm calling to check on you."

"It's been quiet. The FBI and SEC have to go through Flynn now. And since the episode with the camera guy, no one has bothered me. How about you?"

"Nothing," Iris said. "Whatever your lawyer friend did worked."

Gia knew Flynn had called the FBI's Boca Raton office. He must've had enough clout to get the agents off her mother's back.

"I'm glad, Mom. But if you'd feel better coming here I'd love to have you."

Silence from the other end, as if her mother was thinking about it. "You know how I feel about flying. But if the agents show up again I'll come. Last time they made me so nervous."

"There's nothing to be nervous about. You didn't have anything to do with Evan."

"I know, but I don't want to say anything wrong . . . anything that could make this any worse for you. I loathed that man."

Gia didn't want a lecture about her bad choice in mates. Her mother usually tried to keep out of Gia's love life. But Iris had despised Evan from the start; it had been visceral.

"Mom, I'm expecting someone any second and have to go. I'll call you tomorrow."

She hung up, fastened her hat on her head, and went outside. The fresh air immediately made her feel better. Starting for the barn, she heard the sound of a loud engine. Not Flynn's. The purr of his pickup made her heart race like a locomotive.

Annie's old turquoise Ford crested the hill, kicking up a cloud of dust. Gia had given Annie the code to the gate, which she almost always kept locked now. Waving to Annie, Gia turned around and started back for the house.

The brakes squealed as Annie came to a stop. She hopped out of the driver's seat in a pair of overalls that had been patched in so many places the denim was nearly invisible, a kerchief around her head, and the combat boots. Somehow the look worked on her.

"Howdy," Annie said and shielded her eyes with her hand before grabbing her hat from the bench seat.

Gia moved closer and peeked into the back of the Ford "What's all that stuff?" Large zip-tied plastic bags, cardboard boxes, and wooden crates filled the bed. It looked like Annie planned to make a dump run.

"All my worldly possessions," Annie said. "I'm moving."

"You came all the way here on moving day?" Gia knew Annie lived in Davis, a college town outside of Sacramento that was at least a three-hour drive away.

"I don't know where I'm moving yet, so no biggie."

"But you have a place to live in the meantime, right?" Gia couldn't help but be baffled. Why lug all that stuff around if you didn't have a place to put it?

"Nope. But I'll find something."

Gia nudged her head at the sacks and cartons. It looked like Annie had thrown things into the first container she could find, very haphazard. "Aren't you afraid it'll get stolen?"

"Honestly, I haven't thought that far ahead. I have a friend in vet school who has a garage. He might let me store some of it there."

"I've got plenty of room, Annie. You can stash it here for as long as you like." But clearly Annie had a bigger problem than temporary storage. She needed housing. "Is everything all right?"

"Everything's great." Annie smiled so sunnily that Gia didn't know what to make of the situation. She didn't want to pry.

"You want a drink or something to eat before we go scouting?"

Annie thought about it a second. "Something to eat might be good."

"Come inside. I've got cold cuts; I'll make you a sandwich." Hopefully during lunch Annie would open up. Something was going on and Gia would like to help if she could.

She pulled all the sliced meats out of the fridge and grabbed an avocado from one of her hanging baskets. "So how long do we have to plant the seedlings?"

"Not long," Annie said and snagged one of the pieces of avocado Gia had sliced. "I'd like to get started planting no later than two weeks, which means we have our work cut out for us."

"I'll have to show the spot we pick to Flynn to make sure it doesn't violate the deal he made with Rosser."

Annie nodded and eyed all the ingredients Gia had piled on the sandwich bread. "You don't mess around."

"In New York we take our deli sandwiches seriously." She laughed.

"Do you miss it?"

Gia thought about it. Even before her problems started, she'd grown tired of living in Manhattan. The traffic, the noise, the throngs of people; a person could never feel peaceful. "Not really. There's something to be said for country life."

Annie's lips curved up. "I visited once. It was exciting for about twenty-four hours; then I wanted to come home."

Gia finished making Annie's sandwich and garnished the plate with a pile of chips and a sour pickle. She made herself a smaller one so Annie wouldn't have to eat alone. The two munched in companionable silence.

"What made you decide to move so suddenly?" Gia finally asked.

Annie sucked in a breath. "I lived with my boyfriend and I'm not interested in living with him anymore."

Ah, now they were getting somewhere. "Why not ask him to leave?"

"It was his place originally. I never cared for it much. And it's easier this way. He's a procrastinator. If I ask him to leave . . . well, it would be months before he got his shit together. And I'm ready for it to be over, like really ready."

"I can understand that." But Gia thought Annie may have jumped the gun. She should've found a place before she left the old one. "Was it a terrible situation that you needed to get out so soon?"

"Define terrible." Annie laughed. "It wasn't abusive, if that's what you mean. Zeke's a good person in his own way; he's just immature, self-centered, and unrealistic about life. I was tired of carrying him . . . emotionally and financially. I'll find a place. When school lets out for summer break there will be plenty of vacancies."

Gia nodded and then blurted out, "You could live here, at least until school starts again. Flynn has been using the guest apartment, but I could give it to you and give him one of the rooms in the house when he stays over. Lord knows I have enough of them. The apartment is private and you could come and go as you please. I'd throw it in as part of your wages for getting the tree farm and the hay fields going. I'm overwhelmed by the whole thing and you seem to know so much about it that it makes sense to have you on the property in the beginning."

The offer was impetuous, but Gia had a good feeling about Annie. She didn't seem to judge Gia or question her innocence. And if her proposal for Rosser Ranch went as planned, Gia would be opening her home to all manner of strangers. Why not start with someone who could eventually become a friend and an asset to the project?

"Seriously? But you hardly know me."

"I'll ask you to sign a confidentiality agreement," Gia said. "Even though I'm no longer on TV or writing columns, I'd like to preserve my privacy. Unfortunately, as long as my ex is at large there's still media interest in me."

"I don't have a problem signing an agreement. I did a farming project for Francis Ford Coppola a year ago and he had me sign one too. Only the rich and famous can afford to own vineyards and wineries these days so nondisclosure forms are fairly common. You sure it'll be okay with Flynn? I don't want to displace him."

No one used the entire second floor of her house and the accommodations were a hundred times posher than the guest apartment, not that Flynn struck her as fussy. "He's only here a few nights a week, and if he wants his own digs we could tidy up one of the bunkhouses. There's always the pool house too."

It wasn't like the ranch was short of sleeping quarters. There was a foreman's house and a few run-down cottages where permanent ranch hands had lived before Ray had been carted off to jail. She planned to fix them up for the program anyway.

"As long as he doesn't mind . . ." Annie washed down the rest of her sandwich with lemonade.

Gia took her and Annie's plate to the sink. "You want to see it?"

"Uh, sure."

She led Annie outside to the bank of garages and climbed the stairs. Flynn had been the last person to use the apartment and she had no idea what state it was in. She hadn't hired housekeepers yet, fearful that they might squawk to the paparazzi. But the place was too much upkeep for one person.

"I can't promise Flynn didn't leave it messy," she said and used her key to open the door.

Other than a denim jacket he'd left on the back of a dining room chair, the place looked immaculate.

"My goodness, it's so big," Annie said, walking from room to room.

It had a spacious living room, a small kitchen, an eating nook, a master suite, and a laundry room closet. There were lots of windows—light galore. It gave the space a warm glow.

Annie stood to one side of the front room, checking out the view of the swimming pool.

"You can swim whenever you want," Gia said.

"Wow. This is amazingly generous of you. You sure you don't want to take a few days to think about it?"

"Why? I'd be thrilled to have you on site . . . in case anything goes wrong with the trees." And because the place was lonely with just her. At least in New York there were other people in her building.

Annie chuckled. "Once they're planted it's pretty much up to Mother Nature. But I'd love to live here. I'm thinking I might bum a room off my vet-school friend on the days I'm in class until summer break and spend the rest of the time here . . . if that's okay?"

"Perfectly fine with me. You can leave your stuff now if you want." Gia took Flynn's jacket and folded it over her arm, then discreetly raised it to her nose. It smelled like his aftershave and a number of other scents she couldn't identify but were purely Flynn's.

She wondered how he would feel about sleeping under the same roof as her. The house was big enough that they would never have to see each other on the few nights he stayed over, except when he used the kitchen. For her part, the idea of having him there was exceedingly tempting. Hey, it had been Flynn who'd set the rules, not her. The whole town was talking about them anyway. If everyone assumed they were doing the nasty, they may as well do it.

"You want to stay here tonight?" she asked Annie.

"I've got class tomorrow. But if I could leave my stuff that would be great, and I'll come back Saturday to set up."

"You have furniture?" Gia supposed they could store it in one of the outbuildings; the guesthouse was already furnished.

"It's junk I'm leaving behind. Zeke can have it."

"Where will you stay tonight?"

"One of my friend's. Goodness knows they've slept on my couch enough times."

Gia couldn't live like that. Even in college she'd had to have absolute structure. Being without a permanent place to live would've driven her over the edge. Probably because she'd grown up not knowing where her next bed would be.

"Zeke won't give you any trouble, will he?"

Annie laughed. "Nah. That would require energy."

Gia began to form a relatively good picture of the guy. The men in her world may have been ambitious, but there'd still been plenty of narcissistic losers.

From the apartment window she saw Flynn's truck come over the hill. Her chest gave a little kick.

"Flynn," Annie said, sounding so delighted that it gave Gia another kind of kick. This time in the ribs. But Flynn had sworn there was nothing between them.

They left the apartment, jogged down the staircase, and waited for him.

"My own welcoming party," he said, alighting from the driver's seat in his lawyer clothes and tipping his head at the jacket draped over Gia's arm. "What are you doing with that?"

Gia looked at Annie and back at Flynn. "Uh, slight change of plans."

"What's that?" He pulled a duffel from the front seat and grabbed his cowboy hat.

"You heading out to the barn? I'll walk with you." Gia didn't know why exactly, but she wanted to tell him that she'd booted him from the guest apartment in private.

"I have to change first." He scanned the back of Annie's truck. "You going to the swap meet?"

"I'm moving," she said and dropped her eyes.

"Zeke moving with you?"

"Nope." Annie popped the "P."

"Is that so?" Flynn asked and quietly muttered, "About time."

Gia watched the two of them, relieved that she was getting a big-brother vibe off Flynn rather than a yay-you're-available-now air. "Annie's planning to move in here for the summer . . . uh, in the guest apartment, actually."

"Yeah?" He tilted his head and locked eyes with Annie. "Sounds like a good idea. You need help with that stuff?" Flynn didn't wait for her to answer. Dropping the duffel and hefting a few of the boxes from the truck bed, he headed upstairs.

Gia followed suit with one of the plastic bags. It weighed a ton and she had to stop a few times to readjust. Annie carried another one, and in less than thirty minutes they'd finished unloading. For all intents and purposes, Annie was officially moved in.

Flynn picked his duffel off the ground and started in the direction of one of the bunkhouses.

"Flynn," Gia called. "You can stay in the house."

A look passed between them, Flynn silently saying *Are you out of your mind?* But instead of protesting in front of Annie, Flynn nodded and went inside.

"Show me where you want me," he said.

She was tempted to lead him to the master bedroom.

"I'll start walking the field near the western fence line," Annie said. They'd decided the tree farm should be near the road for easy vehicle access. "Meet me out there when you're done."

Gia waved her on and took Flynn into the house.

"Are you trying to kill me, woman?"

"She didn't have anywhere to go. It's bad enough that tonight she's planning to couch surf. What's the deal with this Zeke guy?"

"He's a loser and a user . . . always taking Annie's money. And it's not like she has much. It's good of you to take her in." He brushed a lock of hair that had come loose from her ponytail behind her ear.

"I'm happy to have her oversee the farming venture, but I'm sorry you're losing the apartment."

"I'm not here full-time and can sleep in the bunkhouse . . . don't need a lot of creature comforts."

"Flynn, I've got an entire second floor of en-suite bedrooms. Take one."

He pressed her against the wall and boxed her in with both hands. "What if I want yours?"

She shrugged. "You're the one who made the rules, not me."

His mouth quirked. "Where's that Winchester? You setting me up?" Then he dipped his head and kissed her until her toes curled.

Chapter 13

Ah, what the hell was wrong with him? Flynn couldn't believe his own stupidity, yet the knowledge of it didn't stop him. He pressed her body against the wall and pushed the hard ridge of his erection into her belly while he let his tongue roam the inside of her mouth. She tasted better than his mother's honey. And the more she kissed him back the more he wanted to devour her.

His hands explored her breasts over her clothes as his mouth took her, tasting and sucking with a desperation he'd never felt before. She sagged against him and he tangled his fingers in her hair, holding her head so he could kiss her into next Sunday. He felt his skin turn hot, the fly of his pants strain, and his body roar with desire.

Then his hands were moving again, too frantic to stop, and he searched for skin. Slipping under her top, he touched her smooth, soft stomach until he felt her suck in a breath. He jerked the fabric up, exposing her lacy bra and the perkiest tits he'd ever seen. She made a grab for his belt buckle and the anticipation of her hands wrapped around him sent a volt of pleasure up his spine.

It also sent a rush of clarity. They had to stop. Now!

He pushed her hands away, quickly adjusted his belt, pulled her shirt down, and rested his forehead against hers. "We can't do this."

Gia tried to catch her breath. Her cheeks flushed and dewy, Flynn held her face in his hands and looked into her stormy eyes.

"I'm sorry, that shouldn't have happened," he said and felt like a goddamn teenager. What had become of his self-control? Gia Treadwell, that's what. Why couldn't she get another lawyer? Then Flynn could have her until the cows came home.

"Annie will wonder what happened to me," she said and tried to straighten her clothes . . . her hair. A rash of red crept up her neck.

"I'll change upstairs." He swiped his duffel off the ground and headed for the second floor.

A cold shower would do him good, he thought as he picked the first room he came to. It was done up in plaids and hunting patterns that kind of gave him vertigo. Most people would've considered the room, with its thick carpet, king-size bed and enormous bathroom, the lap of luxury. But there was nothing indulgent about being feet above Gia when he couldn't touch her. Now Flynn knew what being in hell felt like.

He stripped, found a pile of plush towels in the bathroom, and took a fast shower. Going outside with a throbbing hard-on would've been awkward, not to mention uncomfortable. He changed into jeans, a long-sleeved T-shirt, and pulled on his boots. There were still a few of his things in the guest apartment and he went to collect them.

Gia had gone above and beyond letting Annie live here. Quite honestly, it had surprised him. He knew how protective she was of her privacy and he couldn't say he blamed her. Someone in Gia's position had to constantly watch her back, especially when the tabloids paid decent money for any tidbits of information. She had no fear from Annie. Annie might have bad taste in men—Flynn sincerely hoped she was through with Zeke—but she wouldn't sell Gia out. Not her way and definitely not her style.

Annie's brother, Chad, was a different story altogether. The kid was a self-centered train wreck who would lose his family's farm if he didn't stop bleeding it dry. Flynn had tried to set up a trust that would prevent Chad from using the land as his own personal bank account, but Doug and Gloria wouldn't hear of it. God forbid they make the little mooch angry. At which point Flynn had backed off. He'd done his fiduciary duty by explaining the dire situation to them and that was all he could do. But he felt like he'd failed Annie.

She saw the writing on the wall and Flynn knew she'd been distancing herself from the farm . . . from her parents. He didn't like seeing fission in their relationship, but he was the family lawyer not their psychologist. Working and living here for a summer would do Annie—and Gia—good. Gia didn't know a damned thing about farming and Annie did. It would be a nice change for Annie to feel valuable and wanted without her brother sucking all the oxygen out of the room.

Flynn got his stuff from the apartment, stashed it in his new room, and went down to the stable to saddle up Dude. After that kiss he needed to put some distance between him and Gia.

"Hey." The sound of Gia's voice made him jump.

"What's up?"

"Annie thinks she found the perfect spot for the trees. You mind taking a look?"

"Nope." He cinched the saddle tight, climbed onto Dude's back, and held out his arm. "You want a ride?"

He lifted her so she could swing her leg over Dude's loin and sit behind the saddle cantle. The leather barrier did little to ease his aching groin. And when she pressed her front to his back, Flynn muttered a silent curse.

He gave the horse a soft tap of his heel. "Which way?"

She pointed to the west and told him to go as far as the fence.

"Why there?"

"Annie said if we decide to do a cut-it-yourself farm, the area would make for easy access off the main road and we could put in a small parking lot."

It made sense, though it was hard to think with her arms wrapped around his waist. "You want people traipsing all over your property?"

"I think it would give the women in my program more to do, and I like the idea of families making my trees part of their holiday tradition. I can sort of picture a table with hot apple cider, homemade cookies, and Christmas music playing. But if I decide to truck the trees to the city I'll still need access from the main road."

"Sounds smart," he said and changed the subject. "Gia, we gonna be able to move past that kiss?"

"Why?" she teased. "Are you addicted to me now?"

He turned around on his horse. "You seemed to enjoy it even more than I did. They could hear you moaning all the way to China."

"Watch the road," she said and slugged him in the arm. "I never met a man who thought so highly of himself."

Flynn became circumspect. "If you want to get another lawyer and report me to the bar I wouldn't blame you."

"I don't want another attorney; I want you."

"You made that pretty damn obvious thirty minutes ago." He

girded himself for another punch in the arm, but she surprised him by laughing.

"It's no wonder you're still single with that ego," she said.

"I'm single by choice. You'd be wise to remember that."

They rode on. Flowers blanketed the hills and the colors popped like a Monet painting. Flynn had once seen a collection of the artist's work at the de Young. Up until that point his tastes had run to the western watercolors of Charles Marion Russell and the bronze sculptures of Fredric Remington. He'd never been a fan of cubism or abstract impressionism. Truth be told, those paintings gave him a headache. But the work of the French impressionists reminded him of the real-life landscapes of the Sierra. It was May, and even with the drought, the mountains and valleys blossomed with lady's slippers, red clover, irises, dogwood, and lupine. A feast of reds, yellows, whites, and purples. A cowboy could never get lonely on the range with so much scenery to look at, Flynn's father would say. True that.

"Dude has a nice gait," Gia said.

"He's a good horse."

He could see Annie now. She was marking off the land with small wooden stakes. He reined Dude closer and waved.

"What do you think?" Annie straightened from a stoop and stretched her back.

"Looks like a nice piece of land. How much you plan to use?"

"For now, twelve acres; about eighteen-thousand trees," Annie said.

Considering how much land there was, twelve acres wouldn't cost him much in pasture. By fall, when Gia planned to plant hay, he'd be moving his cattle to the Central Valley anyway.

"It's fine with me." He dismounted, reached out his arms for Gia, and lifted her off the horse.

"The sun's good here. And I think the soil will be just fine. But we'll need a fence to keep your cattle out. You know anyone who can do that for us?" Annie smiled up at him.

"Yeah. I'll take care of it. Just mark off where you want it." There was already a split-rail fence alongside the road, which would make his job easier.

A truck zoomed by, came to a skidding halt, and backed up. Clay stuck his head out the window. "Missing a calf?"

"Nope. Gia's thinking of planting some trees here." Flynn didn't know how much she wanted to tell Clay, but he didn't want to lie.

"I'm planning to put in a Christmas tree farm," she said and beamed. Who would've imagined that a television celebrity and financial guru could find pine trees so damned exciting?

"Christmas trees, huh? Buzz Henderson grows 'em on the other end of town. Does a good business from what I hear. Cut-your-own or wholesale?"

"We're still deciding," Gia said and looked at Annie.

"The profit's better with cut-your-own, but I don't know if she'll get enough customers up here. I'm Annie Sparks, by the way." She stuck out her hand to shake Clay's through his truck window.

"Annie's my expert," Gia chimed in. "She went to UC Davis and knows everything about farming."

Clay slid Flynn a sideways glance. Flynn grinned. "Sparks Family Farms up by Yuba City."

"Ah, I should've recognized the name." The Sparkses were to rice in California what the Spreckels were to sugar. "Welcome to Nugget, Annie."

"Thanks. I'll be living here this summer."

"You'll have to come up to the ranch with Gia, meet my wife and the boys."

Gia looked at Flynn, silently asking whether now would be a good time to set up the meeting with the neighbors. He nodded.

"Hey, Clay, I would love to discuss my plans with all our immediate neighbors and introduce them to Annie. Any chance you and Emily would be available sometime next week?"

"Sure. You let us know the day and we'll be there."

"Great."

"I'll see you all later," Clay said and drove off.

Flynn put his foot in the stirrup and pulled himself onto Dude's back. "I've got work to do."

Gia followed him away from Annie for a private word. "What do you think?"

"About Clay? I think he's good with the tree farm. I'm not so sure how he'll feel about the rest of your plan. We'll find out next week, won't we?"

"I suppose so. You staying the night?"

"I was planning to, if that's okay?"

"Of course," she said and turned back to where Annie continued to stick stakes in the ground.

Flynn stood up in his saddle and twisted around. "But, Gia, no kissing, you hear? And for God's sake keep your hands off of me."

Chapter 14

Gia ran around the house like a madwoman.

"Will you let me find you a cleaning service?" Dana watched Gia fluff the couch pillows and shook her head. "They can sign one of those nondisclosure agreements like I did. But this house is too big for you to take care of on your own."

A service had cleaned just before Gia moved in and for the most part the house was tidy. But she wanted the neighbors to see it at its best.

"It's too late for that now," she said and dusted the coffee table.

"At least for the future. Seriously, Gia, I can find you someone. Someone who could really use the work."

Dana got her with those last words. *Someone who could really use the work.*

"All right," she said, "as long as they sign a confidentiality contract."

"While I'm at it, you need a gardener."

Gia had to laugh at that one. What kind of gardener maintained a thousand acres? It would take an enormous landscaping crew.

"Just for the front yard and the pool area," Dana said, reading Gia's mind. "It's looking a little neglected."

"All right, that too. But I'm not exactly rolling in money these days." Though she'd just sold her shares of a semiconductor stock that had risen to four times the original purchase price. She probably should've held on to them, but the profits would help her finance the residential program.

"You could just have them come twice a month to save money," Dana said. "Are you sure you don't want me to stay for the meeting?"

Gia knew Dana and Aidan had scheduled a wedding cake sampling in Reno and didn't want to ruin their plans. "I'll be fine. Flynn will be here."

"Flynn, huh?" Dana's eyes lit with curiosity. "There's talk in town, you know? They're calling Rosser Ranch the love shack."

Ha; if only they knew. It was the love shack with Dudley Do-Right.

If you want to get another lawyer and report me to the bar I wouldn't blame you.

He'd uttered those words over a kiss. Granted it was a hell of a kiss, but still . . . The cowboy had more integrity than any man she'd ever met. And then there was Evan, who wasn't even a man . . . a snake was more like it.

"There's nothing going on between us," she told Dana.

"Really?" Dana sounded disappointed.

"He's my attorney."

"So? What's wrong with a little extracurricular activity?"

"He's a good lawyer," Gia said. "So far he's managed to keep the feds away. We're trying not to complicate things."

Dana arched her brunette brows. "Then you're both interested in each other?"

"Not like that. It's purely sexual. We're both single, and, due to circumstances, spend a lot of time together. You know what that's like?"

"I do. That's how it started with Aidan and me. But then it quickly got serious."

"That's not going to happen with me and Flynn." She rearranged the knickknacks on the shelf. "Evan was the most serious I've ever gotten with a man and look how that turned out."

Dana got up and straightened a painting on the wall. It was an ugly landscape Gia wanted to get rid of along with the animal heads.

"You can't let what happened with Evan taint future relationships. Evan was a crook; you can't judge all men by him."

And you couldn't judge all men by Aidan, who, from what Gia could tell, was a prince among men.

"They were already tainted by my father, who left my mother and me in abject poverty."

"He died, Gia. It's not like he cleaned out your family's bank account and ran off with his secretary. For all you know he had a plan to recoup some of the wealth he'd lost from those bad investments."

Gia opened a few more windows to air out the oversize great room. By the time her guests arrived she wanted the place to smell fresh.

"How do you lose everything and not tell your wife? How do keep secrets that will indelibly change your family's life from the person you love most?" She placed her hands on her hips and stared at Dana in challenge.

Dana let out a breath. "Maybe he planned to tell your mom and then he had the heart attack. Or maybe he couldn't bear to tell her because he loved you two so much and desperately wanted to fix it. You'll never know for sure, Gia. But I think you should cut him a break."

Gia hitched her shoulders, not wanting to talk about her dead father anymore. What was done was done. If nothing else, it had made her the woman she was today. And now she would help others in dire circumstances turn their lives around. When her father died Iris Treadwell hadn't even known how to pay a bill or apply for a credit card. She'd been one of those women who left all money matters to her husband.

"Come in the kitchen." She motioned for Dana to follow her and opened the refrigerator to show her platters of cheese and meats, breads, and veggies. "What do you think? I got it at a nice gourmet shop in Reno."

"It looks fantastic. But these aren't people you have to try to impress, Gia. They're about as down-to-earth as you can get."

"Are you kidding me? Emily McCreedy is a big-deal cookbook author. Maddy Breyer-Shepard owns an inn that would be considered upscale even in a big city."

"You're having them too?" Dana looked surprised.

"The Shepards live just up the road from the McCreedys. Considering how spread out we are around here, they're immediate neighbors. Plus, if I can get the police chief on my side, that'll go a long way with the rest of the town, don't you think?"

"For sure. So this Annie woman is going to talk too?"

Gia lined a dozen wineglasses on the counter and checked each individual one for spots. "Yeah. She'll talk about the farming venture so everyone will see that it's legit. Clay was already impressed with her pedigree. According to Flynn, her family owns one of California's largest rice farms."

"It sounds to me like you've got everything lined up. These are good people, Gia; they'll buy in, especially because you're using the property for agricultural purposes. And I see no reason why you can't continue to lease the land next spring to the Barlows, or any other rancher."

Flynn had certainly been generous about letting her fence off some of the property. He'd even volunteered to see to the fence himself. Sporting, because according to the contract he'd made with Rosser, he was entitled to let his cattle graze on every inch of pasture.

"I could," she said. "The extra money would come in handy."

When the glasses were polished to Gia's standards, she pulled out a stack of plates from the cupboards. "Cloth napkins or paper?"

Dana laughed. "Definitely paper."

They both heard a vehicle pull up and Dana went to the front room to see who it was. Only a few people had the code to the gate and she and Flynn had clickers.

"It's a turquoise pickup," Dana called.

"That's Annie." Gia smiled to herself and joined Dana in the front room. "I'm glad you'll get to meet her."

"What's she wearing?" Dana asked, as they both watched from the window as Annie got out of the truck.

From what Gia could tell, it was a square dancing dress made from bandana fabric and petticoats of tulle. Instead of her signature combat boots she'd donned a vintage pair of shitkickers and wore her hair in two braids. Gia suspected the outfit was Annie's idea of business casual.

"Uh, she's got her own style. Sort of cowpunk, I guess."

"She's adorable," Dana said.

Annie had been coming and going to test the soil for the trees, meeting with people about tilling the ground, and using the guest apartment when she didn't have to be in Davis. Gia had been documenting the process by taking pictures and sending them to her mother in Boca. Iris's mah-jongg buddies couldn't believe Gia was going to be a farmer. Gia had a hard time believing it herself.

She opened the door to greet Annie. "Come meet a friend of mine."

Annie came into the big foyer and put her bags down. She'd been carting her toiletries and everyday necessities back and forth in grocery sacks. Later, Gia planned to give her a suitcase with wheels. Lord knew she had one in every size and color.

"Annie, meet my friend Dana, Nugget's premier real estate agent."

The two women said hello and Gia led them into the front room.

"Everything looks perfect," Annie said, scanning the big space. "Nervous?"

"A little," Gia admitted.

"You'll do great. You used to be on TV, for goodness' sake."

Gia's shows were pretaped and the audience consisted of a producer and the crew. Everything was done for her, from her hair and makeup to the choice of outfits and jewelry she wore. TV was easy compared to facing down Nugget's most influential residents.

"I hope so," she said. "How's everything with you?"

"I'll be done with school soon." Annie sighed.

Living on friends' couches and making the commute from Davis to Nugget had to be killing her.

"It'll be good when you're here full-time," Gia said.

Dana looked at her watch. "If you're sure you don't need me, I'll get going. Aidan and I have more than a dozen cakes to taste."

Annie looked at Gia. "Wedding cakes. Dana's getting married in June."

"Congratulations," Annie said and spontaneously hugged Dana. Dana seemed a bit caught off guard but hugged Annie back.

They walked Dana out and Annie grabbed her stuff. She said she wanted to spend some time in her apartment until the meeting started. Gia was relieved to have a little time to herself to practice her speech in her head.

About fifteen minutes before showtime Flynn drove up and found her in the kitchen. A few damp locks of hair escaped his cowboy hat, his jeans were pressed and his boots polished.

"Sorry I'm late. A bull got loose at my parents' place . . . screwed up my schedule."

"No problem," she said, though she'd been pacing, worried that he wouldn't show, which was silly. In the short time she'd known Flynn he'd proven to be extremely dependable. Frankly, she didn't know how he managed to juggle ranching and his law practice so deftly.

"The food and wine are out, Annie is on her way over, and . . . I'm nervous."

"Don't be; these are good people."

It was the same thing Dana had said. "What if they say no? . . . This is important to me."

He clasped her shoulders and pulled her in close. "Then you'll make it happen. You've certainly got my vote."

She thought he might kiss her again, but he didn't. Since that one time, he seemed to have gotten himself under control. On the nights Flynn stayed over he hid upstairs with the TV on and didn't come down until morning. Gia wanted to say it was for the best, but she'd lost a lot of sleep listening to him creaking around up there . . . her body aching for him.

"You think they won't trust me . . . because of Evan?" She'd lost a lot of her confidence since becoming the target of a federal investigation. When people looked at you with suspicion and condemnation you started seeing yourself that way.

"Relax, Gia; you'll do fine," he said and went inside the mudroom to hang his hat.

"This the food? I'm starved." Flynn started to reach for a slice of cheese and Gia slapped his hand.

"Don't mess up the tray. It looks perfect."

One side of his mouth slid up. "We just gonna look at it all night?"

"No. I want to keep it perfect until the guests get here." She opened the refrigerator and got him a mozzarella cheese stick. "Eat this."

He made a face. "My little nephew eats these."

"So? It doesn't mean it's not edible."

He grabbed her hips and pulled her up against him. Her hands landed on his chest and she could feel his rock-hard muscles flex under his shirt and smell his aftershave. His thighs rubbed against her bare legs, and in that moment she wanted to sink into him. Just let him hold her up while she buried her head in the curve of his neck.

"Nice dress," he said, and the next thing she felt was his hand snaking underneath the hem to squeeze one of her ass cheeks. "Nice thong too."

"What are you doing?" She blinked up at him in surprise. At a time like this he suddenly wanted to get physical?

"Distracting you." He slowly pulled his hand away, brushing the back of her leg, making her shiver.

They heard Annie call from the foyer and quickly pulled apart.

"Come in," Gia shouted, a shade too loud, and turned to Flynn. "Help me carry some of this stuff in."

Together, they each lugged a tray into the front room. Annie saw what they were doing and went into the kitchen to get another one. Gia had already set up the bar and Flynn went to make himself a drink.

"You want one?" he asked Gia and tossed her a naughty grin. "Did it work?"

"Did what work?" She realized he was talking about his distraction method. Hell yeah it had worked. All she could think about was his hand up her dress. For his benefit, though, she merely shook her head. "I'll have a glass of white wine."

"Coming right up."

Annie brought in the bread and cracker baskets and put them next to the meats and cheeses. "Wow, there's enough food here for an army."

Flynn came around the bar and handed each woman a glass of wine. He didn't seem to notice Annie's odd square dancing dress, but he couldn't seem to take his eyes off Gia. She didn't have time to bask in his attention because the doorbell rang.

Gia briskly scanned the room, patted her hair in place, and went to let in her guests. They had all come at the same time, which was convenient but also overwhelming. Emily brought pies, Maddy wine, and the Rodriguezes—Gia still hadn't officially met Tawny— beer. Greetings and introductions were made and everyone made themselves at home in the front room while Gia carried the pies to the kitchen.

Flynn took drink orders, and for the first forty minutes everyone drank, ate, and chatted. Annie seemed comfortable with the crowd, who probably had a lot more in common with her than they did with Gia, city girl and disgraced television personality. Clay wandered the room, examining the animal heads. Gia had actually started naming them.

"You haven't found any homes for the trophies?" he asked.

"Nope. But I haven't really tried. You're welcome to take any of them home."

"No, thanks," Emily chimed in and Maddy laughed.

"Seriously? You don't want 'em?" Lucky said and rose to his feet to take a closer look at Bullwinkle.

"They give me the creeps," Gia said.

"They might look good in the cantina; what do you think?" He bobbed his head at Tawny.

"I think Ray Rosser would have a heart attack in prison if he knew you had them," she replied.

"Yeah, that's exactly what I'm thinking." Lucky rubbed his hands together and Rhys laughed.

Gia had heard that the two men hated each other's guts. There was a lot to the story, but she wasn't familiar with the details.

"Feel free to take them," she told Lucky.

"What do you think of that elk head in the inn?" Maddy tilted her head sideways and squinted up at the animal's beady eyes.

"I'm not feeling it," Rhys said.

"Me neither," Emily agreed.

Everyone laughed. Annie complimented Tawny on her cowboy boots and Lucky told her that his wife was a custom boot designer.

"She's currently working on a pair for Lucinda Williams."

Annie's eyes grew wide. "Wow . . . I love her. What do they look like?"

"Come over to my studio," Tawny said. "We're just up the hill and you can have a look."

Flynn finished up at the bar and took the seat next to Gia. His nearness gave her a surge of courage. She hated to break up the conviviality in the room to talk about her residential program. Everyone was so warm and approachable. She could see being friends with these people, actually inviting them into her life. In New York, where everyone seemed to want something from her, she hadn't had many friends. But the whole point of this gathering was to win her neighbors' approval for the plan.

Gia let the conversation flow while everyone dug into the platters of food. Flynn got up to refill drinks and wineglasses, came right back to Gia, and squeezed her knee, signaling that it was time.

She cleared her throat and a hush fell over the room. "Thanks, everyone, for coming. I know you've been curious why a city person like me bought an active cattle ranch in the middle of . . ."

"Nowhere," Maddy finished, and there were scattered chuckles.

Gia resumed, relieved that she hadn't committed her first faux pas. "I know you've also been curious about the T Corporation. By now you've probably figured out that there is no T Corporation . . .

well, there is, but it's just me. I set up the corporation to protect my identity while purchasing the property for obvious reasons."

There were a few head nods and even smiles.

"Some of you know"—she stared straight at Rhys—"that I'm still under scrutiny by the authorities and the press. I hope their occasional presence here doesn't cause any of you inconvenience." Flynn had said she should be open about the pending investigation so she followed his advice. "I've hired Flynn to represent me and hopefully this will get squared away soon."

Gia saw Clay shoot a look at Flynn. Flynn nodded to him and Gia would've sworn she saw Clay grimace.

"In any event, I wanted to share my plans with you." The circle of guests tightened around her. Flynn put his hand at the small of her back, willing Gia to breathe. "I've hired Annie, who will be living here this summer, to help me plant a Christmas tree farm. In the fall we'll also be planting organic alfalfa and meadow hay."

She told the group about Annie's agricultural background and turned the stage over to her. Annie seemed much more at ease than Gia and methodically mapped out their strategy.

"If we decide to go cut-it-yourself there will be more traffic on the main road during the holidays. Because the McCreedys and the Shepards use McCreedy Road to access their homes it probably won't affect their families as much. But Lucky and Tawny . . ."

Lucky raised his shoulders. "It's off season for us so not a huge deal. Maybe I'll put out a big sign advertising the cowboy camp."

"Absolutely," Annie said. "We could make it a whole community affair. As far as the hay . . . no chemicals. We may use crop dusters a couple times a year to drop organic fungicides and pesticides. If it spooks the cattle we can skip aerial applications altogether."

"Not a problem for my herd," Clay said. Gia had heard that he was a former naval fighter pilot and owned a couple of planes that he regularly flew over his property.

Annie finished her talk to murmurs of approval. Her neighbors seemed genuinely relieved that Gia wasn't trying to skirt the rules to put in a high-rise or a factory-outlet center.

"Sounds good," Clay said. "Depending on the traffic, you may have to eventually widen the main road. But we're talking some years out before those trees are ready to cut, right?"

"Probably eight," Annie said. "In the next couple of weeks we'll be tilling and planting. After that it'll be quiet for some time."

Annie was great, Gia thought. Her confidence exuded competence and Gia could tell Clay was impressed. He was definitely Gia's tough nut in this crowd. Lucky and Tawny had an easygoing vibe. Rhys was always so poker-faced, it was hard to tell where he stood on anything. Except when it came to his wife. Gia had never seen a man more adoring; he'd filled a plate for her, rubbed her back, and looked at her like she was the only woman on earth. The other two men were pretty smitten as well. It was a little difficult having a front-row seat to all that affection. For a minute she wondered what it would be like to have Flynn look at her that way, then dismissed the thought.

He was her lawyer and her friend.

Flynn called for everyone's attention. "Gia has more she'd like to tell you about."

Gia could feel the air crackle with tension. Clearly they thought the plan had been too good to be true. Gia owned a thousand acres of prime California real estate. They all knew what a risky venture agriculture was and Gia was an investment banker after all. Hopefully her women's home would set them at ease because it was better than turning the place into a mobile-home park or any of the other myriad possibilities they likely feared.

She grabbed a bottle of wine off the bar and refilled a few glasses before speaking. Then she launched into the details of her plan, leaving out the personal reasons why the program was so important to her. Gia didn't like talking about those days, not because she was ashamed but because she didn't want her family's ruin and impoverishment to define her. She didn't want to be known as a rags-to-riches story. Instead, she told them how she would house the women, how they would attend daily classes ranging from household budgeting to improving their job skills. How they would work on the farm, help run the business aspects of it, and hopefully leave the ranch capable of supporting themselves.

"How will you find these women?" Rhys asked, his expression grim. "I don't want people with criminal records moving to Nugget."

"I'll—"

Before she could finish Clay jumped in. "It sounds like a halfway house . . . alcoholics and women with drug addictions."

Gia sucked in a breath. Iris hadn't had a criminal record and hadn't been an alcoholic or a drug addict. She'd simply been poor through no fault of her own. But look at the stigma it held. According to Rhys and Clay, in order to be indigent you had to also be a degenerate. It made her queasy.

"Maybe I didn't explain it well," she said. "These would simply be women who are financially struggling . . . single mothers, widows, and divorcees."

"It would certainly be easy enough to do criminal background checks," Flynn interjected.

"Not really," Rhys said. "People can change their names and use bogus social security numbers. Come on, Flynn, you know that better than anyone."

"The way I understand it, it would be more like a women's shelter than a halfway house, right, Gia?" Lucky asked.

"I don't know if I would call it a women's shelter exactly. It'll be a farm and they'll be the workers . . . like your ranch hands."

"Some of my ranch hands have lived on the property for generations," Clay said. "New ones come with reliable references."

This wasn't going well at all. Gia had expected possible resistance but not open hostility.

"Look, Gia doesn't want to bring bad or dangerous people onto her property," Flynn interjected. "She lives here, remember? She's trying to do a good deed. Up until recently she helped millions of television viewers and self-help readers take charge of their personal finances. She wants to do the same thing, only on a more intimate level."

"Or maybe she wants to change public sentiment about her . . . get her own reality show, because that's what this sounds like to me," Clay said, and she heard someone gasp. "Sorry, Gia, I'm a straight shooter and this scheme of yours reeks of gimmickry . . . something for you to use to save face. I'm not saying you were involved in that Ponzi scheme, but there's no question you've fallen from public grace. You're not going to turn our community into a sideshow to resurrect yourself. Not if I can help it."

"I'm with Clay," Rhys said. "I'm going to give you the benefit of the doubt . . . say your motives are good. But I don't see Nugget as the appropriate place for a women's shelter." He rose and so did everyone else.

Tawny glanced at Gia and squeezed her lips flat. If Gia read her right she was trying to say she was sorry. Well, why hadn't she spoken up? "Thank you for having us."

"Yes, thank you," Maddy echoed.

"You're welcome." Gia stood next to Annie as Flynn walked them out. When she was sure they'd left the house, she said, "That went even worse than I expected."

Annie made a hushing gesture with her finger. "Flynn's talking to them."

They both strained to listen. Gia couldn't hear anything, but they were out there a while. Annie moved closer to the foyer but shook her head.

"Maybe he'll talk them into coming around," she said.

"I doubt it." Gia picked up one of the trays and started for the kitchen. "They don't like me much."

Annie grabbed a handful of glasses and followed Gia. "I wouldn't take it personally. Country people are always afraid of change. You need to let the idea sink in for a while and then reapproach them . . . maybe after we get the trees planted."

Gia heard Flynn come back in. "We're in the kitchen," she called.

He walked in like he had the weight of the world on his shoulders. "I'm sorry, Gia."

She sighed. "I should've expected it, though the reality show idea had never crossed my mind. Clay's creative, I'll give him that."

"Clay was extremely disrespectful and I plan on letting him know that I didn't appreciate it." He came up behind her and wrapped his arms around her waist. Gia felt his muscles bunch in anger.

Through the corner of her eye she saw Annie slip out of the room.

"Don't risk your friendship with him over me, Flynn. They have a right to be concerned . . . to be suspicious."

"Yep. But they don't have a right to be assholes. And Clay was an asshole tonight. I promise you, he and I will be having further words in private."

"I don't want you to do that," she said. "These are my neighbors and I want us to get along. It doesn't mean I'm giving up on my program. If there's a will there's a way, right?"

"Honestly, Gia, I don't know that they can stop you. As your attorney I could look into it, though it's not my area of law."

She turned around to face him and reached up to put her hands on his shoulders. "Let's wait, okay? I have enough enemies right now."

"It's up to you. If it's any consolation I thought you were great out there."

Not great enough obviously. "Thanks. You staying the night?"

"Yeah." His eyes wandered down her dress and his gaze simmered. "Despite it being a very bad idea."

Chapter 15

Clay put his arm around Emily as they all walked back to their homes together. She'd been awfully quiet at the meeting. And lately she hadn't been herself. Weepy one moment, manic the next. The sharp mood swings left him at a loss, especially because she was usually so even-keeled. Not like his late ex-wife, who was a ship-wreck.

Clay had tried to discuss the behavior changes with Emily, but she'd dismissed his concerns, accusing him of imagining it.

It was a nice night: still light enough to see and not cool enough for anything more than a light jacket or sweater. When they got far away enough from Gia's house, Lucky was the first to speak. "I understand your concern, Clay, I really do, but it sounds to me like Gia wants to do a good thing."

"You and Rhys jumped all over her," Maddy said. "You were openly hostile."

"We didn't jump on her, nor were we hostile," Rhys replied. "It's my job to look out for the town and that's what I did."

"Outside, I thought Flynn was gonna hit you," Lucky told Clay.

Flynn had been so pissed Clay thought he'd seen steam coming out of his ears. "He's my friend. But it's clear she's dragging him around by his di . . ."

"Clay!" Emily stopped short.

He held up his hands. "Sorry." But it was the damned truth. What the hell was Flynn getting involved for? How would he like it if a halfway house went up next door to his folks' property?

They continued walking until they came to the fork in the road that curved off to Lucky and Tawny's cowboy camp.

"I don't want to go against you guys," Lucky said. "You're my friends and my neighbors, but I'd like to know more about her program before I give a definitive no. My mother could've used the kind of help Gia's talking about. And it wasn't that long ago that Tawny struggled with being a single mom with a sick child while trying to hold her business together. So despite whatever Gia's motives are, I'm sympathetic to the cause." He looked at his wife and she smiled at him with pride.

Clay worried that Gia's proposal might divide neighbors and he didn't like that. They were a cohesive group who depended on each other in tough times. He didn't want this to turn into a war between them, but he also didn't want the tranquility of his bucolic community to be shaken.

"I say the six of us meet"—Lucky circled his hand around their small group—"and come up with a bunch of questions for her to address. Then we'll see if we're satisfied."

"I have to think about more than just us," Rhys reiterated. "I have to think about the whole community."

Clay had already made up his mind. He didn't want a damn women's shelter anywhere in the vicinity, but he also didn't want to brush off Lucky.

"We can meet at our house next weekend," he said. "In the meantime, I'd like to research the zoning restrictions. What Gia's talking about may not even be legal."

"All she'd have to say is that these women are farmhands." Rhys looked at Clay pointedly. "If that's illegal both you and Lucky are in big trouble."

Except Gia had already made it known that these women would be here specifically for her program. Clay had a lot of clout in this town and he wouldn't shy away from using it.

"If push came to shove, she could certainly challenge my cowboy camp." Lucky rubbed a hand over his chin. "You don't know that my guests don't have criminal backgrounds."

"Not the same thing," Rhys said. "Under the zoning you're allowed to run an agritourism business. But like I said, there are a lot of ways she can manipulate this."

"We on for next weekend, then?" Clay wanted to get Emily home. She seemed agitated. Maybe she didn't feel well.

"Yes," the group said in unison.

Lucky and Tawny took the fork to their ranch and the rest of them cut across Clay's field and hiked to the house. Ordinarily, Emily would've invited the Shepards in, but there was nothing normal about her these days. Rhys and Maddy waved goodbye and took off toward their house, which was only a quarter mile away.

Both the boys were out—Cody at a sleepover and Justin on a date—and the house was eerily quiet. Clay turned on the lights, took Emily's purse from her, put it on the hall table, and wrapped her in his arms.

"You okay?" he asked against her lips as he kissed her.

She pulled away and sighed. "You behaved abhorrently. We were guests in Gia's home. She went to a lot of trouble to make us comfortable. . . . Oh, Clay."

"You want a shelter next door? I want my family to be safe, Emily. I don't know what kinds of people will be staying there."

"You could've been more diplomatic about voicing those objections instead of accusing Gia of using this as a publicity stunt." Emily walked into the living room, plopped onto the couch, and took off her shoes with a groan.

Clay sat next to her, pulled her feet into his lap, and began rubbing them. "I think it is a publicity stunt and I tell it like it is."

"Well I found your *telling it like it is* embarrassing . . . and insulting. Lucky's right. Who cares what her reasons are for doing it? If it helps women in trouble get back on their feet again . . . why would you be against something like that?"

"You can't possibly want this thing?" He was getting angry. Emily of all people should be leery after the hell she'd been through with her daughter. It had been more than seven years and they still didn't know who had abducted Hope or whether she was even still alive.

"I don't know enough about it. She never got to finish after you went off the way you did. And Flynn . . . I've never seen him so angry."

"Flynn will get over it. He's a smart guy who's spent most of his career in law enforcement. He should know better than to get involved with a woman like Gia Treadwell. Her lawyer?" He snorted. "He wants to get in her pants is what he wants."

Emily shook her head. "You sound like a jackass when you say things like that."

He supposed he did, but it was the truth. All he had to do was look at Flynn and see infatuation written on his friend's face. The man had it bad. "I just don't understand why he's representing her, Em."

"Probably because he thinks she's innocent and thinks it's awful that she's being used as a scapegoat. I follow the news, Clay. If they'd had even an iota of evidence that Gia was involved in all those financial shenanigans, she would've been arrested by now. I know what it's like to be her . . . to have everyone impugn your character."

When Hope went missing the police immediately looked at Emily and her then-husband. They'd made Emily take a polygraph. Not only had she had to grapple with her daughter's abduction but she'd had to deal with being the key suspect in the case.

"I'm not saying she's guilty, Emily. But I don't like her proposal. This is our home . . . Justin and Cody's home. I don't want it disrupted. I'm all for Gia's Christmas tree farm and the hay she wants to grow, but I don't want a rehab center next door."

"Do you know how classist you sound?" Emily pulled her feet away and sat up. Her face had gone a little green.

"You okay?"

She jumped up and ran to the bathroom. Clay followed. Behind the door he could hear her throwing up and went in to hold her hair back. When she was finished he washed her face.

"Stomach flu?" he asked, tucking her head against his chest. "Want me to get you some ginger ale?"

"I'm okay. I just need to sit down."

They went back into the living room and she cuddled next to him while he stroked her hair.

"You think it might've been something you ate?" He'd noticed she hadn't had anything at Gia's house.

"No," she said. "Back to Gia's residential program. I want you to give it more thought, Clay. If she can guarantee that all the participants have been fully vetted . . . no criminal history . . . I don't see what the big deal is. Will you promise me that you won't dismiss it out of hand?"

"I've got you and the boys to think about, Emily. If anything happened to you . . ."

"No one understands that better than I do. The boys may not be mine biologically, but I love them like my own. Just promise me."

"Why's this so important to you?"

"Because if it hadn't been for you and this ranch, I'd be one of those women. There are all kinds of circumstances that can lay a person low, Clay." He knew Hope's kidnapping had left Emily an empty shell.

"I'll promise on one condition," he said and kissed the top of her head. "You have to tell me what's been bothering you these last couple of weeks. I've never seen you so . . . emotional." He hesitated to use the word, knowing women didn't like it.

Emily looked up at him. "Will you also promise to apologize to Gia and Flynn?"

"I didn't do anything to Flynn."

She rolled her eyes. "You offended the woman he cares about. I don't know if they're romantic, but Flynn is clearly her friend . . . and her lawyer."

"According to everyone in town, they're doing it fifty ways to Sunday."

"You believe everything you hear in town?" She smacked his arm.

Clay laughed and pulled her into his lap. "I can see you're feeling better."

"A little bit, but I could use that ginger ale."

"At your service," he said and lifted her up and put her back down so he could go to the kitchen. Before he left he fluffed a throw pillow and stuck it behind her head. "Sit tight and when I come back you'll tell me what's been upsetting you."

In the kitchen he found a bottle in the pantry, filled a glass with ice, and took a second to admire the room. It used to be dated, with chipped tiles and old linoleum, but he'd kept it that way as an ode to his late parents. Emily had wanted to remodel it, but he'd fought her, fearing modern updates would erase the past. Because he'd give her the moon and the stars if she wanted them—and because she was the cook—she'd won. But she'd preserved some of the old, mixing it with the new, making the room the heart of the house. And it wasn't just the kitchen. She'd brought love into every corner of their lives.

Whatever was going on with her . . . with them, he'd go to the ends of the earth to fix it. He'd promised himself that after Hope he would do his damnedest to never let anything hurt her again.

Grabbing the bottle of ginger ale and the glass, he returned to the living room to find Emily curled up on the couch, sound asleep. He put the soda on the table and tucked her in with a throw blanket from one of the chairs. Whatever she had must've hit her hard. If she still felt sick in the morning he'd take her to the clinic in Glory Junction.

In the meantime, he wanted to clean the bathroom before Emily woke up. He opened the window to air out the room. Under the sink he found cleaning supplies and scrubbed the toilet, sink, and floor where Emily had gotten sick. He was getting ready to empty the trash when something caught his eye. The tip of a toothbrush peeked out from under a wad of tissue. Clay had never seen one with a digital display before so he fished the plastic stick out of the garbage to take a closer look.

It wasn't a toothbrush. The words on the display said, "Pregnant."

Pregnant. He stared at the stick a few seconds, stunned.

"Well, I'll be damned," he muttered aloud, letting the news sink in. But why the hell hadn't his wife told him?

Flynn heard Gia moving around downstairs. For such a well-built house, noise traveled. Either that or he was hyper tuned in to her. More likely the later. He wondered if she was having trouble sleeping.

The meeting had gone piss-poor. No doubt that had made Gia restless. For him it was the goddamn dress and thong she'd had on. Just the thought of her firm ass cheek in his hand had made him hard. By now she'd probably changed into those pajama shorts and thin tank she wore to bed.

"Ah, Jesus," he groaned and rolled over. At this rate it'd be a long night.

He shut his eyes, tried to sleep, even counted sheep. That was when he could've sworn he smelled Gia's perfume wafting under his door and got up to check the hallway. Nothing. He got back in bed, shoved an extra pillow under his head, and stared up at the ceiling fan, hoping the whir of the blades would lull him into dreamland.

About four in the morning he bolted up from a half sleep. A noise came from outside the house, like a faint clanging of metal. He got up, went to the window, and pulled the drapes aside, but it was too dark to make anything out. Not even shadows. He was about to ignore it when he heard more noise coming from the direction of the garbage cans.

"Goddamn it." He tugged on his pants, shirt, and boots.

It was probably just raccoons or a bear. Best to chase off whatever it was before it made a mess. He reached inside his duffel for his Glock. A mama bear could get mean if she traveled with a cub.

He went down the stairs—quiet as he could, not to wake up Gia— through the kitchen, switched on the outdoor lights, and exited through the mudroom door. Something rustled near the wooden trash-bin enclosure. Then two heads popped up, clearly startled by the sudden flood of light. One of them looked directly into the muzzle of Flynn's pistol.

"Don't shoot," the other one said.

"Come out with your hands up."

Flynn saw one of the men stuff something in his jacket pocket before he and his buddy walked out from the enclosure into the open.

"Get down on the ground, put your hands on your head, and spread your legs wide."

Both men complied and Flynn had started to check them for weapons when he felt someone behind him.

"What's going on?" Gia asked and blanched when she saw the gun in Flynn's hand.

He continued frisking the men. "Gia, call the police, please."

"Okay, but who are they and how did they get in here? The gate's closed."

Anyone determined enough could get around that gate on foot. But he didn't have time to make conversation now. Without zip ties or handcuffs he had to hold his semiautomatic and search the men at the same time.

"Just call the police," he said. "And open the gate."

She padded across the lawn in her slippers and disappeared inside the house. While she was gone, Flynn searched both men's pockets, dumping all the contents onto the ground. He wanted to go through it before Rhys or one of his officers came but had his hands full.

"You move and I'll shoot," he told his captives.

The smaller of the two had pissed his pants. Flynn didn't think they would try to escape, but he wasn't taking any chances, keeping the gun trained on them while he squatted down to sort through the flotsam from their pockets. He wanted to know what the big one had found so interesting. Damned if he could tell. The pile consisted of wallets—Flynn went through them looking for ID—a few loose bills, a ring of keys, a business card, chewing gum, and a memory stick.

Flynn pocketed the card and the memory stick just before Gia came back outside.

"They're on their way," she said.

He slid her a glance and nodded. "You should wait in the house. It's cold."

"Not really." She pulled the robe tighter around her. "I want to know what they were doing here."

"Evidently, going through your garbage."

"Gia, where's Evan Laughlin?" the big one asked.

Flynn stuck the toe of his boot in the man's side. "Shut up."

"Ah Jesus, you didn't have to do that," the man said, groaning.

Gia came closer and bent down to look at the guy. "Who are you?"

"I'm with *Tattletale*."

Flynn had never heard of it, but he assumed it was a tabloid. Maybe one of those online pieces of shit.

"Why won't you people leave me alone?" Gia said. After everything that had happened at the meeting last night, finding two yahoos in her garbage had to be the coup de grâce. "I don't know where Evan—"

Flynn pulled Gia up and put his finger to her lips. "Hush."

"Who's the guy, Gia? Is he your bodyguard? Your lover?" Even on his belly, the jerk off was looking for a story.

Flynn nudged his boot into the guy's flank. "What did I tell you?"

The third time in a month, the sound of a siren broke the air.

Gia closed her eyes. "I can't believe this."

Annie came marching across the grass in her nightgown, a denim jacket, cowboy boots, and scary hair. She took one look at the scene and her eyes got big as saucers.

"Were they trying to break in?

"Into my trash," Gia said. "Apparently they thought they'd find the scoop of the century digging through my garbage."

"Why would anyone do that? It's disgusting." Annie winced.

The siren got closer and stopped. A car door slammed and Flynn shouted, "Back here. All clear."

Rhys came running around the house. Flynn assumed backup was ten minutes out because Rhys lived here and the station was at least fifteen minutes away.

"According to Connie, you've got prowlers," Rhys said.

Flynn nodded and pointed at the two bozos on the ground. "I found them digging through Gia's garbage bins."

Rhys's brows shot up. "The trash cans, huh?" He looked at Gia and Annie. "Everyone okay?"

"No, he kicked me." The guy in the dirt started to get up and Rhys told him to stay down.

He pulled a pair of metal cuffs out of his back pocket, crouched, restrained the idiot, and read them both their Miranda rights.

Two more sirens came up the hill. Rhys used his radio to give the officers his location. "We've got the situation contained, but I need another set of cuffs."

Sloane, followed by a young officer Flynn didn't know, came rounding the clubhouse turn. It looked like the entire department had shown.

Sloane cuffed the other guy, got both men up, and escorted them to two Nugget PD SUVS parked in the driveway. The other officer— Wyatt, Rhys called him—went with her.

"I'll meet you at the station in a few," Rhys said, and turned to Flynn. "I need to take your statement."

Annie, who hadn't witnessed much, went back to her apartment, but Gia stayed. Flynn told Rhys how he'd heard a noise, went down to investigate, and found the two men in the garbage enclosure. Rhys took the stuff Flynn had confiscated from the men's pockets, finished his report, and was on his way.

"I'm sorry you have to keep running off my trespassers," Gia told Flynn as they went inside the house.

"You don't have to apologize. I'm glad I was here and you didn't have to handle it on your own."

"Are you going back to bed?"

It wasn't like he had gotten that much sleep in the first place. "I was thinking about it. Why?"

"I'm wide awake now." Once they got in the kitchen she put up a pot of coffee. "I wonder if those guys would've tried to come in the house if you hadn't caught them."

"I doubt it. But make sure to keep your doors and windows locked."

"Maybe I should put a dead bolt on the guest apartment . . . for Annie."

"I'll do it tomorrow . . . today. Hell, what time is it?" He looked at the clock over the stove. Six. Yeah, he wasn't going back to bed.

He stuck his head in the fridge out of pure habit, not hunger, though this was when he usually ate breakfast at the ranch.

"I'll make you bacon and eggs if you want," Gia said.

"Yeah?" He scratched the scruff on his chin. "All right. Thanks."

He sat at the center island and watched her prepare breakfast. The robe she had on was one of those kimono things—silky and very clingy. Flynn was trying not to look at the way it molded to her hips, ass, and breasts as she moved around the kitchen but was failing abysmally. The fact was, he liked morning sex. Always had. And visions of Gia on the granite counter with her legs spread . . . God, he was doomed.

"I don't think those paparazzi guys helped my case with Rhys," she said as the smell of frying bacon filled the kitchen. "I'm attracting too much trouble."

"One thing doesn't have anything to do with the other." Although her program was likely to garner attention, bringing even more press to town.

She'd remembered that he liked his eggs sunny-side up, he noticed as she served them onto a plate with a couple of pieces of toast. Flynn dug in while she nibbled at hers.

"I thought they'd finally given up on me and had moved on to the next story," she said.

He'd sort of thought so too, which raised the ugly question of why the slimy bastards were back again. Flynn had his suspicions and they weren't good. There was no need to voice them at this point and get Gia unnecessarily worried. Not until he did some checking around and had Toad make some calls. But if he was right, they needed to have their ducks in order because things were about to get nasty.

Chapter 16

Sunday afternoon Gia went into town to meet the girls at the Ponderosa. They planned to have an early dinner. Harlee had heard about the men who'd broken into her garbage and wanted the dirt. Flynn had warned her to be careful of what she said, as if she could somehow incriminate herself.

At least they would spend much of the evening talking about Dana's wedding. Gia was sick of the spotlight and hoped to avoid her immediate neighbors after Saturday's debacle. They all needed time to chill. But that didn't mean she was giving up.

Of course the minute Gia got out of her car she bumped into Tawny and Lucky, who were walking across the square. She was tempted to tell them she was meeting people and didn't have time to talk. While it would've been fine in New York, blowing off your neighbors in Nugget was a strict no-no. Gia had learned at least that much.

Tawny hugged Gia, which stunned her, given the tenor of Saturday's meeting.

"I'm sorry about yesterday and how contentious it got," Lucky said. "You can't blame us for being protective of our own backyards. Tawny and I aren't totally against your idea; we just want to make sure it doesn't change the environment. We all value the safety and tranquility we have here. But I will tell you this—and I think I can speak for everyone—we're thrilled with the Christmas tree farm. That'll be a great addition to the community."

"Give everyone time on the residential program," Tawny added. "People around here don't like change. . . . They could still come around. We just don't want you to think there's any ill will. We're all neighbors."

"Of course not," Gia said, though Clay wasn't exactly subtle about what he thought of her and her plans. "I hope everyone will continue to mull it over. I never intended to bring in ex-cons or drug addicts. And I swear to you there are no plans for a reality television show." The last thing Gia needed in her life was more drama.

Tawny rested her hand on Gia's arm. "Clay's a good person. He didn't mean it the way it sounded. On another topic, we heard you had intruders last night."

Gia let out a breath. Everyone here knew everyone else's business. And surely the Rodriguezes had heard the sirens. "I hope the noise didn't disturb you or any of your guests." Now that the weather was good the cowboy camp had to be booked solid.

"Nah," Lucky said. "Everyone okay?"

"Yeah. Flynn caught them and we called the police." Jeez, she'd made them sound like a couple. *We called the police.* "They were reporters from a cheesy tabloid. Harmless but annoying."

"Good. I'm glad Flynn got 'em. But you call us anytime there's a problem. Give me your cell phone." Lucky waved his hand at her and she automatically gave it to him without thinking.

"I'm giving you all of ours; don't hesitate to call." He plugged them in and handed her back her phone.

"You want mine?"

"Yeah," Lucky said and entered her cell and landline into his smartphone as she recited the numbers.

"Dana, Harlee, and Darla are waiting for me." She nodded her head in the direction of the Ponderosa. "I'd better get going, but thanks for the kind words of support. I appreciate it."

Tawny hugged her again and they waved goodbye as she went inside the Ponderosa. It wasn't as busy as usual, but the jukebox still blared. Sophie greeted her with a warm smile.

"Heard about the trouble at your place. I bet you can use a drink. I'll bring one over on the house." Sophie motioned to a table in the back where her three friends waved. "Floyd, our bartender, has been experimenting."

"Thank you, Sophie."

"Oh, and the Christmas tree guy is Buzz Henderson. I've got his number behind the bar. I'll bring it with the drink."

Just when Gia thought the whole world hated her, Tawny and Lucky had been so sweet, and now Sophie. She'd work on winning

Clay over too. *Reality television*, she huffed to herself. Before all her trouble she'd had a respected show, best-selling books, and a syndicated column in top metropolitan newspapers. She'd also been a successful investment banker who'd probably handled more money in a day than Clay made in a year selling beef cattle. He didn't know the first thing about her and what she'd come from. How dare he insinuate that she was staging a public relations coup?

She wandered back to the table. Dana held up a pitcher of margaritas, ready to fill Gia's glass.

She put her hand over the top to stop her from pouring. "Sophie is bringing me something special because I was the victim of garbage pickers."

Harlee laughed and Gia could've sworn margarita came out of her nose. "We want the whole story, especially the part about Flynn wrangling them to the ground."

"Was he naked?" Darla asked, giant plastic flamingo earrings swinging as she bobbed her head.

"No. He had his clothes on." Flynn in jeans was still pretty spectacular, though she suspected Flynn au natural was breathtaking. "But he had a gun and held it on the guys like he knew what he was doing."

"Of course he knows what he's doing; he used to be an FBI agent." Harlee poured herself more margarita. "I just want to say right now that the dipshits who trespassed onto your property do not represent the rest of us reporters. I have never in my entire career dug through someone's trash. Not once."

"What's the worst thing you ever did?" Dana asked Harlee.

"I ordered a pizza once at a crime scene. Reporters gotta eat. In her own way, Gia was a reporter too."

"Uh, more like an advice columnist. I never actually interviewed people, though I had experts on my show."

A waitress came to the table and brought Gia a frothy concoction garnished with mango, pineapple, and an umbrella. Gia took a sip.

"Mmm." Floyd had outdone himself. "This is fantastic." She passed the drink around the table while the server took their orders. "Tell Sophie and Floyd thanks. I love it."

After the waitress left Dana said, "More about Flynn."

"He made the two men get down on the ground, frisked them, and waited for the cops to come. That's it." She didn't mention the fact that she was so thankful he'd been there that night or that he was sexually driving her out of her mind.

"He stays at your place a lot, doesn't he?" Darla took a second sip of Gia's drink. "So good, right?"

"It's a busy time with the cattle. They're having their babies now." Poor Flynn had a heavy load, but he never complained. He was a hard worker.

"How did the meeting go?" Dana asked.

"What meeting?" the other two said at the same time.

Dana looked at Gia like *uh-oh, I spilled the beans, didn't I?*

Gia didn't think there was any reason to keep it a secret any longer now that six of her neighbors knew.

"I'll tell you, but it's not for publication." Gia looked directly at Harlee, then told them her plan for the residential program and how Clay and Rhys had rejected the idea.

"Forget Clay and Rhys, I love the idea," Darla said. "And I want to volunteer to give all the participants dress-for-success hairstyles."

Looking at Darla and her usually loud ensembles—purple hair, glitter press-on nails, and clothes a smidge too tight—no one would believe she was capable of creating anything tasteful. But the hairstylist was truly gifted. Gia had had the best stylists in the business do her hair and Darla could hold a candle to any one of them.

"If you go forward with your proposal and still have opposition from the people who live next door to you, I'm gonna have to write about it," Harlee said.

"I know. But for now nothing is happening except that I'm planting Christmas trees."

Harlee looked unimpressed. "Not really a story. But I'm writing about the *Tattletale* guys. Give me some good quotes."

"Like what?" Gia asked.

"Did you fear for your life? Did you feel violated?"

Gia rolled her eyes. "You're starting to sound like a tabloid now. Flynn told me not to be quoted." By now everyone knew Flynn was her attorney. And of course there were the rumors that they were having wild animal sex. "Just write it from the police report. You can use what I told you, but don't attribute it to me."

Mercifully their food came and Harlee stopped interrogating her long enough to eat.

"It's time to talk about wedding stuff now," Dana said. Gia caught her eye and mouthed, *Thank you.*

They talked about whether it was out of fashion to throw the bridal bouquet, what everyone thought her something borrowed should be, and whether Gia planned to bring Flynn as her date.

"He's my lawyer." Gia didn't need a date and taking a man to a wedding told the world one of two things: You were serious about the guy or you wanted everyone to believe you were serious about the guy.

She didn't want to send either of those messages, though Flynn had a way of bolstering her courage. Let's face it, most of the guests were going to search her out of the crowd, talk behind her back, and lay bets on whether she was complicit in the biggest financial fraud in U.S. history. She was a walking freak show. If it wasn't Dana, Gia would decline the invitation, stay home, and eat good pastry instead of overly sweet wedding cake. But her former real estate agent had become a dear friend and she wanted to be there on her important day.

"Just bring him," Harlee said and grinned. "He can help you fend off people like me."

Harlee had a point, but Gia didn't know if Flynn would even want to go. Most men didn't like weddings and she could see why. Bad food, "The Hokey Pokey," and lots of obnoxious toasts.

"We'll see," she said, because it was the easiest way to get them off her back.

They finished their dinners. Darla ordered mud pie and chocolate cake for them to share. Afterward they called it a night. Gia drove home to an empty house. Flynn had court in the morning and Annie had school.

She opened the gate with her clicker and watched through her rearview mirror to make sure it closed securely behind her. Once inside the house she turned off the alarm. The silence creeped her out so she flicked on the TV, went in her bedroom to change into sweats, and made it back to the living room couch in time for the nightly news.

The landline rang. She muted the TV and got up to grab the phone from the kitchen.

"Hello," she answered and wandered back into the living room.

"Why didn't you answer your cell?" It was Flynn.

"I didn't hear it ring." It was at the bottom of her purse, which she'd left in the bedroom. "What's up? You make it to Sacramento all right?"

"Yeah," he said, but something on the TV caught her eye and she barely heard him. "What are you doing?"

"I just got home." She focused on the flat screen.

"Sit down for a second."

"Flynn? Why is Rufus Cleo on the nightly news?"

"That's what I'm trying to tell you."

"Hang on." She found the remote and unmuted the sound only to catch the tail end of the report. "I missed it."

"You sitting down?"

Gia took her spot on the couch and continued to stare at the screen, hoping there would be more. But they'd taken down the photo of Cleo and the anchor had moved on to a protest in Des Moines. "I am now."

She could hear Flynn breathing on the other end of the line, but he didn't say anything. "Flynn?"

"I'm here. Hang on a sec, I'm getting a text." She heard him mutter an expletive.

"Everything okay?"

"Evan Laughlin's been implicated in Rufus Cleo's murder."

"What?" she asked, confused. "Did they find Evan?"

"No. But they've linked the murder weapon to its owner, who's rolled on Evan."

"Dear God. Murder? That can't be right." Gia's heart raced. "Who is he?"

"A parking garage attendant with a couple of priors."

"Evan didn't fraternize with parking garage attendants. This can't be right, Flynn."

"He worked in Evan's building."

Gia was silent, a million possibilities swirling through her head.

"Have they arrested him?" she finally asked. Because maybe the attendant was lying. With all the news about Evan, the attendant could've thrown out his name as a bargaining chip.

"Yep. Last night around midnight, East Coast time. Gia, don't panic. This doesn't involve you."

None of it involved her. But that hadn't seemed to matter. So hell yeah she was panicking.

* * *

Flynn spent Monday in the office with Toad hunting down every lead they could find. The parking garage attendant was nothing but a petty crook. A fence who'd participated in a few smash and grabs. Flynn found it hard to believe a guy like him could gain entrance into Cleo's high-rise office building after hours. The place had more security than most financial institutions.

More than likely his main role had been supplying the gun to the actual killer. To Flynn's mind that had to be Laughlin, who Cleo would've buzzed into the building without a moment's hesitation. Who knew the real story? Flynn had friends in New York's FBI office, but no one was talking. He relied on the media for information, which was sketchy at best.

"You taking off?" Toad asked as Flynn gathered up his paperwork and shoved it into his briefcase.

"Yeah. I'd like to get to Nugget before dark."

"You babysitting our client?" There was a world of sarcasm in the way Toad said "client." Not everyone would've heard it, but Flynn had known the investigator a long time.

He fixed him with a look that said *don't go there.* "I figure the news will cause her more problems, especially with the media. You should've seen those two bozos digging through her trash the other night."

"You sure she's not in on this?"

Flynn opened the top drawer of his desk, pulled out the thumb drive he'd confiscated from the *Tattletale* reporter's pocket, and plugged it into his computer. "What does this look like to you?"

Toad came around the desk and stared over Flynn's shoulder. "A bunch of names and a bunch of numbers."

"I searched the names. They're members of the carpenters' union, which invested millions in Laughlin's fraudulent scheme. A lot of construction workers lost their entire pensions."

"Where'd you get that and what's its relevance?" Toad asked.

"One of the trespassers filched it from Gia's garbage."

Toad grabbed a chair and pulled it closer to Flynn's monitor to study the screen. "What do you think those numbers mean?"

"I don't know. I showed them to Bellamy and he thinks they're addresses, and these over here"—Flynn pointed to figures on the other side of the spreadsheet—"are dollar amounts."

"She's been sending them money?" Toad sounded as floored as Flynn had initially been.

"I know, insane. But Bellamy is trying to nail it down for sure." The forensic accountant was the best in the business and Flynn had the utmost faith in him. "But to answer your question: Yeah, I think she's sending them money."

Toad scratched his chin. "Why? There are thousands of victims. Why them?"

"Best I can guess is that people like them were hit the hardest . . . blue-collar workers, too old to keep swinging a hammer. They were relying on their pensions to get them through retirement." It certainly fit in with Gia's modus operandi. Her own impoverished upbringing made her want to save the world.

"Shit," Toad said. "Can she get her hands on that kind of money?"

Flynn shrugged, but he suspected that was part of the reason for the day trading.

"You think this clears her?"

"It's certainly not the actions of a crook." Flynn pulled out the zip drive and shut off his computer. "But I plan to have a long talk with her about it tonight. Maybe we're wrong. But I want to know why she kept a spreadsheet."

Toad turned his gaze on Flynn and studied him for a beat. "I got a good vibe off her, but approach this with your head, not your dick."

Too late. Though nothing had happened yet, Flynn's dick had become fully invested. "I'll call you tomorrow. In the meantime, anything you can find on the garage attendant, Laughlin, or Cleo could be helpful. I've got a feeling the feds are about to ramp up their investigation and put a lot of pressure on Gia."

"Oh yeah," Toad said. "You're not kidding."

Flynn made good time to Nugget and was glad to see Gia's security gate closed when he got to Rosser Ranch. She was following protocol. He let himself in using the clicker, pulled his truck into the driveway, got out, and knocked on the door. When there was no answer he used the key she'd given him.

"Gia? You here?" He wandered around the house looking for her, found her car in the garage, and walked to the barn to see if she was there.

She could've gone out with one of her friends. He hadn't told her he was coming. But when he got to the stable Rory was gone. He sad-dled up Dude and followed the trail Gia favored. About a mile into the ride he caught up with her.

Gia twisted around as he came up behind her. "Hey." She smiled. "I wasn't expecting to see you today."

"You still using that dopey saddle?"

She flipped her hand at him. "You worry about your own saddle—which, by the way, could use some TLC."

The leather was worn and frayed, but it was a working saddle intended for comfort and practicality, not show jumping.

"You have news?" she asked.

"Let's ride for a while." It was a beautiful evening, balmy and clear. The days were getting longer and Flynn figured they had at least an hour before the sun set.

"So you do have news?"

He put his finger to his lip. "Hush. Take some time to enjoy the great outdoors."

Gia let out a snort that rivaled one of Dude's. "Are you like the bossiest person in your family?"

"No, my brother Wes is. Bossiest sumbitch you'll ever meet."

"You two don't get along?" Gia clicked her tongue, urging Rory to catch up to Dude so they could ride side by side.

"Yeah, we get along. He's my best friend."

"Who's older?"

"He is, by two years. He married his high-school sweetheart and they have two kids, a boy and a girl."

"Nice," she said.

"I thought you didn't believe in marriage." Dude bent down to munch on grass and Flynn pulled up on the reins.

"It's fine for other people, just not me. Did you have a high-school sweetheart?"

"Tina Alessi." He smiled at the memory of the cute brunette. She'd married a college professor and, last he'd heard, they lived in Boston. "Her family owned the only Italian restaurant in Quincy . . . gave me free food."

"Is that why you dated her?" Gia teased.

"Nope." He gazed at Gia and let his eyes soak in the sight of her in the tight riding breeches that hugged her hips and thighs like a second skin and the clingy shirt that outlined the rise and fall of her perky breasts. With her hair tied back she looked impossibly young . . . and beautiful. "I dated her because she put out."

"Classy." Gia snorted again and Flynn laughed. He loved riling her.

"The truth: She was whip-smart. Class valedictorian . . . nothing hotter than that."

"I would've thought you were the class valedictorian."

"I was salutatorian. She beat me out by half a grade point."

The horses took the trail at a slow, easy gait. Flynn saw a cluster of his cattle in the distance. They looked content, munching on grass as the day turned to dusk. Despite the drought, the Barlows were poised for a good year.

"How 'bout you?" he asked. "I bet you were valedictorian."

"Nah. I didn't really do well academically until college."

"You have a high-school sweetheart?"

"No," she said. "Those years were tough for me."

She seemed like the popular type to him. Smart, personable, and pretty. But scrounging for your next meal left no time to campaign for homecoming queen.

"What changed in college?" he asked.

"Blind ambition," she said, but he suspected she never wanted to be poor again. Clearly it had left permanent scars and had motivated her to start a program for impoverished women and to secretly send money to construction workers who'd lost everything they had. "Why did you go to law school?"

Nice subject change. "Because I wanted to get hired by the FBI. They like lawyers and CPAs and I was never good at math."

"Why the FBI?" she sneered. Flynn couldn't blame her. She and the Bureau weren't on the best of terms.

"All the cliché reasons. I wanted to fight crime, make a difference . . . carry a gun."

She arched her brows. "Apparently you still like the gun part."

"I wouldn't talk if I were you." He was remembering their first meeting . . . she and that Winchester. "Until you figure out where the safety is, keep your day job."

"I don't know if you noticed, but I don't have one anymore."

"Does that mean you're no longer day trading?" They were going to have a long conversation about that, but for now he just wanted to enjoy their ride . . . and flirting with her. She was an exceptional flirt. No giggling or batting her eyelashes. Just truckloads of attitude.

"I wouldn't really call that a job."

"I'd call it crazy."

"I know what I'm doing and I'm extraordinarily good at it."

"And modest too." He reined his horse to stop.

"What are you doing?"

Flynn pointed to a herd of deer: three mamas and their fawns. "Don't scare 'em."

"They're so sweet," she whispered, "I wish I had my phone to take a picture to send to my mom."

Flynn pulled his off his belt and snapped a few shots. The deer were good enough to cooperate, lingering in a copse of trees. "I'll email them to you."

"Thanks. Can you believe this is mine?" She regarded the countryside with wonder. "It's so beautiful here. When Evan disappeared and the criminal investigation started New York felt so cold and scary. One trip here was worth a year's therapy."

"Yup." He too stared up at the majestic mountains. "The Sierra is a special place."

"Is your family's ranch like this?"

"It's about half the size but equally beautiful." He grinned. "A fine place to grow up."

He thought it time they headed back. The sun had started to drop and they needed to talk. He nudged Dude with his knees and made a wide loop in the direction of the stable. Gia and Rory followed.

"You want to see it . . . my family's ranch? You could come for Sunday dinner." He didn't know what possessed him to invite her. It had been a long time since he'd brought a woman home. Flynn told himself it was for his mother's sake . . . she could tell her friends that Gia Treadwell ate in her kitchen.

"Uh . . . sure." Gia seemed as surprised by the invitation as Flynn was that he'd asked. "Is Sunday dinner like a big thing?" She also sounded nervous, which was cute, because she was the celebrity.

"It used to be mandatory, even when I was going to law school and living in Palo Alto. But Wes and Jo are busy with the kids, I've got my practice and the cattle, and life is more unpredictable now that we're all older. But we still try to do it as often as possible."

"With the whole family?"

"Yeah, that's the idea. What are you worried about? You've already met my mom, and there's a good home-cooked meal in it for you."

"What about your dad? Does he know about me?" Flynn knew the subtext of that question: *Does he think I ripped off thousands of people in a Ponzi scheme?*

"My dad doesn't get too involved in the news. He's a grizzled rancher whose motto is: 'Don't believe anything you read or hear and only half of what you see.'"

Gia chuckled. The rooftop of the stable came into view and Flynn had to tighten his reins to keep Dude from racing across the field. He noticed Gia was holding Rory back too. It had been a nice ride; Flynn wished it didn't have to end.

Clay's boys were at the barn waiting.

"Sorry, guys. I forgot to text again." Flynn swung down from Dude and Justin led the gelding to a post to tie his lead rope and unsaddle him. "You don't have to do that, son. I've got it and I'm paying you anyway."

Flynn helped Gia down and Cody took her horse while Justin brushed Dude down with a curry comb. They were getting five-star treatment.

"We'll do anything to stay out of the house right now," said the younger McCreedy.

"Shut up, Cody!" Justin said, and Gia and Flynn exchanged glances.

"Everything okay?" Flynn didn't want to pry, but clearly Cody wanted to talk about it.

"Dad and Emily have been fighting all day."

Justin shot Cody a dirty look. "It's no big deal and it's none of your business, Cody."

"You and Justin fight?" Flynn asked Cody. All brothers did.

"Sometimes."

"It happens when people live under the same roof. It's natural and nothing to worry about." Clay had once confided in Flynn that after his first wife was killed in an auto accident, Cody had begun suffering from anxiety issues. He didn't want the kid to get himself worked up over something that was probably nothing.

Unmoved, Cody frowned. Flynn wished there was more he could say. But he could tell that discussing it was making Justin uncomfortable. The boy was old enough to know Cody had talked out of turn.

"You guys want to go into town for dinner and ice cream?" Ice cream had always been the answer to every problem in the Barlow home.

Cody momentarily perked up until Justin said, "No, thanks. We've got chores at home and it's a school night."

The boys finished helping with the horses and went on their way, cutting across Gia's property to take the shortcut home. Flynn put Dude and Rory into their separate stalls and closed the barn up for the night.

"What do you think they're fighting about?" Gia asked as they walked back to the house.

"Haven't the slightest idea and it's none of our business."

"You're no fun."

"You think it's fun when people talk about you behind your back?"

"Were you always a Dudley Do-Right or did that happen after law school?" she teased.

If Gia knew half the things he wanted to do with her, she wouldn't call him that. If she knew how many times he'd stared at her ass in those riding pants when he thought she wasn't looking . . .

"You want to go to town to eat?" He opened the door for her.

"Can we get ice cream too?" she teased.

"Only if you're good."

Chapter 17

"Don't cry. We'll work through this," Clay didn't know whether it was the hormones or if he was doing everything wrong. "Emily, honey, I'm sorry. I just thought you'd be more excited is all."

She sniffled and wiped her nose with the back of her hand. "I'm trying to be, I really am. It's just so unexpected."

For him it was the best kind of unexpected. Since discovering the test stick on Saturday, he'd been walking on sunshine. Not Emily. She'd been depressed, crying on and off, and hiding in their darkened bedroom.

Both times his first wife had been pregnant he'd been deployed, first to Afghanistan and then Iraq, so he didn't know if this was normal. But he suspected not. And this morning he'd lost patience with Emily.

Two years ago, when they'd gotten married, he'd wanted them to try to have a baby. Neither of them was getting any younger and after Hope . . . well, he thought a baby would make her happy. But she'd insisted on waiting. Waiting for what? He didn't know. The boys couldn't love her any more if she were their biological mother and they had a wonderful life. Trips in his plane, great friends, a beautiful home, and a job that fulfilled her. Most of all they loved and respected each other. Not a night went by when they didn't lay in each other's arms and he didn't feel the intensity of their love coursing through them. It was as constant as breathing.

That's why he didn't understand why having his baby had made her so unhappy. Clay realized babies were hard work. Because he hadn't been around to help with his first two sons, he wanted to change diapers, wake up for nightly feedings, and be there every step of the way for this child. If his help wasn't enough they'd hire a nanny. Whatever Emily wanted.

"Don't be angry with me, Clay." She'd gone into their bathroom to wash her face and brush her hair so they could go downstairs and prepare dinner. "This is hard. It feels like I'm trying to replace Hope."

"No one will ever replace Hope, Emily. No one. This baby is his or her own person. Just like Justin and Cody are."

"Logically I understand that. But here"—she placed her hand over her heart and started crying all over again—"it hurts. It hurts so much that it takes away the happiness."

He wrapped his arms around her and held her small frame against him. "I'm not angry." But he didn't know what to do to make this better. He wanted their child to be wanted, loved, and cherished.

"Let's go downstairs." She dabbed her eyes with a tissue and splashed more cold water on her face. "I don't want the boys to think we're still fighting and overhear us. I'm not ready for them to know I'm pregnant yet."

He didn't know how much longer they could keep it a secret. Between Emily's morning sickness and her crying bouts, Justin and Cody would start to worry. It was a big house, but even two self-absorbed teenagers could sense the tension.

They went down to the kitchen and Emily took a lasagna out of the freezer, threw together a salad, and started to make a loaf of garlic bread when she stepped away from the cutting board and held her nose, her complexion green.

"What's wrong?" Clay asked.

"The smell is making me nauseous."

"Go sit down. I'll take it from here."

She moved to the breakfast area, far enough away from the garlic, and sat at the table. "Don't forget to melt the butter."

He brought her a glass of ginger ale—she was living on that and Saltine crackers these days—and winked. "I think I can handle it."

The reality was she could make simple dishes taste better than anyone else and he and the boys had become spoiled. Even good restaurants had lost their appeal.

As Clay put the final touches on the garlic bread, Justin and Cody came through the mudroom into the kitchen.

"Where have you guys been?" Emily asked.

"Over at Miss Treadwell's, helping Flynn with the horses," Justin said.

"I thought you were taking turns." Clay avoided meeting Emily's eyes. Gia and Flynn were still sore spots between them. Emily wanted him to go over to Rosser Ranch and apologize, but he'd been too wrapped up. If it was that important to her, though, he'd make his mea culpa.

"We did it together this time. You got a problem with that?" Justin said, dripping with sullenness.

Clay was surprised. He thought his eldest was over the attitude issues they'd grappled with after his mother died . . . before Emily had come into their lives. Back then, Justin had been difficult. Surly, disrespectful, and angry at the world.

"What I have a problem with is your attitude."

"What I have a problem with is your yelling at Emily." Justin, who was nearly as tall as Clay now, got in his face. Clay spied Emily stifling a grin.

"I can take care of myself, Justin." She got up and hugged him. "But I appreciate your chivalry. We were having an argument. It's okay to do that every once and a while."

"Are you getting a divorce?" Cody, who'd been standing off to the side, asked.

"Goodness no," Emily said and pulled Clay into an embrace. "Your father and I are madly in love with each other. We were having a disagreement and it got heated is all."

"What was it about?" Cody asked.

"It's personal," Emily said and broke away from the hug so she could pull Cody closer and finger comb his hair. "The important thing is that we're talking through it and it's nothing for you to stress over."

Clay gazed at Emily and smiled. This was the calm and rational woman he'd married and he wanted her back. But he also wanted their baby.

"Are you planning to ever tell me your news?" Gia looked up from her plate.

Because she'd eaten at the Ponderosa the night before they'd ditched Nugget and had gone to a small Italian restaurant in Blairsden. It was quiet and so far they hadn't bumped into anyone they knew. A miracle in these mountains.

"Eat your vegetables," he told her.

They were having a nice evening and he didn't want to ruin it with a cross-examination about the information he'd gotten off the recovered thumb drive. No mistake about it, Flynn needed answers tonight, but he was procrastinating.

"You're seriously bossy, you know that, right?"

"I don't have a problem with it. Being bossy is highly underrated." He took a sip of his wine. For a small place in the middle of nowhere, the restaurant had a good list, not that he was a wine snob. "Did you send the pictures of the deer to your mom?"

"I did." Her face lit up. "I wish she would come, but she hates to fly and I worry that she would be bored. Between mah-jongg, tennis, and all her ladies' lunches she has a full social calendar. You don't have to go to Sacramento tomorrow?"

That sort of depended on what she told him tonight. "I'm making a house call tomorrow in Nugget to do a living trust," he said and left it at that.

"Whose house?" she asked and cut the last crostino in half before popping a piece into her mouth.

"None of your business." He took the other half. "Attorney-client privilege, remember?"

She blew an indelicate noise out of her mouth.

"That's what I like about you, Gia; you're always so graceful and elegant."

"How's this for elegant?" She flipped him off. God, he liked her more every day.

He bobbed his head at her middle finger and let his gaze ride over her chest. "When I'm no longer your attorney we'll be doing a lot of that."

"Confident much?" She speared one of the tomatoes from his salad and made a big show of sucking it off her fork. "What if I'm in prison?"

He took a bite of veal and on a full mouth said, "Conjugal visits."

She leaned against the back of her chair, all kidding aside. "Are they going to try to pin Cleo's murder on me too?"

"Do they have any evidence that could help them do that?" He folded his arms over his chest.

"Does it matter? They don't have a shred of evidence that I was involved in the investment fraud. But has that stopped them from harassing me?"

"You didn't answer my question, Gia."

"Then read my lips. No, there is nothing that connects me to Cleo's murder. You know why? Because I had nothing to do with it . . . with any of it!"

"Keep your voice down."

"Sorry," she said quietly. "I'm just so sick and tired of this. Honestly, Flynn, I can't see Evan involved in murder." Gia let out a sigh. "Then again, I couldn't see him stealing billions of dollars. . . . I don't know what to believe. Do you think I'm an idiot because I fell for him . . . because I was tricked so easily?"

"A lot of really smart people fell for him, Gia. He was an exceptional con artist." Flynn had seen serial killers who'd led such seemingly exemplary lives that their wives slept next to them every night without so much as a clue.

Laughlin was likely a psychopath: charismatic, meticulous, highly organized, and able to pull off a double life as if he were two completely separate people. He didn't blame Gia. She'd gotten sucked in like everyone else.

They finished their meals; Flynn paid the bill and they walked across the parking lot in companionable silence. When they got to his truck he gripped Gia's waist and hoisted her into the passenger seat. He knew it was an excuse to touch her but did it anyway, holding on a little longer than necessary.

"We got stuff to talk about at home," he said.

"It's about time. I wondered when you'd finally get to it."

On their way to the ranch he stopped at the Nugget Market. "I promised you ice cream. What flavor do you want?"

"I'll come in with you."

They strolled through the store and he noticed the owner, Ethel, watching them, an impish grin playing on her lips. The whole damn town thought they were a couple and he was doing very little to dissuade them from that notion. Why? Because it wasn't any of their damn business.

At the freezer section Gia walked back and forth, pondering the selections.

"While I'm young, Gia?" It was late and Ethel probably wanted to close the store.

"I can't decide. What do you like?"

"Plain old vanilla."

"Really? I would've figured you for someone more adventurous." Why did he think she wasn't talking about ice cream?

"I'm plenty adventurous." He winked. "Just not when it comes to my ice cream."

"Or your clients," she muttered and grabbed a carton of French vanilla. "Is the fact that it's *French* vanilla too exotic for you?"

"It'll work."

Ethel waited for them at the cash register and rung up the ice cream. "How's your mom, Flynn?"

"She's been coming to the farmers' markets. Haven't you seen her?"

"I was out of commission for a few weeks with the flu. Hopefully I'll catch her this week. I hear you're doing Donna and Trevor's will."

Gia grinned like she'd discovered his big secret.

"I can't talk about that, Ethel."

"Oh, go on." She leaned across the conveyor belt and smacked his arm. "Donna told me all about it. Stu and I have been talking and we'd like you to do ours too. Can you do it at our house, like you're doing for Donna and Trevor?"

Gia coughed, trying to swallow a laugh.

He pulled a business card from his wallet. "Call and set something up with my secretary. That work?"

"It sure does. You're a good boy, Flynn."

No one had called him a boy in a long time. "Thanks, Ethel."

When they got outside Gia burst into laughter. "How's that attorney-client privilege working for you?"

"I can't help it that everyone here discusses their private business. Now quit laughing." He circled her waist with one arm and lifted her off the ground.

"But you're such a good boy." She continued to roar.

"I'm glad you think that's funny."

He drove to Rosser Ranch while she teased him incessantly. He liked the way she laughed. It was rich and throaty and sexy.

At the gate he pressed the clicker on his sun visor and made sure it closed behind them. The motion-sensor lights went on as they parked in the driveway. Flynn had made sure Gia always kept them on and had gotten the security cameras working again. The news about Cleo and Laughlin was bound to bring more reporters to town. He didn't like thinking about what would've happened if the *Tattletale* guys had gotten Gia's thumb drive. Whatever the hell she was doing—and he thought he damned well knew—could be misinterpreted a dozen different ways. It was a pretty good bet that the tabloid wouldn't have erred in Gia's favor.

Gia grabbed the ice cream and jetted through the front door. Not to be paranoid, but he wished she would've let him go first to make sure the house was clear. It was too late now so he went in behind her, closing and locking the door while she turned off the security alarm. According to the panel, nothing had been breached.

"Should we have ice cream?" she asked.

He nodded. They would talk in the kitchen. She got out bowls and spoons, noticed that her answering machine was flashing, and pressed the button.

"Flynn, you're not answering your cell. I need to talk to you, stat. If you get this, call me immediately, doesn't matter what time. Gia, if you know where Flynn is, please pass along my message. This is Toad."

Gia looked at him questioningly, her eyes wide with worry. He pulled his phone from his belt only to find the battery was out of juice.

"I've got to call him. Is there a landline upstairs?"

"On the little table by the window."

He pounded up the stairs, his mother's favorite saying ringing in his ears. *No news is good news.*

Gia stuck the ice cream in the freezer and waited for Flynn to return. A part of her wanted to stand at the bottom of the staircase and eavesdrop, but she knew Flynn wouldn't appreciate it. When it came to professionalism his bar was as high as the Empire State Building. Despite herself, she couldn't help straining to hear, hoping to catch snatches of the urgent call and know whether it would pull him away.

When he stayed she felt safe, despite how sexually frustrated he made her. Even tonight their playfulness made her tingle from head to toe and feel desperate for more than their suggestive banter.

After Evan, she should be swearing off men forever. But Flynn made her head spin until she was dizzy. They could talk for hours, just talk and talk and talk. She'd never done that with a man before. And she loved how he could laugh at himself. Evan rarely laughed at all and never at himself. Then there was the fact that Flynn didn't want anything from her. Not her connections, not her celebrity, and not her money. He had made it clear that the only thing he wanted was her body, which she'd be more than happy to share with him when the time was right. For both of them.

She didn't want to read too much into the fact that he wanted to take her to his parents' home for dinner. People around here were hospitable. Still . . . dinner with his family. It was old-fashioned and sweet and it meant Flynn wasn't embarrassed of her or that she wasn't just his client.

Gia took a seat at the center island and waited, passing the time by scrolling through her emails. Dana had sent her a picture of the bridal bouquet she'd chosen, Harlee had a few background questions about Gia's trespassers, and Emily had sent a thank-you note for having them over the other night. Awfully polite, considering the tone of the meeting. She'd never lived in a place like this.

After her father died and she and her mother had discovered they were broke they'd felt shunned by their Bedford neighbors. Perhaps she was deluding herself, but she couldn't see that happening here. Nugget residents might gossip behind her back and speculate on her and Flynn's relationship, but they'd never treated her like a criminal. Yet they were completely resistant to accepting her program.

Flynn returned to the kitchen, grim.

"What's wrong?" Gia asked.

"You've been busy."

She scanned the kitchen, wondering what the hell he was talking about. Since he'd gone upstairs she'd done nothing but put the ice cream away. "Come again?"

He seemed angry, holding himself tight as a violin bow. "I'm talking about your depositing hundreds of thousands of dollars into the accounts of construction workers who were ripped off by Laughlin."

She could feel her face blanch. "How'd you find out about that?"

"One of those morons from *Tattletale* found a flash drive in your trash. I swiped it, looked at the spreadsheet you'd saved on it, and suspected you'd been passing members of the carpenters' union cash. I don't know how they did it and I don't want to know, but Toad and

Bellamy, my forensic accountant, confirmed it." He held on to the edge of the granite countertop and Gia could see his knuckles had turned white. "Hundreds of thousands of goddamn dollars! What the hell were you thinking, Gia?"

She swallowed hard, racking her brain to figure out how the thumb drive had wound up in the trash. Careful, she'd copied everything to the memory stick before wiping clean the hard drive of the old computer she'd used. She must have accidentally dumped it with a pile of shredded files into the garbage.

"That I wanted those men and women to be able to retire. That I didn't want them to have to sell the homes they'd raised their children in or go bankrupt."

He squeezed the bridge of his nose and, after a few seconds, lowered himself onto the barstool next to her. "How did you get their addresses?"

She shrugged her shoulders. "It wasn't that difficult."

"Do you know what kind of position this puts you in?" His voice had risen to a near yell, and Gia shrank back, having never seen Flynn truly angry.

"I did it anonymously. There's no way to trace it."

He laughed without humor. "Are you kidding me? My investigators were able to trace it in less than a day. If those reporters had managed to make off with the flash drive . . . Jesus Christ, Gia. Do you know how much trouble you'll be in if the FBI finds out?"

"But how? There's nothing unlawful about giving away money, money that I made legally."

"First of all, you'd have to prove you made the money legally. But more importantly, how do you think it looks? I'll tell you: It looks like you're either running scared, afraid of a murder charge, or you're overcome with guilt. Because innocent people, Gia, don't give away hundreds of thousands of dollars. One of the strongest arguments in your favor is that you were a victim too. That's the thing, Gia; victims don't give other victims large quantities of money."

"I do." She stuck out her chin. "I don't have to prove anything to you. I did it because I didn't want those people to suffer."

"I believe you, Gia. But don't you see how someone who already suspects your involvement might see this? How it could be misinterpreted?"

She did. That was why she'd gone to extremes to cover it up, for

all the good it had done. What a boneheaded move it had been, tossing that flash drive into the garbage. She wanted to strangle herself.

"What do I do?" She rested her face in her hands, resigned that
once again she'd screwed up.

"There's not a goddamn thing we *can* do. As you pointed out, it's
not illegal to give away money; therefore we're not going to the feds
with this. Your beneficiaries will have to eventually claim the income for tax purposes. Let's hope your little Robin Hood stunt doesn't
come to light until the case is solved."

She began to cry, which was a new one for her. Gia never cried.
Ever. But she'd made a mess of things even though all she'd wanted
to do was help. She still couldn't fathom how she'd wound up in this
situation. One day she was on top of the world and the next ruined. It
was beyond Kafkaesque.

"Don't cry!" he said, sounding kind of panicked. "Hell no. I can't
handle tears. Come on, Gia . . . don't."

He got up and paced the kitchen with his back to her. "Are you
still crying?"

"No," she said, but she was.

"Ah, for Christ's sake." He pulled her off the stool, enfolded her
in his arms, and kissed the top of her head.

Next thing she knew he was half-dragging, half-carrying her into
the powder room. The important thing was he hadn't let go. And just
having his arms around her made Gia feel stronger, like she wasn't
alone.

He grabbed a wad of tissue from the dispenser and pushed it into
her hand. "Blow your nose."

She wiped her eyes and cheeks and blew her nose. "I'm a terrible
client, aren't I?"

"The worst I've ever had. I wish I could fire you."

What a horrible thing to say. She glared at him, and before she
could shoot back something equally mean, he kissed her. Right there
with her butt pressed against the sink vanity. His mouth, warm and
incredibly soft, latched onto hers. Insistent, with an insatiability that
was hard to match, he repeatedly plunged his tongue inside her, making it clear that this wasn't a warm-up. He claimed and raided, taking
what he'd been so nobly denying himself. The kiss was both rough
and demanding and so quintessentially Flynn.

She gripped his shoulders to hang on, encouraging him to go for-

ever and not stop. His hands moved to the back of her head to take
the kiss deeper and push the rock-hard bulge in his pants into her
pelvis. She wanted their clothes off, her body so hot and wet that in
another minute she'd melt.

Reaching for his belt, she tried to undo the buckle with one hand
while the other stayed fisted in his shirt for leverage. She fumbled,
stymied by the Western clasp. It didn't fasten like a conventional
buckle.

He pushed her hand away and undid it himself, opening his fly
and pushing down his shorts until his erection sprang free. With both
hands he hoisted her onto the vanity, slid her away from the sink, un-
buttoned her blouse, and parted the sides. His eyes heated and his
nostrils flared.

"God, you're beautiful."

Too frenzied to bother with her bra, he pushed up her skirt and
slid down her panties. She heard something tear, looked down, and
saw that he'd yanked down his pants and underwear to his knees
and had sheathed himself in a condom. She didn't know where the
rubber had come from, only that it had magically appeared. But that
was Flynn, always prepared. He felt her with his fingers. The sensa-
tion of his hands down there, against her bare skin, touching, made
her wetter. She leaned her head against the mirror and shuddered.

Within seconds he'd spread her legs wide and pushed inside her.
His size was impossible and he moved slowly, giving her time to become accustomed to him. Finally he reached under Gia's bottom to
change the angle, burying himself to the hilt. He pulled in and out a
few times, stretching her, and when she moaned in pleasure he began
pumping, hard and fast.

"More," she called because she couldn't get enough of him.

His hands moved to her breasts and he pulled her bra cups down
as he continued to pound into her. Her eyes were closed, but she felt
him take one of her nipples into his warm mouth and suck. The sen-
sation was so delicious she cried out.

"Good?"

"Yes," she said. "Don't stop."

His hands were everywhere now. Fondling her breasts, tweaking
her nipples, squeezing her ass as he kissed her neck and throat. It
took all her energy to keep pace with him . . . to match him stroke for
stroke. He'd gone a little crazy, and the thought that it was she who'd

made him lose control ripped away her last inhibitions. She was wild as she bucked against him, her legs tangled around his waist as she screamed out his name.

Her orgasm happened so fast and lasted so long she felt herself spiral through the air and explode into a million shards of colored light. It had never been as intense as this with anyone else. Flynn lifted her slightly and went deeper . . . harder. His face and neck tensed, as if he was straining. She felt his body convulse and heard him grunt. Then he threw his head back and she watched him come.

He lay his forehead against hers, his breathing fast and heavy. "You all right?"

At a loss for adjectives she simply, very quietly, said yes.

He straightened, tugged off the condom, and threw it in the trash. Next he pulled up his pants and tucked himself in before buttoning his fly. She sat there limp, unable to move. Flynn pulled down her skirt, collected her panties from the floor, righted her bra, and closed her blouse. Tilting his head back, he stood there for a few minutes, silent. To Gia it looked like he was reprimanding himself. Either that or he was disappointed.

"What's wrong?"

He scoured his hand over his face. "That shouldn't have happened."

"You regret it?" Gia adjusted her clothes self-consciously. She had no regrets. Not a single one. She'd loved every minute of what they'd done.

"No," he said. "And that's the problem."

"You're making me feel bad."

"You've got nothing to feel bad about, Gia. You're not my lawyer. You didn't do anything wrong."

"Nor did you. I'm a consenting adult . . . I wanted this . . . egged you on."

"You mean seduced me? Nah, I seduced you. I've been flirting and kissing and touching you for weeks. . . . I lost control. I'm an ass-hole."

"No, you're not." She got down from the vanity. "You're a good attorney. You can't help it if I'm a siren."

His lips curved up in a wry smile. "You are that. But this is my fault and I think I should find you another lawyer."

"No way." That scared her. With his federal law enforcement

background, no one had better experience to represent her than Flynn.

"Then we can't continue to sleep together," he said without much conviction.

"I think that ship has sailed and so do you." Even this soon after, she wanted him again.

"Come out of the bathroom."

She followed him. The powder room was small to begin with, but Flynn made it feel minuscule. He led her into the great room, where he made sure to sit in one of the over-stuffed chairs instead of on the couch with her. It stung. She wanted to cuddle with him.

"This wasn't supposed to happen, not while . . . ah jeez, I sound like a broken record." He sat there for a while, not saying anything, and Gia was sure he was berating himself. Then he rose. "It's late and we should go to sleep."

She looked at him, hopeful he meant together. But he headed for the stairs. "Good night."

He suddenly turned around and kissed her lightly on the lips. "We'll talk about this tomorrow, okay?"

But the next morning he was gone before she even woke up. Gia consoled herself by eating the ice cream they'd never gotten around to having for breakfast.

Chapter 18

Flynn needed distance to think so he drove to Quincy to have breakfast with his brother. Later he'd touch base with Toad and Bellamy. See what more they'd found. Knowing Gia, plenty.

As he drove, snippets of the night before flashed in his head. He couldn't call sex with Gia a mistake because it had been the best he'd ever had. But it complicated things. He wouldn't lose his license over it. Believe it or not, in California a lawyer could sleep with his client as long as he wasn't making sex a condition of representation or exploiting her, like seducing someone despondent over a bad divorce. Still, it was frowned upon, as it should be.

The big problem was, he wanted to continue sleeping with her and she'd made it clear she'd be up for it. But sex made you lose objectivity and he couldn't afford to do that where Gia was concerned. Too much at stake.

Flynn turned left onto Crescent Street and made another left on Main, parked by the natural food store, and walked the block to the coffee shop. In recent years a few trendy cafés and hair salons had sprouted up, but downtown was mainly a mish mash of utilitarian stores housed in historic buildings, some left over from the Gold Rush.

At the coffee shop Wes had secured their usual booth and Flynn hung his hat next to his brother's on the coatrack near the cash register.

"Wes is waiting for you, hon." Flossie, the owner, handed him a menu. Silly, because he'd been ordering the same thing since he was ten years old: chicken fried steak with gravy, eggs sunny-side up, country fried potatoes, and a biscuit.

Flynn walked through the restaurant to the table. Wes stood and slapped him on the back, which evolved into a guy hug. They were about the same height and used to be the same size, but married life had added a few inches to Wes's waistline.

"How you doin'?" Wes sat back down.

"Good." Flynn scooted into the booth, across from his brother.

"You're spending a lot of time in Nugget these days. Mom says the new Rosser Ranch owner has captured your attention." He raised his brows. "That true?"

Why lie? Flynn huffed out a breath. "Yeah, but it's complicated."

"It always is." His brother grinned. "Mom says she's the TV lady whose boyfriend stole all that money."

"Yep. I'm her lawyer."

Wes whistled. "So you can't talk about it, huh?"

"Not about the investigation." The waitress came with coffee and he and Wes put in their orders. "How're Jo and the kids?"

"Great. Whitley asked me to hit you up for Girl Scout cookies."

"Put me down for a dozen boxes. I'll bring them to the office."

"So tell me about the TV lady without giving away the legal stuff." Wes poured cream into his coffee and took a sip.

"She's gorgeous, funny, and smart." Except when she did stupid things like send money to the victims of her ex's investment fraud. "She has a horse named Rory and rides with an English saddle."

"No kidding." Wes leaned across the table. "You two . . . intimate?" They both laughed because Wes had phrased the question so delicately. Not his usual style.

As of yesterday, "Yeah."

"Is it serious?"

"Nah."

"Jeez, Flynn, how much longer you gonna play the field? What's wrong with this one?"

Besides her legal problems . . . "She doesn't believe in marriage."

I don't want to share a bank account with another person. I don't want to make financial decisions by committee. And I don't want to be dependent on someone else.

"From what I can tell, neither do you, little brother."

Wes was wrong. Flynn did believe in marriage . . . when the time and person were right.

Their food came and Wes stopped talking long enough to smother his pancakes in butter and syrup before shoveling a forkful into his mouth.

"Don't listen to that bullshit," he said between bites. "If you want to marry her, marry her."

"I just met her, Wes. Besides, what do you want me to do: hog-tie her and bring her before the county clerk?"

Wes chuckled and continued to plow through his food. "I guess you've lost your touch with the ladies. The old Flynn would've had her begging for your hand."

Flynn rolled his eyes. "Can we talk about this bull you want to buy?"

"Want to change the subject, do ya?" Wes laughed some more. The idiot was enjoying himself. "You've canceled on me so many times I forgot about the goddamned bull. But yeah, let's get it out of the way so I can continue giving you shit."

"If we don't buy that gooseneck stock trailer you want we can afford the bull."

"I want both," Wes said. "Can't we do away with something else? That old trailer we have won't make it another season. And the bull has great lines."

Flynn fidgeted with a packet of sweetener on the table. He knew their old stock trailer was in bad shape. "What do you propose we do?"

Wes owned a successful construction company; he was a good businessman. Yet somehow Flynn had been put in charge of the finances for the ranch.

"We take out a short-term loan. Beef prices are good this year."

Flynn hated borrowing against the ranch, but in this case Wes was right. Not a lot of risk involved. They were talking about a relatively small dollar amount. And they'd make a killing when they took their calves to market.

"Okay," he said. "You want me to handle the loan or do you plan to do it?"

"I'll put Jo on it." Wes's wife was the bookkeeper for both the ranch and the construction company. His brother waggled his brows. "Looks like you've got your hands full with your TV lady."

Flynn shook his head. To keep Wes from starting up again, he said, "Annie Sparks is working for Gia. She's planting Christmas trees on Rosser Ranch and is gonna live there over the summer to oversee the project. She broke up with the douchebag."

"No kidding. For good this time?"

"I think so. She's been staying at the ranch on weekends until school gets out. No sign of Zeke."

"I hope she's finally rid of that little pissant. Remember that time we nearly kicked his ass?"

They'd gone to one of his lousy shows because Annie had asked them to. Zeke had gotten shit-faced on stage, swilling beer like a frat-boy pledge. After the gig ended he'd elected himself designated driver. When Flynn stepped in the kid got belligerent. Then Wes rushed to the rescue and fists starting flying, Zeke throwing the first one. He missed Wes altogether and slammed his knuckles into a wall. Annie freaked out, grabbed Zeke's keys, and slid behind the wheel.

"Yep. If it hadn't been for Annie, we would've left him sprawled facedown in the parking lot."

"What's going on with Chad?" Wes asked. "He still robbing the Sparkses' farm blind?"

Flynn couldn't get into it, though most people in California's tight-knit agricultural community knew about the Chad problem. "Can't talk about it."

"What can you talk about these days?"

"I'm bringing Gia to Sunday dinner." Flynn mopped his biscuit in the leftover gravy.

Wes's face lit with amusement. "Gia, the one who doesn't want to marry you?"

"I didn't say she didn't want to marry me specifically. She doesn't want to marry period."

"I've gotta meet this woman." Wes grinned like a loon. "Mom seems to think she's the second coming of Christ."

"Mom likes her books . . . liked her show."

"I can't wait to tell Jo. She's got a couple of friends she's been wanting to set you up with. Looks like you're off the hook."

They finished their breakfasts, talked more about the cattle, paid their bill, and went their separate ways. Wes had a couple of big residential jobs and was anxious to check on the work. This time of year he made hay while the sun shone because winters could be slow. Between the construction and the cattle, he'd made a good life for himself. Beautiful family and a big house with a swimming pool. The older Flynn got the more Wes's life appealed to him. Someday, he told himself.

He walked back to his truck and called Toad.

"You got anything?"

"I found the ex," Toad said.

"Cleo's ex?"

"Yep. She's living in Florida . . . Miami. What do you say I go out there? Angry exes often have loose lips."

Flynn thought about it. They'd been going through the divorce when Cleo got shot. Because she was still technically Cleo's wife, she stood to do well financially from his death after probate. So he didn't know how chatty she'd be. But he supposed it was worth a shot.

"Yeah, go ahead," he told Toad. "See if you can work your magic." He got off the phone and backed out of his parking space.

He was heading up Main to catch the highway back to Nugget when a florist he'd never seen before caught his eye. Must be new, he thought as he snagged an empty parking space right in front. He didn't know what the hell possessed him to go inside, but twenty minutes later he walked out with a huge arrangement and his wallet a hundred bucks lighter.

Damn, flowers were expensive.

Gia got off the phone with her mother when the doorbell rang. She hadn't heard an accompanying car—then again, the security gate was closed. But she wasn't expecting anyone. On the way to check the peephole, she made sure to avoid windows, which proved difficult in a house full of them. She didn't want to have to deal with a reporter.

But it was Maddy Shepard, the chief's wife.

"Hi. I hope I haven't come at a bad time," she said when Gia opened the door.

"Not at all. Come in. You want coffee or a soft drink?"

"Coffee would be lovely if you have it made. I don't want to put you to any trouble."

"I've got a pot on." Gia led her to the kitchen and fixed her a mug. "Cream? Sugar?"

"Cream, please. Thank you."

Gia got a carton of half and half out of the refrigerator, curious about the impromptu visit. She'd stayed at Maddy's inn a few times while property hunting and had had the misfortune of being there the day the arsonist had torched the place. Other than those few interactions, she and Maddy hardly knew each other.

Gia pulled out one of the barstools. "You want to sit in here or would you be more comfortable in the great room?"

"This is fine. I didn't have a chance to tell you before what a gorgeous house you have. I'd never been inside when the Rossers lived here."

"Thank you," Gia said, though she couldn't take credit for anything about the home. She'd kept it exactly the way it was, with the exception of putting up a few photographs and knickknacks on the shelves.

Maddy scanned the kitchen and craned her neck a little to peek into the breakfast room.

"Would you like to see the rest of the house?" Gia couldn't remember whether she'd made her bed; she'd rushed out early, hoping to have coffee with Flynn. Of course he'd taken off before they could discuss what had happened the previous night.

Coward.

"I'd love to," Maddy said, obviously dying to get a look at the place.

Gia told her to bring her coffee and gave her the grand tour, starting first on the main level. There was a bottom floor—Ray Rosser's man cave—with a pool table, wet bar, and ginormous flat-screen. It also had a gym and an office. Gia used the library on the main floor for her day trading and rarely went downstairs. If she ever entertained, though, the basement would be perfect.

"It's a bit much for one person." Gia laughed. The locals must think she was crazy for buying a place this big.

"Were you thinking of your program when you purchased it?"

"Yep." She let out a sigh. "It has the bunkhouses and the foreman's home, which is perfect. And of course this house." Gia took Maddy to the third floor, which had five bedrooms. "See what I mean?"

Maddy nodded. "That's what I came over to talk to you about. I felt like we left the meeting on a bad note. When my brother and I bought the Lumber Baron to turn it into an inn, the reception was even worse. It got so nasty that many of the town's business owners hung anti-inn banners on their buildings. So I identify with what you're going through and don't want to be like the residents who did that to me."

"But you're still against the program?" Gia didn't mean to sound defensive, but Maddy hadn't spoken up at the meeting.

"The truth is I like the idea. Very much. But—"

"You don't want to contradict your husband."

Maddy smiled. "No, I don't want to publicly contradict the police chief. My husband I can handle."

It was Gia's turn to smile, realizing Maddy was on her side but there were politics involved.

"As far as the police chief... I'm working on him in private," Maddy said. "But if you want this to happen you'll have to significantly change your proposal."

Gia bristled. "What do you mean change it?"

"First off, you should call your program a school rather than making it sound like a halfway house." Maddy held up her hands to stop Gia from interrupting. "I know that sounds awful... snobby, judgmental, like nimbyism.... But do you want to fight or do you want to win? The second thing you could do is appoint a board of respected Nugget residents to help select the candidates for your school." Maddy emphasized the word "school." "These are just suggestions. Ignore them if you want."

"I don't have an aversion to calling it a school. But it would complicate things because I'd have to get special licenses from the state."

"Then call it a camp or a retreat, something that doesn't sound like a homeless shelter to men who make worst-case assumptions. You know what I mean?"

Like your husband. Gia read her loud and clear. "Okay, I'll rework the branding. And I don't have a problem with appointing a board to help with the selection process. You think that will work?"

"I'm going to be one hundred percent honest with you, Gia. Rhys and Clay are hard sells and both hold a lot of sway around here. Right now, their votes are unequivocal *no*s. But as hardheaded as they are, they can also be reasonable and have hearts as big as California. It's up to you to sell them on it. No easy feat, but certainly worth a try. Off the record, because this conversation never happened, we're all going to ask to meet again. At that point I would bring up these things we talked about."

They wandered back to the kitchen and Gia refilled Maddy's coffee. She got out a package of cookies, tried to artfully arrange them on a plate, and put them out for Maddy.

"Thank you for the advice . . . and for supporting my plan."

Maddy sat on one of the barstools and took a cookie. "I grew up fairly privileged and before I moved to Nugget . . . before Rhys . . . I was married to a Wellmont." If she was talking about the *Wellmonts,* they owned one of the largest hotel chains in the world. "It turned out my first husband was in love with someone else. . . . Well, that's another story for another day. The point I'm trying to make is that I'd signed a prenup that didn't give me much. I'd been out of the workforce for years and my confidence was crushed. I may not have been a single mother relying on food stamps, but I felt a certain kind of desperation. . . . Without my family I would've died for the kind of help you want to offer."

Gia forced herself to ask, "Do you think I'm in it for the publicity?"

"I don't really care why you're in it if it helps struggling women. I didn't realize it at first, but just living in this beautiful place helped me get over a very bad time in my life . . . and of course there was Rhys." Maddy got a dreamy, faraway look on her face.

"For the record, if I never saw another camera again it would be too soon."

Maddy reached her hand across the island and put it on top of Gia's. "I know it's been tough, but it's getting better, right?"

"Yes," Gia lied. No need to tell her that the case had become even more complicated.

"It's none of my business, but it seems like you and Flynn are forming an attachment."

Yeah, she'd become attached to Flynn. More than any man she'd ever been with. No longer did she just look forward to seeing him; she counted the days, the hours, and the minutes until his truck pulled into the driveway. And when she was with him, time ceased to exist. There was just the two of them—and so much chemistry it was explosive.

But Flynn was the kind of man who had to be in charge. And Gia wasn't the kind of woman who would allow a man to rule her. Not like her mother had. The only person driving Gia's course would be her.

"We're becoming good friends," she told Maddy.

Maddy smiled in that way that said, *sure you are*. She drained the last of her coffee, took the cup to the sink, and washed it out.

"Thanks for the caffeine and the tour." Maddy pulled the straps of her purse over her shoulder. "I've gotta get to the inn, but I'm glad we could talk."

"Me too. And thanks again."

"Remember," Maddy said, "we never had this conversation."

"Got it." Gia went outside and watched Maddy cut across the field to take the shortcut through Clay's property.

She started to go back inside when Flynn's truck came up the road, whipping up dust as well as her pulse. A smile opened in her chest at the sight of him. He pulled into his usual spot and got out of the truck holding an enormous floral arrangement.

"Who's that for?" she asked, leaning against the open doorway.

"Who do you think?"

"I haven't the foggiest notion." She flashed him a toothy grin and he all but rolled his eyes. "You left so early I figured you had to get home to your wife."

"Very funny." He handed her the arrangement. "They need water."

"Are these happy-sex flowers?" She took them to the kitchen and he followed.

"No, they're you've-bewitched-me flowers." He gave her a once-over. "Nice shorts." They were denim cutoffs, nothing special.

"Thank you . . . for the flowers." She tried to act nonchalant, but the gesture touched her.

Evan had showered her with expensive gifts. Hermès scarves, Tiffany jewelry, hard-to-get concert tickets. Even before she knew how he'd paid for them, the presents hadn't meant much. He'd always made a big deal about how expensive they were and very little about his feelings for her.

With Flynn there'd been a light that shone in his eyes when he'd handed her the bouquet. She wouldn't be so presumptuous as to call it love. But it felt like *something*. Something real.

"Where've you been?" she asked.

"Besides the florist?" He came up behind her as she filled the vase from the tap. "I had breakfast with my brother. We had cattle business to discuss."

"Oh?" She turned around and he pinned her to the counter, his lips so close she thought he would kiss her.

"We need to talk about . . ." He waved his hand between them. "You know what I mean."

"About last night?" She couldn't think with him so close so she ducked under one of his arms and went inside the great room.

"Gia, don't run away when I'm trying to have a conversation with you." He went after her.

"You mean like you did this morning?"

He rubbed his hand down his face, removed his hat, and laid it upside down on the side table before sitting next to her. "I figured we both could use a little space."

"By my count we had eight hours of space while we slept in separate rooms."

Flynn grinned. "That's because I lose myself when I'm around you."

"As you said, I'm bewitching." She kicked off her sandals and pulled her legs under her butt. "How's your brother?"

"Smug." When she shook her head in question, he said, "Never mind. Was that Maddy Shepard I saw leaving when I drove up?"

"Yep. She came over for a nice chat."

"About what?" He put his arm over the back of the couch.

"She had some ideas about how I might sell Rhys and Clay on my residential program."

"Like what?"

She snuggled next to him and outlined Maddy's suggestions. "It's still a long shot because Rhys and Clay are adamantly against it."

"Having her on your side certainly can't hurt and I like the idea of appointing a board." He leaned closer and Gia could see the circles under his eyes. "Besides plotting against the police chief what else did you do today? Nothing you shouldn't have, I hope."

"I didn't even trade." She'd been too anxious over the aftermath of their lovemaking. Then Maddy had called.

He let out a loud yawn, confirming her theory.

"Bad night?" Gia asked, hiding a grin. Served him right for pushing her away like that.

"What do you think?" he growled into her ear. "I'm gonna take a nap."

He got off the couch and before she knew it scooped her up.

"What are you doing?"

"Taking you with me. My room or yours?"

"Mine." It was closer and she was heavy, though Flynn didn't seem to think so. He carried her like she weighed less than a sack of Styrofoam packing peanuts.

When they got to where they were going he unceremoniously dumped her in the middle of the bed, pried off his boots, and climbed in next to her. He curled around her so that her back was pulled against his chest and they lay that way until she felt his breathing slow and heard soft snoring.

She closed her eyes and tried to sleep, but Flynn's warm, hard body proved to be too much of a distraction. His arms and legs cocooned her protectively and his scent—fresh laundry, green grass, and something distinctly Flynn—soothed her senses. Everything about him felt safe and solid—and arousing. She flipped onto her side so she could watch him sleep.

"Quit squirming," he said in a sleepy tone that made his voice rumble.

"I'm just trying to get comfortable."

He tugged her so that her head lay on his chest. "Better?"

She could hear his heart beat. "I'm not really a day sleeper."

"Try this." He pulled her completely on top of him, which only made things worse. She could feel his erection pressing against her.

He gazed up at her, heat in his eyes, and with the agility of a cat rolled her under him. Balancing his weight on his elbows, Flynn brushed his lips over hers. The kiss was feather-soft and her heart dipped. She caged his face in her hands and kissed him again until they were both out of breath. Mouths and tongues dancing to a wild rhythm only they could hear.

"Flynn?" She forced him down on top of her.

"I'll crush you." He rolled them both to their sides and continued to kiss her.

Gia pushed up his Henley. She wanted it off, wanted to feel his skin against hers. Flynn whipped it over his head and she took in a breath at the sight of him. His torso rippled with muscle. Apparently lifting hay bales and wrestling calves was better than any gym. Dark hairs sprinkled his chest and wended down into a happy trail that disappeared inside his pants.

His arms, all muscular and veiny, banded around her, and he whispered, "Take off your top."

She wiggled out of his grip, sat up, and tugged off her T-shirt, leaving her in nothing but a see-through bra and shorts. He hummed his appreciation, pulled her back down, and fondled her breasts, playing with her nipples until they puckered pink and proud through the diaphanous lace. His tongue lazily swirled over each one, wetting the fabric until it molded to her.

"I thought we weren't doing this again." She closed her eyes while the pleasure of his warm mouth ripped through her.

"The road to hell is paved with good intentions," he muttered. "You want to stop?"

"God no."

Flynn lifted his head and her immediate reaction was to pull him back down so he could continue his slow torture.

"Seriously," he said, "do you feel like you have to do this in exchange for my representation?"

She stared at him, hardly believing his words, then bolted upright. "What the hell are you talking about?"

"According to the state bar, I can't require or demand sexual relations with a client as a condition of representation; employ coercion, intimidation, or undue influence in entering into sexual relations with a client; or continue representation of a client with whom I'm having sexual relations with if it causes me to perform legal services incompetently."

"For Christ's sake, Flynn, you're actually reciting the rules to me while I'm half naked? Way to be a buzzkill. I'm paying you cash for your legal services, not sex. And the fact that you even had to ask is insulting. No one could ever coerce or intimidate me into doing anything I didn't want to. So I guess the last question is in your court. Will us sleeping together cause you to be a lousy lawyer?"

After all that, Flynn actually had the audacity to flash a wolfish grin and flick open the front catch of her bra, drag down the straps, and let the whole thing slither off her. "That answer your question?" He pushed her back down on the bed and straddled her.

She ran her hands down his chest, went to work on his belt, and felt him suck in a breath. This time she got the buckle undone all by herself and tore open his fly, one button at a time. He pushed the pants over his very fine ass, down his legs, and kicked them away. And everything coalesced in the pit of her stomach. Lust, overwhelming attraction, and something she wouldn't identify. She knew what it was and willed it away, choosing to focus solely on her hunger for him. It was easier that way.

He unzipped her shorts and drew them down, making her lift up so he could get them all the way off.

"These are nice." Flynn dipped one finger inside her panties, see-through just like the bra, and rimmed the elastic band. "But they've got to go," he said, yanking them off so that she lay there completely open to him.

"No fair; you still have yours on."

He quickly dispensed with his shorts, his impressive erection jutting through a thatch of dark hair, eager and raring to go. The man made her mouth water and her body quiver. Soon his hands, lips, and tongue were everywhere. Touching, laving, and licking. She moaned and let out sounds she didn't know she was capable of making. Thank goodness the nearest neighbor was a right distance away.

He left her for a second, leaning over the side of the bed, searching through his jeans. She clawed his back, urging him to return, her body craving his like an addiction. He stumbled up, clutching a foil package, which he tore open with his teeth, removed a condom, and rolled it down his length. Spreading her legs, he touched her center, first with his fingers, then with his mouth.

"Flynn . . . oh God . . . so good." She came in a rush, screaming his name.

The next thing she knew he was inside her, filling her to the brink, moving in and out . . . making it feel so good. Unlike the last time, he went slowly, savoring every thrust and touch. With the sunlight glinting through the spaces in the drapes, they met each other stroke for stroke. He dropped tiny kisses on her face, her throat, and her shoulders, whispering words that would have otherwise been nonsensical but made perfect sense to her. And in that hour, joined together like a perfect merger, they lost themselves. Near the end, before both of them climaxed, he looked down at her and she could've sworn she saw his heart in his eyes. It made her tear up as she arched into him, reaching the final pinnacle before crashing down. He followed with a racking shudder while he called out her name. They lay there for a few seconds, panting.

Sprawled on top of her, he wiped her cheek with his hand. "You okay?"

"Of course." She tried to move away.

"Hey, hey." He flipped her over, got rid of the condom, and tightened his arms around her. "Where you going?"

She couldn't help it and cuddled into his chest, tucking her head under his chin. "Nowhere."

"Good." He glanced at the clock on her nightstand. "What do you say we crash for a little while? Then I should check the cattle."

"Okay," she said.

He closed his eyes and she spent the next hour watching the best man she'd ever known sleep.

Chapter 19

Clay was almost to town when his phone rang. The touch control on his dashboard lit up with his home number.

"What's up?" he asked.

"Where are you?" It was Emily and she didn't sound right.

They'd been fighting all morning and he'd left in a huff, which was wrong because Emily deserved his understanding. Intellectually he knew that, but his heart felt like it had been rolled over by a semi-truck.

She didn't want their baby.

"Where are you?"

"Just passed Grizzly Heights. Why?"

"Can you come home?"

He pulled over to the side of the road. "What's wrong?"

"I'm bleeding." There was silence and then she said, "It's not a lot, but maybe I should go to the clinic in Glory Junction." Emily's gynecologist saw patients there a couple of days a week.

"Is Dr. Davis even in today?" He was thinking they should go to the emergency room in Quincy instead and hung a U-turn to head back to the ranch.

"She's there; I just called."

"Are you in pain?"

"I'm cramping." She sounded tense, but he wasn't sure if it was the situation or whether she was still angry with him.

"I'm on my way. Did the doctor say there's anything you can do in the meantime?"

"There's nothing," she said.

"Stay calm and I'll be right there." They disconnected and he took the road faster than he should've.

By the time he pulled up to the front of the house, Emily was waiting. He got out and helped her into the passenger side.

"You still hurting?"

"A little bit." Her face was pale and her lips were thin.

He belted her in and kissed her forehead, which felt clammy. "I'll get you there as fast as possible."

She nodded and stared out the side window.

"Em, baby, I'm sorry we fought." God, maybe he'd caused this. He'd yelled . . . and Christ.

"Before Hope I had a miscarriage," she said without looking at him. This was the first time she'd told him that and it seemed like something a wife should share with her husband, even if it happened before he'd come into the picture.

"Was it like this?" he asked.

"This is the way it started, but there was more bleeding."

He wondered if losing the baby would be a relief to her and he felt his heart crack again. They didn't talk for the rest of the drive and when they got to the clinic a nurse ushered Emily back into a room. No one asked him if he wanted to stay with his wife so he sat in the waiting room and tried to read a magazine. He didn't know which one it was, just picked up the first magazine he found on the table and thumbed through the pages.

"You think I can go back there?" he asked the woman at the counter. Ordinarily he wasn't so deferential. After years as a naval officer he was pretty good at being in command, but he wasn't himself.

"Let me go ask," the young woman said and smiled at him like he was a doting husband.

Doting? He'd been a dick. Putting the magazine down, he got up and paced, stopping every now and again to read the posters on the wall. Anything to keep busy. The receptionist took forever to return. Then again, everything seemed to be moving in slow motion. Finally she strolled back and escorted him to the room.

Emily was on an examination table with one of those paper sheets covering her from the waist down.

"Hey." He tried for a smile. "Thought you could use some company."

Emily gave a halfhearted nod. Clay noticed that her eyes were watery.

"The doctor is going to do an ultrasound to see if she can hear a heartbeat. She went to get something." Emily told him to pull up a chair.

He dragged one across the room, sat at the head of the examination table, and held her hand. "What did she say about the bleeding?"

"That it's not a good sign." Emily's voice was so soft he had to strain to hear her.

Not a good sign.

He felt his chest move into his throat. Emily was having a miscarriage.

The doctor entered in a lab coat, greeted Clay, and washed her hands. "Emily may have already explained, but I'm about to do a transvaginal scan to see if we can find a heartbeat. Unfortunately, it can be difficult in early pregnancy, but we'll try and see what we can find." She put on her best reassuring smile.

A million questions swam through Clay's head, including: *What if you don't find one?* But he figured they'd cross that bridge if and when they got there. It was better to let the doctor get on with the ultrasound.

He'd been in-country when Jennifer had been pregnant with Justin and Cody and watched in fascination as the doctor prepared for the procedure.

"Can this hurt the baby?" he asked as the doctor placed Emily's feet into a pair of metal stirrups and inserted a probe inside her.

"It's quite safe. But a lot of people ask that question." She moved the probe around while she watched a TV monitor.

What she was doing looked horribly uncomfortable to Clay, who turned to Emily. "You okay?"

She squeezed his hand. "I'm fine."

"There it is. See?" Dr. Davis pointed to the screen, which displayed something that looked like a NASA shot of the moon. Nothing remotely distinguishable. "That's Emily's uterus and right there is the fetal pole."

"The baby?" Clay's hopes soared.

"To be precise, it's the thickening on the margin of the yolk sac of the fetus," she said.

"Is there a heartbeat?" Emily leaned up so she could see the monitor better.

"It's there," the doctor said. "But it's very slow."

"Which means the baby's alive, right?" Clay moved toward Emily, feeling more optimistic than he had a few minutes ago.

Emily's face turned white and he immediately stepped away from her, angry. How could she not want this child to survive?

"Emily, would you like to dress? Then we can talk."

She nodded and the doctor left the two of them alone. Emily got off the table, found her underwear and jeans, and put them on. There were so many things Clay wanted to say to his wife, but he held his tongue. Now was not the time or the place.

A short time later there was a knock and the doctor came in. "Is the cramping a little better?"

"Yes. But when I was getting dressed there was more blood."

"More than likely there was already blood in the vagina and the probe dislodged it." The doctor indicated they should all sit. "But we're not out of the woods. I'm concerned about the heartbeat being too faint, and the fetal pole was too small for me to take an accurate measurement."

"This is what happened last time I miscarried," Emily said, and for the first time Clay noticed she was crying. Maybe he'd misread her reaction. He stood up and put his arm around her.

"But the baby is alive?" he asked the doctor.

"For now, but this may not be a viable pregnancy. I'm going to ask that Emily come back in a few days and we'll take another scan. We should know better then."

"Is there something we can do in the meantime?" Clay thought with all the innovations of modern medicine there had to be something.

Dr. Davis shook her head with a sad smile. "Unfortunately not. It's up to nature now."

"What about a prescription for the cramping?" He didn't want his wife to be in pain.

"If it is a viable pregnancy Emily shouldn't take any drugs. Some doctors say Tylenol is okay, but I would discourage it in the first trimester. I do, however, encourage massages." She directed that at Clay. "A nice walk can sometimes help, as can a warm bath or shower, and drink plenty of water. I know this is stressful, but the best thing you can do for the baby is try to relax . . . stay calm. Karen will schedule you for the next scan, but if you need me before that don't hesitate to call."

They made the appointment and walked across the parking lot to the truck. They got in and just sat, absorbing everything the doctor had said. Neither one of them seemed to know what to say.

To break the silence, Clay asked if Emily wanted to go to lunch. He wasn't hungry, but it was past noon and Emily should eat. She'd barely had anything for breakfast.

"Sure," she said, but she seemed far away.

He started the engine and drove to the downtown area. Glory Junction was only thirty minutes away from Nugget, but it seemed like a different world. The ski resorts brought in tons of tourists. As a result, the town was filled with boutiques, hotels, and restaurants. Though it was spring and they hadn't had a good snow since February, the main street was still jammed with parked cars. People came to ride the river rapids, boat in the lake, climb the rocky mountains, and bike world-class trails. It had become a mecca for athletes and adventurers and home to several Olympic medalists.

"You in the mood for anything in particular?" He gently rested his hand on Emily's leg.

"Whatever you want I'm good with."

He wanted something quiet and the Morning Glory Diner was decent enough. The Ponderosa cook's parents used to own it once upon a time. Clay didn't know who ran the place now. After a couple of circles he found an empty parking space not far from the restaurant.

"The town's gotten as bad as San Francisco," he muttered.

"Not quite." Emily chuckled.

It was good to hear her laugh. He loved her so much that it stole his breath. Sometimes he found himself making up excuses not to check fences, ride the range, or the myriad other tasks of a rancher so he could stay home with her, watch her cook, and generally bask in her sunshine.

They'd both found each other after personal tragedy—though hers was unimaginable—and rebuilt their lives together. But the hole Hope's disappearance had left in Emily's heart could never be filled. As a father whose sons were his everything, no one understood that better than he did. But they had to keep moving forward. Despite the difficult days—holidays and the anniversary of Hope's abduction—their lives were filled with joy. Of course they could never replace Emily's daughter, or stop hoping that someday they'd find her, but he'd always expected he and Emily would have children together.

Come to find out, the belief had been one-sided.

"What are you thinking about?" Emily asked, pulling him from his thoughts.

"That whatever happens we'll get through it."

On Flynn's way to the stable he found Annie sitting on the split-rail fence staring off into the distance. She had on one of her weird outfits again. A gingham dress, matching kerchief, and combat boots. *Hey, let your freak flag fly,* he always said.

She twisted around and waved to him.

"You up for the rest of the week?"

"I'm up for the rest of the summer." She smiled so brightly Flynn needed sunglasses.

"School's out already?"

"It's pretty flexible for doctorate students so I got out a little early."

He joined her at the fence, leaned his arms on the top railing, and gazed out to see what was so fascinating. "What you doin'?"

"Just checking it out. It's so beautiful here."

"That it is." The sight of the Sierra never stopped holding him spellbound. "Nothing quite like it."

"You're getting a late start."

"I spent the morning in Quincy with Wes." Not a complete lie.

"Funny, your truck's been here most of the day." She'd caught him.

Flynn took off his hat and slapped her playfully with it. "Mind your own business, kid."

"Hey, what happens at Rosser Ranch stays at Rosser Ranch. I'm going over to Tawny's boot studio; wanna come?"

"Nah, I've got work to do."

"I bet you do." She flashed a sly little smile. "How's Wes?"

"He's good. We're talking about getting a new breeding bull."

"That'll set you back." Annie was a farmer through and through, but she knew her ranching too.

"Yes, it will."

"How's the fence coming? Hint, hint." She'd been bugging him about enclosing the area for the tree farm ever since Annie and Gia had picked out the spot.

"As soon as you get that field plowed, I've got a couple of ranch hands from Quincy who'll come up to help me."

"We're tilling Friday. It'll take me a week to prepare the soil, then I'm planting." She whirled her hand through the air like she was lassoing a steer. "Woot! Woot!"

Crazy girl. But he liked her enthusiasm, always had.

"You talk to your parents?" he asked, knowing it was a touchy subject.

She stared down at her feet. "These days as little as possible."

"Annie—"

"I talk to them. But it's hard, Flynn. . . . They're just so flipp'n blind where Chad's concerned. We end up fighting and frankly, I'm tired of it. It's their farm. They can do whatever they want with it."

"Hang in there, kid." He squeezed the back of her neck. "Living here for the summer will be a good break for you." From Chad, from Zeke, and from her naïve but good-hearted parents.

"I think so too. It's so generous of Gia. The guest apartment is great and she said I can use the pool whenever I want. I'm living the life."

Flynn's mouth quirked.

"I like her for you, Flynn. I know people are suspicious of her, but Gia is too good a person to have stolen all that money. The program she wants to start . . . it's not what Clay McCreedy said. It's personal, Flynn, not a ploy to get good PR."

"Yeah, I know."

"The way she talks about it . . . there's passion there. It's like the way I feel about planting things. Helping these women is a calling for her. She understands their frustrations and pain."

At the risk of putting herself on the line. Flynn hoped that sending members of the carpenters' guild cash didn't bite Gia in the ass.

"You think the neighbors have the power to stop the program?" Annie asked.

"I don't know. I'm checking into it, but they might." Flynn still meant to have that talk with Clay. Perhaps he'd pay McCreedy Ranch a visit later. He didn't think he could sway Clay, but he wanted to make it clear that he hadn't appreciated the way he'd gotten in Gia's face.

"That's too bad because the program could be a wonderful thing. Plus, I could use the help with the farm."

"We'll see. Gia doesn't strike me as the type to give up without a fight," Flynn said, knowing she never would've made it on Wall

Street or in broadcast news without plenty of determination and moxie.

Annie hopped down from the fence and smoothed the wrinkles from her dress. "I'm gonna head over to Tawny's now. Sure you don't want to come?"

Flynn eyed his boots. "These'll do me fine. . . . Tawny's boots ain't cheap."

"I heard she has seconds."

Those weren't cheap either, but he'd let Annie discover that for herself. "Have a good time."

Flynn watched Annie cross the field and duck under the fence, then he headed for the stable to saddle up and make afternoon rounds. He was getting a late start. It was a wonder he was getting any work done at all. If Gia hadn't gone to town to do wedding stuff with Dana he might still be in her bed.

After she'd left he'd used a good part of the day to touch base with the office, answer emails, and return calls. This evening he was meeting with Donna and Trevor about their living trust.

Dude nickered as he entered the barn. The boy needed exercise. Flynn got him ready for a long, hard ride. Once they were far enough away from the barn he gave the horse his head, loping a good distance before climbing the hills to search for strays. The day was so clear, he could see all the way to Nevada.

He rode for much of the afternoon, checking the herd and testing fences. A calf had gotten separated from its mother and Flynn helped reunite them. No sign of cougars or coyotes, sometimes a problem up in these hills. Worse for sheep and goats. The calves were big enough to fend for themselves.

On his way back he stopped to examine some of Gia's outbuildings to see if the bunkhouses and single-family dwellings were habitable for her program. The foreman's house was overgrown with brambles. Between Rosser's arrest and the property sitting vacant until Gia moved in, upkeep had fallen by the wayside. When the men came up to build the fence for the Christmas tree farm he'd have them clear the foliage away from the cottage and see what needed to be done on the other buildings. At least they were winterized. Up here in the mountains, where temperatures could drop to single digits, that was half the battle.

He crisscrossed the property, deciding to take a detour to Clay's.

The dogs greeted him with their usual exuberance. The boys were outside doing chores and called the pups away.

"School just get out?" Flynn had lost track of the time.

"About two hours ago," Cody said.

"Your dad home?"

"He's in the house." Justin was having a growth spurt. Every time Flynn saw him he got taller and his shoulders got wider. The boy was a carbon copy of his old man. "You want me to get him?"

"Nah." Flynn jumped down from Dude. "Would you mind tying him up for me?"

Justin grabbed the horse's reins and Flynn walked to the house and rang the doorbell. Clay came out in his stocking feet, looking like hell. Flynn wondered if he'd come down with something.

"You sick?"

"No. Emily isn't feeling well, though. You want to come in?"

"Nope, it's better out here because I came over to yell at you. What the hell's your problem, Clay? If you don't like Gia's proposal that's one thing. But why'd you have to talk to her like that?"

"Because she's being duplicitous . . . Christmas tree farm my ass. That's just a ruse for us to sign off on her publicity stunt. Jeez, Flynn, when did you start thinking with your dick?"

"If it weren't for the fact that we've been friends forever I'd punch you for that. It's not a ruse. Gia's planting the trees next week whether or not the proposal goes down. When the fuck did you become so disrespectful? She doesn't need your goddamn permission. As long as her plan adheres to code she's good to go. And because it's a farm she's allowed to have farmhands. If she was as duplicitous as you say, she would've lied . . . said they were employees. Instead, she was honest. So screw you, Clay. As her lawyer I'm gonna tell her to go right ahead with her plan."

Flynn turned to go, but a small voice called him back.

"Don't leave angry." Emily stood at the door, looking even worse than Clay. "Come inside. Let's talk about this like adults."

"Ah, hell, I didn't mean for you to hear that, Emily." Flynn felt like a heel.

"It's okay."

Clay blocked her. "You're sick, Emily. Flynn and I will work this out on our own."

She moved in front of Clay. "Come inside."

He followed her in because he didn't want to be disrespectful, not to Emily. She led them into the kitchen, poured them each a glass of lemonade, and put a tray of banana bread on the table.

"I just made that, so dig in while it's still warm," she said, Clay standing stiffly at her side. "Sit down, both of you."

She was just a bit of a thing, but she barked orders like a three-star general. Clay, who had been a naval officer, heeded her command. Flynn did likewise.

"This can't continue," she said, shaking her hand between the two of them. "You two grew up together, for goodness' sake. Clay would like to apologize to Gia. He was rude and that's not the kind of people we are." She pierced her husband with a glare. "But our ranch does neighbor hers and Clay has a right to have concerns. We would really like it, Flynn, if we could continue to have an open dialogue about Gia's proposal."

"She would like that as well." Flynn made eye contact with Clay and held it. "Before she did anything she hoped that you all would give her your blessing. But she's certainly under no obligation to get it."

"We realize that," Emily said. "And really appreciate that Gia went out of her way to discuss it with us. Clay has been under some stress lately." She held her husband's gaze. "Otherwise I know he never would've talked to her like that."

Clay remained cagey as a tiger but didn't contradict Emily.

Just to piss him off, Flynn stuck out his hand. "Truce?"

"Yeah, truce," Clay said begrudgingly.

Flynn grabbed a piece of banana bread for the road and rose. "I've got an appointment I need to get to. My understanding is that Gia will be calling you soon to have another meeting." He turned to Clay. "I do hope this one can be civil."

The sly sumbitch grinned, got up, and gathered Flynn in a bear hug. "You still want to punch me, don't you?"

Chapter 20

Gia felt more nervous than the first time she'd made it onto the floor of the New York Stock Exchange.

Flynn's family's ranch was less showy than hers but every bit as magnificent. The land, with its green rolling hills, took her breath away. And the white farmhouse, made from clapboard siding, complete with a wraparound porch, seemed as at home on the land as Flynn did.

There were dogs and kids on the front lawn when they got out of the truck and all of them tackled Flynn at once.

"Uncle Flynn, Uncle Flynn," one of the children shouted while the dogs barked and ran in circles, beside themselves with pleasure.

"This is my nephew, Case," Flynn said and put the boy in a half nelson.

A beautiful girl with long brown hair and big green eyes came toward them, staring warily at Gia. Kids weren't her thing. In fact, they scared her to death with their sticky fingers and temper tantrums. Flynn's niece and nephew looked too old for that, but still . . .

"This is Whitley," Flynn introduced the girl.

"Pleased to meet you both." Gia smiled at them while they ignored her to slaver over Flynn.

When Whitley finally let go of her uncle she turned to Gia. "Grandma said you used to be on TV." By the way Whitley gauged Gia's jeans and blouse she seemed unconvinced.

Flynn had said the dress code was country casual. What did the kid want, Badgley Mischka?

"Yep," she responded, not wanting to prolong the subject.

"Do you know Taylor Swift?"

"No. I wasn't really that kind of TV person. I was the host of a financial show."

"Oh." Whitley was clearly underwhelmed. "Do you, like, know anyone?"

Gia searched her brain for someone who would impress a four-teen-year-old and came up dry.

"Justin Bieber's her best friend." Flynn draped his arm around his niece's shoulders.

"Seriously?" Whitley suddenly looked at Gia like she might actually be worthy.

"No," Flynn said and her face fell. "We're going inside the house. You guys coming with?"

Case shook his head and stayed with the dogs. But Whitley tagged along, probably hoping Gia could get her tickets to a One Direction concert.

Flynn opened the screen door and ushered Gia in. Whitley ran ahead. The scent of food cooking made Gia's stomach growl. The TV was turned up to ear-piercing decibels and someone shouted to lower the volume. The foyer had white wainscoting and toile wall-paper. And the wall going up the staircase featured a gallery of family pictures.

"Are those all Barlows?" Gia started to examine the photos, but Flynn steered her the other way.

"Yep. I'll show them to you later. First, introductions." He tugged her into the living room where two men sat on recliners, watching a game. "Dad, Wes, this is Gia."

Both men put their beers down and stood up to give Gia a proper welcome. She could definitely see a family resemblance, though Flynn was the most handsome of the three. At least to Gia. Flynn's father, Ron, wasn't nearly as grizzled as described. He was in good shape for a man in his sixties, tall with no visible paunch—Flynn in twenty years. Wes smiled at her and she felt herself blush.

"You meet my better half yet?" he asked.

"Not yet," Flynn answered. "We're making the rounds. She did meet the kids, though. Whitley's got seriously bad taste in music. You ought to talk to her about that."

"Yeah, we're working on it," Wes said.

Gia gazed around the room. It wasn't fancy. The furniture was gently worn, the walls covered in framed photographs, and an upright piano sat in the corner. Gia wondered who played. Everything about the house said family, comfort, and warmth. Like a grandma's kiss.

Flynn moved her through the house, a labyrinth of rooms and hallways that held the same vibe as the living room, leaving her no time to explore. She wanted to examine the pictures of Flynn as a little boy, a high school student, and a young man. But he had a mission that ended in the kitchen. There, Patty, Whitley, and a woman she presumed was Wes's wife sat around a big weathered farm table snapping green beans.

"Welcome." Patty got to her feet and introduced her to Jo, Wes's wife. Whitley's resemblance to her mother was uncanny.

"Don't mind the mess," Jo said and hurriedly took off her apron.

Flynn helped himself to something on the stove. "Mmm, good."

"Stay out of that." His mother shooed him away. "There are snacks in the other room. Go join your dad and Wes. We'll keep Gia with us."

Flynn held her gaze, silently asking if she was okay with that plan. She nodded, though the idea of being left with Patty and Jo was a little intimidating. The women obviously wanted to interrogate her. Her mother would do the same thing with Flynn.

Jo pulled out a chair for her and pushed the bowl of string beans closer. Gia sat and watched, intrigued at how the other women snapped off the ends. It seemed easy enough and she tried one. Wow, it was addictive, like bubble wrap, so she snapped a few more. As the afternoon sun drenched the room with warmth and light, they continued breaking the beans into sections. Gia felt as if she'd been thrown back to an earlier time. It was relaxing yet purposeful at the same time.

"The green beans came in early this year," Patty said. "We usually don't get 'em until June."

Gia presumed Patty meant from the garden, which she'd only caught a sliver of on her way inside the house. "What else do you grow?"

"A little bit of everything. Would you like a tour?"

"Sure." Gia had always wanted a garden. In New York the most her terrace could accommodate was a few pots of geraniums.

Patty guided her out the back door to the most elaborate kitchen garden Gia had ever seen, though admittedly she hadn't toured many. But this one seemed so organized. It was completely fenced and divided into sections. One with raised boxes for vegetables and herbs, another large area for fruit trees, and a segment with rows of cutting flowers. A flagstone path wended its way through the various parts, each one designated with a vine-covered arbor and a wooden sign.

Here Flynn had grown up in domestic heaven while Gia was lucky if she could dice an onion, let alone grow one.

"This is really impressive," she told Patty. "Seriously, it looks like something out of *Sunset* magazine."

"Thank you," Patty beamed. "I'm very proud of it. Later, have Flynn show you the beehives."

They went back inside and resumed their places at the table. Patty got Gia a glass of iced tea while she put the final touches on dinner, including doing something that smelled wonderful with their snapped green beans.

"How are you liking Nugget?" Patty asked. "It must be very different from New York."

Very. "I like Nugget better, though I miss the shopping and the food."

"I've never been," Jo said. "Last summer it was between New York and Hawaii for our annual vacation. Hawaii won, though I'd like to go someday . . . maybe when the kids are a little older."

Patty handed Whitley a stack of plates and told her to set the table. Gia asked if she could help but was told that today she was strictly a guest.

"Flynn doesn't usually bring home female friends," Patty said, sounding inordinately pleased that he had. "Next time we'll put you to work, though."

Gia wasn't sure there would be a next time or what she and Flynn were to each other. Attorney-client with privileges, she laughed to herself but didn't think Dudley Do-Right would appreciate her particular brand of humor.

He came into the kitchen and her pulse quickened.

"We eating soon? I'm starved." He winked at her and a shot of warmth spread through her insides. Suddenly she was starved too—for Flynn.

"Five minutes," Patty told him. "Get your dad and your brother."

They assembled in the dining room, which had a big fireplace and a long antique table that sat at least twelve. The tablecloth was lace—Gia thought it could be an heirloom—and the centerpiece was a silver candelabra. She wondered if every Sunday dinner was like this.

Flynn pulled out a chair for Gia and sat in the one next to her. Throughout dinner he reached under the table and traced his hand down her leg. Each time a bolt of electricity arced through her veins. He also whispered in her ear. Nothing overtly sexual, usually things like "pass the potatoes, please," but his lips on the whorl of her ear made her dizzy. Thank goodness no one seemed to notice because he flirted with her the entire supper, even rubbing his foot under the hem of her jeans. It was everything she could do to keep up with the dinner conversation.

"What are you doing?" she asked once she'd gotten him alone.

His eyes heated and he said, "You make me lose control."

"Well, knock it off. It's bad enough I have a reputation as a white-collar criminal. You want your family to think I'm a hussy too?"

He threw back his head and laughed. "A hussy? No one thinks you're a hussy. Though Wes thinks you're hot. My dad said, and I quote, 'She looks like a lady with a good head on her shoulders.' And my mother is planning our wedding. I didn't have the heart to tell her that's never gonna happen."

"Nope." She felt a stabbing pain in her chest as she said it. But yeah, he was 100 percent correct. Marriage was out of the question, not that he'd asked.

Flynn finished giving her a tour of the house. She saw his old bedroom, which still held shelves of trophies, ribbons, and medals from his youth, a stack of yearbooks, and pictures of him riding in local rodeos.

He shut the door and kissed her so tenderly her knees buckled. His arms tightened around her and he whispered, "You want dessert?" He eyed the double bed and she pushed him away.

"Your mom's dessert. Let's go down before we do something we shouldn't."

After pie and homemade ice cream they said their goodbyes and headed to Nugget. Flynn needed to be in Sacramento in the morning. If not for her, he would've made the three-hour drive after dinner.

"I should've driven separately," she said.

"What, you don't want me staying the night?" He slid her a sideways glance while driving.

"I do, but I feel bad that you have to make that commute so early in the morning."

"I'm used to it." He put his arm around her and she lay her head on his shoulder.

She still didn't know what they were together, but today they'd felt like a couple. A real couple. And it definitely hadn't sucked.

But the warm fuzzy feeling flowing through her didn't last long. When they got to the gate at Rosser Ranch, four law enforcement cars blocked the entrance. Flynn stopped and a man in an FBI vest tapped on the window.

"Will the both of you please step out of the vehicle." It wasn't a request.

They complied as agents surrounded them. Rhys was there too. The FBI must've given him notice this time. He stood off to the side, looking as uncomfortable as Gia had ever seen him.

"What's this about?" Flynn asked.

The agent with the vest stepped forward. "We have a warrant for Miss Treadwell's arrest."

Chapter 21

Flynn hauled ass to Sacramento, breaking every speed limit on the highway. He wanted to get there as fast as possible to gather his team and work out the logistics of posting a bond for bail. There was no getting around the fact that Gia would have to be held overnight. Even if Flynn called in every favor owed to him, no way would they be able to get a federal magistrate on the bench on a Sunday night. Furthermore, she'd have to meet with pretrial services before a bail determination could be made and that would take time.

There was nothing he could do short of breaking her out. In his panicked state he'd even contemplated the possibility. Shit, how had this happened? Flynn felt like he'd been broadsided. As soon as he got to the office he planned to call Tim at home to rip him a new one. A heads-up would've been nice—as well as a professional courtesy. Flynn would've surrendered Gia to the court in the morning without all the drama. Then she wouldn't have had to spend one goddamn second behind bars.

But clearly the U.S. Attorney's office was going for shock and awe to make a big splash on CNN. And probably to scare the hell out of Gia so she'd talk. Gia didn't know squat, but the feds had other ideas. At least they'd let him confer with her before the agents had hauled her off like a common criminal.

Thank God they hadn't charged Gia with conspiracy to commit murder. Yet. But aiding and abetting a financial fraudster was bad enough, especially because a grand jury had already cleared her. There was no doubt in his mind that the alphabets—the FBI and the SEC—were getting desperate. Not only did they have thousands of investors screaming for their money back, they'd linked Laughlin to Cleo's murder. The brass was going to lose their jobs if an arrest wasn't made soon. Flynn hated to admit it because he believed in the system—most of the time—but that was where Gia came in.

Over his dead body. He'd move heaven and earth to get her out of this mess. And damn, when had he become such a staunch believer in Gia's innocence? He assumed it was sometime between her trying to turn her ranch into a residential program for indigent women and sending money to carpenters' union pensioners who'd been rooked by Laughlin. But he knew. He knew it in his head and in his heart and in his cumulative fifteen years of putting away and defending criminals.

Gia was no crook. He couldn't have fallen in love with her if she were.

And wasn't that a revelation . . . he was in love with Gia Treadwell. Damn. And right now his woman was sitting in a jail cell. Well, not exactly. At this very moment she was probably still en route to the holding facility, where she'd be booked.

He exited the interstate and tried Toad in Florida for the umpteenth time to no avail. By the time he got to his office building he was frustrated as hell. He took the elevator up and smelled coffee even before he opened the door. Doris, bless her heart. She'd agreed to come in when Flynn said he needed all hands on deck. Bellamy too. Flynn found both of them in the conference room.

"Thanks for making this a priority," he said. "Anyone heard from Toad?"

"No," they said in unison.

"I've gotta run to the jail, but here's what I want you to do." Flynn gave them lengthy instructions on the materials he needed gathered and told Bellamy to make provisions for bail.

"Add this to the mix." He handed Bellamy a handful of paperwork.

Bellamy eyed the documents and his mouth formed an "O." "You sure about this, Flynn?"

"Yep. I'll be back as soon as I can. If Toad calls tell him I'm firing his ass."

Flynn drove the short block to the jail instead of walking. By now Gia should've arrived with the dickhead agent who'd cuffed her. Hopefully she was almost done with booking. Weekends at the jail were usually pretty crowded with family and friends of inmates. Visiting hours went as late as eleven p.m. But tonight the lobby was nearly empty.

"Hey, Flynn," someone at the counter waved him over. "You here to see a client?"

"Yeah. She should've been booked by now. Treadwell, Gia." Flynn gave the deputy Gia's DOB.

"I don't need her date of birth; I know who she is. She's still being processed. Woo wee, you got yourself a high-profile one. The press will be here any minute."

I bet. Flynn could only imagine how quick the feds had dropped a dime once they had Gia in custody.

"Any chance you can get me in now?" Flynn asked.

"You know the rules; I can't until she's been processed."

Flynn turned on his pleading face.

The clerk looked over his shoulder and said, "Let me see where she's at" and disappeared through the back.

While waiting, Flynn checked his cell phone to see if there'd been any word from Toad. Still nothing. It wasn't like him to go MIA in an emergency like this. Flynn was starting to worry. He quickly called his office to see if they'd heard from him. Doris answered and said he hadn't checked in there either, which was baffling. Toad was many things but irresponsible wasn't one of them.

"All right. I won't have my phone for a while so if he calls tell him to hang tight." Flynn disconnected.

Ten minutes later the clerk reappeared, checked Flynn in, and took his cell.

"Someone will bring her in shortly," the deputy said and told him which floor to go to.

Flynn nodded. "Thanks. I owe you one."

"What do you want me to do about the media?"

Flynn searched through his wallet and handed the clerk a stack of his business cards. "Tell them Ms. Treadwell has been counseled by her attorney not to do any interviews and that all inquiries need to go through me."

Reporters would still try to get into the jail to see Gia. Through his years Flynn had handled a number of high-profile cases and knew well how it worked. At some point he would choose a few legitimate news outlets to rebut the crap the feds were doubtlessly spinning. He'd learned the game long ago as an FBI agent. The special agent in charge always had a few favorite reporters in his Rolodex and would feed them information to curry favor and to influence public opinion in a way that made the Bureau look good.

The clerk stashed the cards in his shirt pocket and Flynn caught the elevator. It opened to a small room separated by a plexiglass window. He took a seat and waited for Gia to arrive on the other side of the glass, where they would communicate by phone.

She had to be scared shitless. He guessed the closest she'd ever gotten to the inside of a jail was on Netflix. If he could save her from having to stay the night he would. The thought of her here made his gorge rise.

A few minutes later a deputy escorted her in. Her face was ashen and she looked impossibly small in the orange jump suit—and incredibly lost. The deputy told her where to sit and with trembling hands she picked up the phone. Flynn waited until it was just the two of them.

"I'll have you out by tomorrow," he said.

"How can they do this? The grand jury didn't indict me."

"They went the other route . . . a complaint and affidavit that shows probable cause."

"But how? I didn't do anything."

He shrugged, not knowing what evidence they had. All he'd seen was the arrest warrant. "More than likely they're desperate and hope this scares you into talking. So Gia, don't say a word . . . to anyone!"

"I have nothing to tell."

He didn't have time to ensure her how innocent he knew she was. He had a million things to line up before her hearing the next day. That included calling Tim and chewing him out. "Listen to me, okay? I'm trying to get Pretrial Services to interview you first thing in the morning. They're the folks who help determine your bail. I may have to put up your ranch; you prepared to do that?"

"For bond?" she asked, and he could tell her head was swirling. But she needed to trust him . . . there was no time for hand-holding. "Yeah, I guess."

"My gut tells me the U.S. Attorney isn't going to fight bail. They'd like nothing more than for you to bolt and lead them to Evan Laughlin."

"Flynn, I don't know where he is."

He nodded. Of course she didn't. "Make sure you emphasize to the PSO how many ties you have to the community . . . your mother, Annie, the tree farm. Whatever you can come up with that shows you're not a flight risk. More than likely they'll ask you to turn over your passport. Where is it? I want someone to bring it to court tomorrow so there are no holdups getting you out. I'm also prepared to agree to electronic monitoring. I . . . Gia, have you heard anything I've said?"

She'd zoned out, staring past him as if in a daze.

"Gia?"

"Yes, whatever you say."

She seemed so frightened, his heart cracked in half. "I promise to get this worked out."

"Will you call my mother? I don't want her to see this on the news."

"Of course. I'm assuming her number's on your phone." He'd taken her purse after she'd been arrested.

She nodded. "Flynn? . . . Never mind."

"You'll be fine tonight." He scanned the dingy jailhouse walls. The hell she would, but what else could he say? "I'll also have someone bring you a suit to wear for your initial appearance. You'll be out in time for lunch." He tried for a reassuring grin, though the time frame was pushing it.

Again she nodded with those glazed eyes.

"I've got to get going. Try to sleep, okay? You've got a grueling morning."

He got to his feet, his head swimming with all the things he had to do to ensure she didn't spend any more time in this hellhole than absolutely necessary.

"Flynn," she called.

"Yes?"

She put her hand on the glass and he just stared at it. His eyes started to well and he needed to get out of the room before he lost it. He'd let her down so bad he wanted to punch something. Instead of spending his time getting her into bed, he should've been working the case harder . . . had his ear to the ground. With all his sources . . . how had he let this happen? The whole thing was like a sucker punch.

"I've gotta go, Gia. Stay calm and I'll be back first thing tomorrow." He'd do anything to trade places with her. Anything.

* * *

The night had been the worst of her life. Although she'd had a cell to herself, Gia had been afraid to shut her eyes. Scared that she'd get shivved or shanked or whatever they called it. She was also convinced she'd get lice or a communicable disease from the sleeping cot. And the jail was louder than a factory. Bars clanking, voices carrying, and footsteps clomping. The noise bounced off the walls like a cacophony.

Worse, though, was the memory of the way Flynn had avoided looking at her the previous night. Not once had he made eye contact. He'd been all business, barking orders and reciting a laundry list of procedures. From the time of her arrest he'd morphed into a man she didn't recognize. No longer did his eyes shine with affection . . . and emotion . . . for her. They darkened with suspicion and something worse. Disapproval. How could she blame him? Look at her. The fact that he'd slept with her probably repulsed him.

Just recalling his aloofness, a remoteness that bordered on cold, made her wither inside. But she couldn't think about it now. A deputy marshal had come to transport her to U.S. District Court.

She and three other female inmates were loaded into a shuttle, driven less than a minute away, and herded through the bowels of the federal courthouse to the U.S. Marshals office. As Flynn had predicted, someone from Pretrial Services was there to interview her. The woman, who had wiry red hair and a stern mouth, spent an hour asking her questions and scribbling on a clipboard. Gia did what Flynn had told her and emphasized that she was her mother's sole support. She also told the interviewer that Annie relied on her for a paycheck and a place to live. The woman, apparently satisfied with the answers, gathered up her things and left the cell.

Gia had no idea of the time and searched the walls for a clock. Flynn had taken her watch and earrings along with her purse when she'd been arrested. Out of habit she kept reaching for her phone to check messages only to find it wasn't there.

It seemed like she'd sat there for hours before Flynn finally appeared with a young, attractive woman she'd never seen before. They were both dressed in suits and Gia assumed the woman was an attorney from Flynn's firm. A deputy marshal unlocked her cell and let them in.

"Stephanie will help you get dressed." Flynn handed the woman a suiter and a cosmetic bag that looked familiar and asked that the deputy let him back out.

That was it. Not: *How was your night in hell, Gia?* Or *I missed you.* Not anything that would indicate that she was more than a client. It was for the best, she told herself. She would only bring him down.

Stephanie unzipped the garment bag, revealing one of Gia's most conservative suits, a pinstriped skirt and a matching blazer. Gia wondered who'd rummaged through her closet. She got the distinct impression whoever it was deliberately had chosen something without a big-name designer label. If she recalled right she'd gotten the outfit at Loehmann's during the store's yellow tag sale.

Stephanie helped her get out of the hideous orange jumpsuit and handed her panties, a matching bra, and a camisole. The undergarments were also Gia's, and again she pondered who'd gone all the way to Nugget to get them. The last article Stephanie wanted her to put on was panty hose. She hadn't worn them in years but slid them up her legs, careful not to cause a run. After she was fully dressed Stephanie handed her the bag of makeup and a hand mirror.

"Not too much," she said, as if Gia would trowel it on like a streetwalker. "Try to cover the dark circles under your eyes."

Why? Gia wanted to ask. Were they trying to convince the court that spending a night in county lockup was as relaxing as the Ritz-Carlton?

When Gia finished Stephanie assessed her. "Maybe a little lipstick; you look pale."

It was all Gia could do not to slap the woman. "I'm fine."

Stephanie acted like she wanted to argue but resisted, instead pulling a pair of dated pumps from the bottom of the suiter. "Put these on and I'll call Flynn in for his approval."

His approval?

She tacitly obeyed, feeling too beat down to point out that she knew something about dressing for an audience. Mollified, Stephanie called for one of the deputies and asked that she retrieve Flynn, who returned sometime later.

He gave Gia a cursory once-over. It was as if he was looking right through her. "Let's pull her hair back."

Stephanie whipped a brush, hair spray, and a container of bobby pins from her mammoth handbag, reminding Gia of the game show

Let's Make a Deal, on which audience members were encouraged to carry ridiculous items on their person in hopes the host would ask for them in exchange for a prize.

With heavy strokes, Stephanie began brushing Gia's hair back, winding it into some kind of twist and fastening her handiwork with the bobby pins.

"How's that?" she asked Flynn and looked at him like his opinion held as much weight as God's.

"I think it's good." He turned from Stephanie and addressed Gia. "There are no cameras allowed in federal court, but the media will send sketch artists. We don't want you to look like a convict in the news."

She nodded, feeling the bile rising in the back of her throat.

"Give me a few minutes with Gia," Flynn said to Stephanie, who stuffed everything back into her bag and left them alone.

"Don't be nervous," Flynn said, staring down at paperwork he'd spread across the table. "I talked to Tim. They're not going to challenge letting you out as long as bail's sufficient."

"Who's Tim?"

"The prosecutor I told you about. The magistrate is a tough SOB, but he's always liked me so I think we're good there as well. Just let me do the talking. You have any questions, Gia?"

"Did you call my mother?"

"Yep," he said, his head still bent over the papers. "She's coming. Doris is helping her make the necessary arrangements."

Gia didn't want her mother to come . . . to see her like this. It was bad enough Flynn was seeing her at her lowest. It was a picture he wouldn't be able to erase. "No!" He finally looked up, and in a calmer voice she said, "Let's wait on that, okay? And did anyone feed Rory?"

"She's pretty set on coming, but if you want me to make up an excuse why she shouldn't, I will. Justin and Cody are taking care of the horses."

"Good. Thanks." Flynn seemed to have taken care of everything. He just hadn't taken care of her feelings. She could understand why; she was an embarrassment to him now.

"Who got my clothes?" She hoped it wasn't Stephanie. Gia didn't like her. But it was clear Flynn did. Why else would he have brought her?

"I contract with people who do that."

It was on the tip of her tongue to ask if they were jailbird stylists, but her sense of humor had deserted her.

"I've got to get inside the courtroom now," he said. "The deputies will bring you in soon.

"Gia," he said, and she thought he might finally hold her or do something that indicated they meant something to each other, "remember to breathe."

Remember to breathe. That was it and he left.

She sat there feeling as cheap as her pinstriped suit. Then it hit her all at once; she'd fallen in love with him. She'd been trying to tell herself all this time that her feelings were superficial—an infatuation that would pass like all the others—but she'd been deluding herself. Lying.

A female deputy suddenly appeared. "Time to go."

She escorted Gia through a series of back hallways into the courtroom and sat her next to Flynn. Wiping her palms on the sides of her skirt, she focused on the dark paneled wall behind the bench, studied the district court seal, and tried to breathe while her heart did a 10K run.

The magistrate came in and the deputy court clerk asked everyone to rise. Gia stood up with Flynn and stared straight ahead at the seal. It calmed her to have a focal point. In the gallery behind her, she could hear faint whispering as friends and family members of the other defendants scurried to find seats.

She prayed the hearing would go fast and she'd be released soon so she could go home to Rosser Ranch ... away from the world. Away from the humiliation.

After the magistrate took to the bench Gia sat down. The judge informed her of the charges—securities fraud and aiding and abetting in an investment adviser fraud—and told her if she was convicted the statutory maximum sentence was fifty years in federal prison. Gia gasped and Flynn put his hand on her shoulder. The move wasn't conciliatory; he was trying to tell her to shut up.

Once the magistrate made sure Gia had been briefed on her constitutional rights he brought up the issue of bail. There was a lot of back and forth between the judge, Flynn, the prosecutor, and even the red-haired woman from Pretrial Services. Gia was so busy grasping how very much trouble she was in—fifty years' worth—that she tuned everyone out. No wonder Flynn couldn't stand to look at her.

Fifty years was more time than most murderers got. In his eyes she was a disgrace.

She heard fragments of what Flynn said, but it went through one ear and out the other.

". . . ties to the community."

"Upstanding citizen . . ."

". . . drove three hours . . ."

". . . Miss Treadwell's behalf."

A rustling in the gallery jolted her and she turned around to see what had caused the disturbance. Everyone in the two front rows was standing. Still in a fog, she had trouble making out their faces. But she forced herself to look. Really look. There was Annie and Dana and Dana's fiancé, Aidan. Darla stood next to Harlee, who mouthed, *I want an interview.* Donna, Owen, and the Nugget Mafia were there, probably out of prurient interest, but Gia would take what she could get. Most surprising of all was that Lucky and Tawny, Maddy, Emily, and lo and behold, Clay, had come despite their differences over Gia's plans for her property.

They were all there to support her and suddenly she didn't feel so alone.

The magistrate motioned for them to take their seats and the argument over bail continued. After a lot of legal wrangling the judge agreed to release her in exchange for a property bond and on the condition that she not leave Northern California.

It was over; she was going home. That's why when the deputy came to escort her back to jail she was confused, nearly latching on to Flynn's leg like a child.

"Gia," Flynn, who'd been standing while making his argument, crouched down so they were eye to eye, "you have to return to the jail until we post the bond with the clerk's office. After that they'll process you out. I'll be there to get you, okay?"

"How long?" She never wanted to see the jailhouse again.

"By dinnertime. You'll be okay."

Easy for him to say. She took one last look at her supporters and Clay of all people gave her a thumbs-up. Before she could thank them the deputy moved her along, taking her through the maze in which they'd come. She turned to see if Flynn followed, but he was gone.

Chapter 22

"I'm proud of you for standing up for Gia the way you did," Emily told Clay, clicking her seat belt closed for the long drive back to the Sierra.

"I'm not such a bad guy, you know?"

"I never thought you were." She leaned over and kissed his cheek. "To me you're goodness personified."

Lately Clay had felt like the devil. He still couldn't wrap his head around the fact that Emily didn't want their child and had been cold as ice to her. Instead of arguing they just didn't talk about it. Not since the first scan. He didn't want to exacerbate the situation when Emily's pregnancy was so fragile. Still, that didn't stop him from being resentful.

But the last thing Emily needed was stress. For days she'd been cramping and spotting and Clay feared the worst. Today they'd hopefully know more when they went for the second scan.

"What do you think will happen with the case against her?" Emily asked.

"Rhys believes the feds are trying to scare her into telling them where Laughlin is." Clay maneuvered Sacramento's city streets, taking the best route to the interstate. "He says she would've talked by now if she knew anything."

"I feel terrible for her. The poor woman has been through enough."

Clay knew how much his wife identified with Gia's plight. It had never gone as far as an arrest—or jail—with Emily when Hope went missing. But having people think she was responsible for her own daughter's disappearance . . .

"If anyone can prove her innocence it's Flynn," he said. "From what I hear he's one hell of a lawyer."

Emily nodded and reached for his hand. "It's good we all came."

"Yep," he said, retreating into his own thoughts during the three-hour drive.

By the time they reached the clinic in Glory Junction Emily had fallen asleep.

"Em, baby, we're here." He nudged her gently and she came awake with a start, her face pale and even a little gaunt.

Not for the first time he wondered what was going through her head. These days she kept her own counsel. Clay suspected she'd girded for the worst and would probably be relieved by it. On Sunday he'd seen her go to the oak tree he'd planted for Hope and sit on the bench he'd inscribed with her daughter's name.

This is Hope's tree, Emily. No matter where she is, her spirit lives here. That's her bench. No matter where she is, we'll sit here and always think of her, he'd told her the day they'd gotten engaged.

Clay hadn't wanted to spy, but he knew his wife had spent a good hour sitting under the tree's leafy canopy. She'd gone often enough since he'd planted the oak, sometimes with Hope's baby album. He'd always understood that she needed time alone with her memories. This occasion was no different. But she'd come back more miserable than he'd ever seen her.

"You ready to do this?" he asked, offering her an arm out of the passenger seat.

She exhaled. "As ready as I'll ever be."

They went inside the clinic. A nurse immediately settled them inside an exam room where, as before, Emily stripped from the waist down and covered herself with a paper sheet. Clay busied himself by studying the medical posters on the wall.

And they waited for what seemed like an eternity.

Eventually Dr. Davis swept in, a faint smell of antiseptic soap trailing behind her.

"How are the two of you holding up?"

Not well, but Clay said, "We're holding."

The doctor addressed Emily, "You're still spotting, though?"

"And cramping," Emily said, and the doctor pursed her lips as if she didn't think that was a good sign.

"Doubling-over cramping?"

"Nothing like that. It feels like pinching."

Dr. Davis washed her hands. "I'm not too concerned about mild cramping. It's normal. I'm not too thrilled with the bleeding, though. But we shall see."

Dr. Davis went through the same routine as last time. After prepping she moved the ultrasound monitor closer to the exam table and started the imaging test, moving the probe inside Emily.

"There we are." She pointed at the screen.

The picture looked the same to Clay as it had the last time. A moon with craters.

Davis fiddled with the machine for a while, her expression giving nothing away. Emily strained to see what she was looking at, leaning halfway up on the table.

"I'm getting about ninety beats per minute," Dr. Davis finally said.

"The baby's heart?" Clay asked. "Is that good?"

"It's typical and definitely reassuring. Statistically with an embryonic heartbeat like this the chance of the pregnancy continuing is at least seventy percent." Dr. Davis grinned. "We're in good shape, Mom and Dad."

"What about the spotting?" Emily asked.

"We'll have to watch it. But a little spotting isn't too worrisome."

The gripping vice around Clay's chest loosened and suddenly he could breathe normally again. His mood soared. But it was short-lived. After the doctor left to give Emily time to dress . . . time for them to absorb the wondrous news . . . his wife burst into tears.

He didn't know what to say. *I'm sorry I'm happy you didn't lose the baby.* Because the truth was, his prayers had been answered. He wanted this child like he wanted his next breath. He already loved the tiny seed growing inside Emily.

She hurriedly put on her skirt while Clay stood tensely at her side. He swiped the box of tissues off the counter and handed it to her. Emily blew her nose and did the unexpected; she walked straight into his arms.

"I thought for sure we were going to lose it," she said and sobbed against his chest.

"Isn't that what you wanted?" He sounded harsher than he'd meant to.

She cried so hard that he couldn't understand a word she was saying. So he just held her.

"Let it out, sweetheart. Let it go."

"I was so afraid . . . I want this baby . . . God, do I want this baby." She hiccupped and sniffled, soaking his shirt with her tears.

He lifted her chin with his finger and stared into her wet blue eyes. "You do?"

"I do. I always did. But I'm scared, Clay. I'm so scared."

"Of what?" He rubbed her back, trying to understand.

"Of losing her. I . . . I can't ever go through that again. And I can't let her replace Hope."

"How do you know the baby's a she?" He grinned.

"Just a feeling." She touched her stomach and his chest expanded with joy. Sheer blissful joy. She wanted their baby.

"No one can ever replace Hope," he said. "And we'll never give up trying to find her. As for the baby, we can only control what's in our hands to control. The rest we have to leave to fate."

"We almost lost her, Clay." She wiped her eyes.

"But we didn't." He laid his hand on her belly. "She . . . or he . . . is in there, growing. And we're going to do everything we can to keep our baby safe."

There was a knock at the door. The doctor pulled open the curtain and came bustling in. "How are we doing?"

"Good . . . relieved . . . nervous." Emily laughed and cried at the same time.

The doctor squeezed her arm. "It's those hormones hard at work. Do you have any questions?"

Emily sniffled and Clay pulled her into his side, feeling more at peace than he had in weeks. "Is there anything more we can do?"

"Just make sure Emily eats right and gets plenty of rest. Otherwise, watch the spotting, but remember a little bit is normal. And I'll see you at the next appointment."

They walked outside, arm in arm, into the blinding sunshine. Even the regal Sierra mountains seemed greener and more majestic than usual.

Emily peeked up at him. "I know you want me to be more excited . . . more demonstrative. I want to be, Clay; I really do. Fear and guilt has had me by the throat. But I want this baby. . . . Don't you ever doubt how much I want this baby."

He pulled her close and kissed her in the parking lot of the clinic, loving the subtle changes that had taken over her body. Though her stomach was still flat it felt slightly rounded and her breasts were fuller—all in preparation for bringing their child into the world. He thought his chest might explode with pride.

"I love you, Emily. Now let's go home and tell the boys."

Flynn checked his watch at least four times as he waited at the Pretrial Services Office for Gia. She should've been here by now. He'd moved mountains to post the bond in time to have her out of custody by nightfall. And here it was already dusk. The idea of her spending any more time in county lockup made his stomach churn.

She'd looked so frail and frightened in the courtroom today. Nothing like the woman who'd brazenly held a hunting rifle to his chest. Then she'd been fierce and Flynn was pretty sure that's when she'd begun wrapping herself around his heart. Although at the time he would've been loath to admit it. Now he was full-blown gone for her. But if he couldn't beat the charges against her, he'd have to love her from the other side of a visiting room.

Couldn't the goddamn feds see that if she had any clue where Laughlin was she'd tell them? Then again, they didn't know Gia like he did. How she unselfishly sent victims money. Or that she'd bought Rosser Ranch to give struggling women a fresh start. They only saw a wealthy television celebrity who'd hitched her wagon to a slick-ass con man.

He was just about to call the jail to see what the holdup was when he spotted Gia. She walked slowly across the hall in the clothes she'd been arrested in and carried a paper bag with what he presumed held the rest of her things. She looked so dejected that Flynn wanted to hold her. Highly unprofessional, given the place. He worked with the people at Pretrial Services and the last thing Gia needed was for them to know they were romantically involved. It was bad enough that everyone in the clerk's office was aware he'd put up some of his own property to make her bail. Lawyers didn't do that for their clients. He was expected to be an objective advocate, not her bank.

He took the bag from her. "I've got the truck nearby."

She didn't say anything, just followed him out the door to a parking structure where they rode the elevator up to the third floor. He guided her to his Ford and pressed the key fob to unlock the doors, anxious to be alone with her and away from prying eyes. Without a word, Gia slid in while he got behind the wheel.

"We'll be out of here soon," he said.

She turned away and stared vacantly out the passenger window. The streets were jammed with cars and Flynn knew from experience that the interstate would be worse. Rush hour. Maybe they'd stop somewhere for dinner to wait it out.

"You okay?" He put his hand on her leg as he zigzagged through traffic.

"I want to go home. Did you talk my mom out of coming?"

"Yeah. I told her we'll need her closer to trial." If God forbid they had to go to trial.

Gia returned to staring out the window.

"You want to stop to get something to eat? We could pull off in Folsom or Roseville."

"No, thank you."

Her answer was terse, but Flynn figured Gia was stretched to the limit after her ordeal. It took almost twenty minutes to get on the interstate, which resembled a parking lot. Stop and go for the next fifteen miles.

"You could put your seat back and try to sleep," he said. "You're probably exhausted."

Gia found the lever on the side of her chair, reclined, and closed her eyes. By the time the traffic subsided she was fast asleep. He wanted to pull over somewhere private to cuddle and kiss her but decided she needed the rest. So he rode the rest of the way to Nugget in silence under a moonless sky.

Sometime after eight o'clock he pulled through Gia's security gate and parked in the driveway. He turned off the engine and she stirred, drawing her seat upright.

"You awake?" He moved in to kiss her, but she pulled away.

"I need a shower."

They got out of the truck and he grabbed her paper bag from the back and took it inside the house. Gia headed straight to her bedroom. Flynn assumed she needed time alone to feel human again and went to the kitchen to scrounge up something for them to eat. Annie had left a note on the counter that there was homemade soup in the refrigerator. Flynn found it easily enough in a container on the top shelf and poured it into a pot to heat on the stovetop. From the cupboard he grabbed two bowls and waited.

But when thirty minutes went by he got concerned.

"Gia?" He knocked on her bedroom door.

When she didn't answer he let himself in and found her on the bed with her face buried under the pillow, asleep. Flynn got an extra blanket from the closet and tucked her in. The last twenty-four hours had to have wrung her out. He stood there watching her sleep, taking in her sweet scent. He returned to the kitchen and started to clean up when his phone vibrated on his belt. It was a text from Toad.

Been out of cell range until now, but you'll thank me for it. On my way to the Caymans. Will call with news tomorrow.

Flynn took a deep breath. Toad had left him a voice mail late the previous night, but it had been so garbled and filled with static Flynn hadn't been able to make out much of the message. It sounded like Toad was onto a good lead. But Flynn knew from experience that whatever Toad was chasing could easily turn out to be nothing. He turned off the light in the kitchen and crossed the house back to Gia's room. Shucking off his shirt and pants, he got under the covers and curved his body around hers. The room was silent except for the beat of her heart.

Morning came too fast and Flynn slowly opened his eyes to the light seeping in through the drapes. He reached for Gia, but she was gone, a mound of rumpled blankets in her place. Swinging his legs off the bed, he pulled on his jeans and followed the fresh scent of coffee. But she wasn't in the kitchen. Flynn poured himself a cup, went upstairs to his own room, showered, and dressed.

Before going in search of his elusive girlfriend—he'd brought her home to Mom, he could call her that—he checked his cell for any missed messages from Toad or the office. Nothing yet, but it was still early.

He headed down and wandered the main floor of the house. No Gia, so he went outside and hiked to the barn. Cody was there, but Rory was gone.

"Ms. Treadwell took him out," Cody said while mucking out the mare's stall.

Flynn wondered why she hadn't waited for him. They could've ridden together. He had a lot he wanted to talk to her about.

"Dad said you got her out of jail. I guess she doesn't have to wear one of those ankle bracelets."

"Nope." Flynn scratched a hand under his hat. "You know which way she went?"

"I didn't really pay attention. Sorry."

Flynn whistled for Dude, who was roaming the paddock. "You fed him already, right?"

"About an hour ago." Cody climbed up on the stall gate. "Emily's having a baby."

"No kidding?" That was news to Flynn. "I hadn't heard."

"No one knows yet except the family."

And now me.

"You excited?" he asked.

"Yeah." Cody nodded. "I like the idea of being a big brother."

"You'll be a good one." They were fine boys, Cody and Justin.

He watched as Dude trotted into his stable stall. "Want to go for a ride, boy?" Flynn slipped a bridle onto the gelding's head and led him into the center of the barn to saddle up.

"You gonna try to find Ms. Treadwell?" Cody asked. "If you are you better get a move on. She's got a good hour on you."

"An hour, huh?" Why the hell had she gone off without him? She probably hadn't wanted to wake him, he told himself. He'd barely slept the night she'd stayed in jail, tossing and turning. "That's okay. I'm faster."

He finished wrapping the cinch strap, stuck his foot in the stirrup, and mounted up. "Thanks for taking such good care of the horses," he told Cody. "And congratulations on the baby."

"Thanks, Flynn."

He rode off, following Gia's favorite trail. In the distance he saw Annie with his fence guys. Ranch hands really. But every good hand knew how to build a fence. He'd sent them over yesterday and it appeared they'd gotten a good amount done. Annie waved and Flynn tipped his hat, riding on. He caught up with Gia at the copse of trees near the big pasture where most of his cattle grazed. She had on those clingy breeches she liked to ride in and the breeze ruffled her hair, taking Flynn's breath away. In that moment he knew he was going to tell her that he loved her. Just lay it on the line. And someday, when all the crap was behind them, he planned to make her his wife.

Screw her crazy notions about marriage. He'd change her mind and show her what great partners they'd make.

She reined Rory in so he could come up beside her. "Hey. You checking your cattle?"

"No. I came looking for you. Why didn't you wake me up? We could've ridden out together."

"I needed the space . . . time to think." Rory didn't want to stand still so Gia turned the mare in a few circles so her head faced Dude's.

"We'll work this out, Gia. Toad has a lead . . . he's in the Caymans." Flynn didn't know whether the lead would actually pan out, but he wanted to give her hope. "The feds don't have anything on you anyway."

"Does that really matter? Apparently someone has to take the fall for what Evan did."

"They have to have evidence for a conviction," he said. So far everything they had was highly circumstantial. "I'm going in later to work on the case, but I wanted us to talk."

"About what? I don't know anything, Flynn. If I knew where Evan was I would tell anyone who would listen." She turned away and gazed out toward the mountains.

"Gia, look at me. I wanted to talk about us. . . . The case can wait."

"Good." She spun around. "Because I wanted to talk about us too. From now on we need to keep this solely professional. I . . . uh . . . can't sleep with you anymore. Not even like last night." All he'd done was hold her. "I need you to be my lawyer . . . nothing else."

Where had that come from? If she'd punched him in the stomach he couldn't have been more surprised. Shattered was more like it. He wanted to put up an argument, find out what the hell was going on in that head of hers. Two days ago she'd met his whole family; he'd thought they'd had something.

"Would you rather me get you another attorney?" he asked, shell-shocked.

I need you to be my lawyer . . . nothing else. The words kept looping through his head.

"No, I want you," she replied. "You're a wonderful lawyer. I just think it would be better if we focused on my case."

"And afterward?"

"I'm not the one for you, Flynn." Her eyes misted and she turned Rory so he could no longer look at her. "I have to head back to meet Dana."

He watched her lope away, resisting the pounding need to go after her. *Can't do it*, he told himself. As his client, she got to set the boundaries. It was his fiduciary duty to adhere to them, though he would've turned in his bar card if it meant having her.

Chapter 23

"Don't look back, don't look back, don't look back," Gia repeated the mantra a dozen times. It got her as far as the stable, and when she finally did look back Flynn was gone.

She knew he cared about her in his own way. But he didn't need a woman who was an embarrassment and she didn't need another man to make her heart feel threadbare. What did she have to offer anyway? Especially now, when she was staring down a fifty-year prison sentence for something she didn't do. Better to have a lawyer than a lover.

She dismounted, unsaddled, and groomed Rory as quickly as possible. Flynn could return anytime and she'd rather avoid being alone with him again.

She was on her way to the house when she bumped into Annie.

"Hey," Annie said, wiping sweat from her forehead. "Welcome home. I'd hug you, but I'm disgusting right now."

Gia smiled. No one could be sad around Annie. Today she had on a sun hat with the cord around her neck, men's jeans cinched tight with a thick brown belt, a peasant top, high-top sneakers, and a smudge of dirt on the bridge of her nose.

"How's the fence coming?"

"Good. It should be finished by tomorrow, and in go the seedlings."

Gia prayed she'd be here to see them grow.

"You okay?" Annie tilted her head.

"I've just got a lot on my mind. I'll be fine." Gia peeked at her watch. "Dana's coming so I've gotta run."

"Go," Annie said. "Take her to see the fence when she gets here. And Gia, Flynn will fix everything. You'll see."

Yep. Just not her heart, which was irreparably damaged. From her father, from Evan . . .

When she got up to the house there was a Ford Expedition parked in her driveway, not Dana's Outback. For a second she feared reporters had gotten past the gate. Then she saw Dana sitting on the front porch.

"New car?" Gia asked as she approached the house.

"It's Aidan's. I showed a family homes this morning and the Expedition is roomier." Dana got up and tilted her head. "How are you?"

"I survived the Big House." She tried to make light of it but was humiliated. Forever indebted, though. She couldn't believe the whole community had appeared in court on her behalf. "Thanks for coming to the bail hearing." Gia's eyes watered. "You can't know what it meant to me."

"You would've done the same. We stick together here in Nugget."

It hadn't felt that way when Gia proposed her residential program to the neighbors but they'd certainly rallied when she'd needed them most.

"I just have to take a quick shower and then we can do whatever wedding stuff you want," she said.

"Change of plan, unless you're not up for it."

"What's that?"

"A ladies' lunch. It was Maddy and Emily's idea. We're supposed to meet them and the rest of the crew at the Lumber Baron."

The last thing Gia wanted to do was socialize . . . not after Flynn. Not when her heart ached the way it did. But these good women had come to her defense. They'd driven three hours for a twenty-minute hearing just to stand up for her. It wouldn't be right to turn them down for a simple lunch.

"Can we invite Annie?" she asked. "If she's going to live here all summer she should get to know people."

"Of course. You go shower and I'll find Annie."

"She's in the guest apartment."

Dana headed to the staircase next to the garage. Gia went inside, bathed off the horse sweat, and pulled a sundress over her head. It was quicker than picking out separates. She threw on a denim jacket and a pair of boots, grabbed her purse off the kitchen counter, and met Dana on the porch. If they left now she'd miss Flynn.

"Why didn't you come inside?"

"Too nice a day." Dana lifted her face to the sun. "Annie should be out any second. I'll drive."

"You sure? It's out of your way to take us home."

"Only a few minutes. Where's Flynn?" Dana nudged her chin at his truck.

"Checking on his cattle before he goes to Sacramento."

"He was amazing in court. I've always seen him as a cowboy . . . the boots, the hat, the pickup, the wide smile. But holy crap . . . lawyer Flynn is a force to be reckoned with."

A fat tear streaked down Gia's face. She tried to wipe it away before Dana noticed but too late.

"What's wrong? Gia, why are you crying?" Dana rummaged through her purse, came up with a small package of tissues, and handed them to Gia. "Tell me why you're upset . . . besides the obvious reasons."

Yeah, she should've been crying over being charged with enough federal crimes to put her away for half a century. But that wasn't it.

"I love him." She started to cry, which seemed to have become a habit of late. The last time she'd felt this desolate was at her father's funeral. She'd been Daddy's little girl and he'd been her hero. And then he'd left her and her mother alone to face the world with nothing.

"He doesn't love you?"

"You saw him at the hearing. I'm a jury verdict away from being a felon," she said, sobbing. "How could he love me?" It was better that he didn't. She held no future for him, not when her life hung in the balance. She'd bring him down just like Evan had done to her.

"To me he looked like a man who desperately wanted to get you out of jail. He was frantic, Gia. I don't know him that well, but I have to think a bail hearing is pretty routine for an attorney like Flynn. He acted like it was life or death, which in my mind means he cares for you. A lot."

"He thinks he owes me because we've been sleeping together." She used Dana's tissues to wipe her nose. "Former FBI agents don't fall for America's Most Wanted."

"Evan's the one who's wanted, not you."

"Yet I've been charged with a serious crime . . . fifty years in prison, Dana. You heard the judge."

Annie came out of her apartment and took the stairway down. She beamed at them and waved.

"I don't want her to see me like this ... or know about Flynn," Gia said, searching through her purse for a pair of sunglasses. "They're close. Let's get out of here before Flynn gets back."

Dana and Gia climbed into the Expedition and Annie got in the backseat.

"Thanks for inviting me," she said.

"We're happy to have you join us." Dana surreptitiously patted Gia's leg, started the engine, drove to the gate, and punched in the code.

"Sorry, I should've brought my clicker." It was on Gia's car visor.

"No worries." Dana craned her neck around to Annie. "You'll love the Lumber Baron."

Gia tried to pull herself together while Dana and Annie chatted. She didn't want to fall apart in front everyone. Cool, calm, and collected is the way she liked to present herself, even in the face of crisis. Hell, she used to manage peoples' fortunes. Trading, buying, and selling at the whim of a mercurial stock market. One wrong move and she could lose everything. She knew the consequences of that more than most. That was why she had a spine of steel.

Time to use it.

The drive seemed so much shorter than usual. Dana parked and they went inside the inn. The reservationist told them that everyone was in the kitchen. That area of the inn had been rehabbed after the arson fire. To Gia the kitchen looked just like it had before the blaze. Lots of white gleaming cabinets with glass doors, stainless-steel countertops, and state-of-the-art appliances. Copper pots hung above an enormous center island. Though it was an industrial kitchen, it felt homey.

Emily tossed a big salad and Donna put something in the oven. Maddy, Harlee, Darla, and Tawny sat at the island, drinking wine.

"Sam's in San Francisco," Maddy said. "She's got a huge gala she's planning and sends her regrets."

"How was jail food?" Donna asked. "Did they make you eat the loaf?"

"Donna!" Emily cried.

For the first time since being arrested Gia laughed. Thanks to Donna they were getting her incarceration out of the way, instead of pretending it never happened. "What's the loaf?"

"It's a bunch of leftovers mushed together into a brick. Don't worry; we're making something delicious."

It smelled delicious.

Maddy poured the three of them wine and motioned for them to join the rest of the ladies around the bar. They each grabbed stools while Emily and Donna continued to prepare lunch. It looked like a variety of quiches and two different kinds of salad. Despite everything, Gia was hungry. She hadn't had anything to eat since dinner at the Barlows'. This morning she'd wanted to get out of the house before Flynn woke up and had skipped breakfast.

Gia lifted her glass of white and toasted. "To all of you for coming to my defense. You don't know how much that meant to me."

"Of course we came," Donna said. "You're not guilty, right?"

Emily shook her head and glowered at Donna, but Gia knew everyone else was wondering the same thing.

"I'm not guilty. I only wish I could find Evan and rat him out."

"I saw pictures of him on television." Donna leaned against the counter. "Too good-looking for his own good. The man probably seduced you right out of your drawers."

Good-looking? Next to Flynn he was anemic. Funny; at one time she'd thought Evan was one of the most handsome men she'd ever known.

"We know you're not guilty," Emily said and glared at Donna again. "Flynn will beat the charges. We didn't invite you here to talk about that, though. Today is to celebrate your release and to talk about your proposal . . . the residential program."

"You mean the school." Maddy nodded at Gia, as if to say remember what we talked about. "We want to be part of it."

"What do you mean, part of it?" Gia glanced at Annie, who raised her shoulders and arms in the classic I-don't-know gesture.

"We're all businesswomen and think we have something to add," Maddy said. "I know the hospitality industry inside and out, Harlee owns her own newspaper, Darla knows everything about running a salon, Donna started the Bun Boy from scratch, Tawny sells her custom boots all over the world, Dana is the top-selling real estate agent in the county, and Emily is a famous cookbook author. We could give workshops." She pointed at Emily and Donna. "And they could give cooking classes. With California's cottage food law, some of these women could start baking or catering businesses from home. I could certainly hire a few to work in the Lumber Baron. We're always looking for housekeepers and reservationists. If they do well Nate might be willing to find them a slot in one of his hotels."

"I wouldn't be where I am today if it hadn't been for two bootmakers who took me under their wings and taught me everything I know," Tawny said. "One of them even put me and Katie up in his home. I want to pay that forward."

"Me too," Annie chimed in. "I mean besides running the farm end of it. I have a degree in managerial economics, for goodness' sake."

"What we're trying to say is that we're a bunch of kick-ass ladies and we'd like to get involved." Donna pulled out the quiches and put them on cooling racks. "First thing we'd like to do is help you raise money for this endeavor because it ain't gonna be cheap."

Gia looked around the room and her eyes welled up. *Jeez, not again.* "You guys have done a complete one-eighty. . . . What about Rhys and Clay?" As far as she knew, they hadn't changed their minds about the project.

"No, we haven't," Emily said. "The women in this group have always been in favor of the project. As for Rhys and Clay, you leave them to us. We'll put them on the board to select the candidates, make them feel important, and they'll be fine."

"I don't know what to say." Gia couldn't believe she was getting this much support. She didn't even know if she'd be around to see the project through.

Donna slid a plate of piping-hot quiche under her nose. "Then just eat."

Flynn paced back and forth in his office, his phone clutched between his neck and ear, digesting everything Toad had uncovered.

"So she knows where he is, then?" Flynn couldn't freaking believe it.

"No. But he wants his money and she's got it. So how long do you think it'll take before he turns up at her place?"

"Jesus." Clearly Evan Laughlin wasn't above murder. He'd kill her if he had to.

"What do we do?"

"I'm not sure yet," Flynn said. "So all that money—billions—is in the Caymans? Who's to say she won't move it?"

"Nothing. But where? She'd have to either launder it or keep it under her pillow. That's a lot of dough to have lying around your house."

"Let me think about this for a while. In the meantime, you sit tight."

"I'm not going anywhere," Toad said. "But don't think too long. We don't have the time."

"I know." Flynn got off the phone and pressed the heels of his hands against his eyes. Shit! Toad had found more than Flynn had bargained for. His next call was to Rhys Shepard.

"Hey, it's Flynn. I need you to do me a favor and sit on Gia for the next three hours, just until I can get there."

"You gonna tell me why?" Rhys asked.

"Can't."

"Okay. I'll assume it's a public safety issue. She's over at my wife's inn right now. Sloane's on duty. You want her to tail her home?"

"Yeah. And Rhys, I owe you one."

Flynn hung up. To be in Nugget in three hours, he'd have to get a move on. He hadn't been at his own place in so long he didn't even remember what it looked like. That certainly was about to change.

"You leaving so soon?" Doris asked as he passed the reception desk.

"We got a break in the case and I'm heading to Nugget."

"You don't look happy about it."

"It came as a surprise is all." As many years as Flynn had on the job, nothing ought to come as a revelation anymore. But so much had ridden on this . . . his heart. Which Gia had managed to chew up and spit out. He should've known better than to get involved with her. "I'll be in touch."

"All right and good luck."

Flynn took the stairs instead of the elevator, knowing it would be faster. Parked in front, he shoved his briefcase in the cab of the truck, hopped into the driver's seat, and took off. It seemed like he was always coming and going during rush hour these days. But traffic wasn't as bad as usual and he made good time out of the city.

Near Truckee his phone rang. He checked the caller ID and punched his hands-free.

"Toad, is something happening?"

"My new friend at the bank told me that about twenty minutes ago someone tried to transfer the money electronically, but the password had been changed."

"Do we think it's her or Laughlin?"

"She changed it, and my guess is that Laughlin tried to break the code. I'm trying to find out where he wanted the money transferred."

Flynn's pulse picked up. "Shit. We've gotta tell the feds."

"Yeah, my gut tells me he's getting pretty desperate. Me thinks the last time he got desperate someone wound up dead." Cleo.

"I'll call Tim, but you stay where you are. No one dies on my watch."

"Roger that. Be careful, boss."

"I always am." He prayed Sloane was on the ball. Just one more hour and he'd be there.

On the drive he tried Tim, got voice mail, and left a message that he should call Flynn immediately. His next call was to the special agent in charge of the eastern district of California's FBI office. Same thing. It was nearly six o'clock and Flynn figured everyone was either at dinner or happy hour.

He continued up the mountain, ignoring the speed limit. By the time Gia's big gate came into view, he'd worked himself up into a lather. He pressed the clicker, pulled into the driveway, and got his Glock out of the glove box. Under his seat he found the magazine, popped it into the gun, and racked the slide. He stashed the pistol in the back of his waistband and covered it with his shirt.

Gia came flying out the door. "The Nugget police are here. Sloane won't tell me why."

"Let's go inside." Despite himself, Flynn put his hand at the small of her back.

Sloane stood by the door. "You need me anymore?"

"We're good," he said. "Thanks. I appreciate you coming out here."

Sloane left and Flynn locked the door and checked the windows.

Gia trailed him. "What's going on, Flynn?"

"Take a seat in the living room. I'll be right there."

He got them both glasses of water from the kitchen tap, met her in the other room, set the drinks down on the coffee table, and pulled up one of the club chairs.

"That lead I told you about . . . we know where the money is, Gia."

"You do? Where?"

"The Caymans," he said. "Laughlin's already tried to transfer it from the account. But he couldn't crack the password."

"Wouldn't he know the password?" she asked, confused. "Are you trying to tell me it's someone else's account?"

"The account is Cleo's. He's dead so it's the Widow Cleo's."

"Cleo?" She reached for the glass he'd brought and took a gulp of water.

Flynn couldn't help but notice her long, graceful neck. He still didn't understand why she'd dumped him the way she had. Granted they'd never officially called what they had a relationship, but he'd assumed that actions spoke louder than words. Not only had he slept with a client—something he never did—but he'd brought her home to his family. He couldn't talk to her about it because of their professional relationship; it might seem as if he was pressuring her. So here he sat completely clueless about what he'd done wrong, if anything. For all he knew, it had been a game to her. Or they'd gotten too hot for her to handle.

I don't want to share a bank account with another person. I don't want to make financial decisions by committee. And I don't want to be dependent on someone else.

Flynn pulled himself back to the here and now. "I no longer think he was a hapless victim about to blow the whistle. It's looking like he was in on it and that's why Evan killed him. Of course we don't know for sure. Unfortunately, Cleo's wife swears she knows nothing about her husband's role in the scheme or Laughlin's whereabouts. They were separated at the time of the scam, with a divorce pending. After his death his lawyers turned over all his assets to her. That's when she discovered the account in the Caymans."

"This is good, right?" Gia sat upright. "It clears me."

He shook his head. "Not really. All it shows is that you don't have the money. It doesn't prove you weren't in on it."

Her face twisted in frustration and disappointment. "So why was Sloane here?"

"Laughlin's getting desperate. I was afraid he might show up here to hide . . . to use you to get to the money."

"You don't think I would help him? For God's sake, Flynn."

"Not voluntarily. Gia, this is a man capable of murder. No way was I leaving you susceptible to him holding a gun to the back of your head."

Her mouth opened wide and Flynn watched it sink in. "What about Cleo's widow? Does Laughlin know that she controls the account?"

"Pretty good chance he does, yeah."

Gia jumped to her feet. "We have to call the police. She's not safe, Flynn."

"I already did. Initially I hoped we could lure him out and nab the bastard . . . make him prove you had no part in his crimes. But it's too dicey now, especially because he tried to move on the money. So we wait and pray the feds get him and he clears your name."

"You really think he'd come here?"

"It's a long shot, but I'm not taking any risks." He held her gaze. She might not care about him the same way he did her, but he'd never let anything happen to her. "More than likely he'll go to Florida . . . try to force the widow to move the money. Still, you need to be on high alert."

Flynn's phone rang. He recognized the number instantly and took the call in the adjoining room. When he returned Gia sat on the couch, her eyes faraway, as if she was in another world.

"That was the FBI," he said, trying to keep the excitement out of his voice. He didn't want to get her hopes up. "They've got eyes on Laughlin."

"Where is he?"

"In Florida. They think he's been hiding in either Mexico or Belize, close enough to the money without being obvious."

"Then I'm safe," she said, relieved.

"I can't get into the details, but the feds are laying a net for him. It doesn't mean you shouldn't keep your guard up."

"The feds think he'll make contact with Cleo's widow, don't they?"

"Laughlin's itchy for the money. That's all I can say."

According to Flynn's source the SOB had come in on a boat at PortMiami, gotten into a Lincoln Town Car, and driven to a condominium building two blocks away from where Cleo's widow lived. They were just waiting for Laughlin to move on the widow before they nabbed him. The streets were crawling with agents.

"When they get him what'll happen to me?" Gia asked.

That was the million-dollar question.

Chapter 24

Gia put on a pot of coffee, stuck two slices of bread in the toaster, and gazed at the clock. Flynn had said he'd call as soon as he got word. He'd left early for Sacramento to see what intel he could dig up.

He was all business now, just as he'd been after her arrest. It hurt, but it was what she'd asked of him. Gia kept telling herself it was for the best; they never would've worked out anyway.

Besides, she had Evan's arrest to worry about. It held the key to her freedom. All he had to do was tell the truth about her.

Flynn had warned that in all probability Evan wouldn't lift a finger to help. "Guys like him cover their own asses. He'll know his best defense is to keep his mouth shut . . . maybe even hang the whole thing on you if he thinks he can get a deal out of it."

It made her queasy.

She poured herself a mug of the coffee, buttered the toast, and took a few bites, telling herself that breakfast was the most important meal of the day. The bread tasted dry as sawdust. After a few sips of coffee to help wash it down she dumped the toast in the garbage disposal, turned on the switch, and watched it get sucked through the drain. Then she left for the barn.

Rory stood in her stall and Gia led the mare into the center of the barn to saddle her. She wanted to see the seedlings Annie had planted. Last time she'd checked the ground had just been tilled rows of dirt. Still exciting because it was the start of something. Roots. A way to make a difference.

The day had turned out so lovely, she was anxious to get going before it got too warm and too buggy to ride. Before climbing onto Rory she checked her cell in case she'd missed a text or email from

Flynn. She was scrolling through her messages when a sound made her jump.

"I'll take that." She didn't need to look up to know whose voice it was. "Miss me?"

"Wha . . . what are you doing here, Evan?"

He held out his hand. In the other one he gripped a gun. "Give me the phone, Gia."

She had no choice but to hand it to him.

"What, you're not happy to see me?" He slipped the phone into his jacket pocket, curving his lips in an unctuous grin. She questioned what she'd ever seen in him.

"Can't say I am." Her eyes darted around the barn, looking for a weapon.

A hay hook dangled from the gate of a stall two feet away. He followed the direction of her gaze and laughed.

"Gia, you really think you can overpower me with that?" He backed up to examine the hook, running his fingers over the sharp edge. "I'll tell you what; I'll give you a three-second head start." He moved some distance away from the hook and grasped the pistol with both hands, aiming it straight at her heart. "Go!"

She stood stock still. "You're supposed to be in—"

"In custody? Is that what you were about to say? So you know about all those agents climbing up my ass." He laughed again. This time it sounded rusty, like old nails scraping a tin can. "Not the sharpest tools in the shed, those FBI guys. In fact, they couldn't find their own dicks with a magnifying glass."

"What do you want, Evan?"

"For us to do a little business together."

"That's not going to happen," she said, trying to determine her next move. Knowing she'd never make it to the hay hook before he squeezed off a shot, Gia contemplated her alternatives.

"If you want to keep dear Iris alive you'll reconsider," he sneered and she froze.

"What are you talking about?" Evan had to be bluffing. She'd just spoken to her mother this morning and Iris had been fine.

"We'll talk in the house." He hitched the gun at her, demanding that she lead the way.

"There are people in the house." Gia liked her chances better in the barn. At least Annie or one of her workers might notice Rory sad-dled with no rider. The horse had wandered over to the entrance of the stable where anyone could see her.

"Gia! After all we've meant to each other, why do you lie? I saw the cowboy leave this morning." He raised his brow over the barrel of the gun. "A little earthy for your taste, don't you think?"

Flynn was twenty times any man.

"And Little Orphan Annie is out in the field, digging in the dirt."

Gia wondered how he knew Annie's name. He'd obviously been doing reconnaissance and it scared her to think she wasn't the only one in danger. She had to think of a way to stop him.

"Let's go." He tapped her with the muzzle of the gun and she reluctantly led the way.

When they got in the house Evan glanced around the kitchen. "Let's go in the living room."

He evidentially knew the layout. As they entered his eyes wandered to the open-beam ceiling and the animal heads mounted on the walls and let out a whistle.

"I like what you've done with the place. Sit down." He still had the gun trained on her so she did what he told her.

Her fervent hope was that someone would see them through the windows and call for help. A long shot, she knew. Annie and the others would be in the field for much of the day and Gia didn't expect any visitors.

"What do you want, Evan?"

He pulled her phone from his jacket, scrolled through it, and pushed the screen in front of her face. It was a picture of her mother, bound and gagged. The front page of the *Miami Herald* lay on her lap. The corner of the paper showed the date. Today's. Gia felt her face drain of blood.

"You bastard."

"She'll be fine, Gia, as long as you do exactly what I tell you. I've got a plane waiting at that piece of shit you mountain people call an airport."

It was a private landing strip in Beckwourth that Gia had passed many times without giving it a second thought. All she knew was that Clay had a couple of hangars there.

"In an hour you'll be getting on that plane and flying to Miami to persuade Tiffany Cleo to transfer money to a new account," Evan continued. "As long as I have that money by the end of the day, sweet Iris goes free. If not . . ." He pretended to pull the trigger and suddenly she had trouble breathing.

"You're crazy, Evan. Cleo's house is swarming with agents; there's no way."

"Gia, Gia, Gia, when did you become such a pessimist? I have the utmost faith in you." His smarmy smile reminded her of a snake. How had she not seen the evil in him?

"You must be truly desperate," she said, trying to bide time so she could come up with a plan. "How do I know you won't kill my mother anyway . . . or me, for that matter?"

"You don't. But rest assured, if you don't get me the money you'll both be dead by nightfall."

Gia flinched. The man was diabolical.

"Doesn't it make more sense to pay off someone at the bank to move the money? What makes you think Mrs. Cleo will listen to me?"

"I'll be real honest with you, Gia. I tried the bribery route . . . didn't work. You're my last-ditch effort. What do you have to lose . . . unless you count Iris?" His expression was mocking. "The way I look at it, even if you have to kill the Cleo bitch you're already looking at fifty years behind bars. Yeah, I read the papers. So what's a few more for murder? At least Mommy dearest gets to live out her twilight years in that fancy Boca condo you paid for."

"I don't know how I didn't realize it before, but you're mentally disturbed," she said.

He shook his head. "You always did have a smart mouth. Don't worry, Gia. If you pull this off I'll have plenty of money to get the help I need." He glanced around the room again. "This is nothing like your penthouse."

She followed his gaze to the moose head and saw the Winchester hanging on the wall. Flynn had said it wasn't loaded and she still didn't know where the safety was. But if she could get to it . . .

"I have to go to the bathroom," she said.

"Gia? What do you take me for?"

A sleazy son of a bitch. "What do you want me to do, hold it in?"

"I want you get me a cup of that coffee I saw in the kitchen. And if you behave I'll let you go to the bathroom when we board the plane."

He jerked up the muzzle of his pistol, letting her know to get off the couch. Then he followed her toward the kitchen. This was her chance. But as long as his gun was pointed at her back . . .

The Winchester was just an arm's length away. Gia's heart pounded and a trickle of sweat dripped down the valley of her breasts. Though Evan wasn't a particularly large man, she was no match for him strength wise. She saw her mother tied up in that chair, she thought about Flynn and how he would misinterpret her involvement, and she feared what might happen to Annie if she returned to the house before they caught Evan's plane.

Her panic was so palpable she wondered if Evan could smell it on her. She certainly felt his breath on her neck. That's how close he was. One step . . , two . . . there was the rifle, right in front of her, just hanging on the wall. She sucked in a breath, her hands trembling. *All I have to do is grab it.*

"Move!" Evan jabbed his pistol between her shoulder blades and she passed the rifle, losing her only chance.

When they came to the kitchen he ordered her to pour him a cup of the leftover coffee. He sat on one of the barstools at the center island while she got a mug down from the cupboard. The pot was still hot. She filled the cup and noted that he'd put the gun down on the counter. The grip lay next to his elbow, which was propped on top of the granite. In her head she calculated how much time it would take for him to grab it and pull the trigger. Mere seconds, she suspected.

"What's taking you so long?" He eyed the coffee mug in anticipation. "And while you're at it, make me something to eat. I've been crawling around your bushes all morning and we've got forty minutes before takeoff."

That didn't leave much time. The tiny airport was at least ten minutes away.

"Where's your car?" she asked. No way could he have driven in with the locked gate.

"Gia, food for fuck's sake!"

Back in his banking days he hadn't sounded like a Neanderthal. It must've taken a lot of spit and polish to pull off the refined stockbroker act.

She took a few steps forward, threw the hot coffee in his face, and ran as fast as she could, listening to him scream as she struggled to get the rifle off the wall. Her hands shook and sweat dripped into her eyes. Finally able to pry the gun loose, she made it as far as the front door when she felt a hand clutch the back of her shirt.

"You little bitch," Evan said.

She spun around, wielding the Winchester, waiting for a shot to ring out from his own gun. None came. There was nothing in his hands.

"Forget your gun, Evan?" She shoved the muzzle into his gut. His face was red and still dripping. She wondered if the coffee had been hot enough to make his skin blister. "Back up."

He laughed at her. "You won't shoot me. I doubt that thing is even loaded."

"Only one way to find out. Now back the hell up."

She saw the wheels in his head turning; then he slowly inched away. Just when she thought she had the upper hand he grabbed the barrel and began twisting the rifle away from her. She struggled to keep a firm hold on the butt, but it was a tug of war. And Evan was winning.

"What the hell do you mean they lost him?" Flynn hung a U-turn on the highway, tires screeching, as he yelled into his Bluetooth. "Why didn't you call me last night with this news?"

"I literally found out five minutes ago," Toad said. "The feds were acting squirrelly, but I figured they had a bead on him. Then this morning I find out that the whole operation is FUBAR. They let him slip through their fingers, the idiots."

"Jesus Christ! So Laughlin's been in the wind for at least fourteen hours."

"Roger that."

"I left Gia alone." Flynn wanted to smash his fist into something.

"Laughlin won't come to California. Too risky and too far away from the money."

"Still, the Bureau should've told me. I should've been on top of this."

"I hate to break it to you, boss, but you're no longer on the FBI's payroll. No way you could've known. It wasn't as if the feds wanted to publicize their mammoth screwup, especially to Gia Treadwell's defense attorney."

Shit. Shit. Shit. Flynn banged his hand on the steering wheel.

Laughlin's arrest might've helped Gia's case. Now they were back to square one.

"I'm returning to Rosser Ranch. You stay in Florida and keep your eyes and ears open. Maybe they'll get a lead on him."

"No problem," Toad said. "I'll check in later today."

Flynn disconnected and immediately punched Gia's cell number into his phone. When she didn't answer he tried her landline. He thought about leaving a message, but she was probably riding Rory or overseeing the planting of the Christmas tree seedlings with Annie. Why freak her out when he'd be there soon and could explain everything in person?

He'd left before she'd gotten up this morning. The night before it'd been difficult keeping his distance. He'd wanted to tell her how he felt about her. How he thought they'd started something good. But that would be a violation of the state bar's ethical code. Anything that could be perceived as coercion or extortion was strictly out of the question. Gia was the client and got to call the shots.

He passed the Nugget sign and turned off on Gia's road. Less than a mile from her gate he saw light glinting off something metal out in the field. Probably a pile of tin cans left over from someone's target practice. But the ex-cop in him couldn't let it go. He pulled over and grabbed his sidearm from the glove box to investigate. A few yards off the road he found a car neatly tucked behind a cluster of trees, hidden from the road. If it hadn't been for the fender reflecting off the sun the car would've gone unnoticed.

Flynn circled the Chevy Malibu. It had a bar code sticker on the back windshield, a telltale sign that it was a rental, which could mean anything. He used his phone to shoot pictures of the car's California license plates, sent them off to Rhys, and called the chief at the police department. "Can you run the plates I just texted you?"

There was a pause on the other end of the line. Flynn imagined Rhys was looking at the photographs.

"I'll run them," the chief finally said. "In the meantime, I'm sending a patrol unit. Could be nothing, but I'm thinking more snoopy reporters."

"Thanks, Rhys. I'm on my way to the ranch now. I'll leave the gate open."

Before he returned to his truck Flynn peeked inside the car's windows. There was a bottle of water and a map on the front seat. On the passenger-side floor, a *Miami Herald.*

Miami. Florida. His gut clenched.

Flynn punched in Rhys's number again, blurted his discovery, and took off running for the gate. For fifteen hundred yards he barely breathed, adrenaline pumping through his veins like a bullet train.

"I'm getting too old for this shit," he muttered to himself as he vaulted over the fence and took cover behind the trees that edged Gia's driveway. At the house he crouched along the log siding and hunkered beneath the windows to circle to the back, undetected. The mudroom door was unlocked and he snuck inside, ducking behind the side of the washing machine.

He held his position, listening. Nothing; not a sound. Panic struck. What if they were somewhere else on the property and he couldn't get to them in time? Soundlessly, he crept into the kitchen and found it clear. That was when he saw coffee splattered across the center island and a cup smashed to bits on the floor.

He pulled the Glock from the small of his back and skulked along the wall to the dining room, silently cursing the size of the house. It was reckless doing this without backup, but Flynn couldn't afford to wait. Not until he knew whether Gia was all right.

Halfway there, he heard something crash.

"That was fun."

Flynn's gut tightened. It was a man's voice and it sounded like it was coming from the family room. As he edged closer, the voice grew louder.

"You try that shit again and I'll make you watch while my associate kills your mother."

"Like you killed Rufus Cleo?" It was Gia, out of breath.

"That's what you get when you try to double-cross me. The bastard hijacked the money . . . thought he could keep it all for himself. You should've seen him when I confronted him . . . begged for his life, crying like a baby."

"So he was in on it?"

Good girl, Gia. Flynn crawled across the floor on his belly like a ghost, not even daring to breathe. *Keep him talking until I can get to you.*

The man—by now Flynn knew it was Laughlin—laughed. "Why

do you think I suggested you sit on the board of his foundation? Cleo actually thought you were involved. He thought you were the one hooking the big fish."

"Why, Evan?" Gia asked. "Why me?"

"Your big television name, the syndicated column, the books. You gave me credibility, got me into a lot of closed circles, and you weren't half bad in bed."

Flynn clenched his teeth. He was gonna kill the son of a bitch.

"In the beginning I was tempted to cut you in," Laughlin said as Flynn inched nearer, hiding behind a pony wall that connected the dining area to the great room.

He inched up his head for a mere second and caught a glimpse of them on the couch. Laughlin held a Beretta inches away from Gia's chest and Flynn's heart lurched. The problem was he couldn't go any farther, not without exposing himself, and he was still a good six yards away. He gripped his semiautomatic tighter, his finger on the trigger.

"Your weakness is you're too damn honest," Laughlin continued. "Too satisfied to earn a living when you could be sitting on a sandy beach on your own island."

"You disgust me."

"Yeah, I'm crying all the way to the bank. 'Tis a pity you're such a Goody Two-shoes because you're taking the blame anyway." Laughlin glanced at his watch. "We've gotta go now. And Gia, you pull another stunt like you did with the rifle and I'll make you pay."

The Winchester. Flynn smiled, but it was short-lived as Laughlin got to his feet and pulled Gia up by the collar of her shirt.

"We're taking your car. Get your keys." He jabbed the semiautomatic in her back and it was all Flynn could do to keep from jumping up and breaking the guy's neck.

Gia led Laughlin to her bedroom. Flynn knew her car keys were in her purse, which she typically left on the nightstand. As they started down the long hallway, he quietly jetted back through the kitchen and mudroom, went outside, and plastered himself against the side of the house. He slowly made his way to Gia's French doors, his back hugging the exterior as if he was one with the building. A light came on in the bedroom. Flynn hunkered down, gathered up a handful of pebbles, and hurled them at the glass.

"What's that?" Laughlin asked, and Flynn saw him press his face against a window screen to search the area.

Flynn tightened himself against the wall, sweat soaking through his shirt. On the ground he collected a few more pebbles and repeated the exercise. This time he threw them harder, making enough noise to rouse a heavy sleeper.

Laughlin unlocked the doors and stepped out wary and alert, holding Gia like a human shield. One-handed, he swept the air with his pistol. "Who's out here?"

It was exactly the idiotic move Flynn had expected. He tucked and rolled into Laughlin's shins so that his knees buckled. Before Laughlin could right himself and maintain his balance Gia wrenched free of him. Once she was out of range Flynn jumped to his feet and slammed Laughlin's arm against the wall until he heard a sharp crack. Laughlin let out a piercing scream and dropped the Beretta.

Flynn shoved the muzzle of his Glock into Laughlin's gut. "It's over, asshole."

Sleepless, Gia climbed the staircase. It was past midnight and by the time the agents and police had left, her nervous system was on overdrive. Still, she couldn't seem to close her eyes. Every time she did she saw Evan with his gun trained on her or her mother bound and gagged in a chair.

The FBI had arrested the man Evan had paid to hold Iris hostage. She'd been rushed to an area hospital. Though her injuries weren't serious—dehydration and abrasions on her hands and feet where she'd been bound with tape and rope—doctors thought it would be best to observe her overnight. Thank goodness Toad was still in Florida. He'd driven the forty-six miles from Miami to Boca Raton to stay by her bedside. In a day or so he'd escort her to California. Gia needed her close for a while.

Upstairs she found Flynn's room and tapped on the door. He opened it so fast she nearly fell in. Still dressed in the same jeans and T-shirt from before, he ushered her inside.

"You can't sleep either?"

"I can sleep," he said. "I was worried about you."

She would've said she was fine, but clearly she wasn't. "I wanted to thank you."

"For what?"

Gia pierced him with an are-you-for-real look. "You saved my mother and me."

He moved to the bed and sat on the edge where Gia joined him. "I wanted to kill him, Gia. When I saw him holding the Beretta on you . . ." Flynn stopped, as if he was reliving it all over again.

He'd been so calm among the agents earlier, but now she could feel anger thrumming through him.

"You okay?" He ran his hand down her back, then seemed to think better of it.

"I'm still a little freaked out."

"You pulled the Winchester on him, huh?" He tilted his head and smiled at her.

"I tried. It worked on you after all."

"Yep." He held her gaze like he wanted to say he was proud of her—and something else. But the look quickly vanished and he was back to business again. "The U.S. Attorney's office is dropping the charges against you. Prosecutors seized Tiffany Cleo's account. The justice department plans to hold a press conference tomorrow to announce Laughlin's arrest and to clear your name."

"Will the victims get their money back?"

He nodded. "Not all of it . . . Laughlin and Cleo led lavish lifestyles. But Tim thinks there's enough so that investors will get ninety cents on the dollar, which is a whole lot better than nothing. You too, which should help with your property taxes on this place . . . the tree farm and your program. Unless you want to go back to New York. This'll restore your public image."

"I don't want to go back," she said and took a deep breath. It was over. Truly over. "Without charges hanging over my head I can fully focus on the program. The neighbors are on board—at least the women." She looked at him. He could use a shave, his hair was a mess, and there were dark circles under his eyes. To Gia he'd never been more handsome . . . or more desirable.

"Flynn"—she drew back—"why did you put your property up for my bond? Why would you do something like that?"

Gia had learned that bit of surprising information from one of the prosecutors who'd come to the scene. Until then she'd been kept in the dark about Flynn's generosity, which seemed above and beyond for a lawyer to do for his client. It was even too much for a close friend to do.

"Because yours alone wasn't enough. Prosecutors were planning to eventually amend the charges to include conspiracy in Cleo's murder. There's no bail for murder. Knowing that the charge was imminent made you a high-flight risk. I figured that if I financially vouched for you, it would secure the bond . . . at least until they added the murder count."

"Why didn't you tell me?"

"I didn't want to scare you until I knew for sure whether the feds were bluffing . . . using conspiracy to commit murder as yet another threat to get you to tell them where Laughlin was."

She swallowed; the shadow of spending the rest of her life in prison still made her tremble. "Why would you risk your property like that?"

He drew back as if she'd slapped him. "Because I love you. I didn't want to see you spend a second more in that shithole. You think real estate is more important to me than you are?"

Because I love you.

The words left her speechless. When had he begun loving her?

"I thought you were embarrassed of me . . . the charges, the incarceration, my past relationship with Evan. When I was arrested you were so businesslike, so cold."

He jerked his hand through his messy hair. "Gia, I was trying to get you out of jail. I was going a little crazy. . . . Fifty freaking years in prison, not to mention the charge of conspiracy to commit murder hanging over you. Sorry if I didn't have time to whisper sweet nothings in your ear. Is that why you bolted? Jesus Christ."

"I didn't know," she said, a world of regret in her voice. "I thought you'd be better off without me. We'd only just fooled around and I didn't want to ruin you the way Evan had ruined me. I thought it would be best if you were strictly my lawyer."

"Best for whom? We didn't just fool around; I took you home to my family, Gia. Your problem is you don't trust. *I don't want to share a bank account with another person. I don't want to make financial decisions by committee. I don't want to be dependent on someone else.*" He spat her words back at her with anger.

"I'm not your goddamn father and I'm definitely not that dirtbag piece of shit Laughlin," he continued. "In fact, I'm no longer your lawyer. You're free now . . . do whatever the hell you want."

It was a dismissal, pure and simple.

She got up off the bed. "I was wrong, Flynn. I was only trying to protect you." *And me. Because compared to Evan the damage you could do to my heart would be irreparable. I'd be broken forever.*

Her throat tightened, but she needed to say it. "I love you too, Flynn. So much that I would do anything for you." Even shield him from herself.

Afraid that he'd tell her to go to hell, she didn't wait for a response. She left the room, went downstairs, and searched through the cupboard for a drink. A bottle of Jack Daniel's peeked out from a row of good red wine. Whiskey wasn't her thing; it was Flynn's. Despite it, she poured herself three fingers, hoping it would help her sleep away her mistakes and the horror of the day. God, she'd screwed up royally with Flynn, the best man she'd ever known. The only man besides her father she'd ever loved.

She closed her eyes as the whiskey burned its way down her throat and spread warmth through her belly. A few more sips and she'd try to go bed. Gia took the glass into the great room, curled up on the couch, and scanned the former crime scene. The Winchester was missing from the wall; the police had taken it as evidence.

The staircase creaked, she looked up, and her heart stopped.

"Don't ever drink alone." Flynn came down, took her whiskey, and drained it. "More?"

She shook her head. "I love you. Please believe me when I say I love you."

"But you don't trust me, do you?"

It should've been the most difficult question she'd ever had to answer. More than fifteen hours ago her ex, the man who'd sworn his everlasting love, had threatened to kill her and her mother.

"I do," she said and meant it from the bottom of her heart. "I trust you, Flynn. How could I not? You saved my life and everything that's precious to me."

He sat at the other end of the couch. "I don't need to share a bank account with you, Gia. But I do need us to be dependent on each other. That's the way a true relationship works. You lean on me, I lean on you; you trust me, I trust you. For me it can't be any other way."

She scooted closer to him and put her hand in his. "I think I can do that." Leaning on anyone since her father . . . it was difficult.

"Not 'I think.'" He lifted her chin with his finger. "You need to say you know you can do that. It's the only way it can work between us. When circumstances seem insurmountable, like they did with your arrest, you can't just walk away."

She climbed into his lap and twined her arms around his neck. For a long time she'd been solely reliant on herself. Asking to put her faith in another person . . . well, she would've thought it was impossible. Until Flynn. "Do you really love me?"

"Yes, I really love you. But I need you to say it . . . say you can lean on me. Say that when the chips are down you know I'll always be there for you, and you for me."

She exhaled. It was like jumping off a very tall cliff. "I can lean on you and when the chips are down I know you'll be there for me. I'll always be there for you, Flynn." Her eyes glistened with unshed tears. She loved Flynn so much she could hardly breathe. "I can trust you and I love you so much that I'll never give up on you again."

Flynn's eyes shone with so much need and emotion that it floored her. In a rough voice he said, "You've said the words. Now show me. Make love to me like you mean it."

And there on the couch, and later in her bed, she loved him with her body . . . her heart and soul . . . well into the next day. And she'd continue to love him forever.

Epilogue

"The bar goes over there," Gia told the caterers and pointed to a corner of the yard near the pool.

She glanced at her watch. They only had an hour until the guests began arriving. Thank goodness Samantha Breyer had offered to take charge of the fund-raiser. With her expert event-planning skills everything was right on schedule.

Donna sidled up to Gia and handed her a glass of champagne. "Chillax, girlfriend. Go spend some time with Flynn. He looks bored out of his skull."

He stood over by the French doors with his hands stuffed inside his suit pockets, looking sexier than any man had a right to.

Last week every single woman at Dana's wedding had tried to make a play for him. But he was Gia's. As she walked toward him, his lips slid up in a grin and his eyes roamed over her little black dress.

"It's coming together," he said. "Sam knows her stuff."

"She and Nate have invited a lot of important people with deep pockets. Griffin has already committed a nice chunk of change and Tawny donated a pair of custom boots for the silent auction." She let out a breath. If this went well they'd have plenty of money to finance the program and her new foundation, which, at everyone's urging, she'd turned into a nonprofit.

"Today Clay, Rhys, and the rest of the board narrowed down the first group of women," she told Flynn, brimming with excitement. Everything she'd ever wanted was coming true. "For now we're focusing on California residents, but I'm hoping to eventually broaden our reach."

They both turned when Iris came out of the house dressed to the nines. Flynn met her at the door and gave her his arm. Gia's heart expanded watching Flynn with her mother like that.

"You look beautiful, Mom." Gia grabbed another glass of champagne and handed it to Iris.

"So do you, dear." Iris straightened Flynn's tie. "The two of you make a gorgeous couple. Oh look, there's Patty." She drifted off to greet Flynn's mother. No doubt they would spend the evening plotting.

"Your mom wants to teach a class on beekeeping," she said. "And Jo has volunteered to help keep the Iris Foundation's books. Don't you think that's great?"

"I think you're great." He leaned over and kissed her on the lips.

"Oh, Flynn, so many people have volunteered. . . . I'm just amazed at how everyone is suddenly embracing the program."

"I'm not. It's the right thing to do and it was just a matter of time before the lug heads"—he hitched his head at Clay and Rhys, who'd come early to help with the setup—"accepted the idea. And it sure didn't hurt that their wives were on your side. I've never seen two men more whipped."

Gia slapped Flynn's arm playfully. "Stop it. You see Emily? She's starting to show a tiny bit."

"Hadn't noticed. I only have eyes for you."

"Pouring it on a little thick, don't you think?"

Annie waved from across the yard. Not surprisingly, she'd started hanging out with Harlee and Darla. Gia was glad she'd found friends and adored having her live on the ranch. As for Harlee, her profile on Gia had come out this morning, perfectly timed for the fund-raiser. That had been Maddy's idea. Pretty brilliant, Gia had to admit. The story, which included news about Gia's new Iris Foundation, had been picked up by the Associated Press and printed in every major publication.

"What did I say about trust, Gia?" Flynn's hands glided up the back of her dress.

"Quit it. People will see."

He laughed and raised his brows. "Later, then."

"You're bad." She laughed. So starry-eyed over him, her head was in the clouds most days. "I have something to ask you."

"Yeah?" He tugged her close. "What's that?"

"Will you be the Iris Foundation's lawyer?"

"That depends. Will you be my wife?"

Gia nearly choked on her champagne. "Are you proposing?"

He pulled a ring box out of his jacket and got down on one knee. "Yep. I love you, Gia. We can have a long engagement, but just say yes."

"Yes! Yes!" Before she could tell him how much she loved him the crowd broke into applause. Her eyes filled with tears as she scanned the group. Her neighbors, her friends, her and Flynn's families, they were all gathered around them. "You planned this, didn't you?"

A sly smile played on his lips. He got to his feet, enveloped her in his arms, and whispered, "A little peer pressure, just in case you were . . . uh, undecided. I figured it was better than breaking out the Winchester."

Please turn the page for an exciting sneak peek of
Stacy Finz's newest Nugget romance
FALLING HARD
coming soon!

Chapter 1

The big gate stopped Logan Jenkins in his tracks. He didn't know what he was thinking coming here like this. But his curiosity had gotten the better of him. A man ought to know where he came from and who his people were, he supposed.

Until a week ago, he hadn't given a good goddamn. Then, boom, life had changed with just one phone call.

He pulled his pickup to the side of the road, slung his backpack over his shoulder, and got out to have a look around. Picturesque and peaceful, nothing like the hell holes he'd come from.

The gate was impressive with its curlicue iron work, but not much for keeping anyone out. To prove it, Logan hopped the twelve-foot fence in less than a minute, avoiding the sharp, ornamental spears, and hiked up the long gravel road. At the peak of the hill he paused and let out a low whistle. Even from a hundred yards away, he could see that the house put the gate to shame. It looked like one of those mega ski chalets plucked from an Alpine mountainside. Lots of large windows, tiered decks, and big log siding. It was built to appear rustic, though it was anything but. The landscape wasn't bad either. A river snaked through miles of rolling pastures with the Sierra Nevada mountain range looming in the background.

This is where he would've grown up if things had been different. Instead, for the last twelve years he hadn't belonged anywhere—or everywhere, depending on how he looked at it. His last address—besides the apartment he shared with Gabe when he was stateside—had been Afghanistan. A far cry from Rosser Ranch.

No one tried to stop him, so he continued down the driveway toward the house, taking in the sights. A four-car garage with a guest house. A front lawn as big as a soccer field. And lots of flagstone pathways. Someone went to a lot of trouble to make the gardens seem to match the surrounding countryside.

By now he would've expected at least a dog to have barked at his presence. Crappy security. But he suspected there wasn't much crime in Nugget, California. Just a spot on the map, really. According to a quick search on the internet, its claim to fame was the Western Pacific Railroad Museum, which offered a train ride through gold country. The site he'd read said Nugget was still very much a railroad town, now a crew-change site for Union Pacific. Before the railroad, there'd been the Gold Rush. But ultimately, the pioneers had made their fortunes from timber and cattle. Major cattle ranches still covered the countryside.

Logan laughed to himself. Who would've thought his ancestors were cowboys? The closest he'd ever gotten to livestock were the Kochis' goat and sheep herds in the Hindu Kush. Here, he could see plenty of cows dotting the hills in the foreground like a poster advertising rural life on the farm. Pretty domesticated and attractive, he had to admit. Just not for him. He maneuvered better in chaos. Thrived in it, actually.

When he got close to the house, he circled around it to the backyard. A couple of hammocks swayed under a log cabana. The large, kidney-shaped pool was tempting in the heat. The whole upscale setup was very dude ranch spa.

So far, he wasn't feeling his roots. No cosmic connection with the land. All he was feeling was a shitload of money. The old man was supposed to be buried in the family plot on the property. Maybe Logan would check that out and see if he could summon the ghost of the man who'd given him life. Thank him for being a douchebag.

Logan ambled down a well-worn path designated by a split-rail trail fence that jutted off from the pool area toward a stable. Like the house, the building was constructed of logs with two cupolas and a weathervane on top. It was probably where Rosser had kept the thoroughbreds or whatever kind of horses he'd raised.

"You're late," a woman called to him. She leaned against the side of the barn, shielding her eyes from the sun, a cowboy hat pulled over her forehead.

"Excuse me?" He walked toward her. Up close, he noticed her combat boots right off the bat. They looked funny with the bubblegum pink tank top and short floral skirt that flared a few inches above her knees.

When he met her eyes—big ones that reminded him of golden brown sugar—she smiled and he went to DEFCON 3 in less than a heartbeat. It was like sunshine, that smile. So damn guileless that it instantly put him on alert. Where he'd come from everyone had an agenda.

"You were supposed to be here thirty minutes ago." She pushed herself off the wall of the barn and shrugged as if she were willing to overlook his tardiness. "Come on. I'll show you what needs to be done."

Out of curiosity he followed her as she took the same path he'd started on through a wooded area. Her gait was brisk. Her legs and arms were toned, like she got plenty of exercise, and her ass . . . well, yeah, that looked toned too. They came up on a large cabin and she stopped.

"Your first task would be to clear this." She swept her arm across the weeds and brambles strangling the building, which on closer inspection seemed more like a barracks, and eyed him up and down. "You look like you're up to the challenge."

Even with his Gatorz on, he could see the trail of freckles running across her nose. "What's the cabin for?"

"It's a bunkhouse and we're going to use it for the program."

He got the sense that he was expected to know what the program was so he just nodded.

"There's another one over there." She pointed across a clearing at an identical building that had also seen better days. "Once the shrubs and weeds are cleared away, we'll get to work on the insides."

He probably should've told her he wasn't the job candidate. But once he did, she'd kick him off the property and he wasn't done looking around yet.

"After we finish up here, there are a few more cottages and a foreman's house we have to ready before the roofer and construction crew comes. If you still need work after that I could use you to help till the fields for the hay planting in the fall. You said you're experienced operating a tractor, right?"

He'd never driven a tractor in his life but there couldn't be much to it. Anyway, he wouldn't be here for that. His conscience told him to come clean because she'd find out sooner or later that he wasn't here to clear brush. If she booted him off the land, he'd find another way to explore the place . . . his origins.

"Actually, no," he said.

She tilted her head in surprise. "Were you trying to win me over on the phone so you could get the job?" Her mouth turned down into a frown. "I'll be real honest with you; driving a tractor isn't required. We just need someone who isn't afraid to put his back into the work."

"No, I mean it wasn't me on the phone."

"Oh? Did you read the help-wanted ad in the *Nugget Tribune*?"

He felt compelled to remove a leaf that had gotten stuck in the band of her cowboy hat but kept his hands at his side. "Nope. I was checking the place out."

"Rosser Ranch? Why?"

This is where it got tricky. He didn't want to lie—liars were louses—but he wasn't ready to advertise the truth. Hell, he'd just learned the truth seven days ago and was still trying to wrap his head around the news. The old man hadn't even owned the ranch when he'd died. So to come here like this . . . well, it would seem strange.

"I was passing through, saw the gate, and got curious."

"Passing through?" She seemed dubious. "So you're not looking for work?"

Actually he was, just not this kind of work. He'd gotten out of the Navy a couple of weeks ago and had found himself at loose ends, which was strange when for the last twelve years he'd been told where to shit and when to sit.

Gabe, also a former SEAL, wanted to start a private security business. Everything from risk management and cyber security to VIP protection and contract work for Uncle Sam. He wanted Logan to work for him and was trying to scrounge up investors and a few contract jobs to keep them busy. Any time now, Logan expected to get a call with an assignment.

"Nah," he told her, and took off his shades and stuffed them in his shirt pocket. "You having trouble finding someone?"

"The only guy who called from the ad is a no-show. That's why I thought you were him."

"Sorry. I should've told you from the get-go."

"That's okay." But her shoulders deflated in obvious frustration.

"You sure you don't want the job? It comes with living quarters . . . nothing fancy, but you get to live here." She spread her arms wide.

"Yeah, it's quite a place. You own it?" Somehow, he didn't think so.

"Gosh, no. The owner, Gia Treadwell, is great, though. She bought the place less than a year ago, after her financial-advice show got canceled." She watched him, presumably to see if he knew what she was talking about.

Gia Treadwell. The name rang a bell. If Logan remembered correctly she'd been a talk-show host embroiled in some sort of financial controversy that she was later cleared of. It was hard to keep track of such news when he'd been overseas so much.

"Then she hired me to plant a Christmas tree farm," she continued. "And now I'm prepping the ranch for a residential program to help women down on their luck get back on their feet." She hesitated, and then said, "After . . . uh . . . Gia's troubles, she wanted to pay it forward."

Logan swiveled around to peer at the bunkhouses again. "They going to live in these?"

"Yep. And there are cottages for the women who have children."

"Nice." He wanted to ask her if he could continue to check out the place, maybe wander over to the family cemetery plot, but thought better of it. "I'm Logan Jenkins by the way."

She stuck out her hand. "Annie Sparks."

Annie had a good grip, even though his hands dwarfed hers. And she was so freaking pretty with those big soulful eyes and peaches-and-cream skin that he couldn't stop looking at her. Everything from her trusting demeanor to her flowered skirt and faded straw hat said sweet. Logan usually avoided the sweet girls; they always cried when he left and it broke his heart.

"Why don't you show me where I'd get to live if I took the job?" It was an excuse to see more and to throw her a bone after initially misleading her.

"Sure," Annie said, and perked up. She led him farther down the path to a smaller log cabin. Unlike the others, this one had been cleared. The front porch even had a rocking chair and flower boxes underneath green trimmed windows.

She climbed the stairs and opened the front door. "Feel free to check it out."

He went inside. The place was tiny, just a living room, galley kitchen, eating nook, and sleeping loft. What it lacked in space it made up for in charm, though Logan's bar was pretty low. He'd been deployed so many times, living in enough CHUs—containerized housing units—that even the moldy, shoebox of an apartment he shared with Gabe in Coronado seemed like a palace.

"It's adorable, isn't it?"

"Not bad," he said. Through the trees he could see wide open pastures. The view certainly didn't suck. "You live here, too?"

"I do. In the fall I'll be commuting to finish my PhD program at UC Davis."

"PhD, huh? What in?"

"Agricultural economics."

"Whoa, you must be smart." Logan was lucky to have a high school diploma. Not that he was dumb, but he'd had trouble sitting through classes. The doctors had told his mom it was ADHD. They were wrong. He could concentrate just fine if it were something he was interested in. He loved to read, picked up languages fairly well—at least enough to be conversational—and was a quick study when it came to people. "So does that make you an economist or a farmer?"

"A farmer. Third generation. I don't see that changing. I suppose the degree gives me extra credibility and the option to teach. How about you? What brings you to Nugget?"

"Uh, I recently got out of the Navy, found myself between jobs, and have been doing a little traveling. The town looked interesting." Most of what he'd said was true.

"I thought you might be military. Were you in the Middle East?"

"Afghanistan and Iraq."

"So you saw combat, huh?"

Logan nodded. "So why's the place called Rosser Ranch?" He knew damned well why; he was fishing and it was a better topic than war.

"Ray Rosser used to own the ranch. It had been in his family since the Gold Rush. But he sold it to Gia last year to pay his attorneys' fees when he was charged with murder after killing a cattle rustler."

The lawyer had already told him the colorful story, which still seemed bizarre. It was the twenty-first century. Shooting cattle rustlers? Who did shit like that anymore?

"A week ago he had a stroke in prison and died," Annie said. "His wife and daughter live in Colorado."

Logan had met them at the attorney's office in Sacramento for the reading of the will the day before. That had been a hell of a party. Apparently, they'd known as much about him as he'd known about them. That would be a big zilch.

The wife had been okay. He didn't get the sense that there'd been any love lost between her and Rosser, nor that she'd been surprised he'd been stepping out on her. But the daughter, Raylene, had been a monster bitch. He got it. Finding out that you suddenly had a half-brother was reason enough to be resentful. But he'd gotten the impression that she was mostly mad about the money—that she and her husband weren't getting all of it. Logan hadn't asked for anything. Hell, he hadn't even known about his secret family until the old man croaked and would've been fine moving through life without the knowledge that he and Ray Rosser shared the same DNA. He'd gotten along thirty-one years without it. But his mother had pleaded with him to take his due.

"It's part of your heritage," she'd argued.

And if anyone could cajole him into something he didn't want to do, it was Maisy Jenkins.

She'd raised him singlehandedly, which had been no easy feat. He'd been a wild boy, prone to getting into fights and hanging with the wrong crowd. Yet Maisy had always loved and believed in him. Growing up in Vegas, it had never dawned on him that they lived a little too well for Maisy's paycheck. She worked at a gift shop at the Bellagio and was usually home when he got off of school. Still, they'd owned a modest house in a subdivision, his mother owned a nice car, and they always had plenty of food on the table with money left over for him to buy Little League gear and new clothes. Not rich by a long shot but comfortable. And that was because Ray Rosser had been footing the bill. In return, his mother had sworn to keep her love child's paternity secret.

Logan wasn't angry about it. She did what she had to do. Ray wasn't about to leave his wife, who'd been pregnant with Raylene when Logan was one. Rosser certainly wasn't going to publically acknowledge Logan. So what was the point of pressing the issue? Maisy took the money and moved to Nevada with a signed declaration that Rosser would at least make room for his illegitimate son in his will.

He'd kept to the bargain.

And Logan was thinking he could use the money to partner with Gabe in the security company. With the cash, they could really build something, even hire a few more operators. But first they needed a few assignments under their belt to build a reputation.

In the meantime, Logan planned to learn more about the Rosser side of his family. The only real father figure he'd ever had was Nick, whom his mother had married when Logan was a senior in high school. Nick, a former Navy SEAL in charge of security at the Bellagio, was as good as they came. He'd been the one to make sure Logan walked the straight and narrow and had encouraged him to join the Seaman to SEALs program prior to enlisting, which guaranteed he'd at least become a candidate. No one was prouder of Logan than Nick when he'd made it through six months of BUD/S. But Nick wasn't his biological father, even though Logan wished otherwise.

"You want to sit for a second?" Annie asked, and Logan got the distinct impression she was getting ready to do a sales job on him.

"You're pretty hard up, huh?" He took a seat at the edge of the porch and swung his legs over the side, waiting for her to join him.

"It's difficult to find reliable people out here." Annie took the top step, smoothing the back of her skirt as she sat down. "Most of the good ones have already signed up with a ranch or the railroad for permanent work. We don't have enough to keep someone on past fall but I'm on a deadline. The women are due here in September."

She smelled good, fresh like the outdoors. But it was her breasts straining against the pink tank top that was holding his attention. Those and her combat boots, which were sexy as hell. And . . . shit . . . he'd never found combat boots sexy before.

"What makes you think I'm reliable?" he asked, his gaze moving to her lips. Pretty lush pink ones.

"Because you were in the military, I guess."

He grinned because it was the truth. He was damned reliable. "So just the cabins, the cottages, and the foreman's house?" Logan could probably get them cleared in a few days.

"Yep."

"And I get to live in this one?"

She nodded. "Utilities included but you have to cover your own food."

"I can park my truck here?" He figured it was as good a stopping place as any until Gabe called. Meanwhile, he could get a feel for where he came from.

"Where is it now?"

"I parked it near your security gate, which by the way, sucks."

She laughed. "Why's that?"

"Because I'm in here, not out there."

"We're a little less cautious here in the country but I'll pass the word on to the owner. You'll take the job, then?"

"I'll hack out all the overgrowth. After that you're on your own. Is there a laundromat around here? I don't have a lot of clothes with me." He'd only expected to stay a day or two, just long enough to check the place out, since it was only a three-hour drive from the lawyer's office.

"There's a washer and dryer in each of the bunkhouses, which you're welcome to use."

"I'm guessing the place comes with the furniture, right?" All Logan really cared about was the bed. He could do with not sleeping on the cold, hard ground for a while.

"It does. I'll see if I can find you some bedding, though."

"I have a sleeping bag in my truck. That'll do me."

"Then we're set." Annie stood up, and he let his eyes linger over her mile-long legs. "Let's go back to the barn so you can sign the paperwork. Then I'll open the gate and you can bring your truck around."

"Sounds good."

He suddenly realized he hadn't thought to ask about the pay. This was a reconnaissance mission, he reminded himself. The job was just an excuse to keep him on the property. Now if he could just focus on the land of his ancestors instead of Annie Sparks's smoking-hot body, he'd be okay.

ABOUT THE AUTHOR

Stacy Finz is an award-winning former reporter for the *San Francisco Chronicle*. After twenty years-plus covering notorious serial killers, naked-tractor-driving farmers, fanatical foodies, aging rock stars, and weird Western towns, she figured she had enough material to write fiction. She is the 2013 winner of the Daphne du Maurier Award. Readers can visit her website at: www.stacyfinz.com

STACY FINZ

HEATING UP

A
NUGGET
ROMANCE

shine

Printed in the United States
by Baker & Taylor Publisher Services